NORA ROBERTS

Sweet Stubborn Love

Includes *Luring a Lady* & *Falling for Rachel*

Silhouette Books

SILHOUETTE™

Recycling programs for this product may not exist in your area.

Sweet Stubborn Love

ISBN-13: 978-1-335-47589-3

Copyright © 2025 by Harlequin Enterprises ULC

Luring a Lady
First published in 1991. This edition published in 2025.
Copyright © 1991 by Nora Roberts

Falling for Rachel
First published in 1993. This edition published in 2025.
Copyright © 1993 by Nora Roberts

For questions and comments about the quality of this book, please contact us at CustomerService@Harlequin.com.

Silhouette
22 Adelaide St. West, 41st Floor
Toronto, Ontario M5H 4E3, Canada
www.Harlequin.com

Printed in U.S.A.

CONTENTS

Luring a Lady

Chapter 1

She wasn't a patient woman. Delays and excuses were barely tolerated, and never tolerated well. Waiting—and she was waiting now—had her temper dropping degree by degree toward ice. With Sydney Hayward icy anger was a great deal more dangerous than boiling rage. One frigid glance, one frosty phrase could make the recipient quake. And she knew it.

Now she paced her new office, ten stories up in midtown Manhattan. She swept from corner to corner over the deep oatmeal-colored carpet. Everything was perfectly in place, papers, files, coordinated appointment and address books. Even her brass-and-ebony desk set was perfectly aligned, the pens and pencils marching in a straight row across the polished mahogany, the notepads carefully placed beside the phone.

Her appearance mirrored the meticulous precision and tasteful elegance of the office. Her crisp beige suit was all straight lines and starch, but didn't disguise the fact that there was a great pair of legs striding across the carpet. With it she wore a single strand of pearls, earrings to match and a slim gold watch, all very discreet and exclusive. As a Hayward, she'd been raised to be both.

Her dark auburn hair was swept off her neck and secured with a gold clip. The pale freckles that went with the hair were nearly invisible after a light dusting of powder. Sydney felt they made her look too young and too vulnerable. At twenty-eight she had a face that reflected her breeding. High, slashing cheekbones, the strong, slightly pointed chin, the small straight nose. An aristocratic face, it was pale as porcelain, with a softly shaped mouth she knew could sulk too easily, and large smoky-blue eyes that people often mistook for guileless.

Sydney glanced at her watch again, let out a little hiss of breath, then marched over to her desk. Before she could pick up the phone, her intercom buzzed.

"Yes."

"Ms. Hayward. There's a man here who insists on seeing the person in charge of the Soho project. And your four-o'clock appointment—"

"It's now four-fifteen," Sydney cut in, her voice low and smooth and final. "Send him in."

"Yes, ma'am, but he's not Mr. Howington."

So Howington had sent an underling. Annoyance hiked Sydney's chin up another fraction. "Send him in," she repeated, and flicked off the intercom with one frosted pink nail. So, they thought she'd be pacified with a junior executive. Sydney took a deep breath and prepared to kill the messenger.

It was years of training that prevented her mouth from dropping open when the man walked in. No, not walked, she corrected. Swaggered. Like a black-patched pirate over the rolling deck of a boarded ship.

She wished she'd had the foresight to have fired a warning shot over his bow.

Her initial shock had nothing to do with the fact that he was wildly handsome, though the adjective suited perfectly. A mane of thick, curling black hair flowed just beyond the nape of his neck, to be caught by a leather thong in a short ponytail that did nothing to detract from rampant masculinity. His face was rawboned and lean, with skin the color of an old gold coin. Hooded eyes were nearly as black as his hair. His full lips were shadowed by a day or two's growth of beard that gave him a rough and dangerous look.

Though he skimmed under six foot and was leanly built, he made her delicately furnished office resemble a doll's house.

What was worse was the fact that he wore work clothes. Dusty jeans and a sweaty T-shirt with a pair of scarred boots that left a trail of dirt across her pale carpet. They hadn't even bothered with the junior executive, she thought as her lips firmed, but had sent along a common laborer who hadn't had the sense to clean up before the interview.

"You're Hayward?" The insolence in the tone and the slight hint of a Slavic accent had her imagining him striding up to a camp fire with a whip tucked in his belt.

The misty romance of the image made her tone unnecessarily sharp. "Yes, and you're late."

His eyes narrowed fractionally as they studied each other across the desk. "Am I?"

"Yes. You might find it helpful to wear a watch. My time is valuable if yours is not. Mr...."

"Stanislaski." He hooked his thumbs in the belt loops of his jeans, shifting his weight easily, arrogantly onto one hip. "Sydney's a man's name."

She arched a brow. "Obviously you're mistaken."

He skimmed his gaze over her slowly, with as much interest as annoyance. She was pretty as a frosted cake, but he hadn't come straight and sweaty from a job to waste time with a female. "Obviously. I thought Hayward was an old man with a bald head and a white mustache."

"You're thinking of my grandfather."

"Ah, then it's your grandfather I want to see."

"That won't be possible, Mr. Stanislaski, as my grandfather's been dead for nearly two months."

The arrogance in his eyes turned quickly to compassion. "I'm sorry. It hurts to lose family."

She couldn't say why, of all the condolences she had received, these few words from a stranger touched her. "Yes, it does. Now, if you'll take a seat, we can get down to business."

Cold, hard and distant as the moon. Just as well, he thought. It would keep him from thinking of her in more personal ways—at least until he got what he wanted.

"I have sent your grandfather letters," he began as he settled into one of the trim Queen Anne chairs in front of the desk. "Perhaps the last were misplaced during the confusion of death."

An odd way to put it, Sydney thought, but apt. Her life had certainly been turned upside down in the past few months. "Correspondence should be addressed to me." She sat, folding her hands on the desk. "As you know Hayward Industries is considering several firms—"

"For what?"

She struggled to shrug off the irritation of being interrupted. "I beg your pardon?"

"For what are you considering several firms?"

If she had been alone, she would have sighed and shut her eyes. Instead, she drummed her fingers on the desk. "What position do you hold, Mr. Stanislaski?"

"Position?"

"Yes, yes, what is it you do?"

The impatience in her voice made him grin. His teeth were very white, and not quite straight. "You mean, what is it I do? I work with wood."

"You're a carpenter?"

"Sometimes."

"Sometimes," she repeated, and sat back. Behind her, buildings punched into a hard blue sky. "Perhaps you can tell me why Howington Construction sent a sometimes carpenter to represent them in this interview."

The room smelled of lemon and rosemary and only reminded him that he was hot, thirsty and as impatient as she. "I could— if they had sent me."

It took her a moment to realize he wasn't being deliberately obtuse. "You're not from Howington?"

"No. I'm Mikhail Stanislaski, and I live in one of your buildings." He propped a dirty boot on a dusty knee. "If you're thinking of hiring Howington, I would think again. I once worked for them, but they cut too many corners."

"Excuse me." Sydney gave the intercom a sharp jab. "Janine, did Mr. Stanislaski tell you he represented Howington?"

"Oh, no, ma'am. He just asked to see you. Howington called about ten minutes ago to reschedule. If you—"

"Never mind." Sitting back again, she studied the man who was grinning at her. "Apparently I've been laboring under a misconception."

"If you mean you made a mistake, yes. I'm here to talk to you about your apartment building in Soho."

She wanted, badly, to drag her hands through her hair. "You're here with a tenant complaint?"

"I'm here with many tenants' complaints," he corrected.

"You should be aware that there's a certain procedure one follows in this kind of matter."

He lifted one black brow. "You own the building, yes?"

"Yes, but—"

"Then it's your responsibility."

She stiffened. "I'm perfectly aware of my responsibilities, Mr. Stanislaski. And now…"

He rose as she did, and didn't budge an inch. "Your grandfather made promises. To honor him, you must keep them."

"What I must do," she said in a frigid voice, "is run my business." And she was trying desperately to learn how. "You may tell the other tenants that Hayward is at the point of hiring a contractor as we're quite aware that many of our properties are in need of repair or renovation. The apartments in Soho will be dealt with in turn."

His expression didn't change at the dismissal, nor did the tone of his voice or the spread-legged, feet-planted stance. "We're tired of waiting for our turn. We want what was promised to us, now."

"If you'll send me a list of your demands—"

"We have."

She set her teeth. "Then I'll look over the files this evening."

"Files aren't people. You take the rent money every month, but you don't think of the people." He placed his hands on the desk and leaned forward. Sydney caught a wisp of sawdust and sweat that was uncomfortably appealing. "Have you seen the building, or the people who live in it?"

"I have reports," she began.

"Reports." He swore—it wasn't in a language she understood, but she was certain it was an oath. "You have your accountants and your lawyers, and you sit up here in your pretty office and look through papers." With one quick slash of the hand, he dismissed her office and herself. "But you know nothing. It's not you who's cold when the heat doesn't work, or who must climb five flights of stairs when the elevator is broken. You don't worry that the water won't get hot or that the wiring is too old to be safe."

No one spoke to her that way. No one. Her own temper was making her heart beat too fast. It made her forget that she was facing a very dangerous man. "You're wrong. I'm very concerned about all of those things. And I intend to correct them as soon as possible."

His eyes flashed and narrowed, like a sword raised and turned on its edge. "This is a promise we've heard before."

"Now, it's my promise, and you haven't had that before."

"And we're supposed to trust you. You, who are too lazy or too afraid to even go see what she owns."

Her face went dead white, the only outward sign of fury. "I've had enough of your insults for one afternoon, Mr. Stanislaski. Now, you can either find your way out, or I'll call security to help you find it."

"I know my way," he said evenly. "I'll tell you this, Miss Sydney Hayward, you will begin to keep those promises within two days, or we'll go to the building commissioner, and the press."

Sydney waited until he had stalked out before she sat again. Slowly she took a sheet of stationery from the drawer then methodically tore it into shreds. She stared at the smudges his big wide-palmed hands had left on her glossy desk and chose and shredded another sheet. Calmer, she punched the intercom. "Janine, bring me everything you've got on the Soho project."

An hour later, Sydney pushed the files aside and made two calls. The first was to cancel her dinner plans for the evening. The second was to Lloyd Bingham, her grandfather's—now her—executive assistant.

"You just caught me," Lloyd told her as he walked into Sydney's office. "I was on my way out. What can I do for you?"

Sydney shot him a brief glance. He was a handsome, ambitious man who preferred Italian tailors and French food. Not yet forty, he was on his second divorce and liked to escort society women who were attracted to his smooth blond looks and polished manners. Sydney knew that he had worked hard and long to gain his position with Hayward and that he had taken over the reins during her grandfather's illness the past year.

She also knew that he resented her because she was sitting behind a desk he considered rightfully his.

"For starters, you can explain why nothing has been done about the Soho apartments."

"The unit in Soho?" Lloyd took a cigarette from a slim gold case. "It's on the agenda."

"It's been on the agenda for nearly eighteen months. The first letter in the file, signed by the tenants, was dated almost two years ago and lists twenty-seven specific complaints."

"And I believe you'll also see in the file that a number of them were addressed." He blew out a thin stream of smoke as he made himself comfortable on one of the chairs.

"A number of them," Sydney repeated. "Such as the furnace repairs. The tenants seemed to think a new furnace was required."

Lloyd made a vague gesture. "You're new to the game, Sydney. You'll find that tenants always want new, better and more."

"That may be. However, it hardly seems cost-effective to me to repair a thirty-year-old furnace and have it break down again two months later." She held up a finger before he could speak. "Broken railings in stairwells, peeling paint, an insufficient water heater, a defective elevator, cracked porcelain…" She glanced up. "I could go on, but it doesn't seem necessary. There's a memo here, from my grandfather to you, requesting that you take over the repairs and maintenance of this building."

"Which I did," Lloyd said stiffly. "You know very well that your grandfather's health turned this company upside down over the last year. That apartment complex is only one of several buildings he owned."

"You're absolutely right." Her voice was quiet but without warmth. "I also know that we have a responsibility, a legal and a moral responsibility to our tenants, whether the building is in Soho or on Central Park West." She closed the folder, linked her hands over it and, in that gesture, stated ownership. "I don't want to antagonize you, Lloyd, but I want you to understand that I've decided to handle this particular property myself."

"Why?"

She granted him a small smile. "I'm not entirely sure. Let's just say I want to get my feet wet, and I've decided to make this property my pet project. In the meantime, I'd like you to look over the reports on the construction firms, and give me your recommendations." She offered him another file. "I've included a list of the properties, in order of priority. We'll have a meeting Friday, ten o'clock, to finalize."

"All right." He tapped out his cigarette before he rose. "Sydney, I hope you won't take offense, but a woman who's spent most of her life traveling and buying clothes doesn't know much about business, or making a profit."

She did take offense, but she'd be damned if she'd show it. "Then I'd better learn, hadn't I? Good night, Lloyd."

Not until the door closed did she look down at her hands. They were shaking. He was right, absolutely right to point out her inadequacies. But he couldn't know how badly she needed to prove herself here, to make something out of what her grandfather had left her. Nor could he know how terrified she was that she would let down the family name. Again.

Before she could change her mind, she tucked the file into her briefcase and left the office. She walked down the wide pastel corridor with its tasteful watercolors and thriving ficus trees, through the thick glass doors that closed in her suite of offices. She took her private elevator down to the lobby, where she nodded to the guard before she walked outside.

The heat punched like a fist. Though it was only mid-June, New York was in the clutches of a vicious heat wave with temperatures and humidity spiraling gleefully. She had only to cross the sidewalk to be cocooned in the waiting car, sheltered from the dripping air and noise. After giving her driver the address, she settled back for the ride to Soho.

Traffic was miserable, snarling and edgy. But that would only give her more time to think. She wasn't certain what she was going to do when she got there. Nor was she sure what she would do if she ran into Mikhail Stanislaski again.

He'd made quite an impression on her, Sydney mused. Exotic looks, hot eyes, a complete lack of courtesy. The worst part was the file had shown that he'd had a perfect right to be rude and impatient. He'd written letter after letter during the past year, only to be put off with half-baked promises.

Perhaps if her grandfather hadn't been so stubborn about keeping his illness out of the press. Sydney rubbed a finger over her temple and wished she'd taken a couple of aspirin before she'd left the office.

Whatever had happened before, she was in charge now. She intended to respect her inheritance and all the responsibilities that went with it. She closed her eyes and fell into a half doze as her driver fought his way downtown.

Inside his apartment, Mikhail carved a piece of cherrywood. He wasn't sure why he continued. His heart wasn't in it, but he felt it more productive to do something with his hands.

He kept thinking about the woman. Sydney. All ice and pride, he thought. One of the aristocrats it was in his blood to rebel against. Though he and his family had escaped to America when he had still been a child, there was no denying his heritage. His ancestors had been Gypsies in the Ukraine, hot-blooded, hot tempered and with little respect for structured authority.

Mikhail considered himself to be American—except when it suited him to be Russian.

Curls of wood fell on the table or the floor. Most of his cramped living space was taken up with his work—blocks and slabs of wood, even an oak burl, knives, chisels, hammers, drills, calipers. There was a small lathe in the corner and jars that held brushes. The room smelled of linseed oil, sweat and sawdust.

Mikhail took a pull from the beer at his elbow and sat back to study the cherry. It wasn't ready, as yet, to let him see what was inside. He let his fingers roam over it, over the grain, into the grooves, while the sound of traffic and music and shouts rose up and through the open window at his back.

He had had enough success in the past two years that he could have moved into bigger and more modern dwellings. He liked it here, in this noisy neighborhood, with the bakery on the corner, the bazaarlike atmosphere on Canal, only a short walk away, the women who gossiped from their stoops in the morning, the men who sat there at night.

He didn't need wall-to-wall carpet or a sunken tub or a big stylish kitchen. All he wanted was a roof that didn't leak, a shower that offered hot water and a refrigerator that would keep the beer and cold cuts cold. At the moment, he didn't have any of those things. And Miss Sydney Hayward hadn't seen the last of him.

He glanced up at the three brisk knocks on his door, then grinned as his down-the-hall neighbor burst in. "What's the story?"

Keely O'Brian slammed the door, leaned dramatically against it, then did a quick jig. "I got the part." Letting out a whoop, she raced to the table to throw her arms around Mikhail's neck. "I got it." She gave him a loud, smacking kiss on one cheek. "I got it." Then the other.

"I told you you would." He reached back to ruffle her short cap of dusty blond hair. "Get a beer. We'll celebrate."

"Oh, Mik." She crossed to the tiny refrigerator on long, slim legs left stunningly revealed by a pair of neon green shorts. "I was so nervous before the audition I got the hiccups, then I drank a gallon of water and sloshed my way through the reading." She tossed the cap into the trash before toasting herself. "And I still got it. A movie of the week. I'll probably only get like sixth or seventh billing, but I don't get murdered till the third act." She took a sip, then let out a long, bloodcurdling scream. "That's what I have to do when the serial killer corners me in the alley. I really think my scream turned the tide."

"No doubt." As always, her quick, nervous speech amused him. She was twenty-three, with an appealing coltish body, lively green eyes and a heart as wide as the Grand Canyon. If Mikhail hadn't felt so much like her brother right from the beginning of their relationship, he would have long since attempted to talk her into bed.

Keely took a sip of beer. "Hey, do you want to order some Chinese or pizza or something? I've got a frozen pizza, but my oven is on the blink again."

The simple statement made his eyes flash and his lips purse. "I went today to see Hayward."

The bottle paused on the way to her lips. "In person? You mean like, face-to-face?"

"Yes." Mikhail set aside his carving tools, afraid he would gouge the wood.

Impressed, Keely walked over to sit on the windowsill. "Wow. So, what's he like?"

"He's dead."

She choked on the beer, watching him wide-eyed as she pounded on her chest. "Dead? You didn't…"

"Kill him?" This time Mikhail smiled. Another thing he enjoyed about Keely was her innate flare for the dramatic. "No, but I considered killing the new Hayward—his granddaughter."

"The new landlord's a woman? What's she like?"

"Very beautiful, very cold." He was frowning as he skimmed his fingertips over the wood grain. "She has red hair and white skin. Blue eyes like frost on a lake. When she speaks, icicles form."

Keely grimaced and sipped. "Rich people," she said, "can afford to be cold."

"I told her she has two days before I go to the building commissioner."

This time Keely smiled. As much as she admired Mikhail, she felt he was naive in a lot of ways. "Good luck. Maybe we should take Mrs. Bayford's idea about a rent strike. Of course, then we risk eviction, but…hey." She leaned out the open window. "You should see this car. It's like a Lincoln or something—with a driver. There's a woman getting out of the back." More fascinated than envious, she let out a long, appreciative breath. "*Harper's Bazaar*'s version of the executive woman." Grinning, she shot a glance over her shoulder. "I think your ice princess has come slumming."

Outside, Sydney studied the building. It was really quite lovely, she thought. Like an old woman who had maintained her dignity and a shadow of her youthful beauty. The red brick had faded to a soft pink, smudged here and there by soot and exhaust. The trimming paint was peeling and cracked, but that could be easily remedied. Taking out a legal pad, she began to take notes.

She was aware that the men sitting out on the stoop were watching her, but she ignored them. It was a noisy place, she noted. Most of the windows were open and there was a variety of sounds—televisions, radios, babies crying, someone singing "The Desert Song" in a warbling soprano. There were useless little balconies crowded with potted flowers, bicycles, clothes drying in the still, hot air.

Shading her eyes, she let her gaze travel up. Most of the railings were badly rusted and many had spokes missing. She frowned, then spotted Mikhail, leaning out of a window on the top floor, nearly cheek to cheek with a stunning blonde. Since he was bare chested and the blonde was wearing the tiniest excuse for a tank top, Sydney imagined she'd interrupted them. She acknowledged him with a frigid nod, then went back to her notes.

When she started toward the entrance, the men shifted to make a path for her. The small lobby was dim and oppressively hot. On this level the windows were apparently painted shut. The old parquet floor was scarred and scraped, and there was a smell, a very definite smell, of mold. She studied the elevator dubiously. Someone had hand-lettered a sign above the button that read Abandon Hope Ye Who Enter Here.

Curious, Sydney punched the up button and listened to the grinding rattles and wheezes. On an impatient breath, she made more notes. It was deplorable, she thought. The unit should have been inspected, and Hayward should have been slapped with a citation. Well, she was Hayward now.

The doors squeaked open, and Mikhail stepped out.

"Did you come to look over your empire?" he asked her.

Very deliberately she finished her notes before she met his gaze. At least he had pulled on a shirt—if you could call it that. The thin white T-shirt was ripped at the sleeves and mangled at the hem.

"I believe I told you I'd look over the file. Once I did, I thought it best to inspect the building myself." She glanced at the elevator, then back at him. "You're either very brave or very stupid, Mr. Stanislaski."

"A realist," he corrected with a slow shrug. "What happens, happens."

"Perhaps. But I'd prefer that no one use this elevator until it's repaired or replaced."

He slipped his hands into his pockets. "And will it be?"

"Yes, as quickly as possible. I believe you mentioned in your letter that some of the stair railings were broken."

"I've replaced the worst of them."

Her brow lifted. "You?"

"There are children and old people in this building."

The simplicity of his answer made her ashamed. "I see. Since you've taken it on yourself to represent the tenants, perhaps you'd take me through and show me the worst of the problems."

As they started up the stairs, she noted that the railing was obviously new, an unstained line of wood that was sturdy under her hand. She made a note that it had been replaced by a tenant.

He knocked on apartment doors. People greeted him enthusiastically, her warily. There were smells of cooking—meals just finished, meals yet to be eaten. She was offered strudel, brownies, goulash, chicken wings. Some of the complaints were bitter, some were nervous. But Sydney saw for herself that Mikhail's letters hadn't exaggerated.

By the time they reached the third floor, the heat was making her dizzy. On the fourth, she refused the offer of spaghetti and meatballs—wondering how anyone could bear to cook in all this heat—and accepted a glass of water. Dutifully she noted down how the pipes rattled and thumped. When they reached the fifth floor, she was wishing desperately for a cool shower, a chilled glass of chardonnay and the blissful comfort of her air-conditioned apartment.

Mikhail noted that her face was glowing from the heat. On the last flight of stairs, she'd been puffing a bit, which pleased him. It wouldn't hurt the queen to see how her subjects lived. He wondered why she didn't at least peel off her suit jacket or loosen a couple of those prim buttons on her blouse.

He wasn't pleased with the thought that he would enjoy doing both of those things for her.

"I would think that some of these tenants would have window units." Sweat slithered nastily down her back. "Air-conditioning."

"The wiring won't handle it," he told her. "When people turn them on, it blows the fuses and we lose power. The hallways are the worst," he went on conversationally. "Airless. And up here is worst of all. Heat rises."

"So I've heard."

She was white as a sheet, he noted, and swore. "Take off your jacket."

"I beg your pardon?"

"You're stupid." He tugged the linen off her shoulders and began to pull her arms free.

The combination of heat and his rough, purposeful fingers had spots dancing in front of her eyes. "Stop it."

"Very stupid. This is not a boardroom."

His touch wasn't the least bit loverlike, but it was very disturbing. She batted at his hands the moment one of her arms was free. Ignoring her, Mikhail pushed her into his apartment.

"Mr. Stanislaski," she said, out of breath but not out of dignity. "I will not be pawed."

"I have doubts you've ever been pawed in your life, Your Highness. What man wants frostbite? Sit."

"I have no desire to—"

He simply shoved her into a chair, then glanced over where Keely stood in the kitchen, gaping. "Get her some water," he ordered.

Sydney caught her breath. A fan whirled beside the chair and cooled her skin. "You are the rudest, most ill-mannered, most insufferable man I've ever been forced to deal with."

He took the glass from Keely and was tempted to toss the contents into Sydney's beautiful face. Instead he shoved the glass into her hand. "Drink."

"Jeez, Mik, have a heart," Keely murmured. "She looks beat. You want a cold cloth?" Even as she offered, she couldn't help but admire the ivory silk blouse with its tiny pearl buttons.

"No, thank you. I'm fine."

"I'm Keely O'Brian, 502."

"Her oven doesn't work," Mikhail said. "And she gets no hot water. The roof leaks."

"Only when it rains." Keely tried to smile but got no response. "I guess I'll run along. Nice to meet you."

When they were alone, Sydney took slow sips of the tepid water. Mikhail hadn't complained about his own apartment, but she could see from where she sat that the linoleum on the kitchen floor was ripped, and the refrigerator was hopelessly small and out-of-date. She simply didn't have the energy to look at the rest.

His approach had been anything but tactful, still the bottom line was he was right and her company was wrong.

He sat on the edge of the kitchen counter and watched as color seeped slowly back into her cheeks. It relieved him. For a moment in the hall he'd been afraid she would faint. He already felt like a clod.

"Do you want food?" His voice was clipped and unfriendly. "You can have a sandwich."

She remembered that she was supposed to be dining at Le Cirque with the latest eligible bachelor her mother had chosen. "No, thank you. You don't think much of me, do you?"

He moved his shoulders in the way she now recognized as habit. "I think of you quite a bit."

She frowned and set the glass aside. The way he said it left a little too much to the imagination. "You said you were a carpenter?"

"I am sometimes a carpenter."

"You have a license?"

His eyes narrowed. "A contractor's license, yes. For remodeling, renovations."

"Then you'd have a list of other contractors you've worked with—electricians, plumbers, that sort of thing."

"Yes."

"Fine. Work up a bid on repairs, including the finish work, painting, tile, replacing fixtures, appliances. Have it on my desk in a week." She rose, picking up her crumpled jacket.

He stayed where he was as she folded the jacket over her arm, lifted her briefcase. "And then?"

She shot him a cool look. "And then, Mr. Stanislaski, I'm going to put my money where your mouth is. You're hired."

Chapter 2

"Mother, I really don't have time for this."

"Sydney, dear, one always has time for tea." So saying, Margerite Rothchild Hayward Kinsdale LaRue poured ginseng into a china cup. "I'm afraid you're taking this real estate business too seriously."

"Maybe because I'm in charge," Sydney muttered without looking up from the papers on her desk.

"I can't imagine what your grandfather was thinking of. But then, he always was an unusual man." She sighed a moment, remembering how fond she'd been of the old goat. "Come, darling, have some tea and one of these delightful little sandwiches. Even Madam Executive needs a spot of lunch."

Sydney gave in, hoping to move her mother along more quickly by being agreeable. "This is really very sweet of you. It's just that I'm pressed for time today."

"All this corporate nonsense," Margerite began as Sydney sat beside her. "I don't know why you bother. It would have been so simple to hire a manager or whatever." Margerite added a squirt of lemon to her cup before she sat back. "I realize it might be diverting for a while, but the thought of you with a career. Well, it seems so pointless."

"Does it?" Sydney murmured, struggling to keep the bitterness out of her voice. "I may surprise everyone and be good at it."

"Oh, I'm sure you'd be wonderful at whatever you do, darling." Her hand fluttered absently over Sydney's. The girl had been so little trouble as a child, she thought. Margerite really hadn't a clue how to deal with this sudden and—she was sure—temporary spot of rebellion. She tried placating. "And I was delighted when Grandfather Hayward left you all those nice buildings." She nibbled on a sandwich, a striking woman who looked ten years younger than her fifty years, groomed and polished in a Chanel suit. "But to actually become involved in running things." Baffled, she patted her carefully tinted chestnut hair. "Well, one might think it's just a bit unfeminine. A man is easily put off by what he considers a high-powered woman."

Sydney gave her mother's newly bare ring finger a pointed look. "Not every woman's sole ambition centers around a man."

"Oh, don't be silly." With a gay little laugh, Margerite patted her daughter's hand. "A husband isn't something a woman wants to be without for long. You mustn't be discouraged because you and Peter didn't work things out. First marriages are often just a testing ground."

Reining in her feelings, Sydney set her cup down carefully. "Is that what you consider your marriage to Father? A testing ground?"

"We both learned some valuable lessons from it, I'm sure." Confident and content, she beamed at her daughter. "Now, dear, tell me about your evening with Channing. How was it?"

"Stifling."

Margerite's mild blue eyes flickered with annoyance. "Sydney, really."

"You asked." To fortify herself, Sydney picked up her tea

again. Why was it, she asked herself, that she perpetually felt inadequate around the woman who had given birth to her. "I'm sorry, Mother, but we simply don't suit."

"Nonsense. You're perfectly suited. Channing Warfield is an intelligent, successful man from a very fine family."

"So was Peter."

China clinked against china as Margerite set her cup in its saucer. "Sydney, you must not compare every man you meet with Peter."

"I don't." Taking a chance, she laid a hand on her mother's. There was a bond there, there had to be. Why did she always feel as though her fingers were just sliding away from it? "Honestly, I don't compare Channing with anyone. The simple fact is, I find him stilted, boring and pretentious. It could be that I'd find any man the same just now. I'm not interested in men at this point of my life, Mother. I want to make something of myself."

"Make something of yourself," Margerite repeated, more stunned than angry. "You're a Hayward. You don't need to make yourself anything else." She plucked up a napkin to dab at her lips. "For heaven's sake, Sydney, you've been divorced from Peter for four years. It's time you found a suitable husband. It's women who write the invitations," she reminded her daughter. "And they have a policy of excluding beautiful, unattached females. You have a place in society, Sydney. And a responsibility to your name."

The familiar clutching in her stomach had Sydney setting the tea aside. "So you've always told me."

Satisfied that Sydney would be reasonable, she smiled. "If Channing won't do, there are others. But I really think you shouldn't be so quick to dismiss him. If I were twenty years younger…well." She glanced at her watch and gave a little squeak. "Dear me, I'm going to be late for the hairdresser. I'll just run and powder my nose first."

When Margerite slipped into the adjoining bath, Sydney leaned her head back and closed her eyes. Where was she to put all these feelings of guilt and inadequacy? How could she explain herself to her mother when she couldn't explain herself to herself?

Rising, she went back to her desk. She couldn't convince Margerite that her unwillingness to become involved again had nothing to do with Peter when, in fact, it did. They had been friends, damn it. She and Peter had grown up with each other, had cared for each other. They simply hadn't been in love with each other. Family pressure had pushed them down the aisle while they'd been too young to realize the mistake. Then they had spent the best part of two years trying miserably to make the marriage work.

The pity of it wasn't the divorce, but the fact that when they had finally parted, they were no longer friends. If she couldn't make a go of it with someone she'd cared for, someone she'd had so much in common with, someone she'd liked so much, surely the lack was in her.

All she wanted to do now was to feel deserving of her grandfather's faith in her. She'd been offered a different kind of responsibility, a different kind of challenge. This time, she couldn't afford to fail.

Wearily she answered her intercom. "Yes, Janine."

"Mr. Stanislaski's here, Miss Hayward. He doesn't have an appointment, but he says he has some papers you wanted to see."

A full day early, she mused, and straightened her shoulders. "Send him in."

At least he'd shaved, she thought, though this time there were holes in his jeans. Closing the door, he took as long and as thorough a look at her. As if they were two boxers sizing up the competition from neutral corners.

She looked just as starched and prim as before, in one of her tidy business suits, this time in pale gray, with all those little silver buttons on her blouse done up to her smooth white throat. He glanced down at the tea tray with its delicate cups and tiny sandwiches. His lips curled.

"Interrupting your lunch, Hayward?"

"Not at all." She didn't bother to stand or smile but gestured him across the room. "Do you have the bid, Mr. Stanislaski?"

"Yes."

"You work fast."

He grinned. "Yes." He caught a scent—rather a clash of scents. Something very subtle and cool and another, florid and overly feminine. "You have company?"

Her brow arched. "Why do you ask?"

"There is perfume here that isn't yours." Then with a shrug, he handed her the papers he carried. "The first is what must be done, the second is what should be done."

"I see." She could feel the heat radiating off him. For some reason it felt comforting, life affirming. As if she'd stepped out of a dark cave into the sunlight. Sydney made certain her fingers didn't brush his as she took the papers. "You have estimates from the subcontractors?"

"They are there." While she glanced through his work, he lifted one of the neat triangles of bread, sniffed at it like a wolf. "What is this stuff in here?"

She barely looked up. "Watercress."

With a grunt, he dropped it back onto the plate. "Why would you eat it?"

She looked up again, and this time, she smiled. "Good question."

She shouldn't have done that, he thought as he shifted his hands to his pockets. When she smiled, she changed. Her eyes warmed, her lips softened, and beauty became approachable rather than aloof.

It made him forget he wasn't the least bit interested in her type of woman.

"Then I'll ask you another question."

Her lips pursed as she scanned the list. She liked what she saw. "You seem to be full of them today."

"Why do you wear colors like that? Dull ones, when you should be wearing vivid. Sapphire or emerald."

It was surprise that had her staring at him. As far as she could remember, no one had ever questioned her taste. In some circles, she was thought to be quite elegant. "Are you a carpenter or a fashion consultant, Mr. Stanislaski?"

His shoulders moved. "I'm a man. Is this tea?" He lifted the pot and sniffed at the contents while she continued to gape at him. "It's too hot for tea. You have something cold?"

Shaking her head, she pressed her intercom. "Janine, bring in something cold for Mr. Stanislaski, please." Because she had a nagging urge to get up and inspect herself in a mirror, she cleared her throat. "There's quite a line of demarcation between your must and your should list, Mr.—"

"Mikhail," he said easily. "It's because there are more things you should do than things you must. Like life."

"Now a philosopher," she muttered. "We'll start with the must, and perhaps incorporate some of the should. If we work quickly, we could have a contract by the end of the week."

His nod was slow, considering. "You, too, work fast."

"When necessary. Now first, I'd like you to explain to me why I should replace all the windows."

"Because they're single glazed and not efficient."

"Yes, but—"

"Sydney, dear, the lighting in there is just ghastly. Oh." Margerite stopped at the doorway. "I beg your pardon, I see you're in a meeting." She would have looked down her nose at Mikhail's worn jeans, but she had a difficult time getting past his face. "How do you do?" she said, pleased that he had risen at her entrance.

"You are Sydney's mother?" Mikhail asked before Sydney could shoo Margerite along.

"Why, yes." Margerite's smile was reserved. She didn't approve of her daughter being on a first-name basis in her relationships with the help. Particularly when that help wore stubby ponytails and dirty boots. "How did you know?"

"Real beauty matures well."

"Oh." Charmed, Margerite allowed her smile to warm fractionally. Her lashes fluttered in reflex. "How kind."

"Mother, I'm sorry, but Mr. Stanislaski and I have business to discuss."

"Of course, of course." Margerite walked over to kiss the air an inch from her daughter's cheek. "I'll just be running along. Now, dear, you won't forget we're to have lunch next week? And I wanted to remind you that... Stanislaski," she repeated, turning back to Mikhail. "I thought you looked familiar. Oh, my." Suddenly breathless, she laid a hand on her heart. "You're Mikhail Stanislaski?"

"Yes. Have we met?"

"No. Oh, no, we haven't, but I saw your photo in *Art/World*. I consider myself a patron." Face beaming, she skirted the desk and, under her daughter's astonished gaze, took his hands in hers. To Margerite, the ponytail was now artistic, the tattered jeans eccentric. "Your work, Mr. Stanislaski—magnificent. Truly magnificent. I bought two of your pieces from your last showing. I can't tell you what a pleasure this is."

"You flatter me."

"Not at all," Margerite insisted. "You're already being called one of the top artists of the nineties. And you've commissioned him." She turned to beam at her speechless daughter. "A brilliant move, darling."

"I—actually, I—"

"I'm delighted," Mikhail interrupted, "to be working with your daughter."

"It's wonderful." She gave his hands a final squeeze. "You must come to a little dinner party I'm having on Friday on Long Island. Please, don't tell me you're already engaged for the evening." She slanted a look from under her lashes. "I'll be devastated."

He was careful not to grin over her head at Sydney. "I could never be responsible for devastating a beautiful woman."

"Fabulous. Sydney will bring you. Eight o'clock. Now I must run." She patted her hair, shot an absent wave at Sydney and hurried out just as Janine brought in a soft drink.

Mikhail took the glass with thanks, then sat again. "So," he began, "you were asking about windows."

Sydney very carefully relaxed the hands that were balled into fists under her desk. "You said you were a carpenter."

"Sometimes I am." He took a long, cooling drink. "Sometimes I carve wood instead of hammering it."

If he had set out to make a fool of her—which she wasn't sure he hadn't—he could have succeeded no better. "I've spent the last two years in Europe," she told him, "so I'm a bit out of touch with the American art world."

"You don't have to apologize," he said, enjoying himself.

"I'm not apologizing." She had to force herself to speak calmly, to not stand up and rip his bid into tiny little pieces. "I'd like to know what kind of game you're playing, Stanislaski."

"You offered me work, on a job that has some value for me. I am accepting it."

"You lied to me."

"How?" He lifted one hand, palm up. "I have a contractor's license. I've made my living in construction since I was sixteen. What difference does it make to you if people now buy my sculpture?"

"None." She snatched up the bids again. He probably produced primitive, ugly pieces in any case, she thought. The man was too rough and unmannered to be an artist. All that mattered was that he could do the job she was hiring him to do.

But she hated being duped. To make him pay for it, she forced him to go over every detail of the bid, wasting over an hour of his time and hers.

"All right then." She pushed aside her own meticulous notes. "Your contract will be ready for signing on Friday."

"Good." He rose. "You can bring it when you pick me up. We should make it seven."

"Excuse me?"

"For dinner." He leaned forward. For a shocking moment, she thought he was actually going to kiss her. She went rigid as a spear, but he only rubbed the lapel of her suit between his thumb and forefinger. "You must wear something with color."

She pushed the chair back and stood. "I have no intention of taking you to my mother's home for dinner."

"You're afraid to be with me." He said so with no little amount of pride.

Her chin jutted out. "Certainly not."

"What else could it be?" With his eyes on hers, he strolled around the desk until they were face-to-face. "A woman like you could not be so ill-mannered without a reason."

The breath was backing up in her lungs. Sydney forced it out in one huff. "It's reason enough that I dislike you."

He only smiled and toyed with the pearls at her throat. "No. Aristocrats are predictable, Hayward. You would be taught to tolerate people you don't like. For them, you would be the most polite."

"Stop touching me."

"I'm putting color in your cheeks." He laughed and let the pearls slide out of his fingers. Her skin, he was sure, would be just as smooth, just as cool. "Come now, Sydney, what will you tell your charming mother when you go to her party without me? How will you explain that you refused to bring me?" He could see the war in her eyes, the one fought between pride and manners and temper, and laughed again. "Trapped by your breeding," he murmured. "This is not something I have to worry about myself."

"No doubt," she said between her teeth.

"Friday," he said, and infuriated her by flicking a finger down her cheek. "Seven o'clock."

"Mr. Stanislaski," she murmured when he reached the door. As he turned back, she offered her coolest smile. "Try to find something in your closet without holes in it."

She could hear him laughing at her as he walked down the hallway. If only, she thought as she dropped back into her chair. If only she hadn't been so well-bred, she could have released some of this venom by throwing breakables at the door.

She wore black quite deliberately. Under no circumstances did she want him to believe that she would fuss through her wardrobe, looking for something colorful because he'd suggested it. And she thought the simple tube of a dress was both businesslike, fashionable and appropriate.

On impulse, she had taken her hair down so that it fluffed out to skim her shoulders—only because she'd tired of wearing it pulled back. As always, she had debated her look for the evening carefully and was satisfied that she had achieved an aloof elegance.

She could hear the music blasting through his door before she knocked. It surprised her to hear the passionate strains of *Carmen*. She rapped harder, nearly gave in to the urge to shout over the aria, when the door swung open. Behind it was the blond knockout in a skimpy T-shirt and skimpier shorts.

"Hi." Keely crunched a piece of ice between her teeth and swallowed. "I was just borrowing an ice tray from Mik—my freezer's set on melt these days." She managed to smile and forced herself not to tug on her clothes. She felt like a peasant caught poaching by the royal princess. "I was just leaving." Before Sydney could speak, she dashed back inside to scoop up a tray of ice. "Mik, your date's here."

Sydney winced at the term *date* as the blond bullet streaked past her. "There's no need for you to rush off—"

"Three's a crowd," Keely told her on the run and, with a quick fleeting grin, kept going.

"Did you call me?" Mikhail came to the bedroom doorway. There was one, very small white towel anchored at his waist. He used another to rub at his wet, unruly hair. He stopped when he spotted Sydney. Something flickered in his eyes as he let his gaze roam down the long, cool lines of the dress. Then he smiled. "I'm late," he said simply.

She was grateful she'd managed not to let her mouth fall open. His body was all lean muscle, long bones and bronzed skin—skin that was gleaming with tiny drops of water that made her feel unbearably thirsty. The towel hung dangerously low on his hips. Dazed, she watched a drop of water slide down his chest, over his stomach and disappear beneath the terry cloth.

The temperature in the room, already steamy, rose several degrees.

"You're…" She knew she could speak coherently—in a minute. "We said seven."

"I was busy." He shrugged. The towel shifted. Sydney swallowed. "I won't be long. Fix a drink." A smile, wicked around the edges, tugged at his mouth. A man would have to be dead not to see her reaction—not to be pleased by it. "You look… hot, Sydney." He took a step forward, watching her eyes widen, watching her mouth tremble open. With his gaze on hers, he turned on a small portable fan. Steamy air stirred. "That will help," he said mildly.

She nodded. It was cooling, but it also brought the scent of his shower, of his skin into the room. Because she could see the knowledge and the amusement in his eyes, she got a grip on herself. "Your contracts." She set the folder down on a table. Mikhail barely glanced at them.

"I'll look and sign later."

"Fine. It would be best if you got dressed." She had to swallow another obstruction in her throat when he smiled at her. Her voice was edgy and annoyed. "We'll be late."

"A little. There's cold drink in the refrigerator," he added as he turned back to the bedroom. "Be at home."

Alone, she managed to take three normal breaths. Degree by degree she felt her system level. Any man who looked like that in a towel should be arrested, she thought, and turned to study the room.

She'd been too annoyed to take stock of it on her other visit. And too preoccupied, she admitted with a slight frown. A man like that had a way of keeping a woman preoccupied. Now she noted the hunks of wood, small and large, the tools, the jars stuffed with brushes. There was a long worktable beneath the living room window. She wandered toward it, seeing that a few of those hunks of wood were works in progress.

Shrugging, she ran a finger over a piece of cherry that was scarred with grooves and gouges. Rude and primitive, just as she'd thought. It soothed her ruffled ego to be assured she'd been right about his lack of talent. Obviously a ruffian who'd made a momentary impression on the capricious art world.

Then she turned and saw the shelves.

They were crowded with his work. Long smooth columns of wood, beautifully shaped. A profile of a woman with long, flowing hair, a young child caught in gleeful laughter, lovers trapped endlessly in a first tentative kiss. She couldn't stop herself from touching, nor from feeling. His work ranged from the passionate to the charming, from the bold to the delicate.

Fascinated, she crouched down to get a closer look at the pieces on the lower shelves. Was it possible, she wondered, that a man with such rough manners, with such cocky arrogance possessed the wit, the sensitivity, the compassion to create such lovely things out of blocks of wood?

With a half laugh Sydney reached for a carving of a tiny kangaroo with a baby peeking out of her pouch. It felt as smooth and as delicate as glass. Even as she replaced it with a little sigh, she spotted the miniature figurine. Cinderella, she thought, charmed as she held it in her fingertips. The pretty fairy-tale heroine was still dressed for the ball, but one foot was bare as Mikhail had captured her in her dash before the clock struck twelve. For a moment, Sydney thought she could almost see tears in the painted eyes.

"You like?"

She jolted, then stood up quickly, still nestling the figurine in her hand. "Yes—I'm sorry."

"You don't have to be sorry for liking." Mikhail rested a hip, now more conservatively covered in wheat-colored slacks, on the worktable. His hair had been brushed back and now curled damply nearly to his shoulders.

Still flustered, she set the miniature back on the shelf. "I meant I should apologize for touching your work."

A smile tugged at his lips. It fascinated him that she could go from wide-eyed delight to frosty politeness in the blink of an eye. "Better to be touched than to sit apart, only to be admired. Don't you think?"

It was impossible to miss the implication in the tone of his voice, in the look in his eyes. "That would depend."

As she started by, he shifted, rose. His timing was perfect. She all but collided with him. "On what?"

She didn't flush or stiffen or retreat. She'd become accustomed to taking a stand. "On whether one chooses to be touched."

He grinned. "I thought we were talking about sculpture."

So, she thought on a careful breath, she'd walked into that

one. "Yes, we were. Now, we really will be late. If you're ready, Mr. Stanislaski—"

"Mikhail." He lifted a hand casually to flick a finger at the sapphire drop at her ear. "It's easier." Before she could reply, his gaze came back and locked on hers. Trapped in that one long stare, she wasn't certain she could remember her own name. "You smell like an English garden at teatime," he murmured. "Very cool, very appealing. And just a little too formal."

It was too hot, she told herself. Much too hot and close. That was why she had difficulty breathing. It had nothing to do with him. Rather, she wouldn't allow it to have anything to do with him. "You're in my way."

"I know." And for reasons he wasn't entirely sure of, he intended to stay there. "You're used to brushing people aside."

"I don't see what that has to do with—"

"An observation," he interrupted, amusing himself by toying with the ends of her hair. The texture was as rich as the color, he decided, pleased she had left it free for the evening. "Artists observe. You'll find that some people don't brush aside as quickly as others." He heard her breath catch, ignored her defensive jerk as he cupped her chin in his hand. He'd been right about her skin—smooth as polished pearls. Patiently he turned her face from side to side. "Nearly perfect," he decided. "Nearly perfect is better than perfect."

"I beg your pardon?"

"Your eyes are too big, and your mouth is just a bit wider than it should be."

Insulted, she slapped his hand away. It embarrassed and infuriated her that she'd actually expected a compliment. "My eyes and mouth are none of your business."

"Very much mine," he corrected. "I'm doing your face."

When she frowned, a faint line etched between her brows. He liked it. "You're doing what?"

"Your face. In rosewood, I think. And with your hair down like this."

Again she pushed his hand away. "If you're asking me to model for you, I'm afraid I'm not interested."

"It doesn't matter whether you are. I am." He took her arm to lead her to the door.

"If you think I'm flattered—"

"Why should you be?" He opened the door, then stood just inside, studying her with apparent curiosity. "You were born with your face. You didn't earn it. If I said you sang well, or danced well, or kissed well, you could be flattered."

He eased her out, then closed the door. "Do you?" he asked, almost in afterthought.

Ruffled and irritated, she snapped back. "Do I what?"

"Kiss well?"

Her brows lifted. Haughty arches over frosty eyes. "The day you find out, you can be flattered." Rather pleased with the line, she started down the hall ahead of him.

His fingers barely touched her—she would have sworn it. But in the space of a heartbeat her back was to the wall and she was caged between his arms, with his hands planted on either side of her head. Both shock and a trembling river of fear came before she could even think to be insulted.

Knowing he was being obnoxious, enjoying it, he kept his lips a few scant inches from hers. He recognized the curling in his gut as desire. And by God, he could deal with that. And her. Their breath met and tangled, and he smiled. Hers had come out in a quick, surprised puff.

"I think," he said slowly, consideringly, "you have yet to learn how to kiss well. You have the mouth for it." His gaze lowered, lingered there. "But a man would have to be patient enough to warm that blood up first. A pity I'm not patient."

He was close enough to see her quick wince before her eyes went icy. "I think," she said, borrowing his tone, "that you

probably kiss very well. But a woman would have to be tolerant enough to hack through your ego first. Fortunately, I'm not
tolerant."

For a moment he stood where he was, close enough to swoop
down and test both their theories. Then the smile worked over
his face, curving his lips, brightening his eyes. Yes, he could
deal with her. When he was ready.

"A man can learn patience, *milaya*, and seduce a woman to
tolerance."

She pressed against the wall, but like a cat backed into a corner, she was ready to swipe and spit. He only stepped back and
cupped a hand over her elbow.

"We should go now, yes?"

"Yes." Not at all sure if she was relieved or disappointed, she
walked with him toward the stairs.

Chapter 3

Margerite had pulled out all the stops. She knew it was a coup to have a rising and mysterious artist such as Stanislaski at her dinner party. Like a general girding for battle, she had inspected the floral arrangements, the kitchens, the dining room and the terraces. Before she was done, the caterers were cursing her, but Margerite was satisfied.

She wasn't pleased when her daughter, along with her most important guest, was late.

Laughing and lilting, she swirled among her guests in a frothy gown of robin's-egg blue. There was a sprinkling of politicians, theater people and the idle rich. But the Ukrainian artist was her coup de grace, and she was fretting to show him off.

And, remembering that wild sexuality, she was fretting to flirt.

The moment she spotted him, Margerite swooped.

"Mr. Stanislaski, how marvelous!" After shooting her daughter a veiled censorious look, she beamed.

"Mikhail, please." Because he knew the game and played it at his will, Mikhail brought her hand to his lips and lingered over it. "You must forgive me for being late. I kept your daughter waiting."

"Oh." She fluttered, her hand resting lightly, possessively on his arm. "A smart woman will always wait for the right man."

"Then I'm forgiven."

"Absolutely." Her fingers gave his an intimate squeeze. "This time. Now, you must let me introduce you around, Mikhail." Linked with him, she glanced absently at her daughter. "Sydney, do mingle, darling."

Mikhail shot a quick, wicked grin over his shoulder as he let Margerite haul him away.

He made small talk easily, sliding into the upper crust of New York society as seamlessly as he slid into the working class in Soho or his parents' close-knit neighborhood in Brooklyn. They had no idea he might have preferred a beer with friends or coffee at his mother's kitchen table.

He sipped champagne, admired the house with its cool white walls and towering windows, and complimented Margerite on her art collection.

And all the while he chatted, sipped and smiled, he watched Sydney.

Odd, he thought. He would have said that the sprawling elegance of the Long Island enclave was the perfect setting for her. Her looks, her demeanor, reminded him of glistening shaved ice in a rare porcelain bowl. Yet she didn't quite fit. Oh, she smiled and worked the room as skillfully as her mother. Her simple black dress was as exclusive as any of the more colorful choices in the room. Her sapphires winked as brilliantly as any of the diamonds or emeralds.

But…it was her eyes, Mikhail realized. There wasn't laughter in them, but impatience. It was as though she were thinking—let's get this done and over with so I can get on to something important.

It made him smile. Remembering that he'd have the long

drive back to Manhattan to tease her made the smile widen. It faded abruptly as he watched a tall blond man with football shoulders tucked into a silk dinner jacket kiss Sydney on the mouth.

Sydney smiled into a pair of light blue eyes under golden brows. "Hello, Channing."

"Hello, yourself." He offered a fresh glass of wine. "Where did Margerite find the wild horses?"

"I'm sorry?"

"To drag you out of that office." His smile dispensed charm like penny candy. Sydney couldn't help but respond.

"It wasn't quite that drastic. I have been busy."

"So you've told me." He approved of her in the sleek black dress in much the same way he would have approved of a tasteful accessory for his home. "You missed a wonderful play the other night. It looks like Sondheim's got another hit on his hands." Never doubting her acquiescence, he took her arm to lead her into dinner. "Tell me, darling, when are you going to stop playing the career woman and take a break? I'm going up to the Hamptons for the weekend, and I'd love your company."

Dutifully she forced her clamped teeth apart. There was no use resenting the fact he thought she was playing. Everyone did. "I'm afraid I can't get away just now." She took her seat beside him at the long glass table in the airy dining room. The drapes were thrown wide so that the garden seemed to spill inside with the pastel hues of early roses, late tulips and nodding columbine.

She wished the dinner had been alfresco so she could have sat among the blossoms and scented the sea air.

"I hope you don't mind a little advice."

Sydney nearly dropped her head into her hand. The chatter around them was convivial, glasses were clinking, and the first course of stuffed mushrooms was being served. She felt she'd just been clamped into a cell. "Of course not, Channing."

"You can run a business or let the business run you."

"Hmm." He had a habit of stating his advice in clichés. Sydney reminded herself she should be used to it.

"Take it from someone with more experience in these matters."

She fixed a smile on her face and let her mind wander.

"I hate to see you crushed under the heel of responsibility," he went on. "And after all, we know you're a novice in the dog-eat-dog world of real estate." Gold cuff links, monogrammed, winked as he laid a hand on hers. His eyes were sincere, his mouth quirked in that I'm-only-looking-out-for-you smile. "Naturally, your initial enthusiasm will push you to take on more than is good for you. I'm sure you agree."

Her mind flicked back. "Actually, Channing, I enjoy the work."

"For the moment," he said, his voice so patronizing she nearly stabbed him with her salad fork. "But when reality rushes in you may find yourself trampled under it. Delegate, Sydney. Hand the responsibilities over to those who understand them."

If her spine had been any straighter, it would have snapped her neck. "My grandfather entrusted Hayward to me."

"The elderly become sentimental. But I can't believe he expected you to take it all so seriously." His smooth, lightly tanned brow wrinkled briefly in what she understood was genuine if misguided concern. "Why, you've hardly attended a party in weeks. Everyone's talking about it."

"Are they?" She forced her lips to curve over her clenched teeth. If he offered one more shred of advice, she would have to upend the water goblet in his lap. "Channing, why don't you tell me about the play?"

At the other end of the table, tucked between Margerite and Mrs. Anthony Lowell of the Boston Lowells, Mikhail kept a weather eye on Sydney. He didn't like the way she had her head together with pretty boy. No, by God, he didn't. The man was always touching her. Her hand, her shoulder. Her soft, white, bare shoulder. And she was just smiling and nodding, as though his words were a fascination in themselves.

Apparently the ice queen didn't mind being pawed if the hands doing the pawing were as lily-white as her own.

Mikhail swore under his breath.

"I beg your pardon, Mikhail?"

With an effort, he turned his attention and a smile toward Margerite. "Nothing. The pheasant is excellent."

"Thank you. I wonder if I might ask what Sydney's commissioned you to sculpt."

He flicked a black look down the length of the table. "I'll be working on the project in Soho."

"Ah." Margerite hadn't a clue what Hayward might own in Soho. "Will it be an indoor or outdoor piece?"

"Both. Who is the man beside Sydney? I don't think I met him."

"Oh, that's Channing, Channing Warfield. The Warfields are old friends."

"Friends," he repeated, slightly mollified.

Conspiratorially Margerite leaned closer. "If I can confide, Wilhelmina Warfield and I are hoping they'll make an announcement this summer. They're such a lovely couple, so suitable. And since Sydney's first marriage is well behind her—"

"First marriage?" He swooped down on that tidbit of information like a hawk on a dove. "Sydney was married before?"

"Yes, but I'm afraid she and Peter were too young and impetuous," she told him, conveniently overlooking the family pressure that had brought the marriage about. "Now, Sydney and Channing are mature, responsible people. We're looking forward to a spring wedding."

Mikhail picked up his wine. There was an odd and annoying scratching in his throat. "What does this Channing Warfield do?"

"Do?" The question baffled her. "Why, the Warfields are in banking, so I suppose Channing does whatever one does in banking. He's a devil on the polo field."

"Polo," Mikhail repeated with a scowl so dark Helena Lowell choked on her pheasant. Helpfully Mikhail gave her a sharp slap between the shoulder blades, then offered her her water goblet.

"You're, ah, Russian, aren't you, Mr. Stanislaski?" Helena asked. Images of Cossacks danced in her head.

"I was born in the Ukraine."

"The Ukraine, yes. I believe I read something about your family escaping over the border when you were just a child."

"We escaped in a wagon, over the mountains into Hungary, then into Austria and finally settled in New York."

"A wagon." Margerite sighed into her wine. "How romantic."

Mikhail remembered the cold, the fear, the hunger. But he only shrugged. He doubted romance was always pretty, or comfortable.

Relieved that he looked approachable again, Helena Lowell began to ask him questions about art.

After an hour, he was glad to escape from the pretensions of the society matron's art school jargon. Guests were treated to violin music, breezy terraces and moon-kissed gardens. His hostess fluttered around him like a butterfly, lashes batting, laughter trilling.

Margerite's flirtations were patently obvious and didn't bother him. She was a pretty, vivacious woman currently between men. Though he had privately deduced she shared little with her daughter other than looks, he considered her harmless, even entertaining. So when she offered to show him the rooftop patio, he went along.

The wind off the sound was playful and fragrant. And it was blessedly quiet following the ceaseless after-dinner chatter. From the rail, Mikhail could see the water, the curve of beach, the serene elegance of other homes tucked behind walls and circling gardens.

And he could see Sydney as she strolled to the shadowy corner of the terrace below with her arm tucked through Channing's.

"My third husband built this house," Margerite was saying. "He's an architect. When we divorced, I had my choice between this house and the little villa in Nice. Naturally, with so many of my friends here, I chose this." With a sigh, she turned to face him, leaning prettily on the rail. "I must say, I love this spot. When I give house parties people are spread out on every level, so it's both cozy and private. Perhaps you'll join us some weekend this summer."

"Perhaps." The answer was absent as he stared down at Sydney. The moonlight made her hair gleam like polished mahogany.

Margerite shifted, just enough so that their thighs brushed. Mikhail wasn't sure if he was more surprised or more amused. But to save her pride, he smiled, easing away slowly. "You have a lovely home. It suits you."

"I'd love to see your studio." Margerite let the invitation melt into her eyes. "Where you create."

"I'm afraid you'd find it cramped, hot and boring."

"Impossible." Smiling, she traced a fingertip over the back of his hand. "I'm sure I'd find nothing about you boring."

Good God, the woman was old enough to be his mother, and she was coming on to him like a misty-eyed virgin primed for her first tumble. Mikhail nearly sighed, then reminded himself it was only a moment out of his life. He took her hand between both of his hands.

"Margerite, you're charming. And I'm—" he kissed her fingers lightly "—unsuitable."

She lifted a finger and brushed it over his cheek. "You underestimate yourself, Mikhail."

No, but he realized how he'd underestimated her.

On the terrace below, Sydney was trying to find a graceful way to discourage Channing. He was attentive, dignified, solicitous, and he was boring her senseless.

It was her lack, she was sure. Any woman with half a soul would be melting under the attraction of a man like Channing. There was moonlight, music, flowers. The breeze in the leafy trees smelled of the sea and murmured of romance. Channing was talking about Paris, and his hand was skimming lightly over her bare back.

She wished she was home, alone, with her eyes crossing over a fat file of quarterly reports.

Taking a deep breath, she turned. She would have to tell him firmly, simply and straight out that he needed to look elsewhere for companionship. It was Sydney's bad luck that she happened to glance up to see Mikhail on the rooftop with her mother just when he took Margerite's hand to his lips.

Why the...she couldn't think of anything vile enough to call him. Slime was too simple. Gigolo too slick. He was nuzzling up to her mother. *Her mother.* When only hours before he'd been...

Nothing, Sydney reminded herself and dismissed the tense scene in the Soho hallway from her mind. He'd been posturing and preening, that was all.

And she could have killed him for it.

As she watched, Mikhail backed away from Margerite, laughing. Then he looked down. The instant their eyes met, Sydney declared war.

She whirled on Channing, her face so fierce he nearly babbled. "Kiss me," she demanded.

"Why, Sydney."

"I said kiss me." She grabbed him by the lapels and hauled him against her.

"Of course, darling." Pleased with her change of heart, he cupped her shoulders in his hands and leaned down to her.

His lips were soft, warm, eager. They slanted over hers with practiced precision while his hands slid down her back. He tasted of after-dinner mints. Her body fit well against his.

And she felt nothing, nothing but an empty inner rage. Then a chill that was both fear and despair.

"You're not trying, darling," he whispered. "You know I won't hurt you."

No, he wouldn't. There was nothing at all to fear from Channing. Miserable, she let him deepen the kiss, ordered herself to feel and respond. She felt his withdrawal even before his lips left hers. The twinges of annoyance and puzzlement.

"Sydney, dear, I'm not sure what the problem is." He smoothed down his crinkled lapels. Marginally frustrated, he lifted his eyes. "That was like kissing my sister."

"I'm tired, Channing," she said to the air between them. "I should go in and get ready to go."

Twenty minutes later, the driver turned the car toward Manhattan. In the back seat Sydney sat ramrod straight well over in her corner, while Mikhail sprawled in his. They didn't bother to speak, not even the polite nonentities of two people who had attended the same function.

He was boiling with rage.

She was frigid with disdain.

She'd done it to annoy him, Mikhail decided. She'd let that silk-suited jerk all but swallow her whole just to make him suffer.

Why was he suffering? he asked himself. She was nothing to him.

No, she was something, he corrected, and brooded into the dark. His only problem was figuring out exactly what that something was.

Obviously, Sydney reflected, the man had no ethics, no morals, no shame. Here he was, just sitting there, all innocence and quiet reflection, after his disgraceful behavior. She frowned at the pale image of her own face in the window glass and tried to listen to the Chopin prelude on the stereo. Flirting so blatantly with a woman twenty years older. Sneering, yes positively sneering down from the rooftop.

And she'd hired him. Sydney let out a quiet, hissing breath from between her teeth. Oh, that was something she regretted. She'd let her concern, her determination to do the right thing, blind her into hiring some oversexed, amoral Russian carpenter.

Well, if he thought he was going to start playing patty-cake with her mother, he was very much mistaken.

She drew a breath, turned and aimed one steady glare. Mikhail would have sworn the temperature in the car dropped fifty degrees in a snap.

"You stay away from my mother."

He slanted her a look from under his lashes and gracefully crossed his legs. "Excuse me?"

"You heard me, Boris. If you think I'm going to stand by and watch you put the moves on my mother, think again. She's lonely and vulnerable. Her last divorce upset her and she isn't over it."

He said something short and sharp in his native tongue and closed his eyes.

Temper had Sydney sliding across the seat until she could poke his arm. "What the hell does that mean?"

"You want translation? The simplest is bullshit. Now shut up. I'm going to sleep."

"You're not going anywhere until we settle this. You keep your big, grimy hands off my mother, or I'll turn that building you're so fond of into a parking lot."

His eyes slitted open. She found the glitter of angry eyes immensely satisfying. "A big threat from a small woman," he said in a deceptively lazy voice. She was entirely too close for his comfort, and her scent was swimming in his senses, tangling his temper with something more basic. "You should concentrate on the suit, and let your mother handle her own."

"Suit? What suit?"

"The banker who spent the evening sniffing your ankles."

Her face flooded with color. "He certainly was not. He's entirely too well mannered to sniff at my ankles or anything else. And Channing is my business."

"So. You have your business, and I have mine. Now, let's see what we have together." One moment he was stretched out, and the next he had her twisted over his lap. Stunned, Sydney pressed her hands against his chest and tried to struggle out of his hold. He tightened it. "As you see, I have no manners."

"Oh, I know it." She tossed her head back, chin jutting. "What do you think you're doing?"

He wished to hell he knew. She was rigid as an ice floe, but there was something incredible, and Lord, inevitable, about the way she fit into his arms. Though he was cursing himself, he held her close, close enough that he felt the uneven rise and fall of her breasts against his chest, tasted the sweet, wine-tipped flavor of her breath on his lips.

There was a lesson here, he thought grimly, and she was going to learn it.

"I've decided to teach you how to kiss. From what I saw from the roof, you did a poor job of it with the polo player."

Shock and fury had her going still. She would not squirm or scream or give him the satisfaction of frightening her. His eyes were close and challenging. She thought she understood exactly how Lucifer would have looked as he walked through the gates of his own dark paradise.

"You conceited jerk." Because she wanted to slug him, badly, she fisted her hands closed and looked haughtily down her small, straight nose. "There's nothing you can teach me."

"No?" He wondered if he'd be better off just strangling her and having done with it. "Let's see then. Your Channing put his hands here. Yes?" He slid them over her shoulders. The quick, involuntary shudder chilled her skin. "You afraid of me, *milaya?*"

"Don't be ridiculous." But she was, suddenly and deeply. She swallowed the fear as his thumbs caressed her bare skin.

"Tremble is good. It makes a man feel strong. I don't think you trembled for this Channing."

She said nothing and wondered if he knew his accent had thickened. It sounded exotic, erotic. He wondered he could speak at all with her watching him and waiting.

"His way isn't mine," he muttered. "I'll show you."

His fingers clamped around the back of her neck, pulled her face toward his. He heard her breath catch then shudder out when he paused only a fraction before their lips touched. Her eyes filled his vision, that wide, wary blue. Ignoring the twist in his gut, he smiled, turned his head just an inch and skimmed his lips over her jawline.

She bit back only part of the moan. Instinctively she tipped her head back, giving him access to the long, sensitive column of her throat.

What was he doing to her? Her mind raced frantically to catch up with her soaring body. Why didn't he just get it over with so she could escape with her pride intact?

She'd kill him for this. Crush him. Destroy him.

And oh, it felt wonderful, delicious. Wicked.

He could only think she tasted of morning—cool, spring mornings when the dew slicked over green, green grass and new flowers. She shivered against him, her body still held stiffly away even as her head fell back in surrender.

Who was she? He nibbled lazily over to her ear and burned for her to show him.

A thousand, a million pinpricks of pleasure danced along her skin. Shaken by them, she started to pull away. But his hands slid down her back and melted her spine. All the while his lips teased and tormented, never, never coming against hers to relieve the aching pressure.

She wanted.

The slow, flickering heat kindling in the pit of her stomach.

She yearned.

Spreading, spreading through her blood and bone.

She needed.

Wave after wave of liquid fire lapping, cruising, flowing over her skin.

She took.

In a fire flash her system exploded. Mouth to mouth she strained against him, pressing ice to heat and letting it steam until the air was so thick with it, it clogged in her throat. Her fingers speared through his hair and fisted as she fed greedily on the stunning flavor of her own passion.

This. At last this. He was rough and restless and smelled of man instead of expensive colognes. The words he muttered were incomprehensible against her mouth. But they didn't sound like endearments, reassurances, promises. They sounded like threats.

His mouth wasn't soft and warm and eager, but hot and hard and ruthless. She wanted that, how she wanted the heedless and hasty meeting of lips and tongues.

His hands weren't hesitant or practiced, but strong and impatient. It ran giddily through her brain that he would take what he wanted, when and where it suited him. The pleasure and power of it burst through her like sunlight. She choked out his name when he tugged her bodice down and filled his calloused hands with her breasts.

He was drowning in her. The ice had melted and he was over his head, too dazed to know if he should dive deeper or scrabble for the surface. The scent, the taste, oh Lord, the texture. Alabaster and silk and rose petals. Every fine thing a man could want to touch, to steal, to claim as his own. His hands raced over her as he fought for more.

On an oath he shifted, and she was under him on the long plush seat of the car, her hair spread out like melted copper, her body moving, moving under his, her white breasts spilling out above the stark black dress and tormenting him into tasting.

She arched, and her fingers dug into his back as he suckled. A deep and delicious ache tugged at the center of her body. And she wanted him there, there where the heat was most intense. There where she felt so soft, so needy.

"Please." She could hear the whimper in her voice but felt no embarrassment. Only desperation. "Mikhail, please."

The throaty purr of her voice burst in his blood. He came back to her mouth, assaulting it, devouring it. Crazed, he hooked one hand in the top of her dress, on the verge of ripping it from her. And he looked, looked at her face, the huge eyes, the trembling lips. Light and shadow washed over it, leaving her pale as a ghost. She was shaking like a leaf beneath his hands.

And he heard the drum of traffic from outside.

He surfaced abruptly, shaking his head to clear it and gulping in air like a diver down too long. They were driving through the city, their privacy as thin as the panel of smoked glass that separated them from her chauffeur. And he was mauling her, yes, mauling her as if he were a reckless teenager with none of the sense God had given him.

The apology stuck in his throat. An "I beg your pardon" would hardly do the trick. Eyes grim, loins aching, he tugged her dress back into place. She only stared at him and made him feel like a drooling heathen over a virgin sacrifice. And Lord help him, he wanted to plunder.

Swearing, he pushed away and yanked her upright. He leaned back in the shadows and stared out of the dark window. They were only blocks from his apartment. Blocks, and he'd very nearly…it wouldn't do to think about what he'd nearly.

"We're almost there." Strain had his voice coming out clipped and hard. Sydney winced away as though it had been a slap.

What had she done wrong this time? She'd felt, and she'd wanted. Felt and wanted more than she ever had before. Yet she had still failed. For that one timeless moment she'd been willing to toss aside pride and fear. There had been passion in her, real and ready. And, she'd thought, he'd felt passion for her.

But not enough. She closed her eyes. It never seemed to be enough. Now she was cold, freezing, and wrapped her arms tight to try to hold in some remnant of heat.

Damn it, why didn't she say something? Mikhail dragged an unsteady hand through his hair. He deserved to be slapped. Shot was more like it. And she just sat there.

As he brooded out the window, he reminded himself that it hadn't been all his doing. She'd been as rash, pressing that wonderful body against his, letting that wide, mobile mouth make him crazy. Squirting that damnable perfume all over that soft skin until he'd been drunk with it.

He started to feel better.

Yes, there had been two people grappling in the back seat. She was every bit as guilty as he.

"Look, Sydney." He turned and she jerked back like an overwound spring.

"Don't touch me." He heard only the venom and none of the tears.

"Fine." Guilt hammered away at him as the car cruised to the curb. "I'll keep my big, grimy hands off you, Hayward. Call someone else when you want a little romp in the back seat."

Her fisted hands held on to pride and composure. "I meant what I said about my mother."

He shoved the door open. Light spilled in, splashing over his face, turning it frosty white. "So did I. Thanks for the ride."

When the door slammed, she closed her eyes tight. She would not cry. A single tear slipped past her guard and was dashed away. She would not cry. And she would not forget.

Chapter 4

She'd put in a long day. Actually she'd put in a long week that was edging toward sixty hours between office time, luncheon meetings and evenings at home with files. This particular day had a few hours yet to run, but Sydney recognized the new feeling of relief and satisfaction that came with Friday afternoons when the work force began to anticipate Saturday mornings.

Throughout her adult life one day of the week had been the same as the next; all of them a scattershot of charity functions, shopping and lunch dates. There had been no work schedule, and weekends had simply been a time when the parties had lasted longer.

Things had changed. As she read over a new contract, she was glad they had. She was beginning to understand why her grandfather had always been so lusty and full of life. He'd had a purpose, a place, a goal.

Now they were hers.

True, she still had to ask advice on the more technical wordings of contracts and depended heavily on her board when it came to making deals. But she was starting to appreciate—more, she was starting to relish the grand chess game of buying and selling buildings.

She circled what she considered a badly worded clause then answered her intercom.

"Mr. Bingham to see you, Ms. Hayward."

"Send him in, Janine. Oh, and see if you can reach Frank Marlowe at Marlowe, Radcliffe and Smyth."

"Yes, ma'am."

When Lloyd strode in a moment later, Sydney was still huddled over the contract. She held up one finger to give herself a minute to finish.

"Lloyd. I'm sorry, if I lose my concentration on all these *whereases*, I have to start over." She scrawled a note to herself, set it and the contract aside, then smiled at him. "What can I do for you?"

"This Soho project. It's gotten entirely out of hand."

Her lips tightened. Thinking of Soho made her think of Mikhail. Mikhail reminded her of the turbulent ride from Long Island and her latest failure as a woman. She didn't care for it.

"In what way?"

"In every way." With fury barely leashed, he began to pace her office. "A quarter of a million. You earmarked a quarter of a million to rehab that building."

Sydney stayed where she was and quietly folded her hands on the desk. "I'm aware of that, Lloyd. Considering the condition of the building, Mr. Stanislaski's bid was very reasonable."

"How would you know?" he shot back. "Did you get competing bids?"

"No." Her fingers flexed, then relaxed again. It was difficult, but she reminded herself that he'd earned his way up the ladder while she'd been hoisted to the top rung. "I went with my instincts."

"Instincts?" Eyes narrowed, he spun back to her. The derision in his voice was as thick as the pile of her carpet. "You've been in the business for a matter of months, and you have instincts?"

"That's right. I'm also aware that the estimate for rewiring, the plumbing and the carpentry were well in line with other, similar rehabs."

"Damn it, Sydney, we didn't put much more than that into this building last year."

One slim finger began to tap on the desk. "What we did here in the Hayward Building was little more than decorating. A good many of the repairs in Soho are a matter of safety and bringing the facilities up to code."

"A quarter of a million in repairs." He slapped his palms on the desk and leaned forward. Sydney was reminded of Mikhail making a similar gesture. But of course Lloyd's hands would leave no smudge of dirt. "Do you know what our annual income is from those apartments?"

"As a matter of fact I do." She rattled off a figure, surprising him. It was accurate to the penny. "On one hand, it will certainly take more than a year of full occupancy to recoup the principal on this investment. On the other, when people pay rent in good faith, they deserve decent housing."

"Decent, certainly," Lloyd said stiffly. "You're mixing morals with business."

"Oh, I hope so. I certainly hope so."

He drew back, infuriated that she would sit so smug and righteous behind a desk that should have been his. "You're naive, Sydney."

"That may be. But as long as I run this company, it will be run by my standards."

"You think you run it because you sign a few contracts and make phone calls. You've put a quarter million into what you yourself termed your pet project, and you don't have a clue what this Stanislaski's up to. How do you know he isn't buying inferior grades and pocketing the excess?"

"That's absurd."

"As I said, you're naive. You put some Russian artist in charge of a major project, then don't even bother to check the work."

"I intend to inspect the project myself. I've been tied up. And I have Mr. Stanislaski's weekly report."

He sneered. Before Sydney's temper could fray, she realized Lloyd was right. She'd hired Mikhail on impulse and instinct, then because of personal feelings, had neglected to follow through with her involvement on the project.

That wasn't naive. It was gutless.

"You're absolutely right, Lloyd, and I'll correct it." She leaned back in her chair. "Was there anything else?"

"You've made a mistake," he said. "A costly one in this case. The board won't tolerate another."

With her hands laid lightly on the arms of her chair, she nodded. "And you're hoping to convince them that you belong at this desk."

"They're businessmen, Sydney. And though sentiment might prefer a Hayward at the head of the table, profit and loss will turn the tide."

Her expression remained placid, her voice steady. "I'm sure you're right again. And if the board continues to back me, I want one of two things from you. Your resignation or your loyalty. I won't accept anything in between. Now, if you'll excuse me?"

When the door slammed behind him, she reached for the phone. But her hand was trembling, and she drew it back. She plucked up a paper clip and mangled it. Then another, then a third. Between that and the two sheets of stationery she shredded, she felt the worst of the rage subside.

Clearheaded, she faced the facts.

Lloyd Bingham was an enemy, and he was an enemy with experience and influence. She had acted in haste with Soho. Not that she'd been wrong; she didn't believe she'd been wrong.

But if there were mistakes, Lloyd would capitalize on them and drop them right in her lap.

Was it possible that she was risking everything her grandfather had given her with one project? Could she be forced to step down if she couldn't prove the worth and right of what she had done?

She wasn't sure, and that was the worst of it.

One step at a time. That was the only way to go on. And the first step was to get down to Soho and do her job.

The sky was the color of drywall. Over the past few days, the heat had ebbed, but it had flowed back into the city that morning like a river, flooding Manhattan with humidity. The pedestrian traffic surged through it, streaming across the intersections in hot little packs.

Girls in shorts and men in wilted business suits crowded around the sidewalk vendors in hopes that an ice-cream bar or a soft drink would help them beat the heat.

When Sydney stepped out of her car, the sticky oppression of the air punched like a fist. She thought of her driver sitting in the enclosed car and dismissed him for the day. Shielding her eyes, she turned to study her building.

Scaffolding crept up the walls like metal ivy. Windows glittered, their manufacturer stickers slashed across the glass. She thought she saw a pair of arthritic hands scraping away at a label at a third-floor window.

There were signs in the doorway, warning of construction in progress. She could hear the sounds of it, booming hammers, buzzing saws, the clang of metal and the tinny sound of rock and roll through portable speakers.

At the curb she saw the plumber's van, a dented pickup and a scattering of interested onlookers. Since they were all peering up, she followed their direction. And saw Mikhail.

For an instant, her heart stopped dead. He stood outside the top floor, five stories up, moving nimbly on what seemed to Sydney to be a very narrow board.

"Man, get a load of those buns," a woman beside her sighed. "They are class A."

Sydney swallowed. She supposed they were. And his naked back wasn't anything to sneeze at, either. The trouble was, it was hard to enjoy it when she had a hideous flash of him plummeting off the scaffolding and breaking that beautiful back on the concrete below.

Panicked, she rushed inside. The elevator doors were open, and a couple of mechanics were either loading or unloading their tools inside it. She didn't stop to ask but bolted up the steps.

Sweaty men were replastering the stairwell between two and three. They took the time to whistle and wink, but she kept climbing. Someone had the television up too loud, probably to drown out the sound of construction. A baby was crying fitfully. She smelled chicken frying.

Without pausing for breath, she dashed from four to five. There was music playing here. Tough and gritty rock, poorly accompanied by a laborer in an off-key tenor.

Mikhail's door was open, and Sydney streaked through. She nearly tumbled over a graying man with arms like tree trunks. He rose gracefully from his crouched position where he'd been sorting tools and steadied her.

"I'm sorry. I didn't see you."

"Is all right. I like women to fall at my feet."

She registered the Slavic accent even as she glanced desperately around the room for Mikhail. Maybe everybody in the building was Russian, she thought frantically. Maybe he'd imported plumbers from the mother country.

"Can I help you?"

"No. Yes." She pressed a hand to her heart when she realized she was completely out of breath. "Mikhail."

"He is just outside." Intrigued, he watched her as he jerked a thumb toward the window.

She could see him there—at least she could see the flat, tanned torso. "Outside. But, but—"

"We are finishing for the day. You will sit?"

"Get him in," Sydney whispered. "Please, get him in."

Before he could respond, the window was sliding up, and Mikhail was tossing one long, muscled leg inside. He said something in his native tongue, laughter in his voice as the rest of his body followed. When he saw Sydney, the laughter vanished.

"Hayward." He tapped his caulking gun against his palm.

"What were you doing out there?" The question came out in an accusing rush.

"Replacing windows." He set the caulking gun aside. "Is there a problem?"

"No, I…" She couldn't remember ever feeling more of a fool. "I came by to check the progress."

"So. I'll take you around in a minute." He walked into the kitchen, stuck his head into the sink and turned the faucet on full cold.

"He's a hothead," the man behind her said, chuckling at his own humor. When Sydney only managed a weak smile, he called out to Mikhail, speaking rapidly in that exotic foreign tongue.

"*Tak*" was all he said. Mikhail came up dripping, hair streaming over the bandanna he'd tied around it. He shook it back, splattering water, then shrugged and hooked his thumbs in his belt loops. He was wet, sweaty and half-naked. Sydney had to fold her tongue inside her mouth to keep it from hanging out.

"My son is rude." Yuri Stanislaski shook his head. "I raised him better."

"Your—oh." Sydney looked back at the man with the broad face and beautiful hands. Mikhail's hands. "How do you do, Mr. Stanislaski."

"I do well. I am Yuri. I ask my son if you are the Hayward who owns this business. He only says yes and scowls."

"Yes, well, I am."

"It's a good building. Only a little sick. And we are the doctors." He grinned at his son, then boomed out something else in Ukrainian.

This time an answering smile tugged at Mikhail's mouth. "No, you haven't lost a patient yet, Papa. Go home and have your dinner."

Yuri hauled up his tool chest. "You come and bring the pretty lady. Your mama makes enough."

"Oh, well, thank you, but—"

"I'm busy tonight, Papa." Mikhail cut off Sydney's polite refusal.

Yuri raised a bushy brow. "You're stupid tonight," he said in Ukrainian. "Is this the one who makes you sulk all week?"

Annoyed, Mikhail picked up a kitchen towel and wiped his face. "Women don't make me sulk."

Yuri only smiled. "This one would." Then he turned to Sydney. "Now I am rude, too, talking so you don't understand. He is bad influence." He lifted her hand and kissed it with considerable charm. "I am glad to meet you."

"I'm glad to meet you, too."

"Put on a shirt," Yuri ordered his son, then left, whistling.

"He's very nice," Sydney said.

"Yes." Mikhail picked up the T-shirt he'd peeled off hours before, but only held it. "So, you want to see the work?"

"Yes, I thought—"

"The windows are done," he interrupted. "The wiring is almost done. That and the plumbing will take another week. Come."

He moved out, skirting her by a good two feet, then walked into the apartment next door without knocking.

"Keely's," he told her. "She is out."

The room was a clash of sharp colors and scents. The furniture was old and sagging but covered with vivid pillows and various articles of female attire.

The adjoining kitchen was a mess—not with dishes or pots and pans—but with walls torn down to studs and thick wires snaked through.

"It must be inconvenient for her, for everyone, during the construction."

"Better than plugging in a cake mixer and shorting out the building. The old wire was tube and knob, forty years old or more, and frayed. This is Romex. More efficient, safer."

She bent over his arm, studying the wiring. "Well. Hmm."

He nearly smiled. Perhaps he would have if she hadn't smelled so good. Instead, he moved a deliberate foot away. "After the inspection, we will put up new walls. Come."

It was a trial for both of them, but he took her through every stage of the work, moving from floor to floor, showing her elbows of plastic pipe and yards of copper tubing.

"Most of the flooring can be saved with sanding and refinishing. But some must be replaced." He kicked at a square of plywood he'd nailed to a hole in the second-floor landing.

Sydney merely nodded, asking questions only when they seemed intelligent. Most of the workers were gone, off to cash their week's paychecks. The noise level had lowered so that she could hear muted voices behind closed doors, snatches of music or televised car chases. She lifted a brow at the sound of a tenor sax swinging into "Rhapsody in Blue."

"That's Will Metcalf," Mikhail told her. "He's good. Plays in a band."

"Yes, he's good." The rail felt smooth and sturdy under her hand as they went down. Mikhail had done that, she thought. He'd fixed, repaired, replaced, as needed because he cared about the people who lived in the building. He knew who was playing the sax or eating the fried chicken, whose baby was laughing.

"Are you happy with the progress?" she asked quietly.

The tone of her voice made him look at her, something he'd been trying to avoid. A few tendrils of hair had escaped their pins to curl at her temples. He could see a pale dusting of freckles across her nose. "Happy enough. It's you who should answer. It's your building."

"No, it's not." Her eyes were very serious, very sad. "It's yours. I only write the checks."

"Sydney—"

"I've seen enough to know you've made a good start." She was hurrying down the steps as she spoke. "Be sure to contact my office when it's time for the next draw."

"Damn it. Slow down." He caught up with her at the bottom of the steps and grabbed her arm. "What's wrong with you? First you stand in my room pale and out of breath. Now you run away, and your eyes are miserable."

It had hit her, hard, that she had no community of people who cared. Her circle of friends was so narrow, so self-involved. Her best friend had been Peter, and that had been horribly spoiled. Her life was on the sidelines, and she envied the involvement, the closeness she felt in this place. The building wasn't hers, she thought again. She only owned it.

"I'm not running away, and nothing's wrong with me." She had to get out, get away, but she had to do it with dignity. "I take this job very seriously. It's my first major project since taking over Hayward. I want it done right. And I took a chance by…" She trailed off, glancing toward the door just to her right. She could have sworn she'd heard someone call for help. Television, she thought, but before she could continue, she heard the thin, pitiful call again. "Mikhail, do you hear that?"

"Hear what?" How could he hear anything when he was trying not to kiss her again?

"In here." She turned toward the door, straining her ears. "Yes, in here, I heard—"

That time he'd heard it, too. Lifting a fist, he pounded on the door. "Mrs. Wolburg. Mrs. Wolburg, it's Mik."

The shaky voice barely penetrated the wood. "Hurt. Help me."

"Oh, God, she's—"

Before Sydney could finish, Mikhail rammed his shoulder against the door. With the second thud, it crashed open to lean drunkenly on its hinges.

"In the kitchen," Mrs. Wolburg called weakly. "Mik, thank God."

He bolted through the apartment with its starched doilies and paper flowers to find her on the kitchen floor. She was a tiny woman, mostly bone and thin flesh. Her usually neat cap of white hair was matted with sweat.

"Can't see," she said. "Dropped my glasses."

"Don't worry." He knelt beside her, automatically checking her pulse as he studied her pain-filled eyes. "Call an ambulance," he ordered Sydney, but she was already on the phone. "I'm not going to help you up, because I don't know how you're hurt."

"Hip." She gritted her teeth at the awful, radiating pain. "I think I busted my hip. Fell, caught my foot. Couldn't move. All the noise, nobody could hear me calling. Been here two, three hours. Got so weak."

"It's all right now." He tried to chafe some heat into her hands. "Sydney, get a blanket and pillow."

She had them in her arms and was already crouching beside Mrs. Wolburg before he'd finished the order. "Here now. I'm just going to lift your head a little." Gently she set the woman's limp head on the pillow. Despite the raging heat, Mrs. Wolburg was shivering with cold. As she continued to speak in quiet, soothing tones, Sydney tucked the blanket around her. "Just a few more minutes," Sydney murmured, and stroked the clammy forehead.

A crowd was forming at the door. Though he didn't like leaving Sydney with the injured woman, he rose. "I want to keep the neighbors away. Send someone to keep an eye for the ambulance."

"Fine." While fear pumped hard in her heart, she continued to smile down at Mrs. Wolburg. "You have a lovely apartment. Do you crochet the doilies yourself?"

"Been doing needlework for sixty years, since I was pregnant with my first daughter."

"They're beautiful. Do you have other children?"

"Six, three of each. And twenty grandchildren. Five great…" She shut her eyes on a flood of pain, then opened them again and managed a smile. "Been after me for living alone, but I like my own place and my own way."

"Of course."

"And my daughter, Lizzy? Moved clear out to Phoenix, Arizona. Now what would I want to live out there for?"

Sydney smiled and stroked. "I couldn't say."

"They'll be on me now," she muttered, and let her eyes close again. "Wouldn't have happened if I hadn't dropped my glasses. Terribly nearsighted. Getting old's hell, girl, and don't let anyone tell you different. Couldn't see where I was going and snagged my foot in that torn linoleum. Mik told me to keep it taped down, but I wanted to give it a good scrub." She managed a wavery smile. "Least I've been lying here on a clean floor."

"Paramedics are coming up," Mikhail said from behind her. Sydney only nodded, filled with a terrible guilt and anger she was afraid to voice.

"You call my grandson, Mik? He lives up on Eighty-first. He'll take care of the rest of the family."

"Don't worry about it, Mrs. Wolburg."

Fifteen efficient minutes later, Sydney stood on the sidewalk watching as the stretcher was lifted into the back of the ambulance.

"Did you reach her grandson?" she asked Mikhail.

"I left a message on his machine."

Nodding, she walked to the curb and tried to hail a cab.

"Where's your car?"

"I sent him home. I didn't know how long I'd be and it was too hot to leave him sitting there. Maybe I should go back in and call a cab."

"In a hurry?"

She winced as the siren shrieked. "I want to get to the hospital."

Nonplussed, he jammed his hands into his pockets. "There's no need for you to go."

She turned, and her eyes, in the brief moment they held his, were ripe with emotion. Saying nothing, she faced away until a cab finally swung to the curb. Nor did she speak when Mikhail climbed in behind her.

She hated the smell of hospitals. Layers of illness, antiseptics, fear and heavy cleaners. The memory of the last days her grandfather had lain dying were still too fresh in her mind. The Emergency Room of the downtown hospital added one more layer. Fresh blood.

Sydney steeled herself against it and walked through the crowds of the sick and injured to the admitting window.

"You had a Mrs. Wolburg just come in."

"That's right." The clerk stabbed keys on her computer. "You family?"

"No, I—"

"We're going to need some family to fill out these forms. Patient said she wasn't insured."

Mikhail was already leaning over, eyes dangerous, when Sydney snapped out her answer. "Hayward Industries will be responsible for Mrs. Wolburg's medical expenses." She reached into her bag for identification and slapped it onto the counter. "I'm Sydney Hayward. Where is Mrs. Wolburg?"

"In X ray." The frost in Sydney's eyes had the clerk shifting in her chair. "Dr. Cohen's attending."

So they waited, drinking bad coffee among the moans and tears of inner city ER. Sometimes Sydney would lay her head back against the wall and shut her eyes. She appeared to be dozing, but all the while she was thinking what it would be like to be old, and alone and helpless.

He wanted to think she was only there to cover her butt. Oh yes, he wanted to think that of her. It was so much more comfortable to think of her as the head of some bloodless company than as a woman.

But he remembered how quickly she had acted in the Wolburg apartment, how gentle she had been with the old woman. And most of all, he remembered the look in her eyes out on the street. All that misery and compassion and guilt welling up in those big eyes.

"She tripped on the linoleum," Sydney murmured.

It was the first time she'd spoken in nearly an hour, and Mikhail turned his head to study her. Her eyes were still closed, her face pale and in repose.

"She was only walking in her own kitchen and fell because the floor was old and unsafe."

"You're making it safe."

Sydney continued as if she hadn't heard. "Then she could only lie there, hurt and alone. Her voice was so weak. I nearly walked right by."

"You didn't walk by." His hand hesitated over hers. Then, with an oath, he pressed his palm to the back of her hand. "You're only one Hayward, Sydney. Your grandfather—"

"He was ill." Her hand clenched under Mikhail's, and her eyes squeezed more tightly closed. "He was sick nearly two years, and I was in Europe. I didn't know. He didn't want to disrupt my life. My father was dead, and there was only me, and he didn't want to worry me. When he finally called me, it was almost over. He was a good man. He wouldn't have let things get so bad, but he couldn't…he just couldn't."

She let out a short, shuddering breath. Mikhail turned her hand over and linked his fingers with hers.

"When I got to New York, he was in the hospital. He looked so small, so tired. He told me I was the only Hayward left. Then he died," she said wearily. "And I was."

"You're doing what needs to be done. No one can ask for more than that."

She opened her eyes again, met his. "I don't know."

They waited again, in silence.

It was nearly two hours before Mrs. Wolburg's frantic grandson rushed in. The entire story had to be told again before he hurried off to call the rest of his family.

Four hours after they'd walked into Emergency, the doctor came out to fill them in.

A fractured hip, a mild concussion. She would be moved to a room right after she'd finished in Recovery. Her age made the break serious, but her health helped balance that. Sydney left both her office and home numbers with the doctor and the grandson, requesting to be kept informed of Mrs. Wolburg's condition.

Unbearably weary in body and mind, Sydney walked out of the hospital.

"You need food," Mikhail said.

"What? No, really, I'm just tired."

Ignoring that, he grabbed her arm and pulled her down the street. "Why do you always say the opposite of what I say?"

"I don't."

"See, you did it again. You need meat."

If she kept trying to drag her heels, he was going to pull her arm right out of the socket. Annoyed, she scrambled to keep pace. "What makes you think you know what I need?"

"Because I do." He pulled up short at a light and she bumped into him. Before he could stop it, his hand had lifted to touch her face. "God, you're so beautiful."

While she blinked in surprise, he swore, scowled then dragged her into the street seconds before the light turned.

"Maybe I'm not happy with you," he went on, muttering to himself. "Maybe I think you're a nuisance, and a snob, and—"

"I am not a snob."

He said something vaguely familiar in his native language. Sydney's chin set when she recalled the translation. "It is not bull. You're the snob if you think I am just because I come from a different background."

He stopped, eyeing her with a mixture of distrust and interest. "Fine then, you won't mind eating in here." He yanked her into a noisy bar and grill. She found herself plopped down in a narrow booth with him, hip to hip.

There were scents of meat cooking, onions frying, spilled beer, all overlaid with grease. Her mouth watered. "I said I wasn't hungry."

"And I say you're a snob, and a liar."

The color that stung her cheeks pleased him, but it didn't last long enough. She leaned forward. "And would you like to know what I think of you?"

Again he lifted a hand to touch her cheek. It was irresistible. "Yes, I would."

She was saved from finding a description in her suddenly murky brain by the waitress.

"Two steaks, medium rare, and two of what you've got on tap."

"I don't like men to order for me," Sydney said tightly.

"Then you can order for me next time and we'll be even." Making himself comfortable, he tossed his arm over the back of the booth and stretched out his legs. "Why don't you take off your jacket, Hayward? You're hot."

"Stop telling me what I am. And stop that, too."

"What?"

"Playing with my hair."

He grinned. "I was playing with your neck. I like your neck." To prove it, he skimmed a finger down it again.

She clamped her teeth on the delicious shudder that followed it down her spine. "I wish you'd move over."

"Okay." He shifted closer. "Better?"

Calm, she told herself. She would be calm. After a cleansing breath, she turned her head. "If you don't…" And his lips brushed over hers, stopping the words and the thought behind them.

"I want you to kiss me back."

She started to shake her head, but couldn't manage it.

"I want to watch you when you do," he murmured. "I want to know what's there."

"There's nothing there."

But his mouth closed over hers and proved her a liar. She fell into the kiss, one hand lost in his hair, the other clamped on his shoulder.

She felt everything. Everything. And it all moved too fast. Her mind seemed to dim until she could barely hear the clatter and bustle of the bar. But she felt his mouth angle over hers, his teeth nip, his tongue seduce.

Whatever she was doing to him, he was doing to her. He knew it. He saw it in the way her eyes glazed before they closed, felt it in the hot, ready passion of her lips. It was supposed to soothe his ego, prove a point. But it did neither.

It only left him aching.

"Sorry to break this up." The waitress slapped two frosted mugs on the table. "Steak's on its way."

Sydney jerked her head back. His arms were still around her, though his grip had loosened. And she, she was plastered against him. Her body molded to his as they sat in a booth in a public place. Shame and fury battled for supremacy as she yanked herself away.

"That was a despicable thing to do."

He shrugged and picked up his beer. "I didn't do it alone." Over the foam, his eyes sharpened. "Not this time, or last time."

"Last time, you…"

"What?"

Sydney lifted her mug and sipped gingerly. "I don't want to discuss it."

He wanted to argue, even started to, but there was a sheen of hurt in her eyes that baffled him. He didn't mind making her angry. Hell, he enjoyed it. But he didn't know what he'd done to make her hurt. He waited until the waitress had set the steaks in front of them.

"You've had a rough day," he said so kindly Sydney gasped. "I don't mean to make it worse."

"It's…" She struggled with a response. "It's been a rough day all around. Let's just put it behind us."

"Done." Smiling, he handed her a knife and fork. "Eat your dinner. We'll have a truce."

"Good." She discovered she had an appetite after all.

Chapter 5

Sydney didn't know how Mildred Wolburg's accident had leaked to the press, but by Tuesday afternoon her office was flooded with calls from reporters. A few of the more enterprising staked out the lobby of the Hayward Building and cornered her when she left for the day.

By Wednesday rumors were flying around the offices that Hayward was facing a multimillion-dollar suit, and Sydney had several unhappy board members on her hands. The consensus was that by assuming responsibility for Mrs. Wolburg's medical expenses, Sydney had admitted Hayward's neglect and had set the company up for a large public settlement.

It was bad press, and bad business.

Knowing no route but the direct one, Sydney prepared a statement for the press and agreed to an emergency board meeting. By Friday, she thought as she walked into the hospital, she would know if she would remain in charge of Hayward or whether her position would be whittled down to figurehead.

Carrying a stack of paperbacks in one hand and a potted

plant in the other, Sydney paused outside of Mrs. Wolburg's room. Because it was Sydney's third visit since the accident, she knew the widow wasn't likely to be alone. Invariably, friends and family streamed in and out during visiting hours. This time she saw Mikhail, Keely and two of Mrs. Wolburg's children.

Mikhail spotted her as Sydney was debating whether to slip out again and leave the books and plant she'd brought at the nurses' station.

"You have more company, Mrs. Wolburg."

"Sydney." The widow's eyes brightened behind her thick lenses. "More books."

"Your grandson told me you liked to read." Feeling awkward, she set the books on the table beside the bed and took Mrs. Wolburg's outstretched hand.

"My Harry used to say I'd rather read than eat." The thin, bony fingers squeezed Sydney's. "That's a beautiful plant."

"I noticed you have several in your apartment." She smiled, feeling slightly more relaxed as the conversation in the room picked up again to flow around them. "And the last time I was here the room looked like a florist's shop." She glanced around at the banks of cut flowers in vases, pots, baskets, even in a ceramic shoe. "So I settled on an African violet."

"I do have a weakness for flowers and growing things. Set it right there on the dresser, will you, dear? Between the roses and the carnations."

"She's getting spoiled." As Sydney moved to comply, the visiting daughter winked at her brother. "Flowers, presents, pampering. We'll be lucky to ever get home-baked cookies again."

"Oh, I might have a batch or two left in me." Mrs. Wolburg preened in her new crocheted bed jacket. "Mik tells me I'm getting a brand-new oven. Eye level, so I won't have to bend and stoop."

"So I think I should get the first batch," Mikhail said as he sniffed the roses. "The chocolate chip."

"Please." Keely pressed a hand to her stomach. "I'm dieting. I'm getting murdered next week, and I have to look my best." She noted Sydney's stunned expression and grinned. *"Death Stalk,"* she explained. "My first TV movie. I'm the third victim of the maniacal psychopath. I get strangled in this really terrific negligee."

"You shouldn't have left your windows unlocked," Mrs. Wolburg told her, and Keely grinned again.

"Well, that's show biz."

Sydney waited until a break in the conversation, then made her excuses. Mikhail gave her a ten-second lead before he slipped a yellow rose out of a vase. "See you later, beautiful." He kissed Mrs. Wolburg on the cheek and left her chuckling.

In a few long strides, he caught up with Sydney at the elevators. "Hey. You look like you could use this." He offered the flower.

"It couldn't hurt." After sniffing the bloom, she worked up a smile. "Thanks."

"You want to tell me why you're upset?"

"I'm not upset." She jabbed the down button again.

"Never argue with an artist about your feelings." Insistently he tipped back her chin with one finger. "I see fatigue and distress, worry and annoyance."

The ding of the elevator relieved her, though she knew he would step inside the crowded car with her. She frowned a little when she found herself pressed between Mikhail and a large woman carrying a suitcase-sized purse. Someone on the elevator had used an excess of expensive perfume. Fleetingly Sydney wondered if that shouldn't be as illegal as smoking in a closed car.

"Any Gypsies in your family?" she asked Mikhail on impulse.

"Naturally."

"I'd rather you use a crystal ball to figure out the future than analyze my feelings at the moment."

"We'll see what we can do."

The car stopped on each floor. People shuffled off or squeezed in. By the time they reached the lobby, Sydney was hard up against Mikhail's side, with his arm casually around her waist. He didn't bother to remove it after they'd stepped off. She didn't bother to mention it.

"The work's going well," he told her.

"Good." She didn't care to think how much longer she'd be directly involved with the project.

"The electrical inspection is done. Plumbing will perhaps take another week." He studied her abstracted expression. "And we have decided to make the new roof out of blue cheese."

"Hmm." She stepped outside, stopped and looked back at him. With a quick laugh, she shook her head. "That might look very distinctive—but risky with this heat."

"You were listening."

"Almost." Absently she pressed fingers to her throbbing temple as her driver pulled up to the curb. "I'm sorry. I've got a lot on my mind."

"Tell me."

It surprised her that she wanted to. She hadn't been able to talk to her mother. Margerite would only be baffled. Channing—that was a joke. Sydney doubted that any of her friends would understand how she had become so attached to Hayward in such a short time.

"There really isn't any point," she decided, and started toward her waiting car and driver.

Did she think he would let her walk away, with that worry line between her brows and the tension knotted tight in her shoulders?

"How about a lift home?"

She glanced back. The ride home from her mother's party was still a raw memory. But he was smiling at her in an easy, friendly fashion. Nonthreatening? No, he would never be that with those dark looks and untamed aura. But they had agreed on a truce, and it was only a few blocks.

"Sure. We'll drop Mr. Stanislaski off in Soho, Donald."

"Yes, ma'am."

She took the precaution of sliding, casually, she hoped, all the way over to the far window. "Mrs. Wolburg looks amazingly well, considering," she began.

"She's strong." It was Mozart this time, he noted, low and sweet through the car speakers.

"The doctor says she'll be able to go home with her son soon."

"And you've arranged for the therapist to visit." Sydney stopped passing the rose from hand to hand and looked at him. "She told me," he explained. "Also that when she is ready to go home again, there will be a nurse to stay with her, until she is well enough to be on her own."

"I'm not playing Samaritan," Sydney mumbled. "I'm just trying to do what's right."

"I realize that. I realize, too, that you're concerned for her. But there's something more on your mind. Is it the papers and the television news?"

Her eyes went from troubled to frigid. "I didn't assume responsibility for Mrs. Wolburg's medical expenses for publicity, good or bad. And I don't—"

"I know you didn't." He cupped a hand over one of her clenched ones. "Remember, I was there. I saw you with her."

Sydney drew a deep breath. She had to. She'd very nearly had a tirade, and a lost temper was hardly the answer. "The point is," she said more calmly, "an elderly woman was seriously injured. Her pain shouldn't become company politics or journalistic fodder. What I did, I did because I knew it was right. I just want to make sure the right thing continues to be done."

"You are president of Hayward."

"For the moment." She turned to look out the window as

they pulled up in front of the apartment building. "I see we're making progress on the roof."

"Among other things." Because he was far from finished, he leaned over her and opened the door on her side. For a moment, they were so close, his body pressed lightly to hers. She had an urge, almost desperate, to rub her fingers over his cheek, to feel the rough stubble he'd neglected to shave away. "I'd like you to come up," he told her. "I have something for you."

Sydney caught her fingers creeping up and snatched them back. "It's nearly six. I really should—"

"Come up for an hour," he finished. "Your driver can come back for you, yes?"

"Yes." She shifted away, not sure whether she wanted to get out or simply create some distance between them. "You can messenger your report over."

"I could."

He moved another inch. In defense, Sydney swung her legs out of the car. "All right then, but I don't think it'll take an hour."

"But it will."

She relented because she preferred spending an hour going over a report than sitting in her empty apartment thinking about the scheduled board meeting. After giving her driver instructions, she walked with Mikhail toward the building.

"You've repaired the stoop."

"Tuesday. It wasn't easy getting the men to stop sitting on it long enough." He exchanged greetings with the three who were ranged across it now as Sydney passed through the aroma of beer and tobacco. "We can take the elevator. The inspection certificate is hardly dry."

She thought of the five long flights up. "I can't tell you how glad I am to hear that." She stepped in with him, waited while he pulled the open iron doors closed.

"It has character now," he said as they began the ascent. "And you don't worry that you'll get in to get downstairs and spend the night inside."

"There's good news."

He pulled the doors open again as the car slid to a smooth, quiet stop. In the hallway, the ceiling was gone, leaving bare joists and new wiring exposed.

"The water damage from leaking was bad," Mikhail said conversationally. "Once the roof is finished, we'll replace."

"I've expected some complaints from the tenants, but we haven't received a single one. Isn't it difficult for everyone, living in a construction zone?"

Mikhail jingled his keys. "Inconvenient. But everyone is excited and watches the progress. Mr. Stuben from the third floor comes up every morning before he leaves for work. Every day he says, 'Mikhail, you have your work cut out for you.'" He grinned as he opened the door. "Some days I'd like to throw my hammer at him." He stepped back and nudged her inside. "Sit."

Lips pursed, Sydney studied the room. The furniture had been pushed together in the center—to make it easier to work, she imagined. Tables were stacked on top of chairs, the rug had been rolled up. Under the sheet he'd tossed over his worktable were a variety of interesting shapes that were his sculptures, his tools, and blocks of wood yet to be carved.

It smelled like sawdust, she thought, and turpentine.

"Where?"

He stopped on his way to the kitchen and looked back. After a quick study, he leaned into the jumble and lifted out an old oak rocker. One-handed, Sydney noted, and felt foolish and impressed.

"Here." After setting it on a clear spot, he headed back into the kitchen.

The surface of the rocker was smooth as satin. When Sydney sat, she found the chair slipped around her like comforting arms. Ten seconds after she'd settled, she was moving it gently to and fro.

"This is beautiful."

He could hear the faint creak as the rocker moved and didn't bother to turn. "I made it for my sister years ago when she had a baby." His voice changed subtly as he turned on the kitchen tap. "She lost the baby, Lily, after only a few weeks, and it was painful for Natasha to keep the chair."

"I'm sorry." The creaking stopped. "I can't think of anything worse for a parent to face."

"Because there is nothing." He came back in, carrying a glass of water and a bottle. "Lily will always leave a little scar on the heart. But Tash has three children now. So pain is balanced with joy. Here." He put the glass in her hand, then shook two aspirin out of the bottle. "You have a headache."

She frowned down at the pills he dropped into her palm. True, her head was splitting, but she hadn't mentioned it. "I might have a little one," she muttered. "How do you know?"

"I can see it in your eyes." He waited until she'd sipped and swallowed, then walked behind the chair to circle her temples with his fingers. "It's not such a little one, either."

There was no doubt she should tell him to stop. And she would. Any minute. Unable to resist, she leaned back, letting her eyes close as his fingers stroked away the worst of the pain.

"Is this what you had for me? Headache remedies?"

Her voice was so quiet, so tired that his heart twisted a little. "No, I have something else for you. But it can wait until you're feeling better. Talk to me, Sydney. Tell me what's wrong. Maybe I can help."

"It's something I have to take care of myself."

"Okay. Will that change if you talk to me?"

No, she thought. It was her problem, her future. But what harm would it do to talk it out, to say it all out loud and hear someone else's viewpoint?

"Office politics." She sighed as he began to massage the base of her neck. His rough, calloused fingers were as gentle as a mother's. "I imagine they can be tricky enough when you have experience. All I have is the family name and my grandfather's last wishes. The publicity on Mrs. Wolburg has left my position in the company very shaky. I assumed responsibility without going through channels or consulting legal. The board isn't pleased with me."

His eyes had darkened, but his hands remained gentle. "Because you have integrity?"

"Because I jumped the gun, so to speak. The resulting publicity only made things worse. The consensus is that someone with more savvy could have handled the Wolburg matter— that's how it's referred to at Hayward. The Wolburg matter in a quiet, tidy fashion. There's a board meeting at noon on Friday, and they could very well request that I step down as president."

"And will you?"

"I don't know." He was working on her shoulders now, competently, thoroughly. "I'd like to fight, draw the whole thing out. Then again, the company's been in upheaval for over a year, and having the president and the board as adversaries won't help Hayward. Added to that, my executive vice president and I are already on poor terms. He feels, perhaps justifiably, that he should be in the number one slot." She laughed softly. "There are times I wish he had it."

"No, you don't." He resisted the urge to bend down and press his lips to the long, slender column of her neck. Barely. "You like being in charge, and I think you're good at it."

She stopped rocking to turn her head and stare at him. "You're the first person who's ever said that to me. Most of the people who know me think I'm playing at this, or that I'm experiencing a kind of temporary insanity."

His hand slid lightly down her arm as he came around to crouch in front of her. "Then they don't know you, do they?"

There were so many emotions popping through her as she kept her eyes on his. But pleasure, the simple pleasure of being understood was paramount. "Maybe they don't," she murmured. "Maybe they don't."

"I won't give you advice." He picked up one of her hands because he enjoyed examining it, the long, ringless fingers, the slender wrist, the smooth, cool skin. "I don't know about office politics or board meetings. But I think you'll do what's right. You have a good brain and a good heart."

Hardly aware that she'd turned her hand over under his and linked them, she smiled. The connection was more complete than joined fingers, and she couldn't understand it. This was support, a belief in her, and an encouragement she'd never expected to find.

"Odd that I'd have to come to a Ukrainian carpenter for a pep talk. Thanks."

"You're welcome." He looked back into her eyes. "Your headache's gone."

Surprised, she touched her fingers to her temple. "Yes, yes it is." In fact, she couldn't remember ever feeling more relaxed. "You could make a fortune with those hands."

He grinned and slid them up her arms, pushing the sleeves of her jacket along so he could feel the bare flesh beneath. "It's only a matter of knowing what to do with them, and when." And he knew exactly how he wanted to use those hands on her. Unfortunately, the timing was wrong.

"Yes, well…" It was happening again, those little licks of fire in the pit of her stomach, the trembling heat along her skin. "I really am grateful, for everything. I should be going."

"You have time yet." His fingers glided back down her arms to link with hers. "I haven't given you your present."

"Present?" He was drawing her slowly to her feet. Now they were thigh to thigh, her eyes level with his mouth. It was curved and close, sending her system into overdrive.

He had only to lean down. Inches, bare inches. Imagining it nearly drove him crazy. Not an altogether unpleasant feeling, he discovered, this anticipation, this wondering. If she offered, and only when she offered, would he take.

"Don't you like presents, *milaya?*"

His voice was like hot cream, pouring richly over her. "I… the report," she said, remembering. "Weren't you going to give me your report?"

His thumbs skimmed over her wrists and felt the erratic beat of her pulse. It was tempting, very tempting. "I can send the report. I had something else in mind."

"Something…" Her own mind quite simply shut down.

He laughed, so delighted with her he wanted to kiss her breathless. Instead he released her hands and walked away. She didn't move, not an inch as he strolled over to the shelves and tossed up the drop cloth. In a moment he was back, pressing the little Cinderella into her hand.

"I'd like you to have this."

"Oh, but…" She tried, really tried to form a proper refusal. The words wouldn't come.

"You don't like?"

"No. I mean, yes, of course I like it, it's exquisite. But why?" Her fingers were already curving possessively around it when she lifted her eyes to his. "Why would you give it to me?"

"Because she reminds me of you. She's lovely, fragile, unsure of herself."

The description had Sydney's pleasure dimming. "Most people would term her romantic."

"I'm not most. Here, as she runs away, she doesn't believe enough." He stroked a finger down the delicate folds of the ball gown. "She follows the rules, without question. It's midnight, and she was in the arms of her prince, but she breaks away and runs. Because that was the rule. And she is afraid, afraid to let him see beneath the illusion to the woman."

"She had to leave. She'd promised. Besides, she'd have been humiliated to have been caught there in rags and bare feet."

Tilting his head, Mikhail studied her. "Do you think he cared about her dress?"

"Well, no, I don't suppose it would have mattered to him." Sydney let out an impatient breath as he grinned at her. It was ridiculous, standing here debating the psychology of a fairy-tale character. "In any case, it ended happily, and though I've nothing in common with Cinderella, the figurine's beautiful. I'll treasure it."

"Good. Now, I'll walk you downstairs. You don't want to be late for dinner with your mother."

"She won't be there until eight-thirty. She's always late." Half-way through the door, Sydney stopped. "How did you know I was meeting my mother?"

"She told me, ah, two days ago. We had a drink uptown."

Sydney turned completely around so that he was standing on one side of the threshold, she on the other. "You had drinks with my mother?" she asked, spacing each word carefully.

"Yes." Lazily he leaned on the jamb. "Before you try to turn me into an iceberg, understand that I have no sexual interest in Margerite."

"That's lovely. Just lovely." If she hadn't already put the figurine into her purse, she might have thrown it in his face. "We agreed you'd leave my mother alone."

"We agreed nothing," he corrected. "And I don't bother your mother." There was little to be gained by telling her that Margerite had called him three times before he'd given in and met her. "It was a friendly drink, and after it was done, I think Margerite understood we are unsuitable for anything but friendship. Particularly," he said, holding up a finger to block her interruption, "since I am very sexually interested in her daughter."

That stopped her words cold. She swallowed, struggled for

composure and failed. "You are not, all you're interested in is scoring a few macho points."

Something flickered in his eyes. "Would you like to come back inside so that I can show you exactly what I'm interested in?"

"No." Before she could stop herself, she'd taken a retreating step. "But I would like you to have the decency not to play games with my mother."

He wondered if Margerite would leap so quickly to her daughter's defense, or if Sydney would understand that her mother was only interested in a brief affair with a younger man—something he'd made very clear he wanted no part in.

"Since I would hate for your headache to come back after I went to the trouble to rid you of it, I will make myself as clear as I can. I have no intention of becoming romantically, physically or emotionally involved with your mother. Does that suit you?"

"It would if I could believe you."

He didn't move, not a muscle, but she sensed he had cocked, like the hammer on a gun. His voice was low and deadly. "I don't lie."

She nodded, cool as an ice slick. "Just stick to hammering nails, Mikhail. We'll get along fine. And I can find my own way down." She didn't whirl away, but turned slowly and walked to the elevator. Though she didn't look back as she stepped inside, she was well aware that he watched her go.

At noon sharp, Sydney sat at the head of the long walnut table of the boardroom. Ten men and two women were ranged down either side with crystal tumblers at their elbows, pads and pens at the ready. Heavy brocade drapes were drawn back to reveal a wall of window, tinted to cut the glare of sunlight— had there been any. Instead there was a thick curtain of rain, gray as soot. She could just make out the silhouette of the

Times Building. Occasionally a murmur of thunder sneaked in through the stone and glass.

The gloom suited her. Sydney felt exactly like the reckless child summoned to the principal's office.

She scanned the rows of faces, some of whom had belonged in this office, at this very table, since before she'd been born. Perhaps they would be the toughest to sway, those who thought of her as the little girl who had come to Hayward to bounce on Grandfather's knee.

Then there was Lloyd, halfway down the gleaming surface, his face so smug, so confident, she wanted to snarl. No, she realized as his gaze flicked to hers and held. She wanted to win.

"Ladies, gentlemen." The moment the meeting was called to order she rose. "Before we begin discussion of the matter so much on our minds, I'd like to make a statement."

"You've already made your statement to the press, Sydney," Lloyd pointed out. "I believe everyone here is aware of your position."

There was a rippling murmur, some agreement, some dissent. She let it fade before she spoke again. "Nonetheless, as the president, and the major stockholder of Hayward, I will have my say, then the meeting will open for discussion."

Her throat froze as all eyes fixed on her. Some were patient, some indulgent, some speculative.

"I understand the board's unease with the amount of money allocated to the Soho project. Of Hayward's holdings, this building represents a relatively small annual income. However, this small income has been steady. Over the last ten years, this complex has needed—or I should say received—little or no maintenance. You know, of course, from the quarterly reports just how much this property has increased in value in this space of time. I believe, from a purely practical standpoint, that the money I allocated is insurance to protect our investment."

She wanted to stop, to pick up her glass and drain it, but knew the gesture would make her seem as nervous as she was.

"In addition, I believe Hayward has a moral, an ethical and a legal obligation to insure that our tenants receive safe and decent housing."

"That property could have been made safe and decent for half of the money budgeted," Lloyd put in.

Sydney barely glanced at him. "You're quite right. I believe my grandfather wanted more than the minimum required for Hayward. He wanted it to be the best, the finest. I know I do. I won't stand here and quote you figures. They're in your folders and can be discussed at length in a few moments. Yes, the budget for the Soho project is high, and so are Hayward standards."

"Sydney." Howard Keller, one of her grandfather's oldest associates, spoke gently. "None of us here doubt your motives or your enthusiasm. Your judgment, however, in this, and in the Wolburg matter, is something we must consider. The publicity over the past few days has been extremely detrimental. Hayward stock is down a full three percent. That's in addition to the drop we suffered when you took your position as head of the company. Our stockholders are, understandably, concerned."

"The Wolburg matter," Sydney said with steel in her voice, "is an eighty-year-old woman with a fractured hip. She fell because the floor in her kitchen, a floor we neglected to replace, was unsafe."

"It's precisely that kind of reckless statement that will open Hayward up to a major lawsuit," Lloyd put in. He kept his tone the quiet sound of calm reason. "Isn't it the function of insurance investigators and legal to come to a decision on this, after a careful, thoughtful overview of the situation? We can't run our company on emotion and impulse. Miss Hayward's heart might have been touched by the Wolburg matter, but there are procedures, channels to be used. Now that the press has jumped on this—"

"Yes," she broke in. "It's very interesting how quickly the press learned about the accident. It's hard to believe that only days after an unknown, unimportant old lady falls in her downtown apartment, the press is slapping Hayward in the headlines."

"I would imagine she called them herself," Lloyd said.

Her smile was icy. "Would you?"

"I don't think the issue is how the press got wind of this," Mavis Trelane commented. "The point is they did, and the resulting publicity has been shaded heavily against us, putting Hayward in a very vulnerable position. The stockholders want a solution quickly."

"Does anyone here believe Hayward is not culpable for Mrs. Wolburg's injuries?"

"It's not what we believe," Mavis corrected. "And none of us could make a decision on that until a full investigation into the incident. What is relevant is how such matters are handled."

She frowned when a knock interrupted her.

"I'm sorry," Sydney said, and moved away from the table to walk stiffly to the door. "Janine, I explained we weren't to be interrupted."

"Yes, ma'am." The secretary, who had thrown her loyalty to Sydney five minutes after hearing the story, kept her voice low. "This is important. I just got a call from a friend of mine. He works on Channel 6. Mrs. Wolburg's going to make a statement on the Noon News. Any minute now."

After a moment's hesitation, Sydney nodded. "Thank you, Janine."

"Good luck, Ms. Hayward."

Sydney smiled and shut the door. She was going to need it. Face composed, she turned back to the room. "I've just been told that Mrs. Wolburg is about to make a televised statement. I'm sure we're all interested in what she has to say. So with your permission, I'll turn on the set." Rather than waiting for the debate to settle it, Sydney picked up the remote and aimed it at the console in the corner.

While Lloyd was stating that the board needed to concern themselves with the facts and not a publicity maneuver, Channel 6 cut from commercial to Mrs. Wolburg's hospital bed.

The reporter, a pretty woman in her early twenties with eyes as sharp as nails, began the interview by asking the patient to explain how she came by her injury.

Several members of the board shook their heads and muttered among themselves as she explained about tripping on the ripped linoleum and how the noise of the construction had masked her calls for help.

Lloyd had to stop his lips from curving as he imagined Sydney's ship springing another leak.

"And this floor," the reporter continued. "Had the condition of it been reported to Hayward?"

"Oh, sure. Mik—that's Mikhail Stanislaski, the sweet boy up on the fifth floor, wrote letters about the whole building."

"And nothing was done?"

"Nope, not a thing. Why Mr. and Mrs. Kowalski, the young couple in 101, had a piece of plaster as big as a pie plate fall out of their ceiling. Mik fixed it."

"So the tenants were forced to take on the repairs themselves, due to Hayward's neglect."

"I guess you could say that. Up until the last few weeks."

"Oh, and what happened in the last few weeks?"

"That would be when Sydney—that's Miss Hayward—took over the company. She's the granddaughter of old man Hayward. Heard he'd been real sick the last couple years. Guess things got away from him. Anyway, Mik went to see her, and she came out herself that very day to take a look. Not two weeks later, and the building was crawling with construction workers. We got new windows. Got a new roof going on right this minute. All the plumbing's being fixed, too. Every single thing Mik put on the list is going to be taken care of."

"Really? And did all this happen before or after your injury?"

"Before," Mrs. Wolburg said, a bit impatient with the sarcasm. "I told you all that hammering and sawing was the reason nobody heard me when I fell. And I want you to know that Miss Hayward was there checking the place out again that day. She and Mik found me. She sat right there on the floor and talked to me, brought me a pillow and a blanket and stayed with me until the ambulance came. Came to the hospital, too, and took care of all my medical bills. Been to visit me three times since I've been here."

"Wouldn't you say that Hayward, and therefore Sydney Hayward, is responsible for you being here?"

"Bad eyes and a hole in the floor's responsible," she said evenly. "And I'll tell you just what I told those ambulance chasers who've been calling my family. I've got no reason to sue Hayward. They've been taking care of me since the minute I was hurt. Now maybe if they'd dallied around and tried to make like it wasn't any of their doing, I'd feel differently. But they did what was right, and you can't ask for better than that. Sydney's got ethics, and as long as she's in charge I figure Hayward has ethics, too. I'm pleased to live in a building owned by a company with a conscience."

Sydney stayed where she was after the interview ended. Saying nothing, she switched off the set and waited.

"You can't buy that kind of goodwill," Mavis decided. "Your method may have been unorthodox, Sydney, and I don't doubt there will still be some backwash to deal with, but all in all, I think the stockholders will be pleased."

The discussion labored on another thirty minutes, but the crisis had passed.

The moment Sydney was back in her own office, she picked

up the phone. The receiver rang in her ear twelve times, frustrating her, before it was finally picked up on the other end.

"Yeah?"

"Mikhail?"

"Nope, he's down the hall."

"Oh, well then, I—"

"Hang on." The phone rattled, clanged then clattered as the male voice boomed out Mikhail's name. Feeling like a fool, Sydney stayed on the line.

"Hello?"

"Mikhail, it's Sydney."

He grinned and grabbed the jug of ice water out of the refrigerator. "Hello, anyway."

"I just saw the news. I suppose you knew."

"Caught it on my lunch break. So?"

"You asked her to do it?"

"No, I didn't." He paused long enough to gulp down about a pint of water. "I told her how things were, and she came up with the idea herself. It was a good one."

"Yes, it was a good one. And I owe you."

"Yeah?" He thought about it. "Okay. Pay up."

Why she'd expected him to politely refuse to take credit was beyond her. "Excuse me?"

"Pay up, Hayward. You can have dinner with me on Sunday."

"Really, I don't see how one has to do with the other."

"You owe me," he reminded her, "and that's what I want. Nothing fancy, okay? I'll pick you up around four."

"Four? Four in the afternoon for dinner?"

"Right." He pulled a carpenter's pencil out of his pocket. "What's your address?"

He let out a low whistle as she reluctantly rattled it off. "Nice." He finished writing it on the wall. "Got a phone number? In case something comes up."

She was scowling, but she gave it to him. "I want to make it clear that—"

"Make it clear when I pick you up. I'm on the clock, and you're paying." On impulse he outlined her address and phone number with a heart. "See you Sunday. Boss."

Chapter 6

Sydney studied her reflection in the cheval glass critically and cautiously. It wasn't as if it were a date. She'd reminded herself of that several hundred times over the weekend. It was more of a payment, and no matter how she felt about Mikhail, she owed him. Haywards paid their debts.

Nothing formal. She'd taken him at his word there. The little dress was simple, its scooped neck and thin straps a concession to the heat. The nipped in waist was flattering, the flared skirt comfortable. The thin, nearly weightless material was teal blue. Not that she'd paid any attention to his suggestion she wear brighter colors.

Maybe the dress was new, purchased after a frantic two hours of searching—but that was only because she'd wanted something new.

The short gold chain with its tiny links and the hoops at her ears were plain but elegant. She'd spent longer than usual on her makeup, but that was only because she'd been experimenting with some new shades of eyeshadow.

After much debate, she'd opted to leave her hair down. Then, of course, she'd had to fool with it until the style suited her. Fluffed out, skimming just above her shoulders seemed casual enough to her. And sexy. Not that she cared about being sexy tonight, but a woman was entitled to a certain amount of vanity.

She hesitated over the cut-glass decanter of perfume, remembering how Mikhail had described her scent. With a shrug, she touched it to pulse points. It hardly mattered if it appealed to him. She was wearing it for herself.

Satisfied, she checked the contents of her purse, then her watch. She was a full hour early. Blowing out a long breath, she sat down on the bed. For the first time in her life, she actively wished for a drink.

An hour and fifteen minutes later, after she had wandered through the apartment, plumping pillows, rearranging statuary then putting it back where it had been in the first place, he knocked on the door. She stopped in the foyer, found she had to fuss with her hair another moment, then pressed a hand to her nervous stomach. Outwardly composed, she opened the door.

It didn't appear he'd worried overmuch about his attire. The jeans were clean but faded, the high-tops only slightly less scuffed than his usual work boots. His shirt was tucked in—a definite change—and was a plain, working man's cotton the color of smoke. His hair flowed over the collar, so black, so untamed no woman alive could help but fantasize about letting her fingers dive in.

He looked earthy, a little wild, and more than a little dangerous.

And he'd brought her a tulip.

"I'm late." He held out the flower, thinking she looked as cool and delicious as a sherbert parfait in a crystal dish. "I was working on your face."

"You were—what?"

"Your face." He slid a hand under her chin, his eyes narrowing in concentration. "I found the right piece of rosewood and lost track of time." As he studied, his fingers moved over her face as they had the wood, searching for answers. "You will ask me in?"

Her mind, empty as a leaky bucket, struggled to fill again. "Of course. For a minute." She stepped back, breaking contact. "I'll just put this in water."

When she left him, Mikhail let his gaze sweep the room. It pleased him. This was not the formal, professionally decorated home some might have expected of her. She really lived here, among the soft colors and quiet comfort. Style was added by a scattering of Art Nouveau, in the bronzed lamp shaped like a long, slim woman, and the sinuous etched flowers on the glass doors of a curio cabinet displaying a collection of antique beaded bags.

He noted his sculpture stood alone in a glossy old shadow box, and was flattered.

She came back, carrying the tulip in a slim silver vase.

"I admire your taste."

She set the vase atop the curio. "Thank you."

"Nouveau is sensuous." He traced a finger down the flowing lines of the lamp. "And rebellious."

She nearly frowned before she caught herself. "I find it attractive. Graceful."

"Graceful, yes. Also powerful."

She didn't care for the way he was smiling at her, as if he knew a secret she didn't. And that the secret was her. "Yes, well, I'm sure as an artist you'd agree art should have power. Would you like a drink before we go?"

"No, not before I drive."

"Drive?"

"Yes. Do you like Sunday drives, Sydney?"

"I…" She picked up her purse to give her hands something to do. There was no reason, none at all, for her to allow him to make her feel as awkward as a teenager on a first date. "I don't get much opportunity for them in the city." It seemed wise to get started. She moved to the door, wondering what it would be like to be in a car with him. Alone. "I didn't realize you kept a car."

His grin was quick and a tad self-mocking as they moved out into the hall. "A couple of years ago, after my art had some success, I bought one. It was a little fantasy of mine. I think I pay more to keep it parked than I did for the car. But fantasies are rarely free."

In the elevator, he pushed the button for the garage. "I think about it myself," she admitted. "I miss driving, the independence of it, I suppose. In Europe, I could hop in and zoom off whenever I chose. But it seems more practical to keep a driver here than to go to war every time you need a parking space."

"Sometime we'll go up north, along the river, and you can drive."

The image was almost too appealing, whipping along the roads toward the mountains upstate. She thought it was best not to comment. "Your report came in on Friday," she began.

"Not today." He reached down to take her hand as they stepped into the echoing garage. "Talking reports can wait till Monday. Here." He opened the door of a glossy red-and-cream MG. The canvas top was lowered. "You don't mind the top down?" he asked as she settled inside.

Sydney thought of the time and trouble she'd taken with her hair. And she thought of the freedom of having even a hot breeze blow through it. "No, I don't mind."

He climbed into the driver's seat, adjusting long legs, then gunned the engine. After taking a pair of mirrored sunglasses off the dash, he pulled out. The radio was set on rock. Sydney found herself smiling as they cruised around Central Park.

"You didn't mention where we were going."

"I know this little place. The food is good." He noted her

foot was tapping along in time with the music. "Tell me where you lived in Europe."

"Oh, I didn't live in any one place. I moved around. Paris, Saint Tropez, Venice, London, Monte Carlo."

"Perhaps you have Gypsies in your blood, too."

"Perhaps." Not Gypsies, she thought. There had been nothing so romantic as wanderlust in her hopscotching travels through Europe. Only dissatisfaction, and a need to hide until wounds had healed. "Have you ever been?"

"When I was very young. But I would like to go back now that I am old enough to appreciate it. The art, you see, and the atmosphere, the architecture. What places did you like best?"

"A little village in the countryside of France where they milked cows by hand and grew fat purple grapes. There was a courtyard at the inn where I stayed, and the flowers were so big and bright. In the late afternoon you could sit and drink the most wonderful white wine and listen to the doves coo." She stopped, faintly embarrassed. "And of course, Paris," she said quickly. "The food, the shopping, the ballet. I knew several people, and enjoyed the parties."

Not so much, he thought, as she enjoyed sitting alone and listening to cooing doves.

"Do you ever think about going back to the Soviet Union?" she asked him.

"Often. To see the place where I was born, the house we lived in. It may not be there now. The hills where I played as a child. They would be."

His glasses only tossed her own reflection back at her. But she thought, behind them, his eyes would be sad. His voice was. "Things have changed so much, so quickly in the last few years. Glasnost, the Berlin Wall. You could go back."

"Sometimes I think I will, then I wonder if it's better to leave it a memory—part bitter, part sweet, but colored through the eyes of a child. I was very young when we left."

"It was difficult."

"Yes. More for my parents who knew the risks better than we. They had the courage to give up everything they had ever known to give their children the one thing they had never had. Freedom."

Moved, she laid a hand over his on the gearshift. Margerite had told her the story of escaping into Hungary in a wagon, making it seem like some sort of romantic adventure. It didn't seem romantic to Sydney. It seemed terrifying. "You must have been frightened."

"More than I ever hope to be again. At night I would lie awake, always cold, always hungry, and listen to my parents talk. One would reassure the other, and they would plan how far we might travel the next day—and the next. When we came to America, my father wept. And I understood it was over. I wasn't afraid anymore."

Her own eyes had filled. She turned away to let the wind dry them. "But coming here must have been frightening, too. A different place, different language, different culture."

He heard the emotion in her voice. Though touched, he didn't want to make her sad. Not today. "The young adjust quickly. I had only to give the boy in the next house a bloody nose to feel at home."

She turned back, saw the grin and responded with a laugh. "Then, I suppose, you became inseparable friends."

"I was best man at his wedding only two years ago."

With a shake of her head, she settled back. It was then she noticed they were crossing the bridge over to Brooklyn. "You couldn't find a place to have dinner in Manhattan?"

His grin widened. "Not like this one."

A few minutes later, he was cruising through one of the old neighborhoods with its faded brick row houses and big, shady trees. Children scrambled along the sidewalks, riding bikes, jumping rope. At the curb where Mikhail stopped, two boys were having a deep and serious transaction with baseball cards.

"Hey, Mik!" Both of them jumped up before he'd even climbed out of the car. "You missed the game. We finished an hour ago."

"I'll catch the next one." He glanced over to see that Sydney had already gotten out and was standing in the street, studying the neighborhood with baffled and wary eyes. He leaned over and winked. "I got a hot date."

"Oh, man." Twelve-year-old disgust prevented either of them from further comment.

Laughing, Mikhail walked over to grab Sydney's hand and pull her to the sidewalk. "I don't understand," she began as he led her across the concrete heaved up by the roots of a huge old oak. "This is a restaurant?"

"No." He had to tug to make her keep up with him as he climbed the steps. "It's a house."

"But you said—"

"That we were going to dinner." He shoved the door open and took a deep sniff. "Smells like Mama made Chicken Kiev. You'll like."

"Your mother?" She nearly stumbled into the narrow entranceway. Scattered emotions flew inside her stomach like a bevy of birds. "You brought me to your parents' house?"

"Yes, for Sunday dinner."

"Oh, good Lord."

He lifted a brow. "You don't like Chicken Kiev?"

"No. Yes. That isn't the point. I wasn't expecting—"

"You're late," Yuri boomed. "Are you going to bring the woman in or stand in the doorway?"

Mikhail kept his eyes on Sydney's. "She doesn't want to come in," he called back.

"That's not it," she whispered, mortified. "You might have told me about this so I could have…oh, never mind." She brushed past him to take the couple of steps necessary to bring her into the living room. Yuri was just hauling himself out of a chair.

"Mr. Stanislaski, it's so nice of you to have me." She offered a hand and had it swallowed whole by his.

"You are welcome here. You will call me Yuri."

"Thank you."

"We are happy Mikhail shows good taste." Grinning, he used a stage whisper. "His mama, she didn't like the dancer with the blond hair."

"Thanks, Papa." Casually Mikhail draped an arm over Sydney's shoulders—felt her resist the urge to shrug it off. "Where is everyone?"

"Mama and Rachel are in the kitchen. Alex is later than you. Alex sees all the girls, at the same time," Yuri told Sydney. "It should confuse him, but it does not."

"Yuri, you have not taken the trash out yet." A small woman with an exotic face and graying hair came out of the kitchen, carrying silverware in the skirt of her apron.

Yuri gave his son an affectionate thump on the back that nearly had Sydney pitching forward. "I wait for Mikhail to come and take it."

"And Mikhail will wait for Alex." She set the flatware down on a heavy table at the other end of the room, then came to Sydney. Her dark eyes were shrewd, not unfriendly, but quietly probing. She smelled of spice and melted butter. "I am Nadia, Mikhail's mother." She offered a hand. "We are happy to have you with us."

"Thank you. You have a lovely home."

She had said it automatically, meaningless politeness. But the moment the words were out, Sydney realized they were true. The entire house would probably fit into one wing of her mother's Long Island estate, and the furniture was old rather than antique. Doilies as charming and intricate as those she had seen at Mrs. Wolburg's covered the arms of chairs. The wallpaper was faded, but that only made the tiny rosebuds scattered over it seem more lovely.

The strong sunlight burst through the window and showed every scar, every mend. Just as it showed how lovingly the woodwork and table surfaces had been polished.

Out of the corner of her eye she caught a movement. As she glanced over, she watched a plump ball of gray fur struggling, whimpering from under a chair.

"That is Ivan," Yuri said, clucking to the puppy. "He is only a baby." He sighed a little for his old mutt Sasha who had died peacefully at the age of fifteen six months before. "Alex brings him home from pound."

"Saved you from walking the last mile, right, Ivan?" Mikhail bent down to ruffle his fur. Ivan thumped his tail while giving Sydney nervous looks. "He is named for Ivan the Terrible, but he's a coward."

"He's just shy," Sydney corrected, then gave in to need and crouched down. She'd always wanted a pet, but boarding schools didn't permit them. "There, aren't you sweet?" The dog trembled visibly for a moment when she stroked him, then began to lick the toes that peeked out through her sandals.

Mikhail began to think the pup had potential.

"What kind is he?" she asked.

"He is part Russian wolfhound," Yuri declared.

"With plenty of traveling salesmen thrown in." The voice came from the kitchen doorway. Sydney looked over her shoulder and saw a striking woman with a sleek cap of raven hair and tawny eyes. "I'm Mikhail's sister, Rachel. You must be Sydney."

"Yes, hello." Sydney straightened, and wondered what miracles in the gene pool had made all the Stanislaskis so blindingly beautiful.

"Dinner'll be ready in ten minutes." Rachel's voice carried

only the faintest wisp of an accent and was as dark and smooth as black velvet. "Mikhail, you can set the table."

"I have to take out the trash," he told her, instantly choosing the lesser of two evils.

"I'll do it." Sydney's impulsive offer was greeted with casual acceptance. She was nearly finished when Alex, as dark, exotic and gorgeous as the rest of the family, strolled in.

"Sorry I'm late, Papa. Just finished a double shift. I barely had time to..." He trailed off when he spotted Sydney. His mouth curved and his eyes flickered with definite interest. "Now I'm really sorry I'm late. Hi."

"Hello." Her lips curved in response. That kind of romantic charm could have raised the blood pressure on a corpse. Providing it was female.

"Mine," Mikhail said mildly as he strolled back out of the kitchen.

Alex merely grinned and continued walking toward Sydney. He took her hand, kissed the knuckles. "Just so you know, of the two of us, I'm less moody and have a steadier job."

She had to laugh. "I'll certainly take that into account."

"He thinks he's a cop." Mikhail sent his brother an amused look. "Mama says to wash your hands. Dinner's ready."

Sydney was certain she'd never seen more food at one table. There were mounds of chicken stuffed with rich, herbed butter. It was served with an enormous bowl of lightly browned potatoes and a platter heaped with slices of grilled vegetables that Nadia had picked from her own kitchen garden that morning. There was a tower of biscuits along with a mountain of some flaky stuffed pastries that was Alex's favorite dish.

Sydney sipped the crisp wine that was offered along with vodka and wondered. The amount and variety of food was nothing compared to the conversation.

Rachel and Alex argued over someone named Goose. After

a winding explanation, Sydney learned that while Alex was a rookie cop, Rachel was in her first year with the public defender's office. And Goose was a petty thief Rachel was defending.

Yuri and Mikhail argued about baseball. Sydney didn't need Nadia's affectionate translation to realize that while Yuri was a diehard Yankee fan, Mikhail stood behind the Mets.

There was much gesturing with silverware and Russian exclamations mixed with English. Then laughter, a shouted question, and more arguing.

"Rachel is an idealist," Alex stated. With his elbows on the table and his chin rested on his joined hands, he smiled at Sydney. "What are you?"

She smiled back. "Too smart to be put between a lawyer and a cop."

"Elbows off," Nadia said, and gave her son a quick rap. "Mikhail says you are a businesswoman. And that you are very smart. And fair."

The description surprised her enough that she nearly fumbled. "I try to be."

"Your company was in a sticky situation last week." Rachel downed the last of her vodka with a panache Sydney admired. "You handled it well. It seemed to me that rather than trying to be fair you simply were. Have you known Mikhail long?"

She segued into the question so neatly, Sydney only blinked. "No, actually. We met last month when he barged into my office ready to crush any available Hayward under his work boot."

"I was polite," he corrected.

"You were not polite." Because she could see Yuri was amused, she continued. "He was dirty, angry and ready to fight."

"His temper comes from his mama," Yuri informed Sydney. "She is fierce."

"Only once," Nadia said with a shake of her head. "Only once did I hit him over the head with a pot. He never forgets."

"I still have the scar. And here." Yuri pointed to his shoulder. "Where you threw the hairbrush at me."

"You should not have said my new dress was ugly."

"It was ugly," he said with a shrug, then tapped a hand on his chest. "And here, where you—"

"Enough." All dignity, she rose. "Or our guest will think I am tyrant."

"She is a tyrant," Yuri told Sydney with a grin.

"And this tyrant says we will clear the table and have dessert."

Sydney was still chuckling over it as Mikhail crossed the bridge back into Manhattan. Sometime during the long, comfortable meal she'd forgotten to be annoyed with him. Perhaps she'd had half a glass too much wine. Certainly she'd eaten entirely too much kissel—the heavenly apricot pudding Nadia had served with cold, rich cream. But she was relaxed and couldn't remember ever having spent a more enjoyable Sunday evening.

"Did your father make that up?" Snuggled back in her seat, Sydney turned her head to study Mikhail's profile. "About your mother throwing things?"

"No, she throws things." He downshifted and cruised into traffic. "Once a whole plate of spaghetti and meatballs at me because my mouth was too quick."

Her laughter came out in a burst of enjoyment. "Oh, I would have loved to have seen that. Did you duck?"

He flicked her a grin. "Not fast enough."

"I've never thrown anything in my life." Her sigh was part wistful, part envious. "I think it must be very liberating. They're wonderful," she said after another moment. "Your family. You're very lucky."

"So you don't mind eating in Brooklyn?"

Frowning, she straightened a bit. "It wasn't that. I told you, I'm not a snob. I just wasn't prepared. You should have told me you were taking me there."

"Would you have gone?"

She opened her mouth then closed it again. After a moment, she let her shoulders rise and fall. "I don't know. Why did you take me?"

"I wanted to see you there. Maybe I wanted you to see me there, too."

Puzzled, she turned to look at him again. They were nearly back now. In a few more minutes he would go his way and she hers. "I don't understand why that should matter to you."

"Then you understand much too little, Sydney."

"I might understand if you'd be more clear." It was suddenly important, vital, that she know. The tips of her fingers were beginning to tingle so that she had to rub them together to stop the sensation.

"I'm better with my hands than with words." Impatient with her, with himself, he pulled into the garage beneath her building. When he yanked off his sunglasses, his eyes were dark and turbulent.

Didn't she know that her damn perfume had his nerve ends sizzling? The way she laughed, the way her hair lifted in the wind. How her eyes had softened and yearned as she'd looked at the silly little mutt of his father's.

It was worse, much worse now that he'd seen her with his family. Now that he'd watched how her initial stiffness melted away under a few kind words. He'd worried that he'd made a mistake, that she would be cold to his family, disdainful of the old house and simple meal.

Instead she'd laughed with his father, dried dishes with his mother. Alex's blatant flirting hadn't offended but rather had amused her. And when Rachel had praised her handling of the accident with Mrs. Wolburg, she'd flushed like a schoolgirl.

How the hell was he supposed to know he'd fall in love with her?

And now that she was alone with him again, all that cool

reserve was seeping back. He could see it in the way her spine straightened when she stepped out of the car.

Hell, he could feel it—it surprised him that frost didn't form on his windshield.

"I'll walk you up." He slammed the door of the car.

"That isn't necessary." She didn't know what had spoiled the evening, but was ready to place the blame squarely on his shoulders.

"I'll walk you up," he repeated, and pulled her over to the elevator.

"Fine." She folded her arms and waited.

The moment the doors opened, they entered without speaking. Both of them were sure it was the longest elevator ride on record. Sydney swept out in front of him when they reached her floor. She had her keys out and ready two steps before they hit her door.

"I enjoyed your family," she said, carefully polite. "Be sure to tell your parents again how much I appreciated their hospitality." The lock snapped open. "You can reach me in the office if there are any problems this week."

He slapped his hand on the door before she could shut it in his face. "I'm coming in."

Chapter 7

Sydney considered the chances of shoving the door closed while he had his weight against it, found them slim and opted for shivery reserve.

"It's a bit early for a nightcap and a bit late for coffee."

"I don't want a drink." Mikhail rapped the door closed with enough force to make the foyer mirror rattle.

Though she refused to back up, Sydney felt her stomach muscles experience the same helpless shaking. "Some people might consider it poor manners for a man to bully his way into a woman's apartment."

"I have poor manners," he told her, and, jamming his hands into his pockets, paced into the living room.

"It must be a trial for your parents. Obviously they worked hard to instill a certain code of behavior in their children. It didn't stick with you."

He swung back, and she was reminded of some compact and muscled cat on the prowl. Definitely a man-eater. "You liked them?"

Baffled, she pushed a hand through her disordered hair. "Of course I like them. I've already said so."

While his hands bunched and unbunched in his pockets, he lifted a brow. "I thought perhaps it was just your very perfect manners that made you say so."

As an insult, it was a well-aimed shot. Indignation shivered through the ice. "Well, you were wrong. Now if we've settled everything, you can go."

"We've settled nothing. You tell me why you are so different now from the way you were an hour ago."

She caught herself, tightening her lips before they could move into a pout. "I don't know what you're talking about."

"With my family you were warm and sweet. You smiled so easily. Now with me, you're cold and far away. You don't smile at all."

"That's absurd." Though it was little more than a baring of teeth, she forced her lips to curve. "There, I've smiled at you. Satisfied?"

Temper flickered into his eyes as he began to pace again. "I haven't been satisfied since I walk into your office. You make me suffer and I don't like it."

"Artists are supposed to suffer," she shot back. "And I don't see how I've had anything to do with it. I've given in to every single demand you made. Replaced windows, ripped out plumbing, gotten rid of that tool-and-knot wiring."

"Tube and knob," he corrected, nearly amused.

"Well, it's gone, isn't it? Have you any idea just how much lumber I've authorized?"

"To last two-by-four, I know. This is not point."

She studied him owlishly. "Do you know you drop your articles when you're angry?"

His eyes narrowed. "I drop nothing."

"Your *the*'s and *an*'s and *a*'s," she pointed out. "And your sentence structure suffers. You mix your tenses."

That wounded. "I'd like to hear you speak my language."

She set the purse she still carried onto a table with a snap. "Baryshnikov, glasnost."

His lips curled. "This is Russian. I am Ukrainian. This is a mistake you make, but I overlook."

"It. You overlook *it*," she corrected. "In any case, it's close enough." He took a step forward, she took one back. "I'm sure we can have a fascinating discussion on the subtleties of language, but it will have to wait." He came closer, and she—casually, she hoped—edged away. "As I said before, I enjoyed the evening. Now—" he maneuvered her around a chair "—stop stalking me."

"You imagine things. You're not a *rabbit*, you're a *woman*."

But she felt like a rabbit, one of those poor, frozen creatures caught in a beam of headlights. "I don't know what's put you in this mood—"

"I have many moods. You put me in this one every time I see you, or think about you."

She shifted so that a table was between them. Because she well knew if she kept retreating her back would be against the wall, she took a stand. "All right, damn it. What do you want?"

"You. You know I want you."

Her heart leaped into her throat, then plummeted to her stomach. "You do not." The tremble in her voice irritated her enough to make her force ice into it. "I don't appreciate this game you're playing."

"I play? What is a man to think when a woman blows hot, then cold? When she looks at him with passion one minute and frost the next?" His hands lifted in frustration, then slapped down on the table. "I tell you straight out when you are so upset that I don't want your mama, I want you. And you call me a liar."

"I don't..." She could hardly get her breath. Deliberately she walked away, moving behind a chair and gripping the back hard. It had been a mistake to look into his eyes. There was a ruthlessness there that brought a terrible pitch of excitement to her blood. "You didn't want me before."

"Before? I think I wanted you before I met you. What is this before?"

"In the car." Humiliation washed her cheeks of color. "When I—when we were driving back from Long Island. We were…" Her fingers dug into the back of the chair. "It doesn't matter."

In two strides he was in front of the chair, his hands gripped over hers. "You tell me what you mean."

Pride, she told herself. She would damn well keep her pride. "All right then, to clarify, and to see that we don't have this conversation again. You started something in the car that night. I didn't ask for it, I didn't encourage it, but you started it." She took a deep breath to be certain her voice remained steady. "And you just stopped because…well, because I wasn't what you wanted after all."

For a moment he could only stare, too stunned for speech. Then his face changed, so quickly, Sydney could only blink at the surge of rage. When he acted, she gave a yip of surprise. The chair he yanked from between them landed on its side two feet away.

He swore at her. She didn't need to understand the words to appreciate the sentiment behind them. Before she could make an undignified retreat, his hands were clamped hard on her arms. For an instant she was afraid she was about to take the same flight as the chair. He was strong enough and certainly angry enough. But he only continued to shout.

It took her nearly a full minute to realize her feet were an inch above the floor and that he'd started using English again.

"Idiot. How can so smart a woman have no brains?"

"I'm not going to stand here and be insulted." Of course, she wasn't standing at all, she thought, fighting panic. She was dangling.

"It is not insult to speak truth. For weeks I have tried to be gentleman."

"A *gentleman*," she said furiously. "You've tried to be a *gentleman*. And you've failed miserably."

"I think you need time, you need me to show you how I feel. And I am sorry to have treated you as I did in the car that night. It makes me think you will have..." He trailed off, frustrated that the proper word wasn't in him. "That you will think me..."

"A heathen," she tossed out, with relish. "Barbarian."

"No, that's not so bad. But a man who abuses a woman for pleasure. Who forces and hurts her."

"It wasn't a matter of force," Sydney said coldly. "Now put me down."

He hiked her up another inch. "Do you think I stopped because I don't want you?"

"I'm well aware that my sexuality is under par."

He didn't have a clue what she was talking about, and plowed on. "We were in a car, in the middle of the city, with your driver in the front. And I was ready to rip your clothes away and take you, there. It made me angry with myself, and with you because you could make me forget."

She tried to think of a response. But he had set her back on her feet, and his hands were no longer gripping but caressing. The rage in his eyes had become something else, and it took her breath away.

"Every day since," he murmured. "Every night, I remember how you looked, how you felt. So I want more. And I wait for you to offer what I saw in your eyes that night. But you don't. I can't wait longer."

His fingers streaked into her hair, then fisted there, drawing her head back as his mouth crushed down on hers. The heat seared through her skin, into blood and bone. Her moan wasn't borne of pain but of tormented pleasure. Willing, desperately willing, her mouth parted under his, inviting him, accepting him. This time when her heart rose to her throat, there was a wild glory in it.

On an oath, he tore his mouth from hers and buried it against her throat. She had not asked, she had not encouraged. Those were her words, and he wouldn't ignore the truth of them. Whatever slippery grip he had on control, he clamped tight now, fighting to catch his breath and hold to sanity.

"Damn me to hell or take me to heaven," he muttered. "But do it now."

Her arms locked around his neck. He would leave, she knew, just as he had left that first time. And if he did she might never feel this frenzied stirring again. "I want you." *I'm afraid, I'm afraid.* "Yes, I want you. Make love to me."

And his mouth was on hers again, hard, hot, hungry, while his hands flowed like molten steel down her body. Not a caress now, but a branding. In one long, possessive stroke he staked a claim. It was too late for choices.

Fears and pleasures battered her, rough waves of emotion that had her trembling even as she absorbed delights. Her fingers dug into his shoulders, took greedy handfuls of his hair. Through the thin layers of cotton, she could feel the urgent drum of his heart and knew it beat for her.

More. He could only think he needed more, even as her scent swam in his head and her taste flooded his mouth. She moved against him, that small, slim body restless and eager. When he touched her, when his artist's hands sculpted her, finding the curves and planes of her already perfect, her low, throaty whimpers pounded in his ears like thunder.

More.

He tugged the straps from her shoulders, snapping one in his hurry to remove even that small obstacle. While his mouth raced over the smooth, bare curve, he dragged at the zipper, yanking and pulling until the dress pooled at her feet.

Beneath it. Oh, Lord, beneath it.

The strapless little fancy frothed over milk-white breasts, flowed down to long, lovely thighs. She lifted a trembling hand as if to cover herself, but he caught it, held it. He didn't see the nerves in her eyes as he filled himself on how she looked, surrounded in the last flames of sunset that warmed the room.

"Mikhail." Because he wasn't quite ready to speak, he only nodded. "I...the bedroom."

He'd been tempted to take her where they stood, or to do no more than drag her to the floor. Checking himself, he had her up in his arms in one glorious sweep. "It better be close."

On an unsteady laugh, she gestured. No man had ever carried her to bed before, and she found it dazzlingly romantic. Unsure of what part she should play, Sydney pressed her lips tentatively to his throat. He trembled. Encouraged, she skimmed them up to his ear. He groaned. On a sigh of pleasure, she continued to nibble while her fingers slipped beneath his shirt to stroke over his shoulder.

His arms tightened around her. When she turned her head, his mouth was there, taking greedily from hers as he tumbled with her onto the bed.

"Shouldn't we close the drapes?" The question ended on a gasp as he began doing things to her, wonderful things, shattering things. There was no room for shyness in this airless, spinning world.

It wasn't supposed to be like this. She'd always thought love-making to be either awkwardly mechanical or quietly comforting. It wasn't supposed to be so urgent, so turbulent. So incredible. Those rough, clever hands rushed over flesh, over silk, then back to flesh, leaving her a quivering mass of sensation. His mouth was just as hurried, just as skilled as it made the same erotic journey.

He was lost in her, utterly, irretrievably lost in her. Even the air was full of her, that quiet, restrained, gloriously seductive scent. Her skin seemed to melt, like liquid flowers, under his fingers, his lips. Each quick tremble he brought to her racked through him until he thought he would go mad.

Desire arced and spiked and hummed even as she grew softer, more pliant. More his.

Impatient, he brought his mouth to her breast to suckle through silk while his hands slid up her thighs to find her, wet and burning.

When he touched her, her body arched in shock. Her arm flew back until her fingers locked over one of the rungs of the brass headboard. She shook her head as pleasure shot into her, hot as a bullet. Suddenly fear and desire were so twisted into a single emotion she didn't know whether to beg him to stop or plead with him to go on. On and on.

Helpless, stripped of control, she gasped for breath. It seemed her system had contracted until she was curled into one tight hot ball. Even as she sobbed out his name, the ball imploded and she was left shattered.

A moan shuddered out as her body went limp again.

Unbearably aroused, he watched her, the stunned, glowing pleasure that flushed her cheeks, the dark, dazed desire that turned her eyes to blue smoke. For her, for himself, he took her up again, driving her higher until her breath was ragged and her body on fire.

"Please," she managed when he tugged the silk aside.

"I will please you." He flicked his tongue over her nipple. "And me."

There couldn't be more. But he showed her there was. Even when she began to drag frantically at his clothes, he continued to assault her system and to give her, give her more than she had ever believed she could hold. His hands were never still as he rolled over the bed with her, helping her to rid him of every possible barrier.

He wanted her crazed for him, as crazed as he for her. He could feel the wild need in the way she moved beneath him, in the way her hands searched. And yes, in the way she cried out when he found some secret she'd been keeping just for him.

When he could wait no longer, he plunged inside her, a sword to the hilt.

She was beyond pleasure. There was no name for the edge she trembled on. Her body moved, arching for his, finding their own intimate rhythm as naturally as breath. She knew he was speaking to her, desperate words in a mixture of languages. She understood that wherever she was, he was with her, as much a captive as she.

And when the power pushed her off that last thin edge, he was all there was. All there had to be.

It was dark, and the room was in shadows. Wondering if her mind would ever clear again, Sydney stared at the ceiling and listened to Mikhail breathe. It was foolish, she supposed, but it was such a soothing, intimate sound, that air moving quietly in and out of his lungs. She could have listened for hours.

Perhaps she had.

She had no idea how much time had passed since he'd slapped his hand on her door and barged in after her. It might have been minutes or hours, but it hardly mattered. Her life had been changed. Smiling to herself, she stroked a hand through his hair. He turned his head, just an inch, and pressed his lips to the underside of her jaw.

"I thought you were asleep," she murmured.

"No. I wouldn't fall asleep on top of you." He lifted his head. She could see the gleam of his eyes, the hint of a smile. "There are so many more interesting things to do on top of you."

She felt color rush to her cheeks and was grateful for the dark. "I was..." How could she ask? "It was all right, then?"

"No." Even with his body pressed into hers, he could feel her quick retreat. "Sydney, I may not have so many good words as you, but I think 'all right' is a poor choice. A walk through the park is all right."

"I only meant—" She shifted. Though he braced on his elbows to ease his weight from her, he made sure she couldn't wiggle away.

"I think we'll have a light now."

"No, that's not—" The bedside lamp clicked on. "Necessary."

"I want to see you, because I think I will make love with you again in a minute. And I like to look at you." Casually he brushed his lips over hers. "Don't."

"Don't what?"

"Tense your shoulders. I'd like to think you could relax with me."

"I am relaxed," she said, then blew out a long breath. No, she wasn't. "It's just that whenever I ask a direct question, you give evasions. I only wanted to know if you were, well, satisfied."

She'd been sure before, but now, as the heat had faded to warmth, she wondered if she'd only wished.

"Ah." Wrapping her close, he rolled over until she lay atop him. "This is like a quiz. Multiple choice. They were my favorite in school. You want to know, A, was it all right, B, was it very good or C, was it very wonderful."

"Forget it."

He clamped his arms around her when she tried to pull away. "I'm not finished with you, Hayward. I still have to answer the question, but I find there are not enough choices." He nudged her down until her lips had no choice but to meet his. And the kiss was long and sweet. "Do you understand now?"

His eyes were dark, still heavy from the pleasure they'd shared. The look in them said more than hundreds of silky words. "Yes."

"Good. Come back to me." He nestled her head on his shoulder and began to rub his hand gently up and down her back. "This is nice?"

"Yes." She smiled again. "This is nice." Moments passed in easy silence. "Mikhail."

"Hmm?"

"There weren't enough choices for me, either."

She was so beautiful when she slept, he could hardly look away. Her hair, a tangled flow of golden fire, curtained part of her face. One hand, small and delicate, curled on the pillow where his head had lain. The sheet, tangled from hours of loving showed the outline of her body to where the linen ended just at the curve of her breast.

She had been greater than any fantasy: generous, open, stunningly sexy and shy all at once. It had been like initiating a virgin and being seduced by a siren. And afterward, the faint embarrassment, the puzzling self-doubt. Where had that come from?

He would have to coax the answer from her. And if coaxing didn't work, he would bully.

But now, when he watched her in the morning light, he felt such an aching tenderness.

He hated to wake her, but he knew women enough to be sure she would be hurt if he left her sleeping.

Gently he brushed the hair from her cheek, bent down and kissed her.

She stirred and so did his desire.

He kissed her again, nibbling a trail to her ear. "Sydney." Her sleepy purr of response had his blood heating. "Wake up and kiss me goodbye."

"'S morning?" Her lashes fluttered up to reveal dark, heavy eyes. She stared at him a moment while she struggled to surface. His face was close and shadowed with stubble. To satisfy an old craving, she lifted her hand to it.

"You have a dangerous face." When he grinned, she propped herself up on an elbow. "You're dressed," she realized.

"I thought it the best way to go downtown."

"Go?"

Amused, he sat on the edge of the bed. "To work. It's nearly seven. I made coffee with your machine and used your shower."

She nodded. She could smell both—the coffee and the scent of her soap on his skin. "You should have waked me."

He twined a lock of her hair around his finger, enjoying the way its subtle fire seemed to lick at his flesh. "I didn't let you sleep very long last night. You will come downtown after work? I will fix you dinner."

Relieved, she smiled. "Yes."

"And you'll stay the night with me, sleep in my bed?"

She sat up so they were face-to-face. "Yes."

"Good." He tugged on the lock of hair. "Now kiss me good-bye."

"All right." Testing herself, she sat up, linked her hands around his neck. The sheet slid away to her waist. Pleased, she watched his gaze skim down, felt the tensing of muscles, saw the heat flash. Slowly, waiting until his eyes had come back to hers, she leaned forward. Her lips brushed his and retreated, brushed and retreated until she felt his quick groan. Satisfied she had his full attention, she flicked open the buttons of his shirt.

"Sydney." On a half laugh, he caught at her hands. "You'll make me late."

"That's the idea." She was smiling as she pushed the shirt off his shoulders. "Don't worry, I'll put in a good word for you with the boss."

Two hours later, Sydney strolled into her offices with an armful of flowers she'd bought on the street. She'd left her hair down, had chosen a sunny yellow suit to match her mood. And she was humming.

Janine looked up from her work station, prepared to offer her usual morning greeting. The formal words stuck. "Wow. Ms. Hayward, you look fabulous."

"Thank you, Janine. I feel that way. These are for you."

Confused, Janine gathered up the armful of summer blossoms. "Thank you. I...thank you."

"When's my first appointment?"

"Nine-thirty. With Ms. Brinkman, Mr. Lowe and Mr. Keller, to finalize the buy on the housing project in New Jersey."

"That gives me about twenty minutes. I'd like to see you in my office."

"Yes, ma'am." Janine was already reaching for her pad.

"You won't need that," Sydney told her, and strode through the double doors. She seated herself, then gestured for Janine to take a chair.

"How long have you worked for Hayward?"

"Five years last March."

Sydney tipped back in her chair and looked at her secretary, really looked. Janine was attractive, neat, had direct gray eyes that were a trifle puzzled at the moment. Her dark blond hair was worn short and sleek. She held herself well, Sydney noted. Appearance was important, not the most important, but it certainly counted for what she was thinking.

"You must have been very young when you started here."

"Twenty-one," Janine answered with a small smile. "Right out of business college."

"Are you doing what you want to do, Janine?"

"Excuse me?"

"Is secretarial work what you want to do with your life, or do you have other ambitions?"

Janine resisted the urge to squirm in her chair. "I hope to work my way up to department manager. But I enjoy working for you, Miss Hayward."

"You have five years experience with the company, nearly five more than I do, yet you enjoy working for me. Why?"

"Why?" Janine stopped being nervous and went to flat-out

baffled. "Being secretary to the president of Hayward is an important job, and I think I'm good at it."

"I agree with both statements." Rising, Sydney walked around the desk to perch on the front corner. "Let's be frank, Janine, no one here at Hayward expected me to stay more than a token month or two, and I'm sure it was generally agreed I'd spend most of that time filing my nails or chatting with friends on the phone." She saw by the faint flush that crept up Janine's cheeks that she'd hit very close to the mark. "They gave me an efficient secretary, not an assistant or an office manager, or executive aide, whatever we choose to call them at Hayward, because it wasn't thought I'd require one. True?"

"That's the office gossip." Janine straightened in her chair and met Sydney's eyes levelly. If she was about to be fired, she'd take it on the chin. "I took the job because it was a good position, a promotion and a raise."

"And I think you were very wise. The door opened, and you walked in. Since you've been working for me, you've been excellent. I can't claim to have a lot of experience in having a secretary, but I know that you're at your desk when I arrive in the morning and often stay after I leave at night. When I ask you for information you have it, or you get it. When I ask, you explain, and when I order, you get the job done."

"I don't believe in doing things halfway, Ms. Hayward."

Sydney smiled, that was exactly what she wanted to hear. "And you want to move up. Contrarily, when my position was tenuous at best last week, you stood behind me. Breaking into that board meeting was a risk, and putting yourself in my corner at that point certainly lessened your chances of moving up at Hayward had I been asked to step down. And it most certainly earned you a powerful enemy."

"I work for you, not for Mr. Bingham. And even if it wasn't a matter of loyalty, you were doing what was right."

"I feel very strongly about loyalty, Janine, just as strongly as I feel about giving someone who's trying to make something of herself the chance to do so. The flowers were a thank-you for that loyalty, from me to you, personally."

"Thank you, Ms. Hayward." Janine's face relaxed in a smile.

"You're welcome. I consider your promotion to my executive assistant, with the appropriate salary and benefits, to be a good business decision."

Janine's mouth dropped open. "I beg your pardon?"

"I hope you'll accept the position, Janine. I need someone I trust, someone I respect, and someone who knows how the hell to run an office. Agreed?" Sydney offered a hand. Janine stared at it before she managed to rise and grip it firmly in hers.

"Ms. Hayward—"

"Sydney. We're going to be in this together."

Janine gave a quick, dazzled laugh. "Sydney. I hope I'm not dreaming."

"You're wide-awake, and the flak's going to fall before the day's over. Your first job in your new position is to arrange a meeting with Lloyd. Make it a formal request, here in my office before the close of business hours today."

He put her off until four-fifteen, but Sydney was patient. If anything, the extra time gave her the opportunity to examine her feelings and make certain her decision wasn't based on emotion.

When Janine buzzed him in, Sydney was ready, and she was sure.

"You picked a busy day for this," he began.

"Sit down, Lloyd."

He did, and she waited again while he took out a cigarette. "I won't take up much of your time," she told him. "I felt it best to discuss this matter as quickly as possible."

His gaze flicked up, and he smiled confidently through the haze of smoke. "Having problems on one of the projects?"

"No." Her lips curved in a wintry smile. "There's nothing I can't handle. It's the internal strife at Hayward that concerns me, and I've decided to remedy it."

"Office reorganization is a tricky business." He crossed his legs and leaned back. "Do you really think you've been around long enough to attempt it?"

"I'm not going to attempt it, I'm going to do it. I'd like your resignation on my desk by five o'clock tomorrow."

He bolted up. "What the hell are you talking about?"

"Your resignation, Lloyd. Or if necessary, your termination at Hayward. That distinction will be up to you."

He crushed the cigarette into pulp in the ashtray. "You think you can fire me? Walk in here with barely three months under your belt and fire me when I've been at Hayward for twelve years?"

"Here's the point," she said evenly. "Whether it's been three months or three days, I am Hayward. I will not tolerate one of my top executives undermining my position. It's obvious you're not happy with the current status at Hayward, and I can guarantee you, I'm going to remain in charge of this company for a long time. Therefore, I believe it's in your own interest, and certainly in mine, for you to resign."

"The hell I will."

"That's your choice, of course. I will, however, take the matter before the board, and use all the power at my disposal to limit yours."

Going with instinct, she pushed the next button. "Leaking Mrs. Wolburg's accident to the press didn't just put me in a difficult position. It put Hayward in a difficult position. As an executive vice president, your first duty is to the company, not to go off on some vindictive tangent because you dislike working for me."

He stiffened, and she knew she'd guessed correctly. "You have no way of proving the leak came from my office."

"You'd be surprised what I can prove," she bluffed. "I told you I wanted your loyalty or your resignation if the board stood behind me in the Soho project. We both know your loyalty is out of the question."

"I'll tell you what you'll get." There was a sneer in his voice, but beneath the neat gray suit, he was sweating. "I'll be sitting behind that desk when you're back in Europe dancing from shop to shop."

"No, Lloyd. You'll never sit behind this desk. As the major stockholder of Hayward, I'll see to that. Now," she continued quietly, "it wasn't necessary for me to document to the board the many cases in which you've ignored my requests, overlooked complaints from clients, tenants and other associates at the meeting on Friday. I will do so, however, at the next. In the current climate, I believe my wishes will be met."

His fingers curled. He imagined the satisfaction of hooking them around her throat. "You think because you skidded through one mess, because your senile grandfather plopped you down at that desk, you can shoehorn me out? Lady, I'll bury you."

Coolly she inclined her head. "You're welcome to try. If you don't manage it, it may be difficult for you to find a similar position with another company." Her eyes iced over. "If you don't think I have any influence, or the basic guts to carry this off, you're making a mistake. You have twenty-four hours to consider your options. This meeting is over."

"Why you cold-blooded bitch."

She stood, and this time it was she who leaned over her desk. "Take me on," she said in a quiet voice. "Do it."

"This isn't over." Turning on his heel, he marched to the door to swing it open hard enough that it banged against the wall.

After three deep breaths, Sydney sank into her chair. Okay, she was shaking—but only a little. And it was temper, she realized as she pressed a testing hand against her stomach. Not fear. Good, solid temper. She found she didn't need to vent any anger by mangling paper clips or shredding stationery. In fact, she found she felt just wonderful.

Chapter 8

Mikhail stirred the mixture of meats and spices and tomatoes in the old cast-iron skillet and watched the street below through his kitchen window. After a sniff and a taste, he added another splash of red wine to the mixture. Behind him in the living room *The Marriage of Figaro* soared from the stereo.

He wondered how soon Sydney would arrive.

Leaving the meal to simmer, he walked into the living room to study the rosewood block that was slowly becoming her face.

Her mouth. There was a softness about it that was just emerging. Testing, he measured it between his index finger and thumb. And remembered how it had tasted, moving eagerly under his. Hot candy, coated with cool, white wine. Addictive.

Those cheekbones, so aristocratic, so elegant. They could add a regal, haughty look one moment, or that of an ice-blooded warrior the next. That firm, proud jawline—he traced a fingertip along it and thought of how sensitive and smooth her skin was there.

Her eyes, he'd wondered if he'd have problems with her

eyes. Oh, not the shape of them—that was basic to craft, but the feeling in them, the mysteries behind them.

There was still so much he needed to know.

He leaned closer until he was eye to eye with the half-formed bust. "You will let me in," he whispered. At the knock on the door, he stayed where he was, peering into Sydney's emerging face. "Is open."

"Hey, Mik." Keely breezed in wearing a polka-dotted T-shirt and shorts in neon green. "Got anything cold? My fridge finally gave up the ghost."

"Help yourself," he said absently, "I'll put you on top of the list for the new ones."

"My hero." She paused in the kitchen to sniff at the skillet. "God, this smells sinful." She tipped the spoon in and took a sample. "It is sinful. Looks like a lot for one."

"It's for two."

"Oh." She gave the word three ascending syllables as she pulled a soft drink out of the refrigerator. The smell was making her mouth water, and she glanced wistfully at the skillet again. "Looks like a lot for two, too."

He glanced over his shoulder and grinned. "Put some in a bowl. Simmer it a little longer."

"You're a prince, Mik." She rattled in his cupboards. "So who's the lucky lady?"

"Sydney Hayward."

"Sydney." Her eyes widened. The spoon she held halted in midair above the pan of bubbling goulash. "Hayward," she finished. "You mean the rich and beautiful Hayward who wears silk to work and carries a six-hundred-dollar purse, which I personally priced at Saks. She's coming here, to have dinner and everything?"

He was counting on the everything. "Yes."

"Gee." She couldn't think of anything more profound. But

she wasn't sure she liked it. No, she wasn't sure at all, Keely thought as she scooped her impromptu dinner into a bowl.

The rich were different. She firmly believed it. And this lady was rich in capital letters. Keely knew Mikhail had earned some pretty big bucks with his art, but she couldn't think of him as rich. He was just Mik, the sexy guy next door who was always willing to unclog a sink or kill a spider or share a beer.

Carrying the bowl, she walked over to him and noticed his latest work in progress. "Oh," she said, but this time it was only a sigh. She would have killed for cheekbones like that.

"You like?"

"Sure, I always like your stuff." But she shifted from foot to foot. She didn't like the way he was looking at the face in the wood. "I, ah, guess you two have more than a business thing going."

"Yes." He hooked his thumbs in his pockets as he looked into Keely's troubled eyes. "This is a problem?"

"Problem? No, no problem." She worried her lower lip. "Well, it's just—boy, Mik, she's so uptown."

He knew she was talking about more than an address, but smiled and ran a hand over her hair. "You're worried for me."

"Well, we're pals, aren't we? I can't stand to see a pal get hurt."

Touched, he kissed her nose. "Like you did with the actor with the skinny legs?"

She moved her shoulders. "Yeah, I guess. But I wasn't in love with him or anything. Or only a little."

"You cried."

"Sure, but I'm a wienie. I tear up during greeting card commercials." Dissatisfied, she looked back at the bust. Definitely uptown. "A woman who looks like that, I figure she could drive a guy to joining the Foreign Legion or something."

He laughed and ruffled her hair. "Don't worry. I'll write."

Before she could think of anything else, there was another knock. Giving Keely a pat on the shoulder, he went to answer it.

"Hi." Sydney's face brightened the moment she saw him. She carried a garment bag in one hand and a bottle of champagne in the other. "Something smells wonderful. My mouth started watering on the third floor, and…" She spotted Keely standing near the worktable with a bowl cupped in her hands. "Hello." After clearing her throat, Sydney told herself she would not be embarrassed to have Mikhail's neighbor see her coming into his apartment with a suitcase.

"Hi. I was just going." Every bit as uncomfortable as Sydney, Keely darted back into the kitchen to grab her soft drink.

"It's nice to see you again." Sydney stood awkwardly beside the open door. "How did your murder go?"

"He strangled me in three takes." With a fleeting smile, she dashed through the door. "Enjoy your dinner. Thanks, Mik."

When the door down the hall slammed shut, Sydney let out a long breath. "Does she always move so fast?"

"Mostly." He circled Sydney's waist with his hands. "She is worried you will seduce me, use me, then toss me aside."

"Oh, well, really."

Chuckling, he nipped at her bottom lip. "I don't mind the first two." As his mouth settled more truly on hers, he slipped the garment bag out of her lax fingers and tossed it aside. Taking the bottle of wine, he used it to push the door closed at her back. "I like your dress. You look like a rose in sunshine."

Freed, her hands could roam along his back, slip under the chambray work shirt he hadn't tucked into his jeans. "I like the way you look, all the time."

His lips were curved as they pressed to her throat. "You're hungry?"

"Mmm. Past hungry. I had to skip lunch."

"Ten minutes," he promised, and reluctantly released her. If he didn't, dinner would be much, much later. "What have you brought us?" He twisted the bottle in his hand to study the label. One dark brow lifted. "This will humble my goulash."

With her eyes shut, Sydney took a long, appreciative sniff. "No, I don't think so." Then she laughed and took the bottle from him. "I wanted to celebrate. I had a really good day."

"You will tell me?"

"Yes."

"Good. Let's find some glasses that won't embarrass this champagne."

She didn't know when she'd been more charmed. He had set a small table and two chairs on the tiny balcony off the bedroom. A single pink peony graced an old green bottle in the center, and music drifted from his radio to lull the sounds of traffic. Thick blue bowls held the spicy stew, and rich black bread was heaped in a wicker basket.

While they ate, she told him about her decision to promote Janine, and her altercation with Lloyd.

"You ask for his resignation. You should fire him."

"It's a little more complicated than that." Flushed with success, Sydney lifted her glass to study the wine in the evening sunlight. "But the result's the same. If he pushes me, I'll have to go before the board. I have memos, other documentation. Take this building, for example." She tapped a finger on the old brick. "My grandfather turned it over to Lloyd more than a year ago with a request that he see to tenant demands and maintenance. You know the rest."

"Then perhaps I am grateful to him." He reached up to tuck her hair behind her ear, placing his lips just beneath the jet drops she wore. "If he had been honest and efficient, I wouldn't have had to be rude in your office. You might not be here with me tonight."

Taking his hand, she pressed it to her cheek. "Maybe I should have given him a raise." She turned her lips into his palm, amazed at how easy it had become for her to show her feelings.

"No. Instead, we'll think this was destiny. I don't like someone that close who would like to hurt you."

"I know he leaked Mrs. Wolburg's story to the press." Worked up again, Sydney broke off a hunk of bread. "His anger toward me caused him to put Hayward in a very unstable position. I won't tolerate that, and neither will the board."

"You'll fix it." He split the last of the champagne between them.

"Yes, I will." She was looking out over the neighborhood, seeing the clothes hung on lines to dry in the sun, the open windows where people could be seen walking by or sitting in front of televisions. There were children on the sidewalk taking advantage of a long summer day. When Mikhail's hand reached for hers, she gripped it tightly.

"Today, for the first time," she said quietly, "I felt in charge. My whole life I went along with what I was told was best or proper or expected." Catching herself, she shook her head. "That doesn't matter. What matters is that sometime over the last few months I started to realize that to be in charge meant you had to take charge. I finally did. I don't know if you can understand how that feels."

"I know what I see. And this is a woman who is beginning to trust herself, and take what is right for her." Smiling, he skimmed a finger down her cheek. "Take me."

She turned to him. He was less than an arm's length away. Those dark, untamed looks would have set any woman's heart leaping. But there was more happening to her than an excited pulse. She was afraid to consider it. There was only now, she reminded herself, and reached for him. He held her, rubbing his cheek against her hair, murmuring lovely words she couldn't understand.

"I'll have to get a phrase book." Her eyes closed on a sigh as his mouth roamed over her face.

"This one is easy." He repeated a phrase between kisses.

She laughed, moving willingly when he drew her to her feet. "Easy for you to say. What does it mean?"

His lips touched hers again. "I love you."

He watched her eyes fly open, saw the race of emotion in them run from shock to hope to panic. "Mikhail, I—"

"Why do the words frighten you?" he interrupted. "Love doesn't threaten."

"I didn't expect this." She put a hand to his chest to insure some distance. Eyes darkening, Mikhail looked down at it, then stepped back.

"What did you expect?"

"I thought you were..." Was there no delicate way? "I assumed that you..."

"Wanted only your body," he finished for her, and his voice heated. He had shown her so much, and she saw so little. "I do want it, but not only. Will you tell me there was nothing last night?"

"Of course not. It was beautiful." She had to sit down, really had to. It felt as though she'd jumped off a cliff and landed on her head. But he was looking at her in such a way that made her realize she'd better stay on her feet.

"The sex was good." He picked up his glass. Though he was tempted to fling it off the balcony, he only sipped. "Good sex is necessary for the body and for the state of mind. But it isn't enough for the heart. The heart needs love, and there was love last night. For both of us."

Her arms fell uselessly to her sides. "I don't know. I've never had good sex before."

He considered her over the rim of his glass. "You were not a virgin. You were married before."

"Yes, I was married before." And the taste of that was still bitter on her tongue. "I don't want to talk about that, Mikhail. Isn't it enough that we're good together, that I feel for you something I've never felt before? I don't want to analyze it. I just can't yet."

"You don't want to know what you feel?" That baffled him. "How can you live without knowing what's inside you?"

"It's different for me. I haven't had what you've had or done what you've done. And your emotions—they're always right there. You can see them in the way you move, the way you talk, in your eyes, in your work. Mine are…mine aren't as volatile. I need time."

He nearly smiled. "Do you think I'm a patient man?"

"No," she said, with feeling.

"Good. Then you'll understand that your time will be very short." He began to gather dishes. "Did this husband of yours hurt you?"

"A failed marriage hurts. Please, don't push me on that now."

"For tonight I won't." With the sky just beginning to deepen at his back, he looked at her. "Because tonight I want you only to think of me." He walked through the door, leaving her to gather the rest of the meal.

He loved her. The words swam in Sydney's mind as she picked up the basket and the flower. It wasn't possible to doubt it. She'd come to understand he was a man who said no more than he meant, and rarely less. But she couldn't know what love meant to him.

To her, it was something sweet and colorful and lasting that happened to other people. Her father had cared for her, in his erratic way. But they had only spent snatches of time together in her early childhood. After the divorce, when she'd been six, they had rarely seen each other.

And her mother. She didn't doubt her mother's affection. But she always realized it ran no deeper than any of Margerite's interests.

There had been Peter, and that had been strong and true and important. Until they had tried to love as husband and wife.

But it wasn't the love of a friend that Mikhail was offering her. Knowing it, feeling it, she was torn by twin forces of giddy happiness and utter terror.

With her mind still whirling, she walked into the kitchen to find him elbow deep in soapsuds. She set basket and bottle aside to pick up a dish towel.

"Are you angry with me?" she ventured after a moment.

"Some. More I'm puzzled by you." And hurt, but he didn't want her guilt or pity. "To be loved should make you happy, warm."

"Part of me is. The other half is afraid of moving too fast and risking spoiling what we've begun." He needed honesty, she thought. Deserved it. She tried to give him what she had. "All day today I looked forward to being here with you, being able to talk to you, to be able to share with you what had happened. To listen to you. I knew you'd make me laugh, that my heart would speed up when you kissed me." She set a dry bowl aside. "Why are you looking at me like that?"

He only shook his head. "You don't even know you're in love with me. But it's all right," he decided, and offered her the next bowl. "You will."

"You're so arrogant," she said, only half-annoyed. "I'm never sure if I admire or detest that."

"You like it very much because it makes you want to fight back."

"I suppose you think I should be flattered because you love me."

"Of course." He grinned at her. "Are you?"

Thinking it over, she stacked the second bowl in the first, then took the skillet. "I suppose. It's human nature. And you're…"

"I'm what?"

She looked up at him again, the cocky grin, the dark amused eyes, the tumble of wild hair. "You're so gorgeous."

His grin vanished when his mouth dropped open. When he

managed to close it again, he pulled his hands out of the water and began to mutter.

"Are you swearing at me?" Instead of answering her, he yanked the dishcloth away from her to dry his hands. "I think I embarrassed you." Delighted, she laughed and cupped his face in her hands. "Yes, I did."

"Stop." Thoroughly frazzled, he pushed her hands away. "I can't think of the word for what I am."

"But you are gorgeous." Before he could shake her off, she wound her arms around his neck. "When I first saw you, I thought you looked like a pirate, all dark and dashing."

This time he swore in English and she only smiled.

"Maybe it's the hair," she considered, combing her fingers through it. "I used to imagine what it would be like to get my hands in it. Or the eyes. So moody, so dangerous."

His hands lowered to her hips. "I'm beginning to feel dangerous."

"Hmm. Or the mouth. It just might be the mouth." She touched hers to it, then slowly, her eyes on his, outlined its shape with her tongue. "I can't imagine there's a woman still breathing who could resist it."

"You're trying to seduce me."

She let her hands slide down, her fingers toying with his buttons. "Somebody has to." She only hoped she could do it right. "Then, of course, there's this wonderful body. The first time I saw you without a shirt, I nearly swallowed my tongue." She parted his shirt to let her hands roam over his chest. His knees nearly buckled. "Your skin was wet and glistening, and there were all these muscles." She forgot the game, seducing herself as completely as him. "So hard, and the skin so smooth. I wanted to touch, like this."

Her breath shuddered out as she pressed her fingers into his shoulders, kneading her way down his arms. When her eyes focused on his again, she saw that they were fiercely intense.

Beneath her fingers, his arms were taut as steel. The words dried up in her mouth.

"Do you know what you do to me?" he asked. He reached for the tiny black buttons on her jacket, and his fingers trembled. Beneath the sunny cap-sleeved suit, she wore lace the color of midnight. He could feel the fast dull thud of his heart in his head. "Or how much I need you?"

She could only shake her head. "Just show me. It's enough to show me."

She was caught fast and hard, her mouth fused to his, their bodies molded. When her arms locked around his neck, he lifted her an inch off the floor, circling slowly, his lips tangling with hers.

Dizzy and desperate, she clung to him as he wound his way into the bedroom. She kicked her shoes off, heedless of where they flew. There was such freedom in the simple gesture, she laughed, then held tight as they fell to the bed.

The mattress groaned and sagged, cupping them in the center. He was muttering her name, and she his, when their mouths met again.

It was as hot and reckless as before. Now she knew where they would go and strained to match his speed. The need to have him was as urgent as breath, and she struggled with his jeans, tugging at denim while he peeled away lace.

She could feel the nubs of the bedspread beneath her bare back, and him, hard and restless above her. Through the open window, the heat poured in. And there was a rumble, low and distant, of thunder. She felt the answering power echo in her blood.

He wanted the storm, outside, in her. Never before had he understood what it was to truly crave. He remembered hunger and a miserable wish for warmth. He remembered wanting the curves and softness of a woman. But all that was nothing, nothing like the violent need he felt for her.

His hands hurried over her, wanting to touch every inch, and everywhere he touched she burned. If she trembled, he drove her further until she shuddered. When she moaned, he took and tormented until she cried out.

And still he hungered.

Thunder stalked closer, like a threat. Following it through the window came the passionate wail of the sax. The sun plunged down in the sky, tossing flame and shadows.

Inside the hot, darkening room, they were aware of no time or sound. Reality had been whittled down to one man and one woman and the ruthless quest to mate.

He filled. She surrounded.

Crazed, he lifted her up until her legs circled his waist and her back arched like a bow. Shuddering from the power they made, he pressed his face to her shoulder and let it take him.

The rain held off until the next afternoon, then came with a full chorus of thunder and lightning. With her phone on speaker, Sydney handled a tricky conference call. Though Janine sat across from her, she took notes of her own. Thanks to a morning of intense work between herself and her new assistant, she had the information needed at her fingertips.

"Yes, Mr. Bernstein, I think the adjustments will be to everyone's benefit." She waited for the confirmation to run from Bernstein, to his lawyer, to his West Coast partner. "We'll have the revised draft faxed to all of you by five, East Coast time, tomorrow." She smiled to herself. "Yes, Hayward Industries believes in moving quickly. Thank you, gentlemen. Goodbye."

After disengaging the speaker, she glanced at Janine. "Well?"

"You never even broke a sweat. Look at me." Janine held out a hand. "My palms are wet. Those three were hoping to bulldoze you under and you came out dead even. Congratulations."

"I think that transaction should please the board." Seven million, she thought. She'd just completed a seven-million-dollar deal. And Janine was right. She was steady as a rock. "Let's get busy on the fine print, Janine."

"Yes, ma'am." Even as she rose, the phone rang. Moving on automatic, she plucked up Sydney's receiver. "Ms. Hayward's office. One moment, please." She clicked to hold. "Mr. Warfield."

The faintest wisp of fatigue clouded her eyes as she nodded. "I'll take it. Thank you, Janine."

She waited until her door closed again before bringing him back on the line. "Hello, Channing."

"Sydney, I've been trying to reach you for a couple of days. Where have you been hiding?"

She thought of Mikhail's lumpy bed and smiled. "I'm sorry, Channing. I've been…involved."

"All work and no play, darling," he said, and set her teeth on edge. "I'm going to take you away from all that. How about lunch tomorrow? Lutece."

As a matter of course, she checked her calendar. "I have a meeting."

"Meetings were made to be rescheduled."

"No, I really can't. As it is, I have a couple of projects coming to a head, and I won't be out of the office much all week."

"Now, Sydney, I promised Margerite I wouldn't let you bury yourself under the desk. I'm a man of my word."

Why was it, she thought, she could handle a multimillion-dollar deal with a cool head, but this personal pressure was making her shoulders tense? "My mother worries unnecessarily. I'm really sorry, Channing, but I can't chat now. I've got— I'm late for an appointment," she improvised.

"Beautiful women are entitled to be late. If I can't get you out to lunch, I have to insist that you come with us on Friday. We have a group going to the theater. Drinks first, of course, and a light supper after."

"I'm booked, Channing. Have a lovely time though. Now,

I really must ring off. Ciao." Cursing herself, she settled the receiver on his pipe of protest.

Why hadn't she simply told him she was involved with someone?

Simple question, she thought, simple answer. Channing would go to Margerite, and Sydney didn't want her mother to know. What she had with Mikhail was hers, only hers, and she wanted to keep it that way for a little while longer.

He loved her.

Closing her eyes, she experienced the same quick trickle of pleasure and alarm. Maybe, in time, she would be able to love him back fully, totally, in the full-blooded way she was so afraid she was incapable of.

She'd thought she'd been frigid, too. She'd certainly been wrong there. But that was only one step.

Time, she thought again. She needed time to organize her emotions. And then...then they'd see.

The knock on her office door brought her back to earth. "Yes?"

"Sorry, Sydney." Janine came in carrying a sheet of Hayward stationery. "This just came in from Mr. Bingham's office. I thought you'd want to see it right away."

"Yes, thank you." Sydney scanned the letter. It was carefully worded to disguise the rage and bitterness, but it was a resignation. Effective immediately. Carefully she set the letter aside. It took only a marginal ability to read between the lines to know it wasn't over. "Janine, I'll need some personnel files. We'll want to fill Mr. Bingham's position, and I want to see if we can do it in-house."

"Yes, ma'am." She started toward the door, then stopped. "Sydney, does being your executive assistant mean I can offer advice?"

"It certainly does."

"Watch your back. There's a man who would love to stick a knife in it."

"I know. I don't intend to let him get behind me." She rubbed at the pressure at the back of her neck. "Janine, before we deal with the files, how about some coffee? For both of us."

"Coming right up." She turned and nearly collided with Mikhail as he strode through the door. "Excuse me." The man was soaking wet and wore a plain white T-shirt that clung to every ridge of muscle. Janine entertained a brief fantasy of drying him off herself. "I'm sorry, Ms. Hayward is—"

"It's all right." Sydney was already coming around the desk. "I'll see Mr. Stanislaski."

Noting the look in her boss's eye, Janine managed to fight back the worst of the envy. "Shall I hold your calls?"

"Hmm?"

Mikhail grinned. "Please. You're Janine, with the promotion?"

"Why, yes."

"Sydney tells me you are excellent in your work."

"Thank you." Who would have thought the smell of wet male could be so terrific? "Would you like some coffee?"

"No, thank you."

"Hold mine, too, Janine. And take a break yourself."

"Yes, ma'am." With only a small envious sigh, she shut the door.

"Don't you have an umbrella?" Sydney asked him, and leaned forward for a kiss. He kept his hands to himself.

"I can't touch you, I'll mess up your suit. Do you have a towel?"

"Just a minute." She walked into the adjoining bath. "What are you doing uptown at this time of day?"

"The rain slows things up. I did paperwork and knocked off at four." He took the towel she offered and rubbed it over his head.

"Is it that late?" She glanced at the clock and saw it was nearly five.

"You're busy."

She thought of the resignation on her desk and the files she had to study. "A little."

"When you're not busy, maybe you'd like to go with me to the movies."

"I'd love to." She took the towel back. "I need an hour."

"I'll come back." He reached out to toy with the pearls at her throat. "There's something else."

"What?"

"My family goes to visit my sister this weekend. To have a barbecue. Will you go with me?"

"I'd love to go to a barbecue. When?"

"They leave Friday, after work." He wanted to sketch her in those pearls. Just those pearls. Though he rarely worked in anything but wood, he thought he might carve her in alabaster. "We can go when you're ready."

"I should be able to get home and changed by six. Six-thirty," she corrected. "All right?"

"All right." He took her shoulders, holding her a few inches away from his damp clothes as he kissed her. "Natasha will like you."

"I hope so."

He kissed her again. "I love you."

Emotion shuddered through her. "I know."

"And you love me," he murmured. "You're just stubborn." He toyed with her lips another moment. "But soon you'll pose for me."

"I...what?"

"Pose for me. I have a show in the fall, and I think I'll use several pieces of you."

"You never told me you had a show coming up." The rest of it hit her. "Of me?"

"Yes, we'll have to work very hard very soon. So now I leave you alone so you can work."

"Oh." She'd forgotten all about files and phone calls. "Yes, I'll see you in an hour."

"And this weekend there will be no work. But next…" He nodded, his mind made up. Definitely in alabaster.

She ran the damp towel through her hands as he walked to the door. "Mikhail."

With the door open, he stood with his hand on the knob. "Yes?"

"Where does your sister live?"

"West Virginia." He grinned and shut the door behind her. Sydney stared at the blank panel for a full ten seconds.

"West Virginia?"

Chapter 9

She'd never be ready in time. Always decisive about her wardrobe, Sydney had packed and unpacked twice. What did one wear for a weekend in West Virginia? A few days in Martinique—no problem. A quick trip to Rome would have been easy. But a weekend, a family weekend in West Virginia, had her searching frantically through her closet.

As she fastened her suitcase a third time, she promised herself she wouldn't open it again. To help herself resist temptation, she carried the bag into the living room, then hurried back to the bedroom to change out of her business suit.

She'd just pulled on thin cotton slacks and a sleeveless top in mint green—and was preparing to tear them off again—when the knock sounded at her door.

It would have to do. It would do, she assured herself as she went to answer. They would be arriving so late at his sister's home, it hardly mattered what she was wearing. With a restless hand she brushed her hair back, wondered if she should secure it with a scarf for the drive, then opened the door.

Sequined and sleek, Margerite stood on the other side.

"Sydney, darling." As she glided inside, she kissed her daughter's cheek.

"Mother. I didn't know you were coming into the city today."

"Of course you did." She settled into a chair, crossed her legs. "Channing told you about our little theater party."

"Yes, he did. I'd forgotten."

"Sydney." The name was a sigh. "You're making me worry about you."

Automatically Sydney crossed to the liquor cabinet to pour Margerite a glass of her favored brand of sherry. "There's no need. I'm fine."

"No need?" Margerite's pretty coral-tipped fingers fluttered. "You turn down dozens of invitations, couldn't even spare an afternoon to shop with your mother last week, bury yourself in that office for positively hours on end. And there's no need for me to worry." She smiled indulgently and she accepted the glass. "Well, we're going to fix all of that. I want you to go in and change into something dashing. We'll meet Channing and the rest of the party at Doubles for a drink before curtain."

The odd thing was, Sydney realized, she'd very nearly murmured an agreement, so ingrained was her habit of doing what was expected of her. Instead, she perched on the arm of the sofa and hoped she could do this without hurting Margerite's feelings.

"Mother, I'm sorry. If I've been turning down invitations, it's because the transition at Hayward is taking up most of my time and energy."

"Darling." Margerite gestured with the glass before she sipped. "That's exactly my point."

But Sydney only shook her head. "And the simple fact is, I don't feel the need to have my social calendar filled every night any longer. As for tonight, I appreciate, I really do, the fact that you'd like me to join you. But, as I explained to Channing, I have plans."

Irritation sparked in Margerite's eyes, but she only tapped a nail on the arm of the chair. "If you think I'm going to leave you here to spend the evening cooped up with some sort of nasty paperwork—"

"I'm not working this weekend," Sydney interrupted. "Actually, I'm going out of town for—" The quick rap at the door relieved her. "Excuse me a minute." The moment she'd opened the door, Sydney reached out a hand for him. "Mikhail, my—"

Obviously he didn't want to talk until he'd kissed her, which he did, thoroughly, in the open doorway. Pale and rigid, Margerite pushed herself to her feet. She understood, as a woman would, that the kiss she was witnessing was the kind exchanged by lovers.

"Mikhail." Sydney managed to draw back an inch.

"I'm not finished yet."

One hand braced against his chest as she gestured helplessly with the other. "My mother…"

He glanced over, caught the white-faced fury and shifted Sydney easily to his side. A subtle gesture of protection. "Margerite."

"Isn't there a rule," she said stiffly, "about mixing business and pleasure?" She lifted her brows as her gaze skimmed over him. "But then, you wouldn't be a rule follower, would you, Mikhail?"

"Some rules are important, some are not." His voice was gentle, but without regret and without apology. "Honesty is important, Margerite. I was honest with you."

She turned away, refusing to acknowledge the truth of that. "I'd prefer a moment with you, alone, Sydney."

There was a pounding at the base of her skull as she looked at her mother's rigid back. "Mikhail, would you take my bag to the car? I'll be down in a few minutes."

He cupped her chin, troubled by what he read in her eyes. "I'll stay with you."

"No." She put a hand to his wrist. "It would be best if you left us alone. Just a few minutes." Her fingers tightened. "Please."

She left him no choice. Muttering to himself, he picked up her suitcase. The moment the door closed behind him, Margerite whirled. Sydney was already braced. It was rare, very rare for Margerite to go on a tirade. But when she did, it was always an ugly scene with vicious words.

"You fool. You've been sleeping with him."

"I don't see that as your concern. But, yes, I have."

"Do you think you have the sense or skill to handle a man like that?" There was the crack of glass against wood as she slapped the little crystal goblet onto the table. "This sordid little liaison could ruin you, ruin everything I've worked for. God knows you did enough damage by divorcing Peter, but I managed to put that right. Now this. Sneaking off for a weekend at some motel."

Sydney's fists balled at her sides. "There is nothing sordid about my relationship with Mikhail, and I'm not sneaking anywhere. As for Peter, I will not discuss him with you."

Eyes hard, Margerite stepped forward. "From the day you were born, I used everything at my disposal to be certain you had what you deserved as a Hayward. The finest schools, the proper friends, even the right husband. Now, you're tossing it all back at me, all the planning, all the sacrificing. And for what?"

She whirled around the room as Sydney remained stiff and silent.

"Oh, believe me, I understand that man's appeal. I'd even toyed with the idea of having a discreet affair with him myself." The wound to her vanity was raw and throbbing. "A woman's entitled to a wild fling with a magnificent animal now and again. And his artistic talents and reputation are certainly in his favor. But his background is nothing, less than nothing. Gypsies and farmers and peasants. I have the experience to handle him—had I chosen to. I also have no ties at the moment to make an affair awkward. You, however, are on the verge of making a commitment to Channing. Do you think he'd have you if he ever learned you'd been taking that magnificent brute to bed?"

"That's enough." Sydney moved forward to take her mother's arm. "That's past enough. For someone who's so proud of the Hayward lineage, you certainly made no attempt to keep the name yourself. It was always my burden to be a proper Hayward, to do nothing to damage the Hayward name. Well, I've been a proper Hayward, and right now I'm working day and night to be certain the Hayward name remains above reproach. But my personal time, and whom I decide to spend that personal time with, is my business."

Pale with shock, Margerite jerked her hand away. Not once, from the day she'd been born, had Sydney spoken to her in such a manner. "Don't you dare use that tone with me. Are you so blinded with lust that you've forgotten where your loyalties lie?"

"I've never forgotten my loyalties," Sydney tossed back. "And at the moment, this is the most reasonable tone I can summon." It surprised her as well, this fast, torrid venom, but she couldn't stop it. "Listen to me, Mother, as far as Channing goes, I have never been on the verge of making a commitment to him, nor do I ever intend to do so. That's what you intended. And I will never, never, be pressured into making that kind of commitment again. If it would help disabuse Channing of the notion, I'd gladly take out a full-page ad in the *Times* announcing my relationship with Mikhail. As to that, you know nothing about Mikhail's family, you know nothing about him, as a man. You never got beyond his looks."

Margerite's chin lifted. "And you have?"

"Yes, I have, and he's a caring, compassionate man. An honest man who knows what he wants out of life and goes after it.

You'd understand that, but the difference is he'd never use or hurt anyone to get it. He loves me. And I…" It flashed through her like light, clear, warm and utterly simple. "I love him."

"Love?" Stunned, Margerite reared back. "Now I know you've taken leave of your senses. My God, Sydney, do you believe everything a man says in bed?"

"I believe what Mikhail says. Now, I'm keeping him waiting, and we have a long trip to make."

Head high, chin set, Margerite streamed toward the door, then tossed a last look over her shoulder. "He'll break your heart, and make a fool of you in the bargain. But perhaps that's what you need to remind you of your responsibilities."

When the door snapped shut, Sydney lowered onto the arm of the sofa. Mikhail would have to wait another moment.

He wasn't waiting; he was prowling. Back and forth in front of the garage elevators he paced, hands jammed into his pockets, thoughts as black as smoke. When the elevator doors slid open, he was on Sydney in a heartbeat.

"Are you all right?" He had her face in his hands. "No, I can see you are not."

"I am, really. It was unpleasant. Family arguments always are."

For him, family arguments were fierce and furious and inventive. They could either leave him enraged or laughing, but never drained as she was now. "Come, we can go upstairs, leave in the morning when you're feeling better."

"No, I'd like to go now."

"I'm sorry." He kissed both of her hands. "I don't like to cause bad feelings between you and your mama."

"It wasn't you. Really." Because she needed it, she rested her head on his chest, soothed when his arms came around her. "It was old business, Mikhail, buried too long. I don't want to talk about it."

"You keep too much from me, Sydney."

"I know. I'm sorry." She closed her eyes, feeling her stomach muscles dance, her throat drying up. It couldn't be so hard to say the words. "I love you, Mikhail."

The hand stroking her back went still, then dived into her hair to draw her head back. His eyes were intense, like two dark suns searching hers. He saw what he wanted to see, what he needed desperately to see. "So, you've stopped being stubborn." His voice was thick with emotion, and his mouth, when it met hers, gave her more than dozens of soft endearments. "You can tell me again while we drive. I like to hear it."

Laughing, she linked an arm through his as they walked to the car. "All right."

"And while you drive, I tell you."

Eyes wide, she stopped. "I drive?"

"Yes." He opened the passenger door for her. "I start, then you have a turn. You have license, yes?"

She glanced dubiously at the gauges on the dash. "Yes."

"You aren't afraid?"

She looked back up to see him grinning. "Not tonight, I'm not."

It was after midnight when Mikhail pulled up at the big brick house in Shepherdstown. It was cooler now. There wasn't a cloud in the star-scattered sky to hold in the heat. Beside him, Sydney slept with her head resting on a curled fist. He remembered that she had taken the wheel on the turnpike, driving from New Jersey into Delaware with verve and enthusiasm. Soon after they'd crossed the border into Maryland and she'd snuggled into the passenger seat again, she'd drifted off.

Always he had known he would love like this. That he would find the one woman who would change the zigzagging course of his life into a smooth circle. She was with him now, dreaming in an open car on a quiet road.

When he looked at her, he could envision how their lives

would be. Not perfectly. To see perfectly meant there would be no surprises. But he could imagine waking beside her in the morning, in the big bedroom of the old house they would buy and make into a home together. He could see her coming home at night, wearing one of those pretty suits, her face reflecting the annoyance or the success of the day. And they would sit together and talk, of her work, of his.

One day, her body would grow ripe with child. He would feel their son or daughter move inside her. And they would fill their home with children and watch them grow.

But he was moving too quickly. They had come far already, and he wanted to treasure each moment.

He leaned over to nuzzle his lips over her throat. "I've crossed the states with you, *milaya*." She stirred, murmuring sleepily. "Over rivers and mountains. Kiss me."

She came awake with his mouth warm on hers and her hand resting against his cheek. She felt the flutter of a night breeze on her skin and smelled the fragrance of roses and honeysuckle. And the stir of desire was just as warm, just as sweet.

"Where are we?"

"The sign said, Wild, Wonderful West Virginia." He nipped at her lip. "You will tell me if you think it is so."

Any place, any place at all was wild and wonderful, when he was there, she thought as her arms came around him. He gave a quiet groan, then a grunt as the gearshift pressed into a particularly sensitive portion of his anatomy. "I must be getting old. It is not so easy as it was to seduce a woman in a car."

"I thought you were doing a pretty good job."

He felt the quick excitement stir his blood, fantasized briefly, then shook his head. "I'm intimidated because my mama may peek out the window any minute. Come. We'll find your bed, then I'll sneak into it."

She laughed as he unfolded his long legs out of the open door. "Now I'm intimidated." Pushing her hair back, she turned to look at the house. It was big and brick, with lights glowing gold in the windows of the first floor. Huge leafy trees shaded it, pretty box hedges shielded it from the street.

When Mikhail joined her with their bags, they started up the stone steps that cut through the slope of lawn. And here were the flowers, the roses she had smelled, and dozens of others. No formal garden this, but a splashy display that seemed to grow wild and willfully. She saw the shadow of a tricycle near the porch. In the spill of light from the windows, she noted that a bed of petunias had been recently and ruthlessly dug up.

"I think Ivan has been to work," Mikhail commented, noting the direction of Sydney's gaze. "If he is smart, he hides until it's time to go home again."

Before they had crossed the porch, she heard the laughter and music.

"It sounds as though they're up," Sydney said. "I thought they might have gone to bed."

"We have only two days together. We won't spend much of it sleeping." He opened the screen door and entered without knocking. After setting the bags near the stairs, then taking Sydney's hand, he dragged her down the hall toward the party sounds.

Sydney could feel her reserve settling back into place. She couldn't help it. All the early training, all the years of schooling had drummed into her the proper way to greet strangers. Politely, coolly, giving no more of yourself than a firm handshake and a quiet "how do you do."

She'd hardly made the adjustment when Mikhail burst into the music room, tugging her with him.

"Ha," he said, and swooped down on a small, gorgeous woman in a purple sundress. She laughed when he scooped her up, her black mane of curling hair flying out as he swung her in a circle.

"You're always late," Natasha said. She kissed her brother on both cheeks then the lips. "What did you bring me?"

"Maybe I have something in my bag for you." He set her on her feet, then turned to the man at the piano. "You take good care of her?"

"When she lets me." Spence Kimball rose to clasp hands with Mikhail. "She's been fretting for you for an hour."

"I don't fret," Natasha corrected, turning to Sydney. She smiled—the warmth was automatic—though what she saw concerned her. This cool, distant woman was the one her family insisted Mikhail was in love with? "You haven't introduced me to your friend."

"Sydney Hayward." A little impatient by the way Sydney hung back, he nudged her forward. "My sister, Natasha."

"It's nice to meet you." Sydney offered a hand. "I'm sorry about being so late. It's really my fault."

"I was only teasing. You're welcome here. You already know my family." They were gathering around Mikhail as if it had been years since the last meeting. "And this is my husband, Spence."

But he was stepping forward, puzzlement and pleasure in his eyes. "Sydney? Sydney Hayward?"

She turned, the practiced smile in place. It turned to surprise and genuine delight. "Spence Kimball. I had no idea." Offering both hands, she gripped his. "Mother told me you'd moved south and remarried."

"You've met," Natasha observed, exchanging looks with her own mother as Nadia brought over fresh glasses of wine.

"I've known Sydney since she was Freddie's age," Spence answered, referring to his eldest daughter. "I haven't seen her since…" He trailed off, remembering the last time had been at her wedding. Spence may have been out of touch with New York society in recent years, but he was well aware the marriage hadn't worked out.

"It's been a long time," Sydney murmured, understanding perfectly.

"Is small world," Yuri put in, slapping Spence on the back with fierce affection. "Sydney is owner of building where Mikhail lives. Until she pays attention to him, he sulks."

"I don't sulk." Grumbling a bit, Mikhail took his father's glass and tossed back the remaining vodka in it. "I convince. Now she is crazy for me."

"Back up, everyone," Rachel put in, "his ego's expanding again."

Mikhail merely reached over and twisted his sister's nose. "Tell them you're crazy for me," he ordered Sydney, "so this one eats her words."

Sydney lifted a brow. "How do you manage to speak when your mouth's so full of arrogance?"

Alex hooted and sprawled onto the couch. "She has your number, Mikhail. Come over here, Sydney, and sit beside me. I'm humble."

"You tease her enough for tonight." Nadia shot Alex a daunting look. "You are tired after your drive?" she asked Sydney.

"A little. I—"

"I'm sorry." Instantly Natasha was at her side. "Of course you're tired. I'll show you your room." She was already leading Sydney out. "If you like you can rest, or come back down. We want you to be at home while you're here."

"Thank you," Sydney replied. Before she could reach for her bag, Natasha had hefted it. "It's kind of you to have me."

Natasha merely glanced over her shoulder. "You're my brother's friend, so you're mine." But she certainly intended to grill Spence before the night was over.

At the end of the hall, she took Sydney into a small room with a narrow four-poster. Faded rugs were tossed over a gleaming oak floor. Snapdragons spiked out of an old milk bottle on a table by the window where gauzy Priscillas fluttered in the breeze.

"I hope you're comfortable here." Natasha set the suitcase on a cherrywood trunk at the foot of the bed.

"It's charming." The room smelled of the cedar wardrobe against the wall and the rose petals scattered in a bowl on the nightstand. "I'm very happy to meet Mikhail's sister, and the wife of an old friend. I'd heard Spence was teaching music at a university."

"He teaches at Shepherd College. And he composes again."

"That's wonderful. He's tremendously talented." Feeling awkward, she traced a finger over the wedding ring quilt. "I remember his little girl, Freddie."

"She is ten now." Natasha's smile warmed. "She tried to wait up for Mikhail, but fell asleep on the couch." Her chin angled. "She took Ivan with her to bed, thinking I would not strangle him there. He dug up my petunias. Tomorrow, I think..."

She trailed off, head cocked.

"Is something wrong?"

"No, it's Katie, our baby." Automatically Natasha laid a hand on her breast where her milk waited. "She wakes for a midnight snack. If you'll excuse me."

"Of course."

At the door, Natasha hesitated. She could go with her instincts or her observations. She'd always trusted her instincts. "Would you like to see her?"

After only an instant's hesitation, Sydney's lips curved. "Yes, very much."

Across the hall and three doors down, the sound of the child's restless crying was louder. The room was softly lit by a nightlight in the shape of a pink sea horse.

"There, sweetheart." Natasha murmured in two languages as she lifted her baby from the crib. "Mama's here now." As the crying turned to a soft whimpering, Natasha turned to see Spence at the doorway. "I have her. She's wet and hungry, that's all."

But he had to come in. He never tired of looking at his youngest child, that perfect and beautiful replica of the woman he'd fallen in love with. Bending close, his cheek brushing his wife's, he stroked a finger over Katie's. The whimpering stopped completely, and the gurgling began.

"You're just showing off for Sydney," Natasha said with a laugh.

While Sydney watched, they cuddled the baby. There was a look exchanged over the small dark head, a look of such intimacy and love and power that it brought tears burning in her throat. Unbearably moved, she slipped out silently and left them alone.

She was awakened shortly past seven by high, excited barking, maniacal laughter and giggling shouts coming from outside her window. Moaning a bit, she turned over and found the bed empty.

Mikhail had lived up to his promise to sneak into her room, and she doubted either of them found sleep in the narrow bed much before dawn.

But he was gone now.

Rolling over, she put the pillow over her head to smother the sounds from the yard below. Since it also smothered her, she gave it up. Resigned, she climbed out of bed and pulled on her robe. She just managed to find the doorknob and open the door, when Rachel opened the one across the hall.

The two disheveled women gave each other bleary-eyed stares. Rachel yawned first.

"When I have kids," she began, "they're not going to be allowed out of bed until ten on Saturday mornings. Noon on Sunday. And only if they're bringing me breakfast in bed."

Sydney ran her tongue over her teeth, propping herself on the doorjamb. "Good luck."

"I wish I wasn't such a sucker for them." She yawned again. "Got a quarter?"

Because she was still half-asleep, Sydney automatically searched the pockets of her robe. "No, I'm sorry."

"Hold on." Rachel disappeared into her room, then came back out with a coin. "Call it."

"Excuse me?"

"Heads or tails. Winner gets the shower first. Loser has to go down and get the coffee."

"Oh." Her first inclination was to be polite and offer to get the coffee, then she thought of a nice hot shower. "Tails."

Rachel flipped, caught the coin and held it out. "Damn. Cream and sugar?"

"Black."

"Ten minutes," Rachel promised, then started down the hall. She stopped, glanced around to make sure they were alone. "Since it's just you and me, are you really crazy about Mikhail?"

"Since it's just you and me, yes."

Rachel's grin was quick and she rocked back on her heels. "I guess there's no accounting for taste."

Thirty minutes later, refreshed by the shower and coffee, Sydney wandered downstairs. Following the sounds of activity, she found most of the family had centered in the kitchen for the morning.

Natasha stood at the stove in a pair of shorts and a T-shirt. Yuri sat at the table, shoveling in pancakes and making faces at the giggling baby who was strapped into one of those clever swings that rocked and played music. Alex slouched with his head in his hands, barely murmuring when his mother shoved a mug of coffee under his nose.

"Ah, Sydney."

Alex winced at his father's booming greeting. "Papa, have some respect for the dying."

He only gave Alex an affectionate punch on the arm. "You come sit beside me," Yuri instructed Sydney. "And try Tash's pancakes."

"Good morning," Natasha said even as her mother refilled Sydney's coffee cup. "I apologize for my barbaric children and the mongrel who woke the entire house so early."

"Children make noise," Yuri said indulgently. Katie expressed agreement by squealing and slamming a rattle onto the tray of the swing.

"Everyone's up then?" Sydney took her seat.

"Spence is showing Mikhail the barbecue pit he built," Natasha told her and set a heaping platter of pancakes on the table. "They'll stand and study and make men noises. You were comfortable in the night?"

Sydney thought of Mikhail and struggled not to blush. "Yes, thank you. Oh, please," she started to protest when Yuri piled pancakes on her plate.

"For energy," he said, and winked.

Before she could think how to respond, a small curly-haired bullet shot through the back door. Yuri caught him on the fly and hauled the wriggling bundle into his arms.

"This is my grandson, Brandon. He is monster. And I eat monsters for breakfast. Chomp, chomp."

The boy of about three was wiry and tough, squirming and squealing on Yuri's lap. "Papa, come watch me ride my bike. Come watch me!"

"You have a guest," Nadia said mildly, "and no manners."

Resting his head against Yuri's chest, Brandon gave Sydney a long, owlish stare. "You can come watch me, too," he invited. "You have pretty hair. Like Lucy."

"That's a very high compliment," Natasha told her. "Lucy is a cat. Miss Hayward can watch you later. She hasn't finished her breakfast."

"You watch, Mama."

Unable to resist, Natasha rubbed a hand over her son's curls. "Soon. Go tell your daddy he has to go to the store for me."

"Papa has to come."

Knowing the game, Yuri huffed and puffed and stuck Brandon on his shoulders. The boy gave a shout of laughter and gripped tight to Yuri's hair as his grandfather rose to his feet.

"Daddy, look! Look how tall I am," Brandon was shouting as they slammed out of the screen door.

"Does the kid ever stop yelling?" Alex wanted to know.

"You didn't stop yelling until you were twelve," Nadia told him, and added a flick with her dishcloth.

Feeling a little sorry for him, Sydney rose to pour more coffee into his mug herself. He snatched her hand and brought it to his lips for a smacking kiss. "You're a queen among women, Sydney. Run away with me."

"Do I have to kill you?" Mikhail asked as he strolled into the kitchen.

Alex only grinned. "We can arm wrestle for her."

"God, men are such pigs," Rachel observed as she walked in from the opposite direction.

"Why?" The question came from a pretty, golden-haired girl who popped through the doorway, behind Mikhail.

"Because, Freddie, they think they can solve everything with muscles and sweat instead of their tiny little brains."

Ignoring his sister, Mikhail pushed plates aside, sat down and braced an elbow on the table. Alex grinned at the muttered Ukrainian challenge. Palms slapped together.

"What are they doing?" Freddie wanted to know.

"Being silly." Natasha sighed and swung an arm around Freddie's shoulder. "Sydney, this is my oldest, Freddie. Freddie, this is Miss Hayward, Mikhail's friend."

Disconcerted, Sydney smiled at Freddie over Mikhail's head. "It's nice to see you again, Freddie. I met you a long time ago when you were just a baby."

"Really?" Intrigued, Freddie was torn between studying Sydney or watching Mikhail and Alex. They were knee to knee, hands clasped, and the muscles in their arms were bulging.

"Yes, I, ah..." Sydney was having a problem herself. Mikhail's eyes flicked up and over her before returning to his brother's. "I knew your father when you lived in New York."

There were a couple of grunts from the men at the table. Rachel sat at the other end and helped herself to pancakes. "Pass me the syrup."

With his free hand, Mikhail shoved it at her.

Smothering a grin, Rachel poured lavishly. "Mama, do you want to take a walk into town after I eat?"

"That would be nice." Ignoring her sons, Nadia began to load the dishwasher. She preferred the arm wrestling to the rolling and kicking they'd treated each other to as boys. "We can take Katie in the stroller if you like, Natasha."

"I'll walk in with you, and check on the shop." Natasha washed her hands. "I own a toy store in town," she told Sydney.

"Oh." Sydney couldn't take her eyes off the two men. Natasha could very well have told her she owned a missile site. "That's nice."

The three Stanislaski women grinned at each other. Sentimental, Nadia began to imagine a fall wedding. "Would you like more coffee?" she asked Sydney.

"Oh, I—"

Mikhail gave a grunt of triumph as he slapped his brother's arm on the table. Dishes jumped. Caught up in the moment, Freddie clapped and had her baby sister mimicking the gesture.

Grinning, Alex flexed his numbed fingers. "Two out of three."

"Get your own woman." Before Sydney could react, Mikhail scooped her up, planted a hard kiss on her mouth that tasted faintly and erotically of sweat, then carried her out the door.

Chapter 10

"You might have lost, you know."

Amused by the lingering annoyance in her voice, Mikhail slid an arm around Sydney's waist and continued to walk down the sloping sidewalk. "I didn't."

"The point—" She sucked in her breath. She'd been trying to get the point through that thick Slavic skull off and on for more than an hour. "The point is that you and Alex arm wrestled for me as if I were a six-pack of beer."

His grin only widened, a six-pack would make him a little drunk, but that was nothing to what he'd felt when he'd looked up and seen the fascination in her eyes as she'd stared at his biceps. He flexed them a little, believing a man had a right to vanity.

"And then," she continued, making sure her voice was low, as his family was wandering along in front and behind them. "You manhandled me—in front of your mother."

"You liked it."

"I certainly—"

"Did," he finished, remembering the hot, helpless way she'd responded to the kiss he'd given her on his sister's back porch. "So did I."

She would not smile. She would not admit for a moment to the spinning excitement she'd felt when he'd scooped her up like some sweaty barbarian carrying off the spoils of war.

"Maybe I was rooting for Alex. It seems to me he got the lion's share of your father's charm."

"All the Stanislaskis have charm," he said, unoffended. He stopped and, bending down, plucked a painted daisy from the slope of the lawn they passed. "See?"

"Hmm." Sydney twirled the flower under her nose. Perhaps it was time to change the subject before she was tempted to try to carry him off. "It's good seeing Spence again. When I was fifteen or so, I had a terrible crush on him."

Narrow eyed, Mikhail studied his brother-in-law's back. "Yes?"

"Yes. Your sister's a lucky woman."

Family pride came first. "He's lucky to have her."

This time she did smile. "I think we're both right."

Brandon, tired of holding his mother's hand, bolted back toward them. "You have to carry me," he told his uncle.

"Have to?"

With an enthusiastic nod, Brandon began to shimmy up Mikhail's leg like a monkey up a tree. "Like Papa does."

Mikhail hauled him up, then to the boy's delight, carried him for a while upside down.

"He'll lose his breakfast," Nadia called out.

"Then we fill him up again." But Mikhail flipped him over so Brandon could cling to his back. Pink cheeked, the boy grinned over at Sydney.

"I'm three years old," he told her loftily. "And I can dress my own self."

"And very well, too." Amused, she tapped his sneakered foot. "Are you going to be a famous composer like your father?"

"Nah. I'm going to be a water tower. They're the biggest."

"I see." It was the first time she'd heard quite so grand an ambition.

"Do you live with Uncle Mikhail?"

"No," she said quickly.

"Not yet," Mikhail said simultaneously, and grinned at her.

"You were kissing him," Brandon pointed out. "How come you don't have any kids?"

"That's enough questions." Natasha came to the rescue, plucking her son from Mikhail's back as her brother roared with laughter.

"I just wanna know—"

"Everything," Natasha supplied, and gave him a smacking kiss. "But for now it's enough you know you can have one new car from the shop."

He forgot all about babies. His chocolate-brown eyes turned shrewd. "Any car?"

"Any *little car.*"

"You did kiss me," Mikhail reminded Sydney as Brandon began to badger his mother about how little was little. Sydney settled the discussion by ramming her elbow into Mikhail's ribs.

She found the town charming, with its sloping streets and little shops. Natasha's toy store, The Fun House, was impressive, its stock running the range from tiny plastic cars to exquisite porcelain dolls and music boxes.

Mikhail proved to be cooperative when Sydney wandered in and out of antique shops, craft stores and boutiques. Somewhere along the line they'd lost the rest of the family. Or the family had lost them. It wasn't until they'd started back, uphill, with his arms loaded with purchases that he began to complain.

"Why did I think you were a sensible woman?"

"Because I am."

He muttered one of the few Ukrainian phrases she understood. "If you're so sensible, why did you buy all this? How do you expect to get it back to New York?"

Pleased with herself, she fiddled with the new earrings she wore. The pretty enameled stars swung jauntily. "You're so clever, I knew you'd find a way."

"Now you're trying to flatter me, and make me stupid."

She smiled. "You were the one who bought me the porcelain box."

Trapped, he shook his head. She'd studied the oval box, its top decorated with a woman's serene face in bas-relief for ten minutes, obviously in love and just as obviously wondering if she should be extravagant. "You were mooning over it."

"I know." She rose on her toes to kiss his cheek. "Thank you."

"You won't thank me when you have to ride for five hours with all this on your lap."

They climbed to the top of the steps into the yard just as Ivan, tail tucked securely between his legs streaked across the grass. In hot pursuit were a pair of long, lean cats. Mikhail let out a manful sigh.

"He is an embarrassment to the family."

"Poor little thing." Sydney shoved the package she carried at Mikhail. "Ivan!" She clapped her hands and crouched down. "Here, boy."

Spotting salvation, he swung about, scrambled for footing and shot back in her direction. Sydney caught him up, and he buried his trembling head against her neck. The cats, sinuous and smug, sat down a few feet away and began to wash.

"Hiding behind a woman," Mikhail said in disgust.

"He's just a baby. Go arm wrestle with your brother."

Chuckling, he left her to soothe the traumatized pup. A moment later, panting, Freddie rounded the side of the house. "There he is."

"The cats frightened him," Sydney explained, as Freddie came up to stroke Ivan's fur.

"They were just playing. Do you like puppies?" Freddie asked.

"Yes." Unable to resist, Sydney nuzzled. "Yes, I do."

"Me, too. And cats. We've had Lucy and Desi for a long time. Now I'm trying to talk Mama into a puppy." Petting Ivan, she looked back at the mangled petunias. "I thought maybe if I fixed the flowers."

Sydney knew what it was to be a little girl yearning for a pet. "It's a good start. Want some help?"

She spent the next thirty minutes saving what flowers she could or—since she'd never done any gardening—following Freddie's instructions. The pup stayed nearby, shivering when the cats strolled up to wind around legs or be scratched between the ears.

When the job was done, Sydney left Ivan to Freddie's care and went inside to wash up. It occurred to her that it was barely noon and she'd done several things that day for the first time.

She'd been the grand prize in an arm wrestling contest. She'd played with children, been kissed by the man she loved on a public street. She'd gardened and had sat on a sunny lawn with a puppy on her lap.

If the weekend kept going this way, there was no telling what she might experience next.

Attracted by shouts and laughter, she slipped into the music room and looked out the window. A softball game, she realized. Rachel was pitching, one long leg cocking back as she whizzed one by Alex. Obviously displeased by the call, he turned to argue with his mother. She continued to shake her head at him, bouncing Brandon on her knee as she held firm to her authority as umpire.

Mikhail stood spread legged, his hands on his hips, and one heel touching a ripped seat cushion that stood in as second base.

He tossed in his own opinion, and Rachel threw him a withering glance over her shoulder, still displeased that he'd caught a piece of her curve ball.

Yuri and Spence stood in the outfield, catcalling as Alex fanned for a second strike. Intrigued, Sydney leaned on the windowsill. How beautiful they were, she thought. She watched as Brandon turned to give Nadia what looked like a very sloppy kiss before he bounded off on sturdy little legs toward a blue-and-white swing set. A screen door slammed, then Freddie zoomed into view, detouring to the swing to give her brother a couple of starter pushes before taking her place in the game.

Alex caught the next pitch, and the ball flew high and wide. Voices erupted into shouts. Surprisingly spry, Yuri danced a few steps to the left and snagged the ball out of the air. Mikhail tagged up, streaked past third and headed for home, where Rachel had raced to wait for the throw.

His long strides ate up the ground, those wonderful muscles bunching as he went into a slide. Rachel crowded the plate, apparently undisturbed by the thought of nearly six feet of solid male hurtling toward her. There was a collision, a tangle of limbs and a great deal of swearing.

"Out." Nadia's voice rang clearly over the din.

In the majors, they called it clearing the benches.

Every member of the family rushed toward the plate—not to fuss over the two forms still nursing bruises, but to shout and gesture. Rachel punched Mikhail in the chest. He responded by covering her face with his hand and shoving her back onto the grass. With a happy shout, Brandon jumped into the fray to climb up his father's back.

Sydney had never envied anything more.

"We can never play without fighting," Natasha said from behind her. She was smiling, looking over Sydney's shoulder at the chaos in her backyard. Her arms still felt the slight weight of the baby she'd just rocked to sleep. "You're wise to watch from a distance."

But when Sydney turned, Natasha saw that her eyes were wet.

"Oh, please." Quickly she moved to Sydney's side to take her hand. "Don't be upset. They don't mean it."

"No. I know." Desperately embarrassed, she blinked the tears back. "I wasn't upset. It was just—it was silly. Watching them was something like looking at a really beautiful painting or hearing some incredibly lovely music. I got carried away."

She didn't need to say more. Natasha understood after Spence's explanation of Sydney's background that there had never been softball games, horseplay or the fun of passionate arguments in her life.

"You love him very much."

Sydney fumbled. That quiet statement wasn't as easy to respond to as Rachel's cocky question had been.

"It's not my business," Natasha continued. "But he is special to me. And I see that you're special to him. You don't find him an easy man."

"No. No, I don't."

Natasha glanced outside again, and her gaze rested on her husband, who was currently wrestling both Freddie and Brandon on the grass. Not so many years before, she thought, she'd been afraid to hope for such things.

"Does he frighten you?"

Sydney started to deny it, then found herself speaking slowly, thoughtfully. "The hugeness of his emotions sometimes frightens me. He has so many, and he finds it so easy to feel them, understand them, express them. I've never been the type to be led by mine, or swept away by them. Sometimes he just overwhelms me, and that's unnerving."

"He is what he feels," Natasha said simply. "Would you like to see some of it?" Without waiting for an answer, she walked over to a wall of shelves.

Lovely carved and painted figures danced across the shelves, some of them so tiny and exquisite it seemed impossible that any hand could have created them.

A miniature house with a gingerbread roof and candy-cane shutters, a high silver tower where a beautiful woman's golden hair streamed from the topmost window, a palm-sized canopy bed where a handsome prince knelt beside a lovely, sleeping princess.

"He brought me this one yesterday." Natasha picked up the painted figure of a woman at a spinning wheel. It sat on a tiny platform scattered with wisps of straw and specks of gold. "The miller's daughter from Rumpelstiltskin." She smiled, tracing the delicate fingertips that rode the spindle.

"They're lovely, all of them. Like a magical world of their own."

"Mikhail has magic," Natasha said. "For me, he carves fairy tales, because I learned English by reading them. Some of his work is more powerful, tragic, erotic, bold, even frightening. But it's always real, because it comes from inside him as much as from the wood or stone."

"I know. What you're trying to show me here is his sensitivity. It's not necessary. I've never known anyone more capable of kindness or compassion."

"I thought perhaps you were afraid he would hurt you."

"No," Sydney said quietly. She thought of the richness of heart it would take to create something as beautiful, as fanciful as the diminutive woman spinning straw into gold. "I'm afraid I'll hurt him."

"Sydney—" But the back door slammed and feet clamored down the hall.

The interruption relieved Sydney. Confiding her feelings was new and far from comfortable. It amazed her that she had done so with a woman she'd known less than a day.

There was something about this family, she realized. Something as magical as the fairy-tale figures Mikhail carved for his sister. Perhaps the magic was as simple as happiness.

As the afternoon wore on, they ebbed and flowed out of the house, noisy, demanding and very often dirty. Nadia eventually cleared the decks by ordering all of the men outside.

"How come they get to go out and sit in the shade with a bottle of beer while we do the cooking," Rachel grumbled as her hands worked quickly, expertly with potatoes and a peeler.

"Because…" Nadia put two dozen eggs on boil. "In here they will pick at the food, get big feet in my way and make a mess."

"Good point. Still—"

"They'll have to clean the mess we make," Natasha told her.

Satisfied, Rachel attacked another potato. Her complaints were only tokens. She was a woman who loved to cook as much as she loved trying a case. "If Vera was here, they wouldn't even do that."

"Our housekeeper," Natasha explained to Sydney while she sliced and chopped a mountain of vegetables. "She's been with us for years. We gave her the month off to take a trip with her sister. Could you wash those grapes?"

Obediently Sydney followed instructions, scrubbing fruit, fetching ingredients, stirring the occasional pot. But she knew very well that three efficient women were working around her.

"You can make deviled eggs," Nadia said kindly when she noted Sydney was at a loss. "They will be cool soon."

"I, ah…" She stared, marginally horrified, at the shiny white orbs she'd rinsed in the sink. "I don't know how."

"Your mama didn't teach you to cook?" It wasn't annoyance in Nadia's voice, just disbelief. Nadia had considered it her duty to teach every one of her children—whether they'd wanted to learn or not.

As far as Sydney knew, Margerite had never boiled an egg much less deviled one. Sydney offered a weak smile. "No, she taught me how to order in restaurants."

Nadia patted her cheek. "When they cool, I show you how to make them the way Mikhail likes best." She murmured in Ukrainian when Katie's waking wail came through the kitchen intercom. On impulse, Natasha shook her head before Nadia could dry her hands and go up to fetch her granddaughter.

"Sydney, would you mind?" With a guileless smile, Natasha turned to her. "My hands are full."

Sydney blinked and stared. "You want me to go get the baby?"

"Please."

More than a little uneasy, Sydney started out of the kitchen.

"What are you up to, Tash?" Rachel wanted to know.

"She wants family."

With a hoot of laughter, Rachel swung an arm around her sister and mother. "She'll get more than her share with this one."

The baby sounded very upset, Sydney thought as she hurried down the hall. She might be sick. What in the world had Natasha been thinking of not coming up to get Katie herself? Maybe when you were the mother of three, you became casual about such things. Taking a deep breath, she walked into the nursery.

Katie, her hair curling damply around her face, was hanging on to the side of the crib and howling. Unsteady legs dipped and straightened as she struggled to keep her balance. One look at Sydney had her tear-drenched face crumpling. She flung out her arms, tilted and landed on her bottom on the bright pink sheet.

"Oh, poor baby," Sydney crooned, too touched to be nervous. "Did you think no one was coming?" She picked the sniffling baby up, and Katie compensated for Sydney's awkwardness by cuddling trustingly against her body. "You're so little. Such a pretty little thing." On a shuddering sigh, Katie tipped her head back. "You look like your uncle, don't you? He got embarrassed when I said he was gorgeous, but you are."

Downstairs, three women chuckled as Sydney's voice came clearly through the intercom.

"Oh-oh." After giving the little bottom an affectionate pat, Sydney discovered a definite problem. "You're wet, right? Look, I figure your mother could handle this in about thirty seconds flat—that goes for everybody else downstairs. But everybody else isn't here. So what do we do?"

Katie had stopped sniffling and was blowing bubbles with her mouth while she tugged on Sydney's hair. "I guess we'll give it a try. I've never changed a diaper in my life," she began as she glanced around the room. "Or deviled an egg or played softball, or any damn thing. Whoops. No swearing in front of the baby. Here we go." She spotted a diaper bag in bold green stripes. "Oh, God, Katie, they're real ones."

Blowing out a breath, she took one of the neatly folded cotton diapers. "Okay, in for a penny, in for a pound. We'll just put you down on here." Gently she laid Katie on the changing table and prepared to give the operation her best shot.

"Hey." Mikhail bounded into the kitchen and was greeted by three hissing "shhs!"

"What?"

"Sydney's changing Katie," Natasha murmured and smiled at the sounds flowing through the intercom.

"Sydney?" Mikhail forgot the beer he'd been sent to fetch and stayed to listen.

"Okay, we're halfway there." Katie's little butt was dry and powdered. Perhaps a little over powdered, but better to err on the side of caution, Sydney'd figured. Her brow creased as she attempted to make the fresh diaper look like the one she'd removed, sans dampness. "This looks pretty close. What do you think?" Katie kicked her feet and giggled. "You'd be the expert. Okay, this is the tricky part. No wriggling."

Of course, she did. The more she wriggled and kicked, the more Sydney laughed and cuddled. When she'd managed to secure the diaper, Katie looked so cute, smelled so fresh, felt so soft, she had to cuddle some more. Then it seemed only right that she hold Katie up high so the baby could squeal and kick and blow more bubbles.

The diaper sagged but stayed generally where it belonged.

"Okay, gorgeous, now we're set. Want to go down and see Mama?"

"Mama," Katie gurgled, and bounced in Sydney's arms. "Mama."

In the kitchen, four people scattered and tried to look busy or casual.

"Sorry it took so long," she began as she came in. "She was wet." She saw Mikhail and stopped, her cheek pressed against Katie's.

When their eyes met, color washed to her cheeks. The muscles in her thighs went lax. It was no way, no way at all, she thought, for him to be looking at her with his mother and sisters in the room.

"I'll take her." Stepping forward, he held out his arms. Katie stretched into them. Still watching Sydney, he rubbed his cheek over the baby's head and settled her with a natural ease on his hip. "Come here." Before Sydney could respond, he cupped a hand behind her head and pulled her against him for a long, blood-thumping kiss. Well used to such behavior, Katie only bounced and gurgled.

Slowly he slid away, then smiled at her. "I'll come back for the beer." Juggling Katie, he swaggered out, slamming the screen door behind him.

"Now." Nadia took a dazed Sydney by the hands. "You make deviled eggs."

The sun was just setting on the weekend when Sydney unlocked the door of her apartment. She was laughing—and she was sure she'd laughed more in two days than she had in her entire life. She set the packages she carried on the sofa as Mikhail kicked the door closed.

"You put more in here to come back than you had when you left," he accused, and set her suitcase down.

"One or two things." Smiling, she walked over to slip her arms around his waist. It felt good, wonderfully good, especially knowing that his would circle her in response. *"Dyakuyu,"* she said, sampling *thank you* in his language.

"You mangle it, but you're welcome." He kissed both her cheeks. "This is the traditional greeting or farewell."

She had to bite the tip of her tongue to hold back the grin. "I know." She also knew why he was telling her—again. She'd been kissed warmly by each member of the family. Not the careless touch of cheek to cheek she was accustomed to, but a firm pressure of lips, accompanied by a full-blooded embrace. Only Alex hadn't settled for her cheeks.

"Your brother kisses very well." Eyes as solemn as she could manage, Sydney touched her lips to Mikhail's cheeks in turn. "It must run in the family."

"You liked it?"

"Well…" She shot Mikhail a look from under her lashes. "He did have a certain style."

"He's a boy," Mikhail muttered, though Alex was less than two years his junior.

"Oh, no." This time a quick laugh bubbled out. "He's definitely not a boy. But I think you have a marginal advantage."

"Marginal."

She linked her hands comfortably behind his neck. "As a carpenter, you'd know that even a fraction of an inch can be vital—for fit."

His hands snagged her hips to settle her against him. "So, I fit you, Hayward?"

"Yes." She smiled as he touched his lips to her brow. "It seems you do."

"And you like my kisses better than Alex's?"

She sighed, enjoying the way his mouth felt skimming down her temples, over her jaw. "Marginally." Her eyes flew open when he pinched her. "Well, really—"

But that was all she managed to get out before his mouth closed over hers. She thought of flash fires, ball lightning and electrical overloads. With a murmur of approval, she tossed heat back at him.

"Now." Instantly aroused, he scooped her up in his arms. "I suppose I must prove myself."

Sydney hooked her arms around his neck. "If you insist."

A dozen long strides and he was in the bedroom, where he dropped her unceremoniously onto the bed. By the time she had her breath back, he'd yanked off his shirt and shoes.

"What are you grinning at?" he demanded.

"It's that pirate look again." Still smiling, she brushed hair out of her eyes. "All you need is a saber and a black patch."

He hooked his thumbs in frayed belt loops. "So, you think I'm a barbarian."

She let her gaze slide up his naked torso, over the wild mane of hair, the stubble that proved he hadn't bothered to pack a razor for the weekend. To his eyes, those dark, dramatic, dangerous eyes. "I think you're dazzling."

He would have winced but she looked so small and pretty, sitting on the bed, her hair tumbled from the wind, her face still flushed from his rough, impatient kiss.

He remembered how she'd looked, walking into the kitchen, carrying Katie. Her eyes had been full of delight and wonder and shyness. She'd flushed when his mother had announced that Sydney had made the eggs herself. And again, when his father had wrapped her in a bear hug. But Mikhail had seen that she'd hung on, that her fingers had curled into Yuri's shirt, just for an instant.

There were dozens of other flashes of memory. How she'd

snuggled the puppy or taken Brandon's hand or stroked Freddie's hair.

She needed love. She was strong and smart and sensible. And she needed love.

Frowning, he sat on the edge of the bed and took her hand. Uneasiness skidded down Sydney's spine.

"What is it? What did I do wrong?"

It wasn't the first time he'd heard that strain of insecurity and doubt in her voice. Biting back the questions and the impatience, he shook his head. "Nothing. It's me." Turning her hand over, he pressed a soft kiss in the center of her palm, then to her wrist where her pulse was beating as quickly from fear as from arousal. "I forget to be gentle with you. To be tender."

She'd hurt his feelings. His ego. She hadn't been responsive enough. Too responsive. Oh, God. "Mikhail, I was only teasing about Alex. I wasn't complaining."

"Maybe you should."

"No." Shifting to her knees, she threw her arms around him and pressed her lips to his. "I want you," she said desperately. "You know how much I want you."

Even as the fire leaped in his gut, he brought his hands lightly to her face, fingers stroking easily. The emotion he poured into the kiss came from the heart only and was filled with sweetness, with kindness, with love.

For a moment, she struggled for the heat, afraid she might never find it. But his mouth was so soft, so patient. As her urgency turned to wonder, his lips rubbed over hers. And the friction sparked not the familiar flash fire, but a warm glow, golden, so quietly beautiful her throat ached with it. Even when he took the kiss deeper, deeper, there was only tenderness. Weakened by it, her body melted like wax. Her hands slid limp and useless from his shoulders in total surrender.

"Beautiful. So beautiful," he murmured as he laid her back on the bed, emptying her mind, stirring her soul with long, drowning kisses. "I should be shot for showing you only one way."

"I can't..." Think, breathe, move.

"Shh." Gently, with an artist's touch, he undressed her. "Tonight is only for you. Only to enjoy." His breath caught as the dying sunlight glowed over her skin. She looked too fragile to touch. Too lovely not to. "Let me show you what you are to me."

Everything. She was everything. After tonight he wanted her to have no doubt of it. With slow, worshipful hands, he showed her that beyond passion, beyond desire, was a merging of spirits. A generosity of the soul.

Love could be peaceful, selfless, enduring.

Her body was a banquet, fragrant, dazzling with erotic flavors. But tonight, he sampled slowly, savoring, sharing. Each sigh, each shudder filled him with gratitude that she was his.

He wouldn't allow her to race. Helpless to resist, she floated down the long, dark river where he guided her through air the essence of silk. Never, not even during their most passionate joining, had she been so aware of her own body. Her own texture and shape and scent. And his. Oh, Lord, and his.

Those rock-hard muscles and brute strength now channeled into unimagined gentleness. The subtlety of movement elicited new longings, fresh knowledge and a symphony of understanding that was exquisite in its harmony.

Let me give you. Let me show you. Let me take.

Sensitive fingertips traced over her, lingering to arouse, moving on to seek out some new shattering pleasure. And from her pleasure came his own, just as sweet, just as staggering, just as simple.

She could hear her own breathing, a quiet, trembling sound as the room deepened with night. A tribute to beauty, tears dampened her cheeks and thickened her voice when she spoke his name.

His mouth covered hers again as at last he slipped inside her.

Enfolded in her, cradled by her, he trembled under the long, sighing sweep of sensation. Her mouth opened beneath his, her arms lifted, circled, held.

More. He remembered that he had once fought desperately for more. Now, with her, he had all.

Even with hot hammers of need pounding at him, he moved slowly, knowing he could take her soaring again and again before that last glorious release.

"I love you, Sydney." His muscles trembled as he felt her rise to meet him. "Only you. Always you."

Chapter 11

When the phone rang, it was pitch-dark and they were sleeping, tangled together like wrestling children. Sydney snuggled closer to Mikhail, squeezing her eyes tighter and muttered a single no, determined to ignore it.

With a grunt, Mikhail rolled over her, seriously considered staying just as he was as her body curved deliciously to his.

"Milaya," he murmured, then with an oath, snatched the shrilling phone off the hook.

"What?" Because Sydney was pounding on his shoulder, he shifted off her. "Alexi?" The sound of his brother's voice had him sitting straight up, firing off in Ukrainian. Only when Alex assured him there was nothing wrong with the family did the sick panic fade. "You'd better be in the hospital or jail. Neither?" He sat back, rapped his head on the brass poles of the headboard and swore again. "Why are you calling in the middle of the night?" Rubbing his hand over his face, Mikhail gave Sydney's clock a vicious stare. The glowing dial read 4:45. "What?" Struggling to tune in, he shifted the phone to his other ear. "Damn it, when? I'll be there."

He slammed the phone down and was already up searching for his clothes when he realized Sydney had turned on the light. Her face was dead pale.

"Your parents."

"No, no, it's not the family." He sat on the bed again to take her hand. "It's the apartment. Vandals."

The sharp edge of fear dulled to puzzlement. "Vandals?"

"One of the cops who answered the call knows Alex, and that I live there, so he called him. There's been some damage."

"To the building." Her heart was beginning to pound, heavy and slow, in her throat.

"Yes, no one was hurt." He watched her eyes close in relief at that before she nodded. "Spray paint, broken windows." He bit off an oath. "Two of the empty apartments were flooded. I'm going to go see what has to be done."

"Give me ten minutes," Sydney said and sprang out of bed.

It hurt. It was only brick and wood and glass, but it hurt her to see it marred. Filthy obscenities were scrawled in bright red paint across the lovely old brownstone. Three of the lower windows were shattered. Inside, someone had used a knife to gouge the railings and hack at the plaster.

In Mrs. Wolburg's apartment water was three inches deep over the old hardwood floor, ruining her rugs, soaking the skirts of her sofa. Her lacy doilies floated like soggy lily pads.

"They clogged up the sinks," Alex explained. "By the time they broke the windows downstairs and woke anyone up, the damage here was pretty much done."

Yes, the damage was done, Sydney thought. But it wasn't over. "The other unit?"

"Up on two. Empty. They did a lot of painting up there,

too." He gave Sydney's arm a squeeze. "I'm sorry. We're getting statements from the tenants, but—"

"It was dark," Sydney finished. "Everyone was asleep, and no one's going to have seen anything."

"Nothing's impossible." Alex turned toward the babble of voices coming from the lobby, where most of the tenants had gathered. "Why don't you go on up to Mikhail's place? It's going to take a while to calm everyone down and clear them out."

"No, it's my building. I'd like to go talk to them."

With a nod, he started to lead her down the hall. "Funny they didn't bother to steal anything—and that they only broke into the two empty apartments."

She slanted him a look. He might not have been wearing his uniform, but he was definitely a cop. "Is this an interrogation, Alex?"

"Just an observation. I guess you'd know who had access to the tenants' list."

"I guess I would," she replied. "I have a pretty fair idea who's responsible, Alex." She touched a hand to the ruined banister. "Oh, not who tossed paint or flooded the rooms, but who arranged it. But I don't know if I'll be able to prove it."

"You leave the proving up to us."

She glanced at the streak of paint along the wall. "Would you?" She shook her head before he could reply. "Once I'm sure, I'll turn everything over to you. That's a promise—if you promise to say nothing to Mikhail."

"That's a tough bargain, Sydney."

"I'm a tough lady," she said steadily, and walked down to talk to her tenants.

By eight o'clock she was in her office poring over every word in Lloyd Bingham's personnel file. By ten, she'd made several phone calls, consumed too many cups of coffee and had a structured plan.

She'd authorized Mikhail to hire more men, had spoken with the insurance investigator personally and was now prepared for a little psychological warfare.

She put the call through to Lloyd Bingham herself and waited three rings.

"Hello."

"Lloyd, Sydney Hayward."

She heard the rasp of a lighter. "Got a problem?"

"Not that can't be fixed. It was really a very pitiful gesture, Lloyd."

"I don't know what you're talking about."

"Of course you don't." The sarcasm was brisk, almost careless. "Next time, I'd suggest you do more thorough research."

"You want to come to the point?"

"The point is my building, my tenants and your mistake."

"It's a little early in the day for puzzles." The smug satisfaction in his voice had her fingers curling.

"It's not a puzzle when the solution is so clear. I don't imagine you were aware of just how many service people live in the building. And how early some of those service people get up in the morning, have their coffee, glance out the window. Or how cooperative those people would be in giving descriptions to the police."

"If something happened to your building, that's your problem." He drew hard on his cigarette. "I haven't been near it."

"I never thought you had been," she said easily. "You've always been good at delegating. But once certain parties are picked up by the police, I think you'll discover how unsettling it is not to have loyal employees."

She could have sworn she heard him sweat. "I don't have to listen to this."

"No, of course you don't. And I won't keep you. Oh, Lloyd, don't let them talk you into a bonus. They didn't do a very thorough job. Ciao."

She hung up, immensely satisfied. If she knew her quarry, he wouldn't wait long to meet with his hirelings and pay them off. And since the investigator had been very interested in Sydney's theory, she doubted that meeting would go unobserved.

She flicked her intercom. "Janine, I need food before we start interviewing the new secretaries. Order anything the deli says looks good today and double it."

"You got it. I was about to buzz you, Sydney. Your mother's here."

The little bubble of success burst in her throat. "Tell her I'm…" *Coward.* "No, tell her to come in." But she took a deep breath before she rose and walked to the door. "Mother."

"Sydney, dear." Lovely in ivory linen and smelling of Paris, she strolled in and bussed Sydney's cheek. "I'm so sorry."

"I—what?"

"I've had to wait all weekend to contact you and apologize." Margerite took a steadying breath herself, twisting her envelope bag in her hands. "May I sit?"

"Of course. I'm sorry. Would you like anything?"

"To completely erase Friday evening from my life." Seated, Margerite gave her daughter an embarrassed glance. "This isn't easy for me, Sydney. The simple fact is, I was jealous."

"Oh, Mother."

"No, please." Margerite waved her daughter to the chair beside her. "I don't enjoy the taste of crow and hope you'll let me get it done in one large swallow."

As embarrassed as her mother, Sydney sat and reached for her hand. "It isn't necessary that you swallow at all. We'll just forget it."

Margerite shook her head. "I hope I'm big enough to admit my failings. I like thinking I'm still an attractive and desirable woman."

"You are."

Margerite smiled fleetingly. "But certainly not an admirable one when I find myself eaten up with envy to see that a man I'd hoped to, well, enchant, was instead enchanted by my daughter. I regret, very much, my behavior and my words. There," she said on a puff of breath. "Will you forgive me?"

"Of course I will. And I'll apologize, too, for speaking to you the way I did."

Margerite took a little square of lace from her bag and dabbed at her eyes. "You surprised me, I admit. I've never seen you so passionate about anything. He's a beautiful man, dear. I won't say I approve of a relationship between you, but I can certainly understand it." She sighed as she tucked the handkerchief back into her bag. "Your happiness is important to me, Sydney."

"I know that."

Her eyes still glistened when she looked at her daughter. "I'm so glad we cleared the air. And I want to do something for you, something to make up for all of this."

"You don't have to do anything."

"I want to, really. Have dinner with me tonight."

Sydney thought of the dozens of things she had to do, of the quiet meal she'd hoped for at the end of it all with Mikhail. Then she looked at her mother's anxious eyes. "I'd love to."

"Wonderful." The spring was back in her step as Margerite got to her feet. "Eight o'clock. Le Cirque." She gave Sydney a quick and genuine hug before she strolled out.

By eight, Sydney would have preferred a long, solitary nap, but stepped from her car dressed for the evening in a sleeveless silk jumpsuit of icy blue.

"My mother's driver will take me home, Donald."

"Very good, Ms. Hayward. Enjoy your evening."

"Thank you."

The maître d' recognized her the moment she walked in and gracefully led her to her table himself. As she passed through the elegant restaurant filled with sparkling people and exotic scents, she imagined Mikhail, sitting at his scarred workbench with a bottle of beer and a bowl of goulash.

She tried not to sigh in envy.

When she spotted her mother—with Channing—at the corner table, she tried not to grit her teeth.

"There you are, darling." So certain her surprise was just what her daughter needed, Margerite didn't notice the lights of war in Sydney's eyes. "Isn't this lovely?"

"Lovely." Sydney's voice was flat as Channing rose to pull out her chair. She said nothing when he bent close to kiss her cheek.

"You look beautiful tonight, Sydney."

The champagne was already chilled and open. She waited while hers was poured, but the first sip did nothing to clear the anger from her throat. "Mother didn't mention you'd be joining us tonight."

"That was my surprise," Margerite bubbled like the wine in her glass. "My little make-up present." Following a prearranged signal, she set her napkin aside and rose. "I'm sure you two will excuse me while I powder my nose."

Knowing he only had fifteen minutes to complete his mission, Channing immediately took Sydney's hand. "I've missed you, darling. It seems like weeks since I've had a moment alone with you."

Skillfully Sydney slipped her hand from his. "It has been weeks. How have you been, Channing?"

"Desolate without you." He skimmed a fingertip up her bare arm. She really had exquisite skin. "When are we going to stop playing these games, Sydney?"

"I haven't been playing." She took a sip of wine. "I've been working."

A trace of annoyance clouded his eyes then cleared. He was sure Margerite was right. Once they were married, she would be too busy with him to bother with a career. It was best to get right to the point. "Darling, we've been seeing each other for months now. And of course, we've known each other for years. But things have changed."

She met his eyes. "Yes, they have."

Encouraged, he took her hand again. "I haven't wanted to rush you, but I feel it's time we take the next step. I care for you very much, Sydney. I find you lovely and amusing and sweet."

"And suitable," she muttered.

"Of course. I want you to be my wife." He slipped a box from his pocket, opened the lid so that the round icy diamond could flash in the candlelight.

"Channing—"

"It reminded me of you," he interrupted. "Regal and elegant."

"It's beautiful, Channing," she said carefully. And cold, she thought. So very cold. "And I'm sorry, but I can't accept it. Or you."

Shock came first, then a trickle of annoyance. "Sydney, we're both adults. There's no need to be coy."

"What I'm trying to be is honest." She shifted in her chair, and this time it was she who took his hands. "I can't tell you how sorry I am that my mother led you to believe I'd feel differently. By doing so, she's put us both in an embarrassing position. Let's be candid, Channing. You don't love me, and I don't love you."

Insulted, he pokered up. "I hardly think I'd be offering marriage otherwise."

"You're offering it because you find me attractive, you think I'd make an excellent hostess, and because I come from the same circle as you. Those are reasons for a merger, not a marriage." She closed the lid on the diamond and pressed the box into his hands. "I make a poor wife, Channing, that much I know. And I have no intention of becoming one again."

He relaxed a little. "I understand you might still be a bit raw over what happened between you and Peter."

"No, you don't understand at all what happened between me and Peter. To be honest, that has nothing to do with my refusing you. I don't love you, Channing, and I'm very much in love with someone else."

His fair skin flushed dark red. "Then I find it worse than insulting that you would pretend an affection for me."

"I do have an affection for you," she said wearily. "But that's all I have. I can only apologize if I failed to make that clear before this."

"I don't believe an apology covers it, Sydney." Stiffly he rose to his feet. "Please give my regrets to your mother."

Straight as a poker, he strode out, leaving Sydney alone with a miserable mix of temper and guilt. Five minutes later, Margerite came out of the ladies' room, beaming. "Well now." She leaned conspiratorially toward her daughter, pleased to see that Channing had given them a few moments alone. "Tell me everything."

"Channing's gone, Mother."

"Gone?" Bright eyed, Margerite glanced around. "What do you mean gone?"

"I mean he's left, furious, I might add, because I declined his proposal of marriage."

"Declined?" Margerite blinked. "You— Sydney, how could you?"

"How could I?" Her voice rose and, catching herself, she lowered it to a whisper. "How could you? You set this entire evening up."

"Of course I did." Frazzled, Margerite waved the oncoming waiter away and reached for her wine. "I've planned for months to see you and Channing together. And since it was obvious that Mikhail had brought you out of your shell, the timing was perfect. Channing is exactly what you need. He's eligible, his family is above reproach, he has a beautiful home and excellent bearing."

"I don't love him."

"Sydney, for heaven's sake, be sensible."

"I've never been anything else, and perhaps that's been the problem. I believed you when you came to see me this morning. I believed you were sorry, that you cared, and that you wanted something more than polite words between us."

Margerite's eyes filled. "Everything I said this morning was true. I'd been miserable all weekend, thinking I'd driven you away. You're my daughter, I do care. I want what's best for you."

"You mean it," Sydney murmured, suddenly, unbearably weary. "But you also believe that you know what's best for me. I don't mean to hurt you, but I've come to understand you've never known what's best for me. By doing this tonight, you caused me to hurt Channing in a way I never meant to."

A tear spilled over. "Sydney, I only thought—"

"Don't think for me." She was perilously close to tears herself. "Don't ever think for me again. I let you do that before, and I ruined someone's life."

"I don't want you to be alone," Margerite choked out. "It's hateful being alone."

"Mother." Though she was afraid she might weaken too much, too soon, she took Margerite's hands. "Listen to me, listen carefully. I love you, but I can't be you. I want to know that we can have an honest, caring relationship. It'll take time. But it can't ever happen unless you try to understand me, unless you respect me for who I am, and not for what you want me to be. I can't marry Channing to please you. I can't marry anyone."

"Oh, Sydney."

"There are things you don't know. Things I don't want to talk about. Just please trust me. I know what I'm doing. I've been happier in the last few weeks than I've ever been."

"Stanislaski," Margerite said on a sigh.

"Yes, Stanislaski. And Hayward," she added. "And me. I'm doing something with my life, Mother. It's making a difference. Now let's go fix your makeup and start over."

★ ★ ★

At his workbench, Mikhail polished the rosewood bust. He hadn't meant to work so late, but Sydney had simply emerged in his hands. There was no way to explain the way it felt to have her come to life there. It wasn't powerful. It was humbling. He'd barely had to think. Though his fingers were cramped, proving how long he had carved and sanded and polished, he could barely remember the technique he'd used.

The tools didn't matter, only the result. Now she was there with him, beautiful, warm, alive. And he knew it was a piece he would never part with.

Sitting back, he circled his shoulders to relieve the stiffness. It had been a viciously long day, starting before dawn. He'd had to channel the edge of his rage into organizing the cleaning up and repair the worst of the damage. Now that the impetus that had driven him to complete the bust was passed, he was punchy with fatigue. But he didn't want to go to bed. An empty bed.

How could he miss her so much after only hours? Why did it feel as though she were a world away when she was only at the other end of the city? He wasn't going to go through another night without her, he vowed as he stood up to pace. She was going to have to understand that. He would make her understand that. A woman had no right to make herself vital to a man's existence then leave him restless and alone at midnight.

Dragging a hand through his hair, he considered his options. He could go to bed and will himself to sleep. He could call her and satisfy himself with the sound of her voice. Or he could go uptown and beat on her door until she let him in.

He grinned, liking the third choice best. Snatching up a shirt, he tugged it on as he headed for the door. Sydney gave a surprised gasp as he yanked it open just as her hand was poised to knock.

"Oh. What instincts." She pressed the hand to her heart. "I'm sorry to come by so late, but I saw your light was on, so I—"

He didn't let her finish, but pulled her inside and held her until she wondered her ribs didn't crack. "I was coming for you," he muttered.

"Coming for me? I just left the restaurant."

"I wanted you. I wanted to—" He broke off and snapped her back. "It's after midnight. What are you doing coming all the way downtown after midnight?"

"For heaven's sake—"

"It's not safe for a woman alone."

"I was perfectly safe."

He shook his head, cupping her chin. "Next time, you call. I'll come to you." Then his eyes narrowed. An artist's eyes, a lover's eyes saw beyond carefully repaired makeup. "You've been crying."

There was such fury in the accusation, she had to laugh. "No, not really. Mother got a bit emotional, and there was a chain reaction."

"I thought you said you'd made up with her."

"I did. I have. At least I think we've come to a better understanding."

He smiled a little, tracing a finger over Sydney's lips. "She does not approve of me for her daughter."

"That's not really the problem. I'm afraid she's feeling a little worn down. She had her plans blow up in her face tonight."

"You'll tell me."

"Yes." She walked over, intending to collapse on his badly sprung couch. But she saw the bust. Slowly she moved closer to study it. When she spoke, her voice was low and thick. "You have an incredible talent."

"I carve what I see, what I know, what I feel."

"Is this how you see me?"

"It's how you are." He laid his hands lightly on her shoulders. "For me."

Then she was beautiful for him, Sydney thought. And she

was trembling with life and love, for him. "I didn't even pose for you."

"You will." He brushed his lips over her hair. "Talk to me."

"When I met Mother at the restaurant, Channing was with her."

Over Sydney's head, Mikhail's eyes darkened dangerously. "The banker with the silk suits. You let him kiss you before you let me."

"I knew him before I knew you." Amused, Sydney turned and looked jealousy in the eye. "And I didn't let you kiss me, as I recall. You just did."

He did so again, ruthlessly. "You won't let him again."

"No."

"Good." He drew her to the sofa. "Then he can live."

With a laugh, she threw her arms around him for a hug, then settled her head on his shoulder. "None of it's his fault, really. Or my mother's, either. It's more a matter of habit and circumstance. She'd set up the evening after persuading Channing that the time was ripe to propose."

"Propose?" Mikhail spun her around to face him. "He wants to marry you?"

"Not really. He thought he did. He certainly doesn't want to marry me anymore." But he was shoving her out of the way so he could get up and pace. "There's no reason to be angry," Sydney said as she smoothed down her jumpsuit. "I was the one in the awkward position. As it is I doubt he'll speak to me again."

"If he does, I'll cut out his tongue." Slowly, Mikhail thought, working up the rage. "No one marries you but me."

"I've already explained..." She trailed off as breath lodged in a hard ball in her throat. "There's really no need to go into this," she managed as she rose. "It's late."

"You wait," Mikhail ordered and strode into the bedroom. When he came back carrying a small box, Sydney's blood turned to ice. "Sit."

"No, Mikhail, please—"

"Then stand." He flipped open the top of the box to reveal a ring of hammered gold with a small center stone of fiery red. "The grandfather of my father made this for his wife. He was a goldsmith so the work is fine, even though the stone is small. It comes to me because I am the oldest son. If it doesn't please you, I buy you something else."

"No, it's beautiful. Please, don't. I can't." She held her fisted hands behind her back. "Don't ask me."

"I am asking you," he said impatiently. "Give me your hand."

She took a step back. "I can't wear the ring. I can't marry you."

With a shake of his head, he pulled her hand free and pushed the ring on her finger. "See, you can wear it. It's too big, but we'll fix it."

"No." She would have pulled it off again, but he closed his hand over hers. "I don't want to marry you."

His fingers tightened on hers, and a fire darted into his eyes, more brilliant than the shine of the ruby. "Why?"

"I don't want to get married," she said as clearly as she could. "I won't have what we started together spoiled."

"Marriage doesn't spoil love, it nurtures it."

"You don't know," she snapped back. "You've never been married. I have. And I won't go through it again."

"So." Struggling with temper, he rocked back on his heels. "This husband of yours hurt you, makes you unhappy, so you think I'll do the same."

"Damn it, I loved him." Her voice broke, and she covered her face with her hand as the tears began to fall.

Torn between jealousy and misery, he gathered her close, murmuring endearments as he stroked her hair. "I'm sorry."

"You don't understand."

"Let me understand." He tilted her face up to kiss the tears. "I'm sorry," he repeated. "I won't yell at you anymore."

"It's not that." She let out a shuddering breath. "I don't want to hurt you. Please, let this go."

"I can't let this go. Or you. I love you, Sydney. I need you. For my life I need you. Explain to me why you won't take me."

"If there was anyone," she began in a rush, then shook her head before she could even wish it. "Mikhail, I can't consider marriage. Hayward is too much of a responsibility, and I need to focus on my career."

"This is smoke, to hide the real answer."

"All right." Bracing herself, she stepped away from him. "I don't think I could handle failing again, and losing someone I love. Marriage changes people."

"How did it change you?"

"I loved Peter, Mikhail. Not the way I love you, but more than anyone else. He was my best friend. We grew up together. When my parents divorced, he was the only one I could talk to. He cared, really cared, about how I felt, what I thought, what I wanted. We could sit for hours on the beach up at the Hamptons and watch the water, tell each other secrets."

She turned away. Saying it all out loud brought the pain spearing back.

"And you fell in love."

"No," she said miserably. "We just loved each other. I can hardly remember a time without him. And I can't remember when it started to become a given that we'd marry someday. Not that we talked about it ourselves. Everyone else did. Sydney and Peter, what a lovely couple they make. Isn't it nice how well they suit? I suppose we heard it so much, we started to believe it. Anyway, it was expected, and we'd both been raised to do what was expected of us."

She brushed at tears and wandered over to his shelves. "You were right when you gave me that figure of Cinderella. I've always followed the rules. I was expected to go to boarding school and get top grades. So I did. I was expected to behave presentably, never to show unacceptable emotions. So I did. I was expected to marry Peter. So I did."

She whirled back. "There we were, both of us just turned twenty-two—quite an acceptable age for marriage. I suppose we both thought it would be fine. After all, we'd known each other forever, we liked the same things, understood each other. Loved each other. But it wasn't fine. Almost from the beginning. Honeymooning in Greece. We both loved the country. And we both pretended that the physical part of marriage was fine. Of course, it was anything but fine, and the more we pretended, the further apart we became. We moved back to New York so he could take his place in the family business. I decorated the house, gave parties. And dreaded watching the sun go down."

"It was a mistake," Mikhail said gently.

"Yes, it was. One I made, one I was responsible for. I lost my closest friend, and before it was over, all the love was gone. There were only arguments and accusations. I was frigid, why shouldn't he have turned to someone else for a little warmth? But we kept up appearances. That was expected. And when we divorced, we did so in a very cold, very controlled, very civilized manner. I couldn't be a wife to him, Mikhail."

"It's not the same for us." He went to her.

"No, it's not. And I won't let it be."

"You're hurt because of something that happened to you, not something you did." He caught her face in his hands when she shook her head. "Yes. You need to let go of it, and trust what we have. I'll give you time."

"No." Desperate, she clamped her hands on his wrists. "Don't you see it's the same thing? You love me, so you expect me to marry you, because that's what you want—what you think is best."

"Not best," he said, giving her a quick shake. "Right. I need to share my life with you. I want to live with you, make babies with you. Watch them grow. There's a family inside us, Sydney."

She jerked away. He wouldn't listen, she thought. He wouldn't understand. "Marriage and family aren't in my plans," she said, suddenly cold. "You're going to have to accept that."

"Accept? You love me. I'm good enough for that. Good enough for you to take to your bed, but not for changing plans. All because you once followed rules instead of your heart."

"What I'm following now is my common sense." She walked by him to the door. "I'm sorry, I can't give you what you want."

"You will not go home alone."

"I think it'll be better if I leave."

"You want to leave, you leave." He stalked over to wrench the door open. "But I'll take you."

It wasn't until she lay teary and fretful in her bed that she realized she still wore his ring.

Chapter 12

It wasn't that she buried herself in work over the next two days, it was that work buried her. Sydney only wished it had helped. Keeping busy was supposed to be good for the morale. So why was hers flat on its face?

She closed the biggest deal of her career at Hayward, hired a new secretary to take the clerical weight off Janine and handled a full-staff meeting. Hayward stock had climbed three full points in the past ten days. The board was thrilled with her.

And she was miserable.

"An Officer Stanislaski on two, Ms. Hayward," her new secretary said through the intercom.

"Stan—oh." Her spirits did a jig, then settled. *Officer.* "Yes, I'll take it. Thank you." Sydney pasted on a smile for her own peace of mind. "Alex?"

"Hey, pretty lady. Thought you'd want to be the first to know. They just brought your old pal Lloyd Bingham in for questioning."

Her smiled faded. "I see."

"The insurance investigator took your advice and kept an eye on him. He met with a couple of bad numbers yesterday, passed some bills. Once they were picked up, they sang better than Springsteen."

"Then Lloyd did hire someone to vandalize the building."

"So they say. I don't think you're going to have any trouble from him for a while."

"I'm glad to hear it."

"You were pretty sharp, homing in on him. Brains and beauty," he said with a sigh that nearly made her smile again. "Why don't we take off to Jamaica for a couple of days? Drive Mikhail crazy?"

"I think he's already mad enough."

"Hey, he's giving you a hard time? Just come to Uncle Alex." When she didn't respond, the teasing note dropped out of his voice. "Don't mind Mik, Sydney. He's got moods, that's all. It's the artist. He's nuts about you."

"I know." Her fingers worried the files on her desk. "Maybe you could give him a call, tell him the news."

"Sure. Anything else you want me to pass on?"

"Tell him…no," she decided. "No, I've already told him. Thanks for calling, Alex."

"No problem. Let me know if you change your mind about Jamaica."

She hung up, wishing she felt as young as Alex had sounded. As happy. As easy. But then Alex wasn't in love. And he hadn't punched a hole in his own dreams.

Is that what she'd done? Sydney wondered as she pushed away from her desk. Had she sabotaged her own yearnings? No, she'd stopped herself, and the man she loved from making a mistake. Marriage wasn't always the answer. She had her own example to prove it. And her mother's. Once Mikhail had cooled off, he'd accept her position, and they could go on as they had before.

Who was she kidding?

He was too stubborn, too bullheaded, too damn sure his way was the right way to back down for an instant.

And what if he said all or nothing? What would she do then? Snatching up a paper clip, she began to twist it as she paced the office. If it was a matter of giving him up and losing him, or giving in and risking losing him…

God, she needed someone to talk to. Since it couldn't be Mikhail, she was left with pitifully few choices. Once she would have taken her problems to Peter, but that was…

She stopped, snapping the mangled metal in her fingers. That was the source of the problem. And maybe, just maybe, the solution.

Without giving herself time to think, she rushed out of her office and into Janine's. "I have to leave town for a couple of days," she said without preamble.

Janine was already rising from behind her new desk. "But—"

"I know it's sudden, and inconvenient, but it can't be helped. There's nothing vital pending at the moment, so you should be able to handle whatever comes in. If you can't, then it has to wait."

"Sydney, you have three appointments tomorrow."

"You take them. You have the files, you have my viewpoint. As soon as I get to where I'm going, I'll call in."

"But, Sydney." Janine scurried to the door as Sydney strode away. "Where are you going?"

"To see an old friend."

Less than an hour after Sydney had rushed from her office, Mikhail stormed in. He'd had it. He'd given the woman two days to come to her senses, and she was out of time. They were going to have this out and have it out now.

He breezed by the new secretary with a curt nod and pushed open Sydney's door.

"Excuse me. Sir, excuse me."

Mikhail whirled on the hapless woman. "Where the hell is she?"

"Ms. Hayward is not in the office," she said primly. "I'm afraid you'll have to—"

"If not here, where?"

"I'll handle this, Carla," Janine murmured from the doorway.

"Yes, ma'am." Carla made her exit quickly and with relief.

"Ms. Hayward's not here, Mr. Stanislaski. Is there something I can do for you?"

"Tell me where she is."

"I'm afraid I can't." The look in his eyes had her backing up a step. "I only know she's out of town for a day or two. She left suddenly and didn't tell me where she was going."

"Out of town?" He scowled at the empty desk, then back at Janine. "She doesn't leave her work like this."

"I admit it's unusual. But I got the impression it was important. I'm sure she'll call in. I'll be happy to give her a message for you."

He said something short and hard in Ukrainian and stormed out again.

"I think I'd better let you tell her that yourself," Janine murmured to the empty room.

Twenty-four hours after leaving her office, Sydney stood on a shady sidewalk in Georgetown, Washington, D.C. A headlong rush of adrenaline had brought her this far, far enough to have her looking at the home where Peter had settled when he'd relocated after the divorce.

The impulsive drive to the airport, the quick shuttle from city to city had been easy enough. Even the phone call to request an hour of Peter's time hadn't been so difficult. But this, this last step was nearly impossible.

She hadn't seen him in over three years, and then it had been across a wide table in a lawyer's office. Civilized, God, yes, they'd been civilized. And strangers.

It was foolish, ridiculous, taking off on this kind of tangent. Talking to Peter wouldn't change anything. Nothing could. Yet she found herself climbing the stairs to the porch of the lovely old row house, lifting the brass knocker and letting it rap on the door.

He answered himself, looking so much the same that she nearly threw out her hands to him as she would have done once. He was tall and leanly built, elegantly casual in khakis and a linen shirt. His sandy hair was attractively rumpled. But the green eyes didn't light with pleasure, instead remaining steady and cool.

"Sydney," he said, backing up to let her inside.

The foyer was cool and light, speaking subtly in its furnishings and artwork of discreet old money. "I appreciate you seeing me like this, Peter."

"You said it was important."

"To me."

"Well, then." Knowing nothing else to say, he ushered her down the hall and into a sitting room. Manners sat seamlessly on both of them, causing her to make the right comments about the house, and him to parry them while offering her a seat and a drink.

"You're enjoying Washington, then."

"Very much." He sipped his own wine while she simply turned her glass around and around in her hand. She was nervous. He knew her too well not to recognize the signs. And she was as lovely as ever. It hurt. He hated the fact that it hurt just to look at her. And the best way to get past the pain was to get to the point.

"What is it I can do for you, Sydney?"

Strangers, she thought again as she looked down at her glass. They had known each other all of their lives, had been married for nearly three years, and were strangers. "It's difficult to know where to start."

He leaned back in his chair and gestured. "Pick a spot."

"Peter, why did you marry me?"

"I beg your pardon."

"I want to know why you married me."

Whatever he'd been expecting, it hadn't been this. Shifting, he drank again. "For several of the usual reasons, I suppose."

"You loved me?"

His eyes flashed to hers. "You know I loved you."

"I know we loved each other. You were my friend." She pressed her lips together. "My best friend."

He got up to pour more wine. "We were children."

"Not when we married. We were young, but we weren't children. And we were still friends. I don't know how it all went so wrong, Peter, or what I did to ruin it so completely, but—"

"You?" He stared, the bottle in one hand, the glass in the other. "What do you mean *you ruined it*?"

"I made you unhappy, miserably unhappy. I know I failed in bed, and it all spilled over into the rest until you couldn't even bear to be around me."

"You didn't want me to touch you," he shot back. "Damn it, it was like making love to—"

"An iceberg," she finished flatly. "So you said."

Fighting guilt, he set his glass down. "I said a lot of things, so did you. I thought I'd gotten past most of it until I heard your voice this afternoon."

"I'm sorry." She rose, her body and voice stiff to compensate for shattered pride. "I've just made it worse coming here. I am sorry, Peter, I'll go."

"It was like making love with my sister." The words burst out and stopped her before she crossed the room. "My pal. Damn, Sydney, I couldn't..." The humiliation of it clawed at him again.

"I could never get beyond that, and make you, well, a wife. It unmanned me. And I took it out on you."

"I thought you hated me."

He slapped the bottle back on the table. "It was easier to try to hate you than admit I couldn't arouse either one of us. That I was inadequate."

"But I was." Baffled, she took a step toward him. "I know I was useless to you in bed—before you told me, I knew it. And you had to go elsewhere for what I couldn't give you."

"I cheated on you," he said flatly. "I lied and cheated on my closest friend. I hated the way you'd started to look at me, the way I started to look at myself. So I went out to prove my manhood elsewhere, and hurt you. When you found out, I did the manly thing and turned the blame on you. Hell, Sydney, we were barely speaking to each other by that time. Except in public."

"I know. And I remember how I reacted, the hateful things I said to you. I let pride cost me a friend."

"I lost a friend, too. I've never been sorrier for anything in my life." It cost him to walk to her, to take her hand. "You didn't ruin anything, Syd. At least not alone."

"I need a friend, Peter. I very badly need a friend."

He brushed a tear away with his thumb. "Willing to give me another shot?" Smiling a little, he took out his handkerchief. "Here. Blow your nose and sit down."

She did, clinging to his hand. "Was that the only reason it didn't work. Because we couldn't handle the bedroom?"

"That was a big one. Other than that, we're too much alike. It's too easy for us to step behind breeding and let a wound bleed us dry. Hell, Syd, what were we doing getting married?"

"Doing what everyone told us."

"There you go."

Comforted, she brought his hand to her cheek. "Are you happy, Peter?"

"I'm getting there. How about you? President Hayward."

She laughed. "Were you surprised?"

"Flabbergasted. I was so proud of you."

"Don't. You'll make me cry again."

"I've got a better idea." He kissed her forehead. "Come out in the kitchen. I'll fix us a sandwich and you can tell me what you've been up to besides big business."

It was almost easy. There was some awkwardness, little patches of caution, but the bond that had once held them together had stretched instead of broken. Slowly, carefully, they were easing the tension on it.

Over rye bread and coffee, she tried to tell him the rest. "Have you ever been in love, Peter?"

"Marsha Rosenbloom."

"That was when we were fourteen."

"And she'd already given up a training bra," he said with his mouth full. "I was deeply in love." Then he smiled at her. "No, I've escaped that particular madness."

"If you were, if you found yourself in love with someone, would you consider marriage again?"

"I don't know. I'd like to think I'd do a better job of it, but I don't know. Who is he?"

Stalling, she poured more coffee. "He's an artist. A carpenter."

"Which?"

"Both. He sculpts, and he builds. I've only known him a little while, just since June."

"Moving quick, Sydney?"

"I know. That's part of the problem. Everything moves fast with Mikhail. He's so bold and sure and full of emotion. Like his work, I suppose."

As two and two began to make four, his brows shot up. "The Russian?"

"Ukrainian," she corrected automatically.

"Good God, Stanislaski, right? There's a piece of his in the White House."

"Is there?" She gave Peter a bemused smile. "He didn't mention it. He took me home to meet his family, this wonderful family, but he didn't tell me his work's in the White House. It shows you where his priorities lie."

"And you're in love with him."

"Yes. He wants to marry me." She shook her head. "I got two proposals in the same night. One from Mikhail, and one from Channing Warfield."

"Lord, Sydney, not Channing. He's not your type."

She shoved the coffee aside to lean closer. "Why?"

"In the first place he's nearly humorless. He'd bore you mindless. The only thing he knows about Daddy's business is how to take clients to lunch. And his only true love is his tailor."

She really smiled. "I've missed you, Peter."

He took her hand again. "What about your big, bold artist?"

"He doesn't have a tailor, or take clients to lunch. And he makes me laugh. Peter, I couldn't bear to marry him and have it fall apart on me again."

"I can't tell you if it's right. And if I were you, I wouldn't listen to anyone's good-intentioned advice this time around."

"But you'll give me some anyway?"

"But I'll give you some anyway," he agreed, and felt years drop away. "Don't judge whatever you have with him by the mess we made. Just ask yourself a couple of questions. Does he make you happy? Do you trust him? How do you imagine your life with him? How do you imagine it without him?"

"And when I have the answers?"

"You'll know what to do." He kissed the hand joined with his. "I love you, Sydney."

"I love you, too."

Answer the questions, she thought as she pushed the elevator button in Mikhail's lobby. It was twenty-four hours since Peter had listed them, but she hadn't allowed herself to think of them. Hadn't had to, she corrected as she stepped inside the car. She already knew the answers.

Did he make her happy? Yes, wildly happy.

Did she trust him? Without reservation.

Her life with him? A roller coaster of emotions, demands, arguments, laughter, frustration.

Without him? Blank.

She simply couldn't imagine it. She would have her work, her routine, her ambitions. No, she'd never be without a purpose again. But without him, it would all be straight lines.

So she knew what to do. If it wasn't too late.

There was the scent of drywall dust in the hallway when she stepped out of the elevator. She glanced up to see the ceiling had been replaced, the seams taped, mudded and sanded. All that was left to be done here was the paint and trim.

He did good work, she thought, as she ran her hand along the wall. In a short amount of time, he'd taken a sad old building and turned it into something solid and good. There was still work ahead, weeks before the last nail would be hammered. But what he fixed would last.

Pressing a hand to her stomach, she knocked on his door. And hoped.

There wasn't a sound from inside. No blare of music, no click of work boots on wood. Surely he hadn't gone to bed, she told herself. It was barely ten. She knocked again, louder, and wondered if she should call out his name.

A door opened—not his, but the one just down the hall. Keely poked her head out. After one quick glance at Sydney, the friendliness washed out of her face.

"He's not here," she said. Her champagne voice had gone flat. Keely didn't know the details, but she was sure of one thing. This was the woman who had put Mikhail in a miserable mood for the past few days.

"Oh." Sydney's hand dropped to her side. "Do you know where he is?"

"Out." Keely struggled not to notice that there was misery in Sydney's eyes, as well.

"I see." Sydney willed her shoulders not to slump. "I'll just wait."

"Suit yourself," Keely said with a shrug. What did she care if the woman was obviously in love? This was the woman who'd hurt her pal. As an actress Keely prided herself on recognizing the mood beneath the actions. Mikhail might have been fiercely angry over the past few days, but beneath the short temper had been raw, seeping hurt. And she'd put it there. What did it matter if she was suffering, too?

Of course it mattered. Keely's sentimental heart went gooey in her chest.

"Listen, he'll probably be back soon. Do you want a drink or something?"

"No, really. I'm fine. How's, ah, your apartment coming?"

"New stove works like a champ." Unable to be anything but kind, Keely leaned on the jamb. "They've still got a little of this and that—especially with the damage those idiots did." She brightened. "Hey, did you know they arrested a guy?"

"Yes." Janine had told her about Lloyd's arrest when she'd called in. "I'm sorry. He was only trying to get back at me."

"It's not your fault the guy's a jerk. Anyway, they sucked up the water, and Mik mixed up some stuff to get the paint off the brick. They had to tear out the ceiling in the apartment below that empty place. And the floors buckled up pretty bad." She shrugged again. "You know Mik, he'll fix it up."

Yes, she knew Mik. "Do you know if there was much damage to Mrs. Wolburg's things?"

"The rugs are a loss. A lot of other things were pretty soggy. They'll dry out." More comfortable, Keely took a bite of the banana she'd been holding behind her back. "Her grandson was by. She's doing real good. Using a walker and everything already, and crabbing about coming home. We're planning on throwing her a welcome-back party next month. Maybe you'd like to come."

"I'd—" They both turned at the whine of the elevator.

The doors opened, and deep voices raised in some robust Ukrainian folk song poured out just ahead of the two men. They were both a little drunk, more than a little grubby, and the way their arms were wrapped around each other, it was impossible to say who was supporting whom. Sydney noticed the blood first. It was smeared on Mikhail's white T-shirt, obviously from the cuts on his lip and over his eye.

"My God."

The sound of her voice had Mikhail's head whipping up like a wolf. His grin faded to a surly stare as he and his brother stumbled to a halt.

"What do you want?" The words were thickened with vodka and not at all welcoming.

"What happened to you?" She was already rushing toward them. "Was there an accident?"

"Hey, pretty lady." Alex smiled charmingly though his left eye was puffy with bruises and nearly swollen shut. "We had a hell'va party. Should've been there. Right, bro?"

Mikhail responded by giving him a sluggish punch in the stomach. Sydney decided it was meant as affection as Mikhail then turned, locked his brother in a bear hug, kissed both his cheeks.

While Mikhail searched his pockets for keys, Sydney turned to Alex. "What happened? Who did this to you?"

"Did what?" He tried to wink at Keely and winced. "Oh, this?" He touched ginger fingers to his eye and grinned. "He's always had a sneaky left." He shot his brother a look of bleary admiration while Mikhail fought to fit what seemed like a very tiny key in an even tinier lock. "I got a couple good ones in under his guard. Wouldn't have caught him if he hadn't been drunk. Course I was drunk, too." He weaved toward Keely's door. "Hey, Keely, my beautiful gold-haired dream, got a raw steak?"

"No." But having sympathy for the stupid, she took his arm. "Come on, champ, I'll pour you into a cab."

"Let's go dancing," he suggested as she guided him back to the elevator. "Like to dance?"

"I live for it." She glanced over her shoulder as she shoved him into the elevator. "Good luck," she told Sydney.

She was going to need it, Sydney decided, as she walked up behind Mikhail just as he managed to open his own door. He shoved it back, nearly caught her in the nose, but her reflexes were better than his at the moment.

"You've been fighting with your brother," she accused.

"So?" He thought it was a shame, a damn shame, that the sight of her was sobering him up so quickly. "You would rather I fight with strangers?"

"Oh, sit down." Using her temporary advantage, she shoved him into a chair. She strode off into the bathroom, muttering to herself. When she came back with a wet washcloth and antiseptic, he was up again, leaning out the window, trying to clear his head.

"Are you sick?"

He pulled his head in and turned back, disdain clear on his battered face. "Stanislaskis don't get sick from vodka." Maybe a little queasy, he thought, when the vodka was followed by a couple of solid rights to the gut. Then he grinned. His baby brother had a hell of a punch.

"Just drunk then," she said primly, and pointed to the chair. "Sit down. I'll clean your face."

"I don't need nursing." But he sat, because it felt better that way.

"What you need is a keeper." Bending over, she began to

dab at the cut above his eye while he tried to resist the urge to lay his cheek against the soft swell of her breast. "Going out and getting drunk, beating up your brother. Why would you do such a stupid thing?"

He scowled at her. "It felt good."

"Oh, I'm sure it feels marvelous to have a naked fist popped in your eye." She tilted his head as she worked. That eye was going to bruise dramatically before morning. "I can't imagine what your mother would say if she knew."

"She would say nothing. She'd smack us both." His breath hissed when she slopped on the antiseptic. "Even when he starts it she smacks us both." Indignation shimmered. "Explain that."

"I'm sure you both deserved it. Pathetic," she muttered, then looked down at his hands. "Idiot!" The skin on the knuckles was bruised and broken. "You're an artist, damn it. You have no business hurting your hands."

It felt good, incredibly good to have her touching and scolding him. Any minute he was going to pull her into his lap and beg.

"I do what I like with my own hands," he said. And thought about what he'd like to be doing with them right now.

"You do what you like, period," she tossed back as she gently cleaned his knuckles. "Shouting at people, punching people. Drinking until you smell like the inside of a vodka bottle."

He wasn't so drunk he didn't know an insult when he heard one. Nudging her aside, he stood and, staggering only a little, disappeared into the next room. A moment later, she heard the shower running.

This wasn't the way she'd planned it, Sydney thought, wringing the washcloth in her hands. She was supposed to come to him, tell him how much she loved him, ask him to forgive her for being a fool. And he was supposed to be kind and understanding, taking her in his arms, telling her she'd made him the happiest man in the world.

Instead he'd been drunk and surly. And she'd been snappish and critical.

Well, he deserved it. Before she had time to think, she'd heaved the washcloth toward the kitchen, where it slapped wetly against the wall then slid down to the sink. She stared at it for a minute, then down at her own hands.

She'd thrown something. And it felt wonderful. Glancing around, she spotted a paperback book and sent it sailing. A plastic cup gave a nice ring when it hit the wall, but she'd have preferred the crash of glass. Snatching up a battered sneaker, she prepared to heave that, as well. A sound in the doorway had her turning, redirecting aim and shooting it straight into Mikhail's damp, naked chest. His breath woofed out.

"What are you doing?"

"Throwing things." She snatched up the second shoe and let it fly. He caught that one before it beaned him.

"You leave me, go away without a word, and you come to throw things?"

"That's right."

Eyes narrowed, he tested the weight of the shoe he held. It was tempting, very tempting to see if he could land it on the point of that jutting chin. On an oath, he dropped it. However much she deserved it, he just couldn't hit a woman.

"Where did you go?"

She tossed her hair back. "I went to see Peter."

He shoved his bruised hands into the pockets of the jeans he'd tugged on. "You leave me to go see another man, then you come back to throw shoes at my head. Tell me why I shouldn't just toss you out that window and be done with it."

"It was important that I see him, that I talk to him. And I—"

"You hurt me," he blurted out. The words burned on his tongue. He hated to admit it. "Do you think I care about getting a punch in the face? You'd already twisted my heart. This I can fight," he said, touching the back of his hand to his cut lip. "What you do to me inside leaves me helpless. And I hate it."

"I'm sorry." She took a step toward him but saw she wasn't yet welcome. "I was afraid I'd hurt you more if I tried to give you what you wanted. Mikhail, listen, please. Peter was the only person who cared for me. For *me*. My parents…" She could only shake her head. "They're not like yours. They wanted what was best for me, I'm sure, but their way of giving it was to hire nannies and buy me pretty clothes, send me to the best boarding school. You don't know how lonely it was." Impatient, she rubbed her fingers over her eyes to dry them. "I only had Peter, and then I lost him. What I feel for you is so much bigger, so much more, that I don't know what I'd do if I lost you."

He was softening. She could do that to him, as well. No matter how he tried to harden his heart, she could melt it. "You left me, Sydney. I'm not lost."

"I had to see him. I hurt him terribly, Mikhail. I was convinced that I'd ruined the marriage, the friendship, the love. What if I'd done the same with us?" With a little sigh, she walked to the window. "The funny thing was, he was carrying around the same guilt, the same remorse, the same fears. Talking with him, being friends again, made all the difference."

"I'm not angry that you talked to him, but that you went away. I was afraid you wouldn't come back."

She turned from the window. "I'm finished with running. I only went away because I'd hoped I could come back to you. Really come back."

He stared into her eyes, trying to see inside. "Have you?"

"Yes." She let out a shaky breath. "All the answers are yes. We walked through this building once, and I could hear the voices, all the sounds behind the doors. The smells, the laughing. I envied you belonging here. I need to belong. I want to have the chance to belong. To have that family you said was inside us."

She reached up, drawing a chain from around her neck. At the end, the little ruby flashed its flame.

Shaken, he crossed the room to cup the ring in his hand. "You wear it," he murmured.

"I was afraid to keep it on my finger. That I'd lose it. I need you to tell me if you still want me to have it."

His eyes came back to hers and locked. Even as he touched his lips to hers gently, he watched her. "I didn't ask you right the first time."

"I didn't answer right the first time." She took his face in her hands to kiss him again, to feel again. "You were perfect."

"I was clumsy. Angry that the banker had asked you before me."

Eyes wet, she smiled. "What banker? I don't know any bankers."

Unfastening the chain from around her neck, he set it aside. "It was not how I'd planned it. There was no music."

"I hear music."

"No soft words, no pretty light, no flowers."

"There's a moon. I still have the first rose you gave me."

Touched, he kissed her hands. "I told you only what I wanted, not what I'd give. You have my heart, Sydney. As long as it beats. My life is your life." He slipped the ring onto her finger. "Will you belong to me?"

She curled her fingers to keep the ring in place. "I already do."

★ ★ ★ ★ ★

Falling for Rachel

Mary Kay, here's one just for you

Prologue

Nick couldn't figure out how he'd been so damn stupid. Maybe it was more important to be part of the gang than he liked to admit. Maybe he was mad at the world in general and figured it was only right to get his licks in when he had the chance. And certainly he'd have lost face if he'd backed out when Reece and T.J. and Cash were so fired up.

But he'd never actually broken the law before.

Not quite true, he reminded himself as he pulled himself through the broken window and into the back of the electronics store. But they'd only been little laws. Setting up a three-card monte scam over on Madison for suckers and tourists, hawking hot watches or Gucci knockoffs up on Fifth, forging a couple of IDs so that he could buy a beer. He'd worked in a chop shop for a while, but it wasn't as if *he'd* stolen the cars. He'd just broken them down for parts. He'd gotten stung a few times for fighting with the Hombres, but that was a matter of honor and loyalty.

Breaking into a store and stealing calculators and portable

stereos was a big leap. While it had seemed like a lark over a couple of beers, the reality of it was setting those brews to churning in his stomach.

The way Nick saw it, he was trapped, as he'd always been. There was no easy way out.

"Hey, man, this is better than swiping candy bars, right?" Reece's eyes, dark and surly, scanned the storeroom shelves. He was a short man with a rough complexion who'd spent several of his twenty years in Juvenile Hall. "We're gonna be rich."

T.J. giggled. It was his way of agreeing with anything Reece said. Cash, who habitually kept his own counsel, was already shoving boxes of video games in the black duffel he carried.

"Come on, Nick." Reece tossed him an army-surplus bag. "Load it up."

Sweat began to roll down Nick's back as he shoved radios and minirecorders into the sack. What the hell was he doing here? he asked himself. Ripping off some poor slob who was just trying to make a living? It wasn't like fleecing tourists or selling someone else's heat. This was stealing, for God's sake.

"Listen, Reece, I—" He broke off when Reece turned and shined the flashlight in Nick's eyes.

"Got a problem, bro?"

Trapped, Nick thought again. Copping out now wouldn't stop the others from taking what they'd come for. And it would only bring him humiliation.

"No. No, man, no problem." Anxious to get it all over with, he shoved more boxes in without bothering to look at them. "Let's not get too greedy, okay? I mean, we got to get the stuff out, then we got to fence it. We don't want to take more than we can handle."

His lips pulled back in a sneer, Reece slapped Nick on the back. "That's why I keep you around. Your practical mind. Don't worry about turning the stuff. I told you, I got a connection."

"Right." Nick licked his dry lips and reminded himself he was a Cobra. It was all he'd ever been, all he ever would be.

"Cash, T.J., take that first load out to the car." Reece flipped the keys. "Make sure you lock it. Wouldn't want any bad guys stealing anything, would we?"

T.J.'s giggles echoed off the ceiling as he wiggled out the window. "No, sir." He pushed his wraparound sunglasses back on his nose. "Thieves everywhere these days. Right, Cash?"

Cash merely grunted and wrestled his way out the window.

"That T.J.'s a real idiot." Reece hefted a boxed VCR. "Give me a hand with this, Nick."

"I thought you said we were just going for the small stuff."

"Changed my mind." Reece pushed the box into Nick's arms. "My old lady's been whining for one of these." Reece tossed back his hair before climbing through the window. "You know your problem, Nick? Too much conscience. What's it ever gotten you? Now, the Cobras, we're family. Only time you got to have a conscience is with your family." He held out his arms. When Nick put the VCR into them, Reece slipped off into the dark.

Family, Nick thought. Reece was right. The Cobras were his family. You could count on them. He'd had to count on them. Pushing all his doubts aside, Nick shouldered his bag. He had to think of himself, didn't he? His share of tonight's work would keep a roof over his head for another month or two. He could have paid for his room the straight way if he hadn't gotten laid off from the delivery-truck job.

Lousy economy, he decided. If he had to steal to make ends meet, he could blame the government. The idea made him snicker as he swung one leg out of the window. Reece was right, he thought. You had to look out for number one.

"Need a hand with that?"

The unfamiliar voice had Nick freezing halfway out the window. In the shadowy light he saw the glint of a gun, the flash of a badge. He gave one fleeting, panicky thought to shoving the bag at the silhouette and making a run for it. Shaking his head, the cop stepped closer. He was young, dark, with a weary kind of resignation in the eyes that warned Nick that he'd been this route before.

"Do yourself a favor," the cop suggested. "Just chalk it up to bad luck."

Resigned, Nick slipped out of the window, set the bag down, faced the wall and assumed the position. "Is there any other kind?" he muttered, and let his mind wander as he was read his rights.

Chapter 1

With a briefcase in one hand and a half-eaten bagel in the other, Rachel raced up the courthouse steps. She hated to be late. Detested it. Knowing she'd drawn Judge Hatchet-Face Snyder for the morning hearing only made her more determined to be inside and at the defense table by 8:59. She had three minutes to spare, and would have had twice that if she hadn't stopped by the office first.

How could she have known that her boss would be lying in wait with another case file?

Two years of working as a public defender, she reminded herself as she hit the doors at a run. That was how she should have known.

She scanned the elevators, gauged the waiting crowd and opted for the stairs. Cursing her heels, she took them two at a time and swallowed the rest of the bagel. There was no use fantasizing about the coffee she craved to wash it down with.

She screeched to a halt at the courtroom doors and took a precious ten seconds to straighten her blue serge jacket and smooth down her tousled, chin-length black hair. A quick check showed her that her earrings were still in place. She looked at her watch and let out a deep breath.

Right on time, Stanislaski, she told herself as she moved sedately through the doors and into the courtroom. Her client, a twenty-three-year-old hooker with a heart of flint, was being escorted in as Rachel took her place. The solicitation charges would probably have earned her no more than a light fine and time served, but stealing the john's wallet had upped the ante.

As Rachel had explained to her bitter client, not all customers were too embarrassed to squawk when they lost two hundred in cash and a gold card.

"All rise!"

Hatchet-Face strode in, black robes flapping around all six-foot-three and two hundred and eighty pounds of him. He had skin the color of a good cappuccino and a face as round and unfriendly as the pumpkins Rachel remembered carving with her siblings every Halloween.

Judge Snyder tolerated no tardiness, no sass and no excuses in his courtroom. Rachel glanced over at the assistant district attorney who would be the opposing counsel. They exchanged looks of sympathy and got to work.

Rachel got the hooker off with ninety days. Her client was hardly brimming with gratitude as the bailiff led her away. She had better luck with an assault case.... After all, Your Honor, my client paid for a hot meal in good faith. When the pizza arrived cold, he pointed out the problem by offering some to the delivery boy. Unfortunately, his enthusiasm had him offering it a bit too heartily, and during the ensuing scuffle said pizza was inadvertently dumped on the delivery boy's head....

"Very amusing, Counselor. Fifty dollars, time served."

Rachel wrangled her way through the morning session. A pickpocket, a drunk-and-disorderly, two more assaults and a petty larceny. They rounded things off at noon with a shoplifter, a two-time loser. It took all of Rachel's skill and determination to convince the judge to agree to a psychiatric evaluation and counseling.

"Not too shabby." The ADA was only a couple of years older than Rachel's twenty-six, but he considered himself an old hand. "I figure we broke even."

She smiled and shut her briefcase. "No way, Spelding. I edged you out with the shoplifter."

"Maybe." Spelding, who had been trying to wheedle his way into a date for weeks, walked out beside her. "Could be his psych will come back clean."

"Sure. The guy's seventy-two years old and steals disposable razors and greeting cards with flowers on them. Obviously he's perfectly rational."

"You PDs are such bleeding hearts." But he said it lightly, because he greatly admired Rachel's courtroom style. As well as her legs. "Tell you what, I'll buy you lunch, and you can try to convince me why society should turn the other cheek."

"Sorry." She shot him a quick smile and opted for the stairs again. "I've got a client waiting for me."

"In jail?"

She shrugged. "That's where I find them. Better luck next time, Spelding."

The precinct house was noisy and smelled strongly of stale coffee. Rachel entered with a little shiver. The weatherman had been a little off that day with his promise of Indian summer. A thick, nasty-looking cloud cover was moving in over Manhattan. Rachel was already regretting the fact that she'd grabbed neither coat nor umbrella on her dash out of her apartment that morning.

With any luck, she figured, she'd be back in her office within the hour, and out of the coming rain. She exchanged a few greetings with some of the cops she knew and picked up her visitor's badge at the desk.

"Nicholas LeBeck," she told the desk sergeant. "Attempted burglary."

"Yeah, yeah…" The sergeant flipped through his papers. "Your brother brought him in."

Rachel sighed. Having a brother who was a cop didn't always make life easier. "So I hear. Did he make his phone call?"

"Nope."

"Anyone come looking for him?"

"Nope."

"Great." Rachel shifted her briefcase. "I'd like him brought up."

"You got it. Looks like they've given you another loser, Ray. Take conference room A."

"Thanks." She turned, dodging a swarthy-looking man in handcuffs and the uniformed cop behind him. She managed to snag a cup of coffee, and took it with her into a small room that boasted one barred window, a single long table and four scarred chairs. Taking a seat, she flipped open her briefcase and dug out the paperwork on Nicholas LeBeck.

It seemed her client was nineteen and unemployed and rented a room on the Lower East Side. She let out a little sigh at his list of priors. Nothing cataclysmic, she mused, but certainly enough to show a bent for trouble. The attempted burglary had taken him up a step, and it left her little hope of having him treated as a minor. There had been several thousand dollars' worth of electronic goodies in his sack when Detective Alexi Stanislaski collared him.

She'd be hearing from Alex, no doubt, Rachel thought. There was nothing her brother liked better than to rub her nose in it.

When the door of the conference room opened, she continued to sip her coffee as she took stock of the man being led in by a bored-looking policeman.

Five-ten, she estimated. A hundred and forty. Needed some weight. Dark blond hair, shaggy and nearly shoulder-length. His lips were quirked in what looked like a permanent smirk. It might have been an attractive mouth otherwise. A tiny peridot stud that nearly matched his eyes gleamed in his earlobe. The eyes, too, would have been attractive if not for the bitter anger she read there.

"Thank you, Officer." At her slight nod, the cop uncuffed her client and left them alone. "Mr. LeBeck, I'm Rachel Stanislaski, your lawyer."

"Yeah?" He dropped into a chair, then tipped it back. "Last PD I had was short and skinny and had a bald spot. Looks like I got lucky this time."

"On the contrary. You were apprehended crawling out of a broken window of a storeroom of a locked store, with an estimated six thousand dollars' worth of merchandise in your possession."

"The markup on that crap is incredible." It wasn't easy to keep the sneer in place after a miserable night in jail, but Nick had his pride. "Hey, you got a cigarette on you?"

"No. Mr. LeBeck, I'd like to get your hearing set as soon as possible so that we can arrange for bail. Unless, of course, you prefer to spend your nights in jail."

He shrugged his thin shoulders and tried to look unconcerned. "I'd just as soon not, sweetcakes. I'll leave that to you."

"Fine. And it's Stanislaski," she said mildly. "*Ms.* Stanislaski. I'm afraid I was only given your file this morning on my way to court, and had time for no more than a brief conversation with the DA assigned to your case. Because of your previous record, and the type of crime involved here, the state had decided to try you as an adult. The arrest was clean, so you won't get a break there."

"Hey, I don't expect breaks."

"People rarely get them." She folded her hands over his file.

"Let's cut to the chase, Mr. LeBeck. You were caught, and unless you want to weave some fairy tale about seeing the broken window and going in to make a citizen's arrest…"

He had to grin. "Not bad."

"It stinks. You're guilty, and since the arresting officer didn't make any mistakes, and you have an unfortunate list of priors, you're going to pay. How much you pay is going to depend on you."

He continued to rock in his chair, but a fresh line of sweat was sneaking down his spine. A cell. This time they were going to lock him in a cell—not just for a few hours, but for months, maybe years.

"I hear the jails are overcrowded—costs the tax-payers a lot of money. I figure the DA would spring for a deal."

"It was mentioned." Not just bitterness, Rachel realized. Not just anger. She saw fear in his eyes now, as well. He was young and afraid, and she didn't know how much she would be able to help him. "About fifteen thousand in merchandise was taken out of the store, over and above what was in your possession. You weren't alone in that store, LeBeck. You know it, I know it, the cops know it. And so does the DA. You give them some names, a lead on where that merchandise might be sitting right now, and I can cut you a deal."

His chair banged against the floor. "The hell with that. I never said anybody was with me. Nobody can prove it, just like nobody can prove I took more than what I had in my hands when the cop took me."

Rachel leaned forward. It was a subtle move, but one that had Nick's eyes locking on hers. "I'm your lawyer, LeBeck, and the one thing you're not going to do is lie to me. You do, and I'll leave you twisting in the wind, just like your buddies did last night." Her voice was flat, passionless, but he heard the anger simmering beneath. He had to fight to keep from squirming in his chair. "You don't want to cut a deal," she continued, "that's your choice. So you'll serve three to five instead of the six months in and two years probation I can get you. Either way, I'll do my job. But don't sit there and insult me by saying you pulled this alone. You're penny-ante, LeBeck." It pleased her to see the anger back in his face. The fear had begun to soften her. "Con games and sticky fingers. This is the big leagues. What you tell me stays with me unless you want it different. But you play it straight with me, or I walk."

"You can't walk. You were assigned."

"And I can get reassigned. Then you'll go through this with somebody else." She began to pile papers back in her briefcase. "That would be your loss. Because I'm good. I'm real good."

"If you're so good, how come you're working for the PD's office?"

"Let's just say I'm paying off a debt." She snapped her briefcase closed. "So what's it going to be?"

Indecision flickered over his face for just a moment, making him look young and vulnerable, before he shook his head. "I'm not going to turn in my friends. No deal."

She let out a short, impatient breath. "You were wearing a Cobra jacket when you were collared."

They'd taken that when they booked him—just as they'd taken his wallet, his belt, and the handful of change in his pocket. "So what?"

"They're going to go looking for your *friends,* those same friends who are standing back and letting you take the heat all alone. The DA can push this to burglary and hang a twenty-thousand-dollar theft over your head."

"No names," he said again. "No deal."

"Your loyalty's admirable, and misplaced. I'll do what I can to have the charges reduced and have bail set. I don't think it'll be less than fifty thousand. Can you scrape ten percent together?"

Not a chance in hell, he thought, but he shrugged. "I can call in some debts."

"All right, then, I'll get back to you." She rose, then slipped a card out of her pocket. "If you need me before the hearing, or if you change your mind about the deal, give me a call."

She rapped on the door, then swung through when it opened. An arm curled around her waist. She braced instinctively, then let out a little hiss of breath when she looked up and saw her brother grinning at her.

"Rachel, long time no see."

"Yeah, it must be a day and a half."

"Grumpy." His grin widened as he pulled her out of the corridor and into the squad room. "Good sign." His gaze skimmed over her shoulder and locked briefly on LeBeck. "So, they tied you up with that one. Tough break, sweetheart."

She gave him a sisterly elbow in the ribs. "Stop gloating and get me a decent cup of coffee." Resting a hip against the corner of his desk, she rapped her fingertips against her briefcase. Nearby a short, round man was holding a bandanna to his temple and moaning slightly as he gave a statement to another cop. Someone was talking in loud and rapid Spanish. A woman with a bruise on her cheek was weeping and rocking a fat toddler.

The squad room smelled of all of it—the despair, the anger, the boredom. Rachel had always thought that if your senses were very keen you could just barely scent the justice beneath it all. It was very much the same in her offices, a few blocks away.

For a moment, Rachel pictured her sister, Natasha, having breakfast with her family in her pretty kitchen in the big, lovely house in West Virginia. Or opening her colorful toy shop for the day. The image made her smile a bit, just as it did to imagine her brother Mikhail carving something passionate or fanciful out of wood in his sun-washed new studio, perhaps having a hasty cup of coffee with his gorgeous wife before she hurried off to her midtown office.

And here she was, waiting for a cup of what would certainly

be very bad coffee in a downtown precinct house filled with the sight and smells and sounds of misery.

Alex handed her the coffee, then eased down on the desk beside her.

"Thanks." She sipped, winced, and watched a couple of hookers strut out of the holding cells. A tall, bleary-eyed man with a night's worth of stubble shifted around them and followed a uniform through the door that led down to the cells. Rachel gave a little sigh.

"What's wrong with us, Alexi?"

He grinned again and slipped an arm around her. "What? Just because we like slogging through the dregs for a living, for little pay and less gratitude? Nothing. Not a thing."

She chuckled and fueled her system with the motor oil disguised as coffee. "At least you just got a promotion. Detective Stanislaski."

"Can't help it if I'm good. You, on the other hand, are spinning your wheels putting criminals back on the streets I'm risking life and limb to keep clean."

She snorted, scowling at him over the brim of the paper cup. "Most of the people I represent aren't doing anything more than trying to survive."

"Sure—by stealing, cheating, and assaulting."

Her temper began to heat. "I went to court this morning to represent an old man who'd copped some disposable razors. A real desperate case, that one. I guess they should have locked him up and thrown away the key."

"So it's okay to steal as long as what you take isn't particularly valuable?"

"He needed help, not a jail sentence."

"Like that creep you got off last month who terrorized two old shopkeepers, wrecked their store and stole the pitiful six hundred in the till?"

She'd hated that one, truly hated it. But the law was clear, and had been made for a reason. "Look, you guys blew that one. The arresting officer didn't read him his rights in his native language or arrange for a translator. My client barely understood a dozen words of English." She shook her head before Alex could jump into one of his more passionate arguments. "I don't have time to debate the law with you. I need to ask you about Nicholas LeBeck."

"What about him? You got the report."

"You were the arresting officer."

"Yeah—so? I was on my way home, and I happened to see the broken window and the light inside. When I went to investigate, I saw the perpetrator coming through the window carrying a sackful of electronics. I read him his rights and brought him in."

"What about the others?"

Alex shrugged and finished off the last couple of swallows of Rachel's coffee. "Nobody around but LeBeck."

"Come on, Alex, twice as much was taken from the store as what my client allegedly had in his bag."

"I figure he had help, but I didn't see anyone else. And your client exercised his right to remain silent. He has a healthy list of priors."

"Kid stuff."

Alex sneered. "You could say he didn't spend his childhood in the Boy Scouts."

"He's a Cobra."

"He had the jacket," Alex agreed. "And the attitude."

"He's a scared kid."

With a sound of disgust, Alex chucked the empty cup into a wastebasket. "He's no kid, Rach."

"I don't care how old he is, Alex. Right now he's a scared kid sitting in a cell and trying to pretend he's tough. It could have been you, or Mikhail—even Tash or me—if it hadn't been for Mama and Papa."

"Hell, Rachel."

"It could have been," she insisted. "Without the family, without all the hard work and sacrifices, any one of us could have gotten sucked into the streets. You know it."

He did. Why did she think he'd become a cop? "The point is, we didn't. It's a basic matter of what's right and what's wrong."

"Sometimes people make bad choices because there's no one around to help them make good ones."

They could have spent hours debating the many shades of justice, but he had to get to work. "You're too softhearted, Rachel. Just make sure it doesn't lead to being softheaded. The Cobras are one of the roughest gangs going. Don't start thinking your client's a candidate for Boys' Town."

Rachel straightened, pleased that her brother remained slouched against the desk. It meant they were eye to eye. "Was he carrying a weapon?"

Alex sighed. "No."

"Did he resist arrest?"

"No. But that doesn't change what he was doing, or what he is."

"It might not change what he was doing—allegedly—but it might very well say something about what he is. Preliminary hearing's at two."

"I know."

She smiled again and kissed him. "See you there."

"Hey, Rachel." She turned at the doorway and looked back. "Want to catch a movie tonight?"

"Sure." She'd made it to the outside in two steps when her name was called again, more formally this time.

"Ms. Stanislaski!"

She paused, flipping her hair back with one hand as she looked over her shoulder. It was the tired-eyed, stubble-faced man she'd noticed before. Hard to miss, she reflected as he hurried toward her. He was over six feet by an inch or so, and his baggy sweatshirt was held up by a pair of broad shoulders. Faded jeans, frayed at the cuffs, white at the stress points, fit well over long legs and narrow hips.

It would have been hard not to miss the anger, too. It radiated from him, and it was reflected in steel-blue eyes set deep in a rough, hollow-cheeked face.

"Rachel Stanislaski?"

"Yes."

He caught her hand and, in the process of shaking it, dragged her down a couple of steps. He might look lean and mean, Rachel thought, but he had the grip of a bear trap.

"I'm Zackary Muldoon," he said, as if that explained everything.

Rachel only lifted a brow. He certainly looked fit to spit nails, and after that brief taste of his strength she wouldn't have put the feat past him. But she wasn't easily intimidated, particularly when she was standing in an area swarming with cops.

"Can I help you, Mr. Muldoon?"

"I'm counting on it." He dragged a big hand through a tousled mop of hair as dark as her own. He swore and took her elbow to pull her down the rest of the steps. "What's it going to take to get him out? And why the hell did he call you and not me? And why in God's name did you let him sit in a cell all night? What kind of lawyer are you?"

Rachel shook her arm free—no easy task—and prepared to use her briefcase as a weapon if it became necessary. She'd heard about the black Irish and their tempers. But Ukrainians were no slouches, either.

"Mr. Muldoon, I don't know who you are or what you're talking about. And I happen to be very busy." She'd managed two steps when he whirled her around. Rachel's tawny eyes narrowed dangerously. "Look, Buster—"

"I don't care how busy you are, I want some answers. If you don't have time to help Nick, then we'll get another lawyer.

God knows why he chose some fancy broad in a designer suit in the first place." His blue eyes shot fire, the Irish poet's mouth hardening into a sneer.

She sputtered, angry color flagging both cheeks. She jabbed one stiffened, clear-tipped finger in his chest. "*Broad?* You just watch who you call *broad,* pal, or—"

"Or you'll get your boyfriend to lock me in a cell?" Zack suggested. Yeah, that was definitely a fancy face, he thought in disgust. Butter-soft skin in pale gold, and eyes like good Irish whiskey. What he needed was a street fighter, and he'd gotten society. "I don't know what kind of defense Nick expects from some woman who spends her time kissing cops and making dates when she's supposed to be working."

"It's none of your business what I—" She took a deep breath. Nick. "Are you talking about Nicholas LeBeck?"

"Of course I'm talking about Nicholas LeBeck. Who the hell do you think I'm talking about?" His black brows drew together over his furious eyes. "And you'd better come up with some answers, lady, or you're going to be off his case and out on your pretty butt."

"Hey, Rachel!" An undercover cop dressed like a wino sidled up behind her. He eyed Zack. "Any problem here?"

"No." Though her eyes were blazing, she offered him a half smile. "No, I'm fine, Matt. Thanks." She edged over to one side and lowered her voice. "I don't owe you any answers, Muldoon. And insulting me is a poor way to gain my cooperation."

"You're paid to cooperate," he told her. "Just how much are you hosing the boy for?"

"Excuse me?"

"What's your fee, sugar?"

Her teeth set. The way she saw it, *sugar* was only a marginal step up from *broad.* "I'm a public defender, Muldoon, assigned to LeBeck's case. That means he doesn't owe me a damn thing. Just like I don't owe you."

"A PD?" He all but backed her off the sidewalk and into the building. "What the devil does Nick need a PD for?"

"Because he's broke and unemployed. Now, if you'll excuse me…" She set a hand on his chest and shoved. She'd have been better off trying to shove away the brick building at her back.

"He lost his job? But…" The words trailed off. This time Rachel read something other than anger in his eyes. Weariness, she thought. A trace of despair. Resignation. "He could have come to me."

"And who the hell are you?"

Zack rubbed a hand over his face. "I'm his brother."

Rachel pursed her lips, lifted a brow. She knew how the gangs worked, and though Zack looked rough-and-ready enough to fit in with the Cobras, he also looked too old to be a card-carrying member.

"Don't the Cobras have an age limit?"

"What?" He let his hand drop and focused on her again with a fresh oath. "Do I look like I belong to a street gang?"

With her head tilted, Rachel ran her gaze from his battered high-tops to his shaggy dark head. He had the look of a street tough, certainly of a man who could bulldoze his way down alleys, pounding rivals with those big-fisted hands. The hard, hollowed face and hot eyes made her think he'd enjoy cracking skulls, particularly hers. "Actually, you could pass. And your manners certainly reflect the code. Rude, abrasive and rough."

He didn't give a damn what she thought of his appearance, or his manners, but it was time they set the record straight. "I'm Nick's brother—stepbrother, if you want to be technical. His mother married my father. Get it?"

Her eyes remained wary, but there was some interest there now. "He said he didn't have any relatives."

For an instant, she thought she saw hurt in those steel-blue depths. Then it was gone, hardened away. "He's got me, whether he likes it or not. And I can afford a real lawyer, so why don't you fill me in, and I'll take it from there."

This time she didn't merely set her teeth, she practically snarled. "I happen to be a *real* lawyer, Muldoon. And if LeBeck wants other counsel, he can damn well ask for it himself."

He struggled to find the patience that always seemed to elude him. "We'll get into that later. For now, I want to know what the hell's going on."

"Fine." She snapped the word out as she looked at her watch. "You can have fifteen minutes of my time, providing you take it while I eat. I have to be back in court in an hour."

Chapter 2

From the way she looked—elegant sex in a three-piece suit—
Zack figured her for one of the trendy little restaurants that
served complicated pasta dishes and white wine. Instead, she
stalked down the street, her long legs eating up the sidewalk so
that he didn't have to shorten his pace to keep abreast.

She stopped at a vendor and ordered a hot dog—loaded—
with a soft drink, then stepped aside to give Zack room to make
his selection. The idea of eating anything that looked like a hot
dog at what he considered the crack of dawn had his stomach
shriveling. Zack settled for a soft drink—the kind loaded with
sugar and caffeine—and a cigarette.

Rachel took the first bite, licked mustard off her thumb.
Over the scent of onions and relish, Zack caught a trace of her
perfume. It was like walking through the jungle, he thought
with a frown. All those ripe, sweaty smells, and then suddenly,
unexpectedly, you could come across some exotic, seductive
vine tangled with vivid flowers.

"He's charged with burglary," Rachel said with her mouth

full. "Not much chance of shaking it. He was apprehended climbing out of the window with several thousand dollars' worth of stolen merchandise in his possession."

"Stupid." Zack downed half the soft drink in a swallow. "He doesn't have to steal."

"That's neither here nor there. He was caught, he was charged, and he doesn't deny the act. The DA's willing to deal, offer probation and community service, if Nick cooperates."

Zack chuffed out smoke. "Then he'll cooperate."

Rachel's left brow lifted, then settled. She had no doubt Zackary Muldoon thought he could prod, push or punch anybody into anything. "I sincerely doubt it. He's scared, but he's stubborn. And he's loyal to the Cobras."

Zack said something foul about the Cobras. Rachel was forced to agree. "Well, that may be, but it doesn't change the bottom line. His record is fairly lengthy, and it won't be easy to get around it. It's also mostly hustle and jive. The fact that this is his first step into the big leagues might help reduce his sentence. I think I can get him off with three years. If he behaves, he'll only serve one."

Zack's fingers dug into the aluminum can, crushing it. Fear settled sickly in his stomach. "I don't want him to go to prison."

"Muldoon, I'm a lawyer, not a magician."

"They got back the stuff he took, didn't they?"

"That doesn't negate the crime, but yes. Of course, there's several thousand more outstanding."

"I'll make it good." Somehow. Zack heaved the can toward a waste can. It tipped the edge, joggled, then fell inside. "Listen, I'll make restitution on what was stolen. Nick's only nineteen. If you can get the DA to try him as a minor, it would go easier."

"The state's tough on gang members, and with his record I don't think it would happen."

"If you can't do it, I'll find someone who can." Zack threw up a hand before she could tear into him. "I know I came down on you before. Sorry. I work nights, and I'm not my best in the morning." Even that much of an apology grated on him, but he needed her. "I get a call an hour ago from one of Nick's friends telling me he's been in jail all night. When I get down here and see him, it's the same old story. I don't need you. I don't need anybody. I'm handling it." He tossed down his cigarette, crushed it out, lit another. "And I know he's scared down to the bone." With something close to a sigh, he jammed his hands in his pockets. "I'm all he's got, Ms. Stanislaski. Whatever it takes, I'm not going to see him go to prison."

It was never easy for her to harden her heart, but she tried. She wiped her hands carefully on a paper napkin. "Have you got enough money to cover the losses? Fifteen thousand?"

He winced, but nodded. "I can get it."

"It'll help. How much influence do you have over Nick?"

"Next to none." He smiled, and Rachel was surprised to note that the smile held considerable charm. "But that can change. I've got an established business, and a two-bedroom apartment. I can get you professional and character references, whatever you need. My record's clean— Well, I did spend thirty days in the brig when I was in the navy. Bar fight." He shrugged it off. "I don't guess they'd hold it against me, since it was twelve years ago."

Rachel turned the possibilities over in her mind. "If I'm reading you right, you want me to try to get the court to turn Nick over to your care."

"The probation and community service. A responsible adult to look out for him. All the damages paid."

"You might not be doing him any favor, Muldoon."

"He's my brother."

That she understood perfectly. Rachel cast her eyes skyward as the first drop of rain fell. "I've got to get back to the office. If you've got the time, you can walk with me. I'll make some calls, see what I can do."

★ ★ ★

A bar, Rachel thought with a sigh as she tried to put together a rational proposition for the hearing that afternoon. Why did the man have to own a bar? She supposed it suited him—the big shoulders, the big hands, the crooked nose that she assumed had been broken. And, of course, the rough, dark Irish looks that matched his temper.

But it would have been so much nicer if she could tell the judge that Zackary Muldoon owned a nice men's shop in mid-town. Instead, she was going to ask a judge to hand over the responsibility and the guardianship of a nineteen-year-old boy—with a record and an attitude—to his thirty-two-year-old stepbrother, who ran an East Side bar called Lower the Boom.

There was a chance, a slim one. The DA was still pushing for names, but the shop owner had been greatly mollified with the promise of settlement. No doubt he'd inflated the price of his merchandise, but that was Muldoon's problem, not hers.

She didn't have much time to persuade the DA that he didn't want to try Nick as an adult. Taking what information she'd managed to pry out of Zack, she snagged opposing counsel and settled into one of the tiny conference rooms in the courthouse.

"Come on, Haridan, let's clean this mess up and save the court's time and the taxpayers' money. Putting this kid in jail isn't the answer."

Haridan, balding on top and thick through the middle, eased his bulk into a chair. "It's my answer, Stanislaski. He's a punk. A gang member with a history of antisocial behavior."

"Some tourist scams and some pushy-shovey."

"Assault."

"Charges were dropped. Come on, we both know it's mi-nor-league. *He's* minor-league. We've got a scared, troubled kid looking for his place with a gang. We want him out of the gang, no question. But jail isn't the way." She held up a hand be-fore Haridan could interrupt. "Look, his stepbrother is willing to help—not only by paying for property you have absolutely no proof my client stole, but by taking responsibility. Giving LeBeck a job, a home, supervision. All you have to do is agree to handling LeBeck as a minor."

"I want names."

"He won't give them." Hadn't she gone back down and harassed Nick for nearly an hour to try to pry one loose? "You can put him away for ten years, and you still won't get one. So what's the point? You haven't got a hardened criminal here—yet. Let's not make him one."

They knocked that back and forth, and Haridan softened. Not out of the goodness of his heart, but because his plate was every bit as full as Rachel's. He had neither the time nor the energy to pursue one punk kid through the system.

"I'm not dropping it down from burglary to nighttime breaking and entering." On that he was going to stand firm, but he would throw her a crumb. "Even if we agree to handle him as a juvie, the judge isn't going to let him walk with probation."

Rachel gathered up her briefcase. "Just leave the judge to me. Who'd we pull?"

Haridan grinned. "Beckett."

Marlene C. Beckett was an eccentric. Like a magician, she pulled unusual sentences out of her judge's robes as if they were little white rabbits. She was in her midforties, dashingly attractive, with a single streak of white hair that swept through a wavy cap of fire-engine red.

Personally, Rachel liked her a great deal. Judge Beckett was a staunch feminist and former flower child who had proven that a woman—an unmarried, career-oriented woman—could be successful and intelligent without being abrasive or whiny. She might have been in a man's world, but Judge Beckett was all woman. Rachel respected her, admired her, even hoped to follow in her footsteps one day.

She just wished she'd been assigned to another judge.

As Beckett listened to her unusual plea, Rachel felt her stomach sinking down to her knees. Beckett's lips were pursed. A bad sign. One perfectly manicured nail was tapping beside the gavel. Rachel caught the judge studying the defendant, and Zack, who sat in the front row behind him.

"Counselor, you're saying the defendant will make restitution for all properties lost, and that though the state is agreeable that he be tried as a minor, you don't want him bound over for trial."

"I'm proposing that trial may be waived, Your Honor, given the circumstances. Both the defendant's mother and stepfather are deceased. His mother died five years ago, when the defendant was fourteen, and his stepfather died last year. Mr. Muldoon is willing and able to take responsibility for his stepbrother. If it please the court, the defense suggests that once restitution is made, and a stable home arranged, a trial would be merely an unproductive way of punishing my client for a mistake he already deeply regrets."

With what might have been a snort, Beckett cast a look at Nick. "Do you deeply regret bungling your attempt at burglary, young man?"

Nick lifted one shoulder and looked surly. A sharp rap on the back of the head from his stepbrother had him snarling. "Sure, I—" He glanced at Rachel. The warning in her eyes did more to make him subside than the smack. "It was stupid."

"Undoubtedly," Judge Beckett agreed. "Mr. Haridan, what is your stand on this?"

"The district attorney's office is not willing to drop charges, Your Honor, though we will agree to regard the defendant as a juvenile. An offer to lessen or drop charges was made—if the defendant would provide the names of his accomplices."

"You want him to squeal on those he—mistakenly, I'm sure—considers friends?" Beckett lifted a brow at Nick. "No dice?"

"No, ma'am."

She made some sound that Rachel couldn't interpret, then pointed at Zack. "Stand up... Mr. Muldoon, is it?"

Ill at ease, Zack did so. "Ma'am? Your Honor?"

"Where were you when your young brother was getting himself mixed up with the Cobras?"

"At sea. I was in the navy until two years ago, when I came back to take over my father's business."

"What rank?"

"Chief petty officer, ma'am."

"Mmm-hmm..." She took his measure, as a judge and as a woman. "I've been in your bar—a few years back. You used to serve an excellent manhattan."

Zack grinned. "We still do."

"Are you of the opinion, Mr. Muldoon, that you can keep your brother out of trouble and make a responsible citizen of him?"

"I... I don't know, but I want a chance to try."

Beckett tapped her fingers and sat back. "Have a seat. Ms. Stanislaski, the court is not of the opinion that a trial would be out of place in this matter—"

"Your Honor—"

Beckett cut Rachel off with a single gesture. "I haven't finished. I'm going to set bail at five thousand dollars."

This brought on an objection from the DA that was dealt with in exactly the same manner.

"I'm also going to grant the defendant what we'll call a provisionary probation. Two months," Beckett said, folding her hands. "I will set the trial date for two months from today. If during that two-month period the defendant is found to be walking the straight and narrow, is gainfully employed, refrains from associating with known members of the Cobras and has not committed any crime, this court will be amenable to extending that probation, with the likelihood of a suspended sentence."

"Your Honor," Haridan puffed out, "how can we be certain the defendant won't waltz in here in two months and claim to have upheld the provisions?"

"Because he will be supervised by an officer of the court, who will serve as co-guardian with Mr. Muldoon for the two-month period. And I will receive a written report on Mr. LeBeck from that officer." Beckett's lips curved. "I think I'm going to enjoy this. Rehabilitation, Mr. Haridan, does not have to be accomplished in prison."

Rachel restrained herself from giving Haridan a smug grin. "Thank you, Your Honor."

"You're quite welcome, Counselor. Have your report to me every Friday afternoon, by three."

"My…" Rachel blinked, paled, then gaped. "My report? But, Your Honor, you can't mean for me to supervise Mr. LeBeck."

"That is precisely what I mean, Ms. Stanislaski. I believe having a male and a female authority figure will do our Mr. LeBeck a world of good."

"Yes, Your Honor, I agree. But… I'm not a social worker."

"You're a public servant, Ms. Stanislaski. So serve." She rapped her gavel. "Next case."

Stunned speechless by the judge's totally unorthodox ruling, Rachel moved to the back of the courtroom. "Good going, champ," her brother muttered in her ear. "Now you've got yourself hooked good."

"How could she do that? I mean, how could she just *do* that?"

"Everybody knows she's a little crazy." Furious, he swung Rachel out in the hall by an elbow. "There's no way in holy hell I'm letting you play babysitter for that punk. Beckett can't force you to."

"No, of course she can't." After dragging a hand through her hair, she shook Alex off. "Stop pulling at me and let me think."

"There's nothing to think about. You've got your own family and your own life. Watching over LeBeck is out of the question.

And for all you know, that brother of his is just as dangerous. It's bad enough I have to watch you defend these creeps. No way I'm having you play big sister to one of them."

If he'd sympathized with her predicament, she might not have been quite as hasty. If he'd told her she'd gotten a raw deal, she probably would have agreed and set the wheels in motion to negate it. But...

"You don't have to watch me do anything, Alexi, and I can play big sister to whomever I choose. Now why don't you take that big bad badge of yours and go arrest some harmless vagrant."

His blood boiled every bit as quickly as hers. "You're not doing this."

"I'll decide what I'm going to do. Now back off."

He cupped a hand firmly on her chin just as she poked it out. "I've got a good mind to—"

"The lady asked you to back off." Zack's voice was quiet, like a snake before it strikes. Alex whipped his head around, eyes hot and ready. It took all of his training to prevent himself from throwing the first punch.

"Keep out of our business."

Zack planted his feet and prepared. "I don't think so."

They looked like two snarling dogs about to go for the throat. Rachel pushed her way between them.

"Stop it right now. This is no way to behave outside a courtroom. Muldoon, is this how you're going to show Nick responsibility? By picking fights?"

He didn't even glance at her, but kept his eyes on Alex. "I don't like to see women pushed around."

"I can take care of myself." She rounded on her brother. "You're supposed to be a cop, for heaven's sake. And here you are acting like a rowdy schoolboy. You think about this. The court believes this is a viable solution, so I'm obligated to try it."

"Damn it, Rachel—" Alex's eyes went flat and cold when

Zack stepped forward again. "Pal, you mess with me, or my sister, you'll be wearing your teeth in a glass by your bedside."

"Sister?" Thoughtfully Zack examined one face, then the other. Oh, yes, the family resemblance was strong enough when you took a minute to study them. They both had those wild good looks that came through the blood. His anger cooled instantly. That changed things. He gave Rachel another speculative look. It changed a lot of things.

"Sorry. I didn't realize it was a family argument. You go ahead and yell at her all you want."

Alex had to fight to keep his lips from twitching. "All right, Rachel, you're going to listen to me."

She had to sigh. Then she had to take his face in her hands and kiss him. "Since when have I ever listened to you? Go away, Alexi. Chase some bad guys. And I'll have to take a rain check on that movie tonight."

There was no arguing with her. There never was. Changing tactics, Alex stared down Zack. "You watch out for her, Muldoon, and watch good. Because while you're at it, I'm going to be watching you."

"Sounds fair. Come by the bar anytime, Officer. First one's on the house."

Muttering under his breath, Alex stalked away. He turned once when Rachel called something out to him in Ukrainian. With a reluctant smile, he shook his head and kept walking.

"Translation?" Zack asked.

"Just that I would see him Sunday. Did you pay the bond?"

"Yeah, they're going to release him in a minute." Zack took a moment to reevaluate now that he realized she'd been kissing her brother that morning, not a lover. "I take it your brother isn't too thrilled to see you tangled up with me and Nick."

She gave Zack a long, bland look. "Who is, Muldoon? But since that's the court ruling, let's go get started."

"Get started?"

"We're going to pick up our charge, and you're going to move him into your apartment."

After spending the better part of a decade sharing close quarters with a couple hundred sailors, Zack gave one last wistful thought to the dissolution of his privacy. "Right." He took Rachel by the arm—a gesture she tried not to resent. "I don't suppose you've got any rope in that briefcase of yours."

It wasn't necessary to tie Nick up to gain his cooperation. But it was close. He sulked. He argued. He swore. By the time they'd walked out of the courthouse to hail a cab, Zack was biting down on fury and Nick had switched his resentment to Rachel.

"If this is the best deal you could cut, you'd better go back to law school. I've got rights, and the first one is to fire you."

"Your privilege, LeBeck," Rachel said, idly checking her watch. "You're certainly free to seek other counsel, but you can't fire me as your court-appointed guardian. We're stuck with each other for the next two months."

"That's bull. If you and that crazy judge think you can cook up—"

Zack made his move first, but Rachel merely elbowed him out of the way and went toe-to-toe with Nick. "You listen to me, you sorry, spoiled, sulky little jerk. You've got two choices—pretending to be a human being for the next eight weeks or going to prison for three years. I don't give a damn which way you go, but I'll tell you this. You think you're tough? You think you've got all the answers? You go inside for a week, and with that pretty face of yours the cons will be on you like dogs on fresh meat. You'd be willing to deal then, pal. Believe me, you'd be willing to deal."

That shut him up, and Rachel had the added satisfaction of seeing his angry flush die to a sickly pallor. She gestured when a cab swung to the curb. "Your choice, tough guy," she said, and turned to Zack. "I've got work to do. I should be able to clear things up by around seven, then I'll be by to see how things are going."

"I'll keep dinner warm," he said with a smirk, then caught her hand before she could walk away. "Thanks. I mean it." She would have shrugged it off. His hand was hard as rock, calluses over calluses. He grinned. "You're all right, Counselor. For a broad." He climbed into the cab behind his brother, sent her a quick salute as they pulled away. "She's right about you being a jerk, Nick," Zack said easily. "But you sure as hell picked a lawyer with first-class legs."

Nick said nothing, but he did sneak a look out the rear window. He'd noticed Rachel's legs himself.

When they arrived at Nick's room ten minutes later, Zack had to swallow another bout of temper. It wouldn't do any good to yell at the kid every five minutes. But why in the hell had he picked such a neighborhood?

Hoods loitering on street corners. Drug deals negotiated out in broad daylight. Hookers already slicked up and stalking their prey. He could smell the stench of overripe garbage and unwashed humanity. His feet crunched on broken glass as they crossed the heaving sidewalk and entered the scarred and graffiti-laden brick building.

The smells were worse here, trapped inside, where even the fitful September breeze couldn't reach. Zack maintained his silence as they climbed up three floors, ignoring the shouted arguments behind closed doors and the occasional crash and weeping.

Nick unlocked the door and stepped into a single room furnished with a sagging iron bed, a broken dresser and a rickety wooden chair braced with a torn phone book. A few heavy-metal posters had been tacked to the stained walls in a pitiful attempt to give the room some personality. Helpless against the rage that geysered inside him, Zack let loose with a string of curses that turned the stale air blue.

"And what the hell have you been doing with the money I sent home every month when I was at sea? With the salary you were supposed to be earning from the delivery job? You're living in garbage, Nick. What's worse, you chose to live in it."

Not for a second would Nick have admitted that most of his money had gone into the Cobra treasury. Nor would he have admitted the shame he felt at having Zack see how he lived. "It's none of your damn business," he shot back. "This is my place, just like it's my life. You were never around, were you? Just because you got tired of cruising around on some stupid destroyer doesn't give you the right to come back here and take over."

"I've been back two years," Zack pointed out wearily. "And I spent a year of that watching the old man die. You didn't bother to come around much, did you?"

Nick felt a fresh wash of shame, and a deep, desperate sorrow that he was certain Zack could never understand. "He wasn't my old man."

Zack's head jerked up. Nick's hands fisted. Violent temper snapped and sizzled in the room. The slightest move would have sparked it into flame. Slowly, effortfully, Zack forced his body to relax.

"I'm not going to waste my time telling you he did the best he could."

"How the hell do you know?" Nick tossed back. "You weren't here. You got out your way, *bro*. I got out mine."

"Which brings us full circle. Pack up what you want, and let's go."

"This is my place—" Zack moved so quickly that the snarl caught in Nick's throat. He was up against the wall, Zack's big hands holding him in place while his thin body quivered with rage. Zack's face was so close to his, all Nick could see were those dark, dangerous eyes.

"For the next two months, like it or not, your place is with me. Now cut the crap and get some clothes together. Your free ride's over." He released Nick, knowing he had the strength and skill to snap his defiant young brother in half. "You got ten minutes, kid. You're working tonight."

By seven, Rachel was indulging a fantasy about a steamy bubble bath, a glass of crisp white wine and an hour with a good book. It helped ease the discomfort of the crowded subway car. She braced her feet against the swaying, kept her gaze focused on the middle distance. There were a few rough-looking characters scattered through the car whom she'd assessed and decided to ignore. A wino was snoring in the seat behind her, his face hidden under a newspaper.

At her stop, she bulled her way out, then started up the steps into the wet, windy evening. Hunched in her jacket, she fought with her umbrella, then slogged the two blocks to Lower the Boom.

The beveled glass door was heavy. She tugged it open and stepped out of the chill into the warmth, sounds and scents of an established neighborhood bar. It wasn't the dive she'd been expecting, but a wide wood-paneled room with a glossy mahogany bar trimmed in brass. The stools were burgundy leather, and every one was occupied. Neat tables were set around the room to accommodate more customers. There were the scents of whiskey and beer, cigarette smoke and grilled onions. A jukebox played the blues over the hum of conversation.

She spotted two waitresses winding their way through the patrons. No fishnet stockings and cleavage, Rachel mused. Both women were dressed in white slacks with modified sailor tops. There was a great deal of laughter, and she caught snatches of an argument as to whether the Mets still had a chance to make the playoffs.

Zack was in the center of the circular bar, drawing a beer

for a customer. He'd exchanged his sweatshirt for a cable-knit turtleneck in navy blue. Oh, yes, she could see him on the deck of a ship, Rachel realized. Braced against the rolling, face to the wind. The bar's nautical theme, with its ship's bells and anchors, suited him.

She conjured up an image of him in uniform, found it entirely too attractive, and blinked it away.

She wasn't the fanciful type, she reminded herself. She was certainly no romantic. Above all, she was not the kind of woman who walked into a bar and found herself attracted to some landlocked sailor with shaggy hair, big shoulders and rough hands.

The only reason she was here was to uphold the court's ruling. However distasteful it might be to be hooked up with Zackary Muldoon for two months, she would do her duty.

But where was Nick?

"Would you like a table, miss?"

Rachel glanced around at a diminutive blonde hefting a large tray laden with sandwiches and beer. "No, thanks. I'll just go up to the bar. Is this place always crowded?"

The waitress's gray eyes brightened as she looked around the room. "Is it crowded? I didn't notice." With a laugh, she moved off while Rachel walked to the bar. She eased her way between two occupied stools, rested a foot on the brass rail and waited to catch Zack's eye.

"Well, darling…" The man on her left had a plump, pleasant face. He shifted on his stool to get a better look. "Don't think I've seen you in here before."

"No." Since he looked old enough to be her father, Rachel granted him a small smile. "You haven't."

"Pretty young girl like you shouldn't be here all alone." He leaned back—his stool creaking dangerously—and slapped the man on her other side on the shoulder. "Hey, Harry, we ought to buy this lady a drink."

Harry, who continued to sip his beer and work a crossword

puzzle in the dim light, merely nodded. "Sure thing, Pete. Set it up. I need a five-letter word for the possibility of danger or pain."

Rachel glanced up. Zack was watching her, his blue eyes dark and steady, his bony face set and unsmiling. She felt something hot streak up her spine. *"Peril,"* she murmured, and fought off a shudder.

"Yeah! Hey, thanks!" Pleased, Harry pushed up his reading glasses and smiled at her. "First drink's on me. What'll you have, honey?"

"Pouilly-Fumé." Zack set a glass of pale gold wine in front of her. "And the first one's on the house." He lifted a brow. "That suit you, Counselor?"

"Yes." She let out the breath she hadn't been aware of holding. "Thank you."

"Zack always gets the prettiest ones," Pete said with a sigh. "Tip me another, kid. Least you can do, since you stole my girl." He shot Rachel a wink that had her relaxing with a smile again.

"And how often does he steal your girls, Pete?"

"Once, twice a week. It's humiliating." He grinned at Zack over a fresh beer. "Old Zack did date one of my girls once. Remember that time you were home on leave, Zack, you took my Rosemary to the movies, out to Coney Island? She's married and working on her second kid now."

Zack mopped up the bar with a cloth. "She broke my heart."

"There isn't a female alive who's scratched your heart, much less broken it." This from the blonde waitress, who slapped an empty tray on the bar. "Two house wines, white. A Scotch, water back, and a draft. Harry, you ought to buy yourself one of those little clip-on lights before you ruin what's left of your eyes."

"You broke my heart, Lola." Zack put some glasses on the tray. "Why do you think I ran off and joined the navy?"

"Because you knew how good you'd look in dress whites."

She laughed, hefted the tray, then glanced at Rachel. "You watch out for that one, sweetie. He's dangerous."

Rachel sipped at her wine and tried to pretend the scents slipping out from the kitchen weren't making her stomach rumble. "Have you got a minute?" she asked Zack. "I need to see where you're living."

Pete let out a hoot and rolled his eyes. "What's the guy got?" he wanted to know.

"More than you'll ever have." Zack grinned at him and signaled to another bartender to cover for him. "I just seem to attract aggressive women. Can't keep their hands off me."

Rachel finished off her wine before sliding from the stool. "I can restrain myself if I put my mind to it. Though it pains me to mar his reputation," she said to Pete, "I'm his brother's lawyer."

"No fooling?" Impressed, Pete took a closer look. "You the one who got the kid out of jail?"

"For the time being. Muldoon?"

"Right this way for the tour." He flipped up a section of the bar and stepped through. Again he took her arm. "Try to keep up."

"You know, I don't need you to hold on to me. I've been walking on my own for some time."

He pushed open a heavy swinging door that led to the kitchen. "I like holding on to you."

Rachel got the impression of gleaming stainless steel and white porcelain, the heavy scent of frying potatoes and grilling meat, before her attention was absorbed by an enormous man. He was dressed all in white, and his full apron was splattered and stained. Because he towered over Zack, Rachel estimated him at halfway to seven feet and a good three-fifty. If he'd played football, he would have been the entire defensive line.

His face was shiny from the kitchen heat, and the color of india ink. There was a scar running from one coal-black eye down to his massive chin. His hamlike hands were delicately building a club sandwich.

"Rio, this is Rachel Stanislaski, Nick's lawyer."

"How-de-do." She caught the musical cadence of the West Indies in his voice. "Got that boy washing dishes like a champ. Only broke him five or six all night."

Standing at a huge double sink, up to the elbows in soapy water, Nick turned his head and scowled. "If you call cleaning up someone else's slop a job, you can just—"

"Now don't you be using that language around this lady here." Rio picked up a cleaver and brought it down with a *thwack* to cut the sandwich in two, then four. "My mama always said nothing like washing dishes to give a body plenty of time for searching the soul. You keep washing and searching, boy."

Nick would have liked to have said more. Oh, he'd have loved to. But it was hard to argue with a seven-foot man holding a meat cleaver. He went back to muttering.

Rio smiled, and noted that Rachel was eyeing the sandwich. "How 'bout I fix you some hot meal? You can eat after you finish your business."

"Oh, I…" Her mouth was watering. "I really should get home."

"Zack, he's going to see you home after you're done. It's too late for a woman to go walking the streets by herself."

"I don't need—"

"Dish her up some of your chili, Rio," Zack suggested as he pulled Rachel toward a set of stairs. "This won't take long."

Rachel found herself trapped, hip to hip with him in a narrow staircase. He smelled of the sea, she realized, of that salty, slightly electric scent that meant a storm was brewing beyond the horizon. "It's very kind of you to offer, Muldoon, but I don't need a meal, or an escort."

"You'll get both, need them or not." He turned, effectively trapping her against the wall. It felt good to have his body brush hers. As good as he'd imagined it would. "I never argue with Rio. I met him in Jamaica about six years ago—in a little bar tussle. I watched him pick up a two-hundred-pound man and toss him through a wall. Now, Rio's mostly a peaceful sort of man, but if you get him riled, there's no telling what he might do." Zack lifted a hand and wound a lock of Rachel's hair around his finger. "Your hair's wet."

She slapped his hand away and tried to pretend her heart wasn't slamming in her throat. "It's raining."

"Yeah. I can smell it on you. You sure are something to look at, Rachel."

She couldn't move forward, couldn't move back, so she did the only thing open to her. She bristled like a cornered cat. "You're in my way, Muldoon. My advice is to move your butt and save the Irish charm for someone who'll appreciate it."

"In a minute. Was that Russian you yelled after your brother today?"

"Ukrainian," she said between her teeth.

"Ukrainian." He considered that, and her. "I never made it to the Soviet Union."

She lifted a brow. "Neither have I. Now can we save this discussion until after I've seen the living arrangements?"

"All right." He started up the steps again, his hand on the small of her back. "It's not much, but I can guarantee it's a large step up from the dump Nick was living in. I don't know why he—" He cut himself off and shrugged. "Well, it's done."

Rachel had a feeling it was just beginning.

Chapter 3

Though it brought on all manner of headaches, Rachel took her new charge seriously. She could handle the inconvenience, the extra time sliced out of her personal life, Nick's surly and continued resentment. What gave her the most trouble was the enforced proximity with Zackary Muldoon.

She couldn't dismiss him and she couldn't work around him. Having to deal with him on what was essentially a day-to-day basis was sending her stress level through the roof.

If only she could pigeonhole him, she thought as she walked from the subway to her apartment after a Sunday dinner with her family, it would somehow make things easier. But after nearly a week of trying, she hadn't even come close.

He was rough, impatient, and, she suspected, potentially violent. Yet he was concerned enough about his stepbrother to shell out money and—much more vital—time and energy to set the boy straight. In his off hours, he dressed in clothes more suited to the rag basket than his tall, muscled frame. Yet when she'd walked through his apartment over the bar, she'd found everything neat as a pin. He was always putting his hands on her—her arm, her hair, her shoulder—but he had yet to make the kind of move she was forever braced to repel.

He flirted with his female customers, but as far as Rachel had been able to glean, it stopped at flirtation. He'd never been married, and though he'd left his family for months, even years, at a time, he'd given up the sea and had landlocked himself when his father became too ill to care for himself.

He irritated her on principle. But on some deeper, darker level, the very things about him that irritated her fanned little flames in her gut that Rachel could only describe as pure lust.

She'd tried to cool them by reminding herself that she wasn't the lusty type. Passionate, yes. When it came to her work, her family and her ambitions. But men, though she enjoyed their companionship and their basic maleness, had never been at the top of her list of priorities.

Sex was even lower than that. And it was very annoying to find herself itchy.

So who was Zackary Muldoon, and would she be better off not knowing?

When he stepped out of the shadows into the glow of a streetlight, she jolted and choked back a scream.

"Where the hell have you been?"

"I— Damn it, you scared me to death." She brought a trembling hand back out of her purse, where it had shot automatically toward a bottle of Mace. Oh, she hated to be frightened. Detested having to admit she could be vulnerable. "What are you doing lurking out here in front of my building?"

"Looking for you. Don't you ever stay home?"

"Muldoon, with me it's party, party, party." She stalked up the steps and jammed her key in the outer door. "What do you want?"

"Nick took off."

She stopped halfway through the door, and he bumped solidly into her. "What do you mean, took off?"

"I mean he slipped out of the kitchen sometime this afternoon, when Rio wasn't looking. I can't find him." He was so furious—with Nick, with Rachel, with himself—that it took all of his control not to punch his fist through the wall. "I've been at it almost five hours, and I can't find him."

"All right, don't panic." Her mind was already clicking ahead as she walked through the tiny lobby to the single gate-fronted elevator. "It's early, just ten o'clock. He knows his way around."

"That's the trouble." Disgusted with himself, Zack stepped in the car with her. "He knows his way around too well. The rule was, he'd tell me when he was going, and where. I've got to figure he's hanging out with the Cobras."

"Nick's not going to break that kind of tie overnight." Rachel continued to think as the elevator creaked its way up to the fourth floor. "We can drive ourselves crazy running around the city trying to hunt him down, or we can call in the cavalry."

"The cavalry?"

She shoved the gate open and walked into the hallway. "Alex."

"No cops," Zack said quickly, grabbing her arms. "I'm not setting the cops on him."

"Alex isn't just a cop. He's my brother." Struggling to hold on to her own patience, she pried his fingers from her arms. "And I'm an officer of the court, Zack. If Nick's breaking the provisions, I can't ignore it."

"I'm not going to see him tossed back in a cell barely a week after I got him out."

"*We* got him out," she corrected, then unlocked her door. "If you didn't want my help and advice, you shouldn't have come."

Zack shrugged and stepped inside. "I guess I figured we could go out looking together."

The room was hardly bigger than the one Nick had rented, but it was all female. Not flouncy, Zack thought. Rachel wouldn't go for flounce. There were vivid colors in the plump pillows tossed over a low-armed sofa. The scented candles were burned down to various lengths, and mums were just starting to fade in a china vase.

There was a huge bronze-framed oval mirror on one wall. Its glass needed resilvering. A three-foot sculpture in cool white marble dominated one corner. It reminded Zack of a mermaid rising up out of the sea. There were smaller sculptures, as well, all of them passionate, some of them bordering on the ferocious. A timber wolf rearing out of a slab of oak, twisted fingers of bronze and copper that looked like a fire just out of control, a smooth and sinuous malachite cobra ready to strike.

There were shelves of books, and dozens of framed photographs—and there was the unmistakable scent of woman.

Zack felt uncharacteristically awkward and clumsy, and completely out of place. He stuck his hands in his pockets, certain he'd knock over one of those slender tapers. His mother had liked candles, he remembered. Candles and flowers and blue china bowls.

"I'll make coffee." Rachel tossed her purse aside and walked into the adjoining kitchen.

"Yeah. Good." Restless, Zack roamed the room, checked out the view through the cheerful striped curtains, frowned over the photographs that were obviously of her family, paced back to the sofa. "I don't know what I'm doing. What makes me think I can play daddy to a kid Nick's age? I wasn't around for half his life. He hates me. He's got a right."

"You've been doing fine," Rachel countered, taking out cups and saucers. "You're not playing daddy, you're being his brother. If you weren't around for half his life, it's because you had a life of your own. And he doesn't hate you. He's angry and full of resentment, which is a long way from hate—which he wouldn't have any right to. Now stop feeling sorry for yourself, and get out the milk."

"Is that how you cross-examine?" Not sure whether he was amused or annoyed, Zack opened the refrigerator.

"No, I'm much tougher than that in court."

"I bet." He shook his head at the contents of her refrigerator. Yogurt, a package of bologna, another of cheese, several diet soft drinks, a jug of white wine, two eggs, and half a stick of butter. "You're out of milk."

She swore, then sighed. "So we drink it black. Did you and Nick have a fight?"

"No— I mean no more than usual. He snarls, I snarl back. He swears, I swear louder. But we actually had what could pass for a conversation last night, then watched an old movie on the tube after the bar closed."

"Ah, progress…" She handed him his coffee in a dainty cup and saucer that felt like a child's tea set in his hands.

"We get a lot of families in for lunch on Sundays." Zack ignored the china handle and wrapped his fingers around the bowl of the cup. "He was down in the kitchen at noon. I figured he might like to knock off early, you know, take some time for himself. I went into the kitchen around four. Rio didn't want to rat on him, so he'd been covering for him for an hour or so. I hoped he'd just taken a breather, but… Then I went out looking." Zack finished off the coffee, then helped himself to more. "I've been pretty hard on him the last few days. It seemed like the best way. On my first ship, my CO was a regular Captain Bligh. I hated the bastard until I realized he'd turned us into a crew." Zack grinned a little. "Hell, I still hated him, but I never forgot him."

"Stop beating yourself up." She couldn't prevent herself from reaching out, touching his arm. "It isn't as if you hanged him from the yardarm or whatever. Now sit down and try to relax. Let me talk to Alex."

He did sit, though he wasn't happy about it. Because he felt like an idiot trying to balance the delicate saucer on his knee, he set it down on the table. There wasn't an ashtray in sight, so he clamped down on the urge for a cigarette.

He paid little attention to Rachel until her voice rose in frustration. Then he smiled a little. She was certainly full of fire, punching out requests and orders with the aplomb of a seasoned seaman. Lord, he'd gotten so he looked forward to hearing that throaty, impatient voice. How many times over the past few days had he made up excuses to call her?

Too many, he admitted. Something about the lady had hooked him, and Zack wasn't sure whether he wanted to pry himself loose or be reeled in.

And the last thing he should be doing now was thinking of his libido, he reminded himself. He had to think about Nick.

Obviously Rachel's brother was resisting, but she wasn't taking no for an answer. When she switched to heated Ukrainian, Zack reached over to toy with the spitting cobra in the center of the coffee table. It drove him crazy when she talked in Ukrainian.

"Tak," she said, satisfied that she'd worn Alex down. "I owe you one, Alexi." She laughed, a rich, and full-blooded laugh that sent heat straight to Zack's midsection. "All right, all right, so I'll owe you two." Zack watched her hang up and cross long legs covered in a hunter-green material that was silky enough to whisper seductively when her thighs brushed together. "Alex and his partner are going to cruise around, check out some of the Cobras' known haunts. They'll let us know if they see him."

"So we wait?"

"We wait." She rose and took a fresh legal pad from a drawer. "To pass the time, you can fill me in a little more on Nick's background. You said his mother died when he was about fifteen. What about his father?"

"His mother wasn't married before." Zack reached automatically for a cigarette, then remembered. Recognizing the gesture, Rachel rose again and found a chipped ashtray. "Thanks." Relieved, he lit a cigarette, cupping his fingers around the tip out of habit. "Nadine was about eighteen when she got pregnant, and the guy wasn't interested in family. He took off and left her to fend for herself. So she had Nick and did what she could. One day she came into the bar looking for work. Dad hired her."

"How old was Nick?"

"Four or five. Nadine was barely making ends meet. Sometimes she couldn't get a sitter for him, so Dad told her to bring the kid along and I'd watch him. He was okay," Zack said with a half smile. "I mean, he was real quiet. Most of the time he'd just watch you like he was expecting to get dumped on. But he was smart. He'd just started school, but he could already read, and he could print some, too. Anyway, a couple months later, Nadine and my father got married. Dad was about twenty years older than she was, but I guess they were both lonely. My mother'd been dead for more than ten years. Nadine and the kid moved in."

"How did you...how did Nick adjust?"

"It seemed okay. Hell, I was a kid myself." Restless again, he rose to pace. "Nadine bent over backward trying to please everyone. That's the way she was. My father...he wasn't always easy, you know, and he put a lot of time into the bar. We weren't a Norman Rockwell kind of family, but we did okay." He glanced back at her photographs, surprised at the quick twinge of envy. "I didn't mind the kid hanging around me. Much. Then I joined the navy, right out of high school. It was kind of a family tradition. When Nadine died, it was hard on Nick. Hard on my father. I guess you could say they took it out on each other."

"Is that when Nick started to get into trouble?"

"I'd say he got into his share before that, but it got worse.

Whenever I'd get back, my father would be full of complaints. The boy wouldn't do this, he did that. He was hanging around with punks. He was looking for trouble. And Nick would skulk off or slam out. If I said anything, he'd tell me to kiss his—" He shrugged. "You get the picture."

She thought she did. A young boy unwanted by his father. He begins to admire his new brother, and then feels deserted by him, as well. He loses his mother and finds himself alone with a man old enough to be his grandfather, a man who couldn't relate to him.

Nothing permanent in his life—except rejection.

"I'm not a psychologist, Zack, but I'd say he needs time to trust that you mean to stay part of his life this time around. And I don't think taking a firm hand is wrong. In fact, I think that's just what he'd understand from you, and respect in the long run. Maybe that just needs to be balanced a bit." She sighed and set her notes aside. "Which is where I come in. So far, I've been just as rough on him. Let's try a little good-cop/bad-cop. I'll be the sympathetic ear. Believe me, I understand hotheads and bad boys. I grew up with them. We can start by—" The phone rang and she snagged it. "Hello. Uh-huh. Good. That's good. Thanks, Alex." She could see the relief in Zack's eyes before she hung up. "They spotted him on his way back to the bar."

Relief sparked quickly into anger. "When I get my hands on him—"

"You'll ask, in a very reasonable fashion, where he was," Rachel told him. "And to make certain you do, I'm going with you."

Nick let himself into Zack's apartment. He figured he'd been pretty clever. He'd managed to slip in and out of the kitchen without setting off Rio's radar. The way they were watching him around here, he thought, he might as well be doing time.

Everything was going wrong, anyway. He ducked into the

kitchen and, since Zack wasn't around to say any different, opened a beer. He'd just wanted to check in with the guys, see what was happening on the street.

And they'd treated him like an outsider.

They didn't trust him, Nick thought resentfully as he swigged one long swallow, then two. Reece had decided that since he'd gotten out so quickly, he must have ratted. He thought he'd convinced most of the gang that he was clean, but when he'd spilled the whole story—from how he'd been caught to how he'd ended up washing dishes in Zack's bar, they'd laughed at him.

It hadn't been the good, communal laughter he'd shared with the Cobras in the past. It had been snide and nasty, with T.J. giggling like a fool and Reece smirking and playing with his switchblade. Only Cash had been the least bit sympathetic, saying how it was a raw deal.

Not one of them had bothered to explain why they'd left him hanging when the cop showed up.

When he'd left them, he'd gone by Marla's place. They'd been seeing each other steadily for the past couple of months, and he'd been sure he'd find a sympathetic ear, and a nice warm body. But she'd been out—with somebody else.

Looked as though he'd been dumped again, all around. Nothing new, Nick told himself. But the sting of rejection wasn't any easier to take this time.

Damn it, they were supposed to be his family. They were supposed to stick up for him, stand by him, not shake him loose at the first hint of trouble. He wouldn't have done it to them, he told himself, and heaved the empty beer bottle into the trash, where it smashed satisfactorily. No, by God, he wouldn't have done it to them.

When he heard the door open, he set his face into bored lines and sauntered out of the kitchen. He'd expected Zack, but he hadn't expected Rachel. Nick felt a heat that was embarrassment and something more try to creep up into his cheeks.

Zack peeled off his jacket, hoping he had a firm grip on his temper. "I guess you've got a good reason why you skipped out this afternoon."

"I wanted some air." Nick pulled out a cigarette, struck a match. "There a law against it?"

"We had an agreement," Zack said evenly. "You were supposed to check with me before you went out, and tell me your plans."

"No, man. You had an agreement. Last I looked it was a free country and people could go for a walk when they felt like it." He gestured toward Rachel. "You bring the lawyer to sue me, or what?"

"Listen, kid—"

"I'm not a kid," Nick shot back. "You came and went as you damn well pleased when you were my age."

"I wasn't a thief at your age." Incensed, Zack took two steps forward. Rachel snagged his arm.

"Why don't you go down and get me a glass of wine, Muldoon? The kind you served me the other night will do just fine." When he tried to shake her off, she tightened her grip. "I want a moment alone with my client, so take your time."

"Fine." He bit off the word before he stalked to the door. "Whatever she says, pal, you're on double KP next week. And if you try to sneak off again, I'll have Rio chain you to the sink." He gave himself the sweet satisfaction of slamming the door.

Nick took another puff on his cigarette and dropped onto the couch. "Big talk," he muttered. "He's always figured he could boss me around. I've been on my own for years, and it's time he got that straight."

Rachel sat down beside him. She didn't bother to mention that she could smell the beer on his breath and he was underage. Why hadn't Zack seen the raw need in Nick's eyes? Why hadn't *she* seen it before?

"It's tough, having to move in here after having a place of your own."

Her voice was mild, and without censure. Nick squinted through the smoke. "Yeah," he said, cautiously. "I can hack it for a couple of months, I guess."

"When I first moved out, I was a little older than you—not much. I was excited, and scared, and lonely. I wouldn't have admitted to lonely if my life had depended on it. I've got two older brothers. They checked up on me constantly." She laughed a little. Nick didn't crack a smile. "It infuriated me, and it made me feel safe. They still get on my back, but I can usually find a way around them."

Nick stared hard at the tip of his cigarette. "He's not my real brother."

Oh, Lord, he looked young, she thought. And so terribly sad. "I suppose that would depend on your definition of real." She laid a hand on his knee, prepared for him to shrug her off, but he only switched his gaze from his cigarette to her fingers. "It'd be easier for you to believe he doesn't care, but you're not stupid, Nick."

There was a hot ball in his throat that he refused to believe was tears. "Why should he care? I'm nothing to him."

"If he didn't care, he wouldn't yell at you so much. Take it from me—I come from a family where a raised voice is a sign of unswerving love. He wants to look out for you."

"I can look out for myself."

"And have been," she agreed. "But most of us can use a hand now and again. He won't thank me for telling you all this, but I think you should know." She waited until he raised his eyes again. "He's had to take out a loan to pay for the stolen property and the damages."

"That's bull," Nick shot back, appalled. "Did he lay that trip on you?"

"No, I checked on it myself. It seems old Mr. Muldoon's illness drained quite a bit of his savings, and Zack's. Zack's gotten the bar back on a pretty solid footing again, but he didn't have enough to swing the costs. A man doesn't put himself out like that for someone he doesn't care about."

The sick feeling in Nick's gut had him crushing out the cigarette. "He just feels obligated, that's all."

"Maybe. Either way, it seems to me you owe him something, Nick. At least you owe him a little cooperation over the next few weeks. He was scared when he came looking for me tonight. You probably don't want to believe that, either."

"Zack's never been scared of anything."

"He didn't come right out and say it, but I think he believed you'd taken off for good, that he wasn't going to see you again."

"Where the hell would I go?" he demanded. "There's nobody—" He broke off, ashamed to admit there was no one to go to. "We made a deal," he muttered, "I'm not going to skip."

"I'm glad to hear it. And I'm not going to ask you where you went," she added with a faint smile. "If I did, I'd have to put it in my report to Judge Beckett, and I'd rather not. So we'll just say you went out for some air, lost track of the time. Maybe the next time you feel like you've got to get out, you could call me."

"Why?"

"Because I know how it feels when you need to break loose." He looked so lost that Rachel skimmed a hand through his hair, brushing it back from his face. "Lighten up, Nick. It's not a crime to be friends with your lawyer, either. So what do you say? You give me a break and try a little harder to get along with Zack, and I'll do what I can to keep him off your back? I know all kinds of tricks for handling nosy older brothers."

Her scent was clouding his senses. He didn't know why he hadn't noticed before how beautiful her eyes were. How deep and wide and soft. "Maybe you and I could go out sometime."

"Sure." She saw the suggestion only as a breakthrough in

trust, and she smiled. "Rio's a terrific cook, but once in a while you just got to have pizza, right?"

"Yeah. So I can call you?"

"Absolutely." She gave his hand a quick squeeze. When his hand tightened over hers, she was only mildly surprised. Before she could comment, Zack was pushing the door open again. Nick jumped up as if he were on a string.

Zack passed Rachel her wine, then handed Nick the ginger-ale bottle he had hooked under one finger. Taking his time, he twisted off the top of the beer he had hooked under another. "So, did you two finish your consultation?"

"For now." Rachel sipped her wine and lifted a brow at Nick.

It wasn't easy, especially after what she'd told him Zack had done, but Nick met his brother's eyes. "I'm sorry I took off."

The surprise was so great that Zack had to swallow quickly or choke on his beer. "Okay. We can work out a schedule so you can have more free time." What the hell did he do now? "Uh... Rio could use some help swabbing down the kitchen. Things usually break up early on Sunday nights."

"Sure, no problem." Nick started for the door. "See you, Rachel."

When the door closed, Zack dropped down beside her, shaking his head. "What'd you do, hypnotize him?"

"Not exactly."

"Well, what the hell did you say to him?"

She sighed, tremendously pleased with herself, and settled back. "That's privileged information. He just needs someone to stroke his bruised ego now and again. You two may not be biological brothers, but your temperaments very similar."

"Oh." He settled back, as well, swinging an arm around the top of the couch so that he could play with her hair. "How's that?"

"You're both hotheaded and stubborn—which is easy for me to recognize, as I come from a long line of the same." Enjoying the wine and the quiet, she let her eyes close. "You don't like to admit you made a mistake, and you'd rather punch your way out of a problem than reason it through."

"Are you trying to say those are faults?"

She had to laugh. "We'll just call them personality traits. My family is ripe with passionate natures. And what a passionate nature requires is an outlet. My sister Natasha had dance, then her own business and her family. My brother Mikhail has his art. Alexi has his quest to right wrongs, and I have the law. As I see it, you had the navy, and now this bar. Nick hasn't found his yet."

He brushed a finger lightly over the nape of her neck, felt the quick quiver that ran through her. "Do you really consider the law enough of an outlet for passion?"

"The way I play it." She opened her eyes, but the smile that had started to curve her lips died away. He'd shifted, and his face was close—much too close—and his hands had slipped down to her shoulders. The warning bell that rang in her brain had come too late. "I've got to get home," she said quickly. "I've got a nine-o'clock hearing."

"I'll take you in a minute."

"I know the way, Muldoon."

"I'll take you," he said again, and something in his tone made it quite clear that he wasn't talking about walking her to her door. He tugged the wineglass out of her hand and set it aside. "We were talking about passionate natures." His fingers skimmed up through her hair, fisted in it. "And outlets."

In an automatic defensive gesture, her hand slammed against his chest, but he continued to draw her closer. "I came here to help you, Muldoon," she reminded him as his mouth hovered dangerously above hers. "Not to play games."

"Just testing your theory, Counselor." He nipped lightly at her lower lip, once, twice. When that teasing sample stirred the juices, he crushed his mouth to hers and devoured.

She could stop him. Of course she would stop him, Rachel

told herself. She knew how to defend herself against unwanted advances. The trouble was, she hadn't a clue as to how to defend herself against advances she didn't want to want.

His mouth was so...avid. So impatient. So greedy. She wondered if he would swallow her whole. He used lips and tongue and teeth devastatingly. If there was an instant, some fraction of a heartbeat, when she could have resisted, it passed unnoticed, and she was swamped by the hot wave that was his need, or hers. Or what they made together. On one long, throaty moan, she went under for the third time, dragging him with her.

He'd been prepared for her to slap or scratch. And he would have accepted it, would have forced himself to be satisfied with that quick, tempting taste. He was a man with large appetites, but he had never been one to take what wasn't offered willingly.

She didn't offer. She exploded. In that blink of time before his mouth covered hers, he'd seen the fire come into her eyes, that dark, liquid fire that equaled passion. When the kiss had gone from teasing to fevered, she had answered, pulling him far deeper into that hot well of desires than he'd intended to go.

And that moan. It sprinted along his spine, that glorious feline sound that was both surrender and demand. Even as it died away, she was wrapping herself around him, pressing that incredibly lean and limber body against his in a way that had a chain of explosions rioting through his system.

She heard his breathy oath, felt the long cushions of the couch press into her back as he shifted her. For one wild moment, all she could think was Yes! This was what she wanted, this wild flurry of sensations, this crazed, mindless mating of flesh. As his mouth raced down to savage her throat, she arched against him, craving the possession.

Then he said her name. Groaned it. The shock of hearing it ripped her back to reality. She was grappling on a couch in a strange apartment with a man she barely knew.

"No." His hands were moving over her, and they nearly

dragged her back into the whirlwind. Desperate to pull away, she shoved and struggled. "Stop. I said no."

He couldn't get his breath. If someone had held a gun to his head, he wouldn't have moved. But the *no* stopped him. He managed to lift his head, and the reckless light in his eyes had her fighting against a shudder. "Why?"

"Because this is insane." God, she could still taste him on her lips, and the churning for more of him was making her crazy. "Get off me."

He could have strangled her for making him want to beg. "Your call, lady." Because his hands were unsteady, he balled them into fists. "I thought you said you didn't play games."

She was humiliated, furious and frustrated beyond belief. As she saw it, the best disguise was full-blown anger. "I don't. You're the one who pushed yourself on me. The simple fact is, I'm not interested."

"I guess that's why you were kissing me so hard my teeth are loose."

"You kissed me." She jabbed a finger at him. "And you're so damn big I couldn't stop you."

"A simple no did," he reminded her, and lit a cigarette. "Let's keep it honest, Counselor. I wanted to kiss you. I've been wanting to do that, and more, ever since I saw you sitting like a queen in that grubby station house. Now, maybe you didn't feel the same way, but when I kissed you, you kissed me right back."

Sometimes retreat was the best defense. Rachel snatched up her purse and jacket. "It's done, so there's nothing more to discuss."

"Wrong." He was up and blocking her path. "We can finish discussing it while I take you home."

"I don't want you to take me home. I'm not having you take me home." Eyes blazing, she swung her jacket over her shoulders. "And if you insist on following me there, I'll have you arrested for harassment."

He merely grabbed her by the arm. "Try it."

She did something she wished she'd done the first time she laid eyes on him. She punched him in the stomach. He let out a little *whoosh* of air, and his eyes narrowed.

"First one's free. Now, we can walk to the subway, or I can carry you there."

"What's wrong with you?" she shouted. "Can't you take no for an answer?"

His response was to shove her back against the door and kiss the breath out of her. "If I didn't," he said between his teeth, "we wouldn't be walking out of here right now when you've got me so wound up I'm going to have to live in a cold shower for the next week." He yanked open the door. "Now…are you going to walk, or are you going to ride over my shoulder?"

She stuck out her chin and sailed past him.

She'd walk, all right. But she'd be damned if she'd speak to him.

Chapter 4

At the end of a harried ten-hour day, Rachel walked out of the courthouse. She should have been feeling great—her last client was certainly happy with the non-guilty verdict she'd gotten for him. But this time the victory hadn't managed to lift her spirits. The only solution she could see was to pick up a quart of ice cream on the way home and gorge herself into a sugar coma.

It usually worked, and since, as a law-abiding citizen, she couldn't relieve her tension by striding into Lower the Boom and shooting Zackary Muldoon through his thick skull, it was the safest alternative.

She almost tripped over her own feet when she saw him rise from his perch at the bottom of the steps.

"Counselor." He reached out a hand when she teetered. "Steady as she goes."

"What now?" she demanded, jerking away. "Doesn't it occur to you that—even though I've been appointed by the court as Nick's co-guardian—I'm entitled to an hour of personal time without you in my face?"

He studied that face, noting signs of fatigue, as well as temper, in those big, tawny eyes. "You know, honey, I figured you'd be in a better mood after winning a case like you just did. Let's try these." With a flourish, he brought his other hand from behind his back. It was filled with gold, bronze and rust-colored mums.

Refusing to be charmed, Rachel gave them one long, suspicious glare. "What are those for?"

"To replace the ones that are dying in your apartment." When she made no move to take them, he bit down on his impatience. He'd come to apologize, damn it, and it looked as though she was going to make him go through with it. "Okay, I'm sorry. I got pushy the other night. And after I got over wanting to choke you, I realized you'd gone out of your way to do me a favor, and I'd repaid it by…" Furious all over again, he thrust the flowers at her. "Hell, lady, all I did was kiss you."

All he did? she thought, tempted to toss the flowers down and grind them underfoot. Just kissing didn't jangle a woman's system for better than thirty-six hours. "Why don't you take your flowers, and your charming apology, and—"

"Hold on." He thought it better to stop her before she said something he'd regret. "I said I was sorry, and I meant it, but maybe I should be more specific." To ensure that she'd stay put until he was finished, he wrapped his fingers around the lapel of her plum-colored jacket. "I'm not sorry I kissed you, any more than I'm going to be sorry the next time I kiss you. I am sorry for the way I acted after you put on the brakes."

She lifted a brow. "The way you acted," she repeated. "You mean like a jerk."

It gave her a great deal of pleasure to see a muscle twitch in his jaw.

"Okay."

A smart attorney knew when to accept a compromise. Lips pursed, she studied the flowers. "Are these a bribe, Muldoon?"

The way she said his name, with just a hint of a sneer, told him he'd gotten over the first hurdle. "Yeah."

"All right, I'll take them."

"Gee, thanks." Now that his hands were free, he tucked his thumbs in his front pockets. "I slipped in the courtroom about an hour ago and watched you."

"Oh?" She couldn't tell him how glad she was she hadn't seen him. "And?"

"Not bad. Turning a vandalism charge around on the other guy—"

"The plaintiff," she explained. "My client was justifiably frustrated after he'd exhausted all reasonable attempts to have his landlord live up to the terms of his lease."

"And spray painting The Landlord from Hell all over the guy's brownstone on the Upper West Side was his way of relieving that frustration."

"He certainly made his point. My client had paid his rent on time and in good faith, and the landlord consistently refused to acknowledge each and every request for repair and maintenance. Under the terms of the lease—"

"Hey, babe." Zack raised a hand, palm out. "You don't have to sell me. By the time you got through, I was pulling for him. There were murmurs in the visitors' gallery about lynching the landlord." His mouth was sober enough, but his eyes danced with humor. The contrast was all but irresistible.

Her smile was quick and wicked. "I love justice."

Reaching out, he toyed with the tiny gold links circling her neck. "Maybe you'd like to celebrate your victory for the underdog. Want to go for a walk?"

Mistake. The word popped full-blown into her mind, but she could smell the spicy flowers, and the evening was beautifully balmy. "I guess I would, as long as it's to my apartment. I should put these in water."

"Let me take that." He'd tugged the briefcase out of her hand

before she could object. Then—she should have expected it—
he took her arm. "What do you carry in here, bricks?"

"The law's a weighty business, Muldoon." His grip on her
forced her to slow her pace to his. He strolled when she would
have strode. "So, how's it going with Nick?"

"It's better. At least I think it's better. He balked at the idea of
Rio teaching him to cook, but the idea of busing tables didn't
seem to bother him much. He still won't talk to me—I mean
really talk to me. But it's only been a week."

"You've got seven more."

"Yeah." He let go of her arm long enough to reach into his
pocket and take out a handful of change. He dropped it into a
panhandler's cup in a gesture so automatic that Rachel assumed
he made a habit of it. "I figure if they could turn me from a
green recruit into a sailor in about the same amount of time, I
have a pretty good shot at this."

"Do you miss it?" She tilted her head up to his. "Being at
sea?"

"Not so much anymore. Sometimes I still wake up at night
and think I'm aboard ship." Then there were the nightmares,
but that wasn't something a man shared with a woman. "Once
things are stable, I'm planning on buying a boat, maybe taking a couple of months and sailing down to the Islands. Maybe
a nice ketch, forty-two feet—not too fancy." He could already
see it, a trim little honey, quick to the touch, brass and mahogany gleaming, white sails bulging in the wind. He imagined Rachel would look just fine standing at the bow. "You
ever done any sailing?"

"Not unless you count taking the ferry over to Liberty Island."

"You'd like it." He skimmed his fingers lightly down her
arm. "It's what you might call an outlet."

Rachel decided it was safer not to comment. When they
reached her building, she turned to him, holding out a hand for

her briefcase. "Thanks for the flowers, and the walk. I'll probably come by the bar tomorrow after work and look in on Nick."

Instead of giving her the briefcase, he closed his hand over hers. "I took the night off, Rachel. I want to spend it with you."

Her quick jolt of alarm both pleased and amused him. "Excuse me?"

"Maybe I should rephrase that. I'd like to spend the night with you—several nights running, in fact—but I'll settle for the evening." He managed to wind a lock of her hair around his finger before she remembered to bat his hand away. "Some food, some music. I know a place that does both really well. If the idea of a date makes you nervous…"

"I'm not nervous." Not exactly, she thought.

"Anyway, we can consider it a few hours between two people who have a mutual interest. It couldn't hurt if we got to know each other a little better." He pulled out his trump card. "For Nick's sake."

She studied him, much as she had the witness she'd so ruthlessly cross-examined earlier. "You want to spend the evening with me for Nick's sake?"

Giving up, he grinned. "Hell, no. There's bound to be some spillover benefit there, but I want to spend the evening with you for purely selfish reasons."

"I see. Well, since you didn't perjure yourself, I may be able to cut a deal. It has to be an early evening, somewhere I can dress comfortably. And you won't…" How had he phrased it? "Get pushy."

"You're a tough one, Counselor."

"You got it."

"Deal," he said, and gave her the briefcase.

"Fine. Come back in twenty minutes. I'll be ready."

A bar, Rachel thought a half hour later. She should have known Zack would spend his night off on a busman's holiday. Actually, she supposed it was more of a club. There was a three-piece band playing the blues on a small raised stage, and there were a handful of couples dancing on a tiny square of floor surrounded by tables. From the way he was greeted by the waitress, he was obviously no stranger.

Within moments they were settled at a table in a shadowy corner, with a glass of wine for her and a mug of beer for him.

"I come for the music," he explained. "But the food's good, too. That's not something I mention to Rio."

"Since I've seen the way he slices a club sandwich, I can't hold that against you." She squinted at the tiny menu. "What do you recommend?"

"Trust me." His thigh brushed hers as he shifted closer to toy with the stones dangling at her ear. He smiled at her narrowed eyes. "And try the grilled chicken."

She discovered he could be trusted, at least when it came to food. Enjoying every bite, lulled by the music, she began to relax. "You said the navy was a family tradition. Is that why you joined, really?"

"I wanted to get out." He nursed a second beer, appreciating the way she plowed through the meal. He'd always been attracted to a woman with an appetite. "I wanted to see the world. I only figured on the four years, but then I re-upped."

"Why?"

"I got used to being part of a crew, and I liked the life. Looking out and seeing nothing but water, or watching the land pull away when you headed out. Coming into port and seeing a place you'd never seen before."

"In nearly ten years I imagine you saw a lot of places."

"The Mediterranean, the South Pacific, the Indian Ocean, the Persian Gulf. Froze my...fingers off in the North Atlantic and watched sharks feed in the Coral Sea."

Both fascinated and amused, she propped her elbows on the table. "Did you know you didn't mention one land mass?

Doesn't one body of water look pretty much like another from the deck of a ship?"

"No." He didn't think he could explain, knew he wasn't lyrical enough to describe the varying hues of the water, the subtle degrees of the power of the deep. What it felt like to watch dolphins run, or whales sound. "I guess you could say that a body of water has its own personality, just like a body of land does."

"You do miss it."

"It gets in your blood. How about you? Is the law a Stanislaski family tradition?"

"No." Under the table, her foot began to tap to the beat of the bass. "My father's a carpenter. So was his father."

"Why law?"

"Because I'd grown up in a family who'd known oppression. They escaped Ukraine with what they could carry in a wagon— in the winter through the mountains—eventually reaching Austria. I was born here, the first of my family to be born here."

"It sounds as though you regret it."

He was astute, she decided. More astute than she'd given him credit for. "I suppose I regret not being a part of both sides. They haven't forgotten what it was like to taste freedom for the first time. I've never known anything but freedom. Freedom and justice go hand in hand."

"Some might say you could be serving justice in a nice, cushy law firm."

"Some might."

"You had offers." When her brows lifted, he shrugged. "You're representing my brother. I checked on you. Graduated top of your class at NYCC, passed the bar first shot, then turned down three very lucrative offers from three very prestigious firms to work for peanuts as a public defender. I had to figure either you were crazy or dedicated."

She swallowed a little bubble of temper and nodded. "And you left the navy with a chestful of medals, including the Sil-

ver Star. Your file includes, along with a few reprimands for
insubordination, a personal letter of gratitude from an admiral
for your courage during a rescue at sea in a hurricane." Enjoying his squirm of embarrassment, she lifted her glass in toast.
"I checked, too."

"We were talking about you," he began.

"No. You were." Smiling, she cupped her chin on her hand.
"So tell me, Muldoon, why did you turn down a shot at officer candidate school?"

"Didn't want to be a damn officer," he muttered. Rising,
he grabbed her hand and hauled her to her feet. "Let's dance."

She chuckled as he dragged her onto the crowded dance
floor. "You're blushing."

"I am not. And shut up."

Rachel tucked her tongue in her cheek. "It must be hell
being a hero."

"Here's the deal." Zack held her lightly by the arms on the
edge of the dance floor. "You drop the stuff about medals and
admirals, and I won't mention that you were class valedictorian."

She thought it over. "Fair enough. But I think—"

He pulled her into his arms. "Stop thinking."

It did the trick, all right. The moment she found herself
pressed hard against him, her mind clicked off. She could still
hear the music, the low, seductive alto sax, the pulse of the
bass, the slow rhythms of the piano notes, but rational thought
vanished.

They weren't dancing. Rachel was certain no one would
call this locked-hard, swaying embrace a dance. But it would
be foolish to try to pull away when there was so little room.
Breathing wasn't all that important, after all. Not when you
could feel your own heart slamming against your ribs.

She hadn't intended to wind her arms quite so firmly around
his neck, but now that they were there, there seemed little point
in moving them. Besides, if she skimmed her fingers up just a

bit, they could trail through his hair so that she could discover how fascinating that silky contrast was compared to the rock-hard body molded to hers.

"You fit." He bent his head so that his mouth was against her ear. "I was a little too wound up to be sure the other night. But I thought you would."

The subtle movements of his lips against her skin had her shivering before she could prevent it. "What?"

"Fit," he said again, letting his hands follow those curvy lines down to her hips and back again.

"That's only because I'm standing on my toes."

"Honey, height doesn't have a thing to do with it." He rubbed his cheek against her hair, filling himself with the scent, the texture. "You feel right, you smell right, you taste right."

Shaken, she turned her head before his mouth could finish its journey down the side of her face. "I could have you arrested for trying to seduce me in a public place."

"That's all right. I know a good lawyer." He trailed his fingers under the back of her soft wool sweater to the heated skin beneath.

Her breath caught, then released unsteadily. "They'll have us both arrested."

"I'll post bail." There was nothing but Rachel under the sweater, he was sure of it. His mouth went dry as dust. "I want you alone." Biting off a groan, he dipped his head to press his lips to her neck. "Do you know what I'd do to you right now if I had you alone?"

She shook her swimming head. "We should sit down. We shouldn't do this."

"I want to touch you, every inch of you. And taste you. I want to make you crazy."

He already was. If she didn't manage to slow things down, her overcharged system was likely to explode. "Two steps back," she said on a long breath, and took just that. His hands remained at her waist, but at least she could breathe again. At least she managed two gulps of air before she looked into his eyes and the breath backed up in her lungs again. "Too much, too fast, Muldoon. I'm not a spontaneous type of person."

What she *was* was a volcano ready to erupt. He was damn sure going to be there when the ground started to shake. But he didn't intend to scare her off, either. "Hey, you want time. I can give you an hour. Two, if you really want me to suffer."

She shook her head, edging back to the table. "Let's just say I'll let you know if and when I'm ready to take this any further."

"She wants me to suffer," Zack said under his breath. When she didn't sit, he reached for his wallet. "I take it we're leaving."

"An early evening," she reminded him. And she wanted badly to get outside, where the air could cool her blood.

"A deal's a deal." He tossed bills onto the table. "Why don't we walk back? A little exercise might help us both sleep to-night."

A twenty-block hike, Rachel mused. It couldn't hurt.

"Cold?" he asked a short time later.

"No. It's nice." But he slipped an arm around her shoulders anyway. "I don't often get a chance to just walk. Mostly it's a dash from my place to the office, from the office to the court-house."

"What do you do when you're not dashing?"

"Oh, I go to the movies, window-shop, visit the family. In fact, I was thinking it might be good for Nick to go with me one Sunday. Have some of Mama's home cooking, listen to one of Papa's stories, see how my brothers harass me."

"Just Nick?"

She slanted him a look. "I suppose we could make room for Nick's brother."

"It's been a long time since I—since either of us had a family meal. How about the cop? I can't see him piping us aboard."

"I'll handle Alex." Now that she'd suggested it, her mind began to turn quickly. "You know, Natasha and her family are due to visit in a couple of weeks. Things will be crowded and crazy. It might be the perfect opportunity to toss Nick into your not-so-average-family type of situation. I'll see what I can work out."

"I know I thanked you before, but I don't think I know how to tell you how much I appreciate what you're doing for him."

"The court—"

"That's bilge, Rachel." They reached the steps of her building, and he turned her to face him. "You're not just filing weekly reports or representing a client. You put yourself out for Nick right from the start."

"Okay, so I've got a weak spot for bad boys. Don't let it get around."

"No, what you've got is class, and a good heart." He liked the way she looked in the shadowy light, the vitality that pulsed from her like breath, the snap of energy and embarrassment in her eyes. "It's a tough combination to beat."

She shrugged under his hands. "Now you're going to make me blush, Muldoon, so let's not get sloppy. If things work out the way we want, you can buy me more flowers at the end of the two months. We'll call it square." He let her back up one step, but then held her firm. She was uneasy, but she wasn't surprised. "Listen, it's been nice, but..."

"I don't figure you're going to ask me in."

"No," she said definitely, remembering how her body had reacted to him in a crowded club. "I'm not."

"So I'll just have to take care of this out here."

"Zack..."

"You know I'm not going to let you go without kissing you, Rachel." To tease them both, he skimmed his lips over her jaw. "Especially when I only have to touch you to know all the want's not on my side."

"This is never going to work," she murmured, but her arms were already sliding around him.

"Sure it will. We just put our lips together, and what happens happens."

This time she knew what to expect, and braced. It made no difference at all. The same heat, the same rush, the same power. The same reckless, unrelenting need. Had she said it was too much? No, it wasn't enough. She was afraid she could never get enough. How could she have lived her entire life without knowing what it was to be truly needy?

"I'm not getting involved this way," she murmured against his mouth. "Not with you. Not with anyone."

"Okay. Fine." Ruthlessly, he dragged her head back and plundered. A flash fire erupted between them until he felt singed down to the bone. He all but whimpered when she nipped impatiently at his lower lip. Images began to cartwheel in his head—him scooping her up and carrying her inside, falling with her into a big, soft bed. Making love with her on some white, deserted beach, with the sun beating down on her naked, golden skin. Waves pounding against the shore as she cried out his name.

"Hey, buddy."

The voice behind him was nothing more than an irritating buzzing in his head. Zack would cheerfully have ignored it, but he felt the slight prick of a knife at his back. Keeping Rachel behind him, he turned and looked into the pale, sooty-eyed face of the mugger.

"How about I let you keep the babe, and you hand over your wallet? Hers, too." The mugger turned the knife so that the backwash of the streetlight caught the steel. "And let's make it fast."

Blocking Rachel with his body, Zack reached in his back pocket. He could hear Rachel's unsteady breathing as she unzipped her bag. It wasn't impulse, but instinct. The moment the mugger's eyes shifted, Zack lunged.

With a scream in her throat and the Mace in her hand, Rachel watched them struggle. She saw the knife flash, heard the awful crunch of fist against bone before the blade clattered to the sidewalk. Then the mugger was racing off into the dark, and she and Zack were as alone as they'd been seconds before.

He turned back to her. She noted that he wasn't even breathing hard, and that the gleam in his eyes had only sharpened. "Where were we?"

"You idiot." The words were little more than a whisper as she fought to get them out over the lump of fear in her throat. "Don't you know any better than to jump someone holding a knife? He could have killed you."

"I didn't feel like losing my wallet." He glanced down at the can in her hand. "What's that?"

"Mace." Disgusted by the fact she hadn't even popped off the safety top, she dropped it back in her purse. "I'd have given him a faceful if you hadn't gotten in the way."

"Next time I'll step aside and let you handle it." He frowned down at the trickle of blood on his wrist and swore without much heat. "I guess he nicked me."

She went pale as water. "You're bleeding."

"I thought it was his." Annoyed more than hurt, he poked a finger through the rip in the arm of his sweater. "I got this on Corfu, my last time through. Damn it." Eyes narrowed, he stared down the street, wondering if he had a chance of catching up with the mugger and taking the price of the sweater, if not its sentimental value, out of his hide.

"Let me see." Her fingers trembled as she pushed the sleeve up to examine the long, shallow slash. "Idiot!" she said again, and began to fumble in her purse for her keys. "You'll have to come inside and let me fix it. I can't believe you did something so stupid."

"It was the principle," he began, but she cut him off with a stream of Ukrainian as she stabbed her key at the lock.

"English," he said, pressing a hand to his stomach as it began to knot. "Use English. You don't know what it does to me when you talk in Russian."

"It's not Russian." Snatching his good arm, she pulled him inside. "You were just showing off, that's all. Oh, it's just like a man." Still pulling him, she stalked into the elevator.

"Sorry." He was fighting off a grin, trying to look humble. "I don't know what got into me." He certainly wasn't going to admit he'd had worse scratches shaving.

"Testosterone," she said between her teeth. "You can't help it." She kept her hand on him until she'd gotten them inside her apartment. "Sit," she ordered, and dashed into the bathroom.

He sat, making himself at home by propping his feet on her coffee table. "Maybe I should have a brandy," he called out. "In case I'm going into shock."

She hurried back out with bandages and a small bowl of soapy water. "Do you feel sick?" Scared all over again, she pressed a hand to his brow. "Are you dizzy?"

"Let's see." Always willing to take advantage of an opportunity, he grabbed a fistful of her hair and pulled her mouth to his. "Yeah," he said when he let her go. "You could say I'm feeling a little light-headed."

"Fool." She slapped his hand aside, then sat down to clean the wound. "This could have been serious."

"It was serious," he told her. "I hate having someone poke me in the back with a knife when I'm kissing a woman. Honey, if you don't stop shaking, I'm going to have to get *you* a brandy."

"I'm not shaking—or if I am, it's just because I'm mad." She tossed her hair back and glared at him. "Don't you ever do that again."

"Aye, aye, sir."

To pay him back for the smirk, she dumped iodine over the

wound. When he swore, it was her turn to smile. "Baby," she said accusingly, but then took pity on him and blew the heat away. "Now hold still while I put a bandage on it."

He watched her work. It was very pleasant to feel her fingers on his skin. It seemed only natural that he should lean over to nibble at her ear.

Fire streaked straight up her spine. "Don't." Shifting out of reach, she pulled his sleeve down over the fresh bandage. "We're not going to pick things up now. Not here." Because if they did, she knew there would be no backing off.

"I want you, Rachel." He caught her hand in his before she could stand. "I want to make love with you."

"I know what you want. I have to know what I want."

"Before we were interrupted downstairs, I think that was pretty clear."

"To you, maybe." After a deep breath, she pulled her hand free and stood. "I told you, I don't do things spontaneously. And I certainly don't take a lover on impulse. If I act on the attraction I feel for you, I'll do so with a clear head."

"I don't think I've had a clear head since I laid eyes on you." He stood, as well, but because it suddenly seemed important to both of them he kept his distance. "I realize how the saying goes about guys like me and women in every port. That's not reality—not my reality, anyway. I'm not going to tell you I spent every liberty curled up with a good book, but…"

"It's not my business."

"I'm beginning to think it is, or could be." The look in his eyes kept her from arguing. "I've been on land for two years, and there hasn't been anybody important." He couldn't believe what he was saying, what he felt compelled to say, but the words just tumbled out. "I'll be damned if there's ever been anyone like you in my life."

"I have priorities…" she began. The words sounded weak to her. "And I don't know if I want this kind of complication right now. We have Nick to think about, as well, and I'd rather we just take it slow."

"Take it slow," he repeated. "I can't give you any promises on that. I *can* promise that the first chance I get, when it's just you and me, I'm going to do whatever it takes to shake up those priorities of yours."

She jammed nervous hands in her pockets. "I appreciate the warning, Muldoon. And here's one for you. I don't shake easily."

"Good." His grin flashed before he walked to the door. "Winning's no fun if it's easy. Thanks for the first aid, Counselor. Lock your door." He shut it quietly behind him and decided to walk home.

At this rate, he was never going to get any sleep.

Chapter 5

She wasn't avoiding him. Exactly. She was busy, that was all. Her caseload didn't allow time for her to drop by Zack's bar night after night and chat with the regulars. It wasn't as if she were neglecting her duty. She had slipped in a time or two to talk with Nick in the kitchen. If she'd managed to get in and out without running into Zack, it was merely coincidence.

And a healthy survival instinct.

If she let her answering machine screen her calls at home, it was simply because she didn't want to be disturbed unnecessarily.

Besides, he hadn't called. The jerk.

At least she was making some progress where Nick was concerned. He had called her, twice. Once at her office, and once at home. She found his suggestion that they catch a movie together a hopeful sign. After all, if he spent an evening with her, he wouldn't be hanging out with the Cobras, looking for trouble.

After ninety minutes of car chases, gunplay and the assorted mayhem of the action-adventure he'd chosen, they settled down in a brightly lit pizzeria.

"Okay, Nick, so tell me how it's going." His answer was a shrug, but Rachel gave his arm a squeeze and pressed. "Come on, you've had two weeks to get used to things. How are you feeling about it?"

"It could be worse." He pulled out a cigarette. "It's not so bad having a little change in my pocket, and I guess Rio's not so bad. It's not like he's on my case all the time."

"But Zack is?"

Nick blew out a stream of smoke. He liked to watch her through the haze. It made her look more mysterious, more exotic. "Maybe he's laid off a little. But it's like tonight. I got the night off, right? But he wants to know where I'm going, who I'm going with, when I'll be back. That kind of sh—" He caught himself. "That kind of stuff. I mean, hey, I'm going to be twenty in a couple of months. I don't need a keeper."

"He's a pushy guy," Rachel said, trying to strike a balance between sympathy and sternness. "But he's not only responsible for you in the eyes of the law—he cares about you." Because his answering snort seemed more automatic than sincere, she smiled. "His style's a little rough, but I'd have to say his intentions are good."

"He's going to have to give me some room."

"You're going to have to earn it." She squeezed his hand to take the sting out of her words. "What did you tell him about tonight?"

"I said I had a date, and he should butt out." Nick grinned, pleased when he saw the answering humor in Rachel's eyes. He'd have been very disappointed if he'd realized she was amused at the term *date*. "It's like he's got his life and I got mine. You know what I'm saying?"

"Yes." She drew a deep appreciative breath as their pizza arrived. "And what do you want to do with your life, Nick?"

"I figure I'll take what comes."

"No ambitions?" She took the first bite, watching him. "No dreams?"

Something flickered in his eyes before he lowered them. "I don't want to be serving drinks for a living, that's for sure. Zack can have it." After crushing out his cigarette, he applied himself to the pizza. "And no way I'm going into the damn navy, either. He swung that one by me the other day, and I shot it down big-time."

"Well, you seem to know what you don't want. That's a step."

He reached out to toy with the little silver ring on her finger. "Did you always want to be a lawyer?"

"Pretty much. For a while I wanted to be a ballerina, like my sister. That's when I was five. It only took about three lessons for me to figure out it wasn't all tutus and toe shoes. Then I thought I might be a carpenter, like the men in my family, so I asked for a tool set for my birthday. I think I was eight. I managed to build a pretty fair book rack before I retired." She smiled, and his heart rate accelerated. "It took me a while to come to the conclusion that I couldn't be what Natasha was, or Papa or Mama or anyone else. I had to find my own way." She said it casually, hoping the concept would take root.

"So you went to law school."

"Mmm…" Her eyes brightened as she studied him. "Can you keep a secret?"

"Sure."

"Perry Mason." Laughing at herself, she scooped up another slice. "I was fascinated by those old reruns. You know, how there would always be this murder, and Perry would take the case when his client looked doomed. Lieutenant Tragg would have all this evidence, and Perry would have Della and Paul Drake out looking for clues to prove his client's innocence. Then they'd go to court. Lots of objections, and 'Your Honor, as usual the counsel for the defense is turning this proceeding into a circus.' It would look bad for Perry. He'd be up against that smug-faced DA."

"Hamilton Berger," Nick said, grinning.

"Right. Perry would play it real close to the vest, dropping little hints to Della, but never spilling the whole thing. You just knew he had all the answers, but he would string it out. Then, always at the eleventh hour, he'd get the real murderer up on the witness stand, and he'd just hammer the truth out of him, until the poor slob would crumble like a cookie and confess all."

"Then he'd explain how he'd figured it all out in the epilogue," Nick finished for her. "And you wanted to be Perry Mason."

"You bet," Rachel agreed over a bite of pizza. "By the time I realized it wasn't that black-and-white, and it certainly wasn't that tidy, I was hooked."

"Ray Charles," Nick said, half to himself.

"What?"

"It just made me think how listening to Ray Charles made me want to play the piano."

Rachel rested her chin on her folded hands and tried to ease the door open a little farther. "Do you play?"

"Not really. I used to think it would be pretty cool. Sometimes I'd hang around this music store and fiddle around until they kicked me out." The twinge of embarrassment made him brush the rest aside. "I got over it."

But once she had a purpose, Rachel wasn't easily shaken. "I always wished I'd learned. Tash got my mother a piano a few months ago—when we found out she'd always wanted to play. All those years we were growing up, she never mentioned it. All those years…" Her words trailed off, and then she shook herself back to the matter at hand. "My sister married a musician. Spencer Kimball."

"Kimball?" Nick's eyes widened before he could prevent it. "The composer?"

"You know his work?"

"Yeah." He struggled to keep it cool. A guy couldn't admit he listened to longhair music—unless it was heavy metal. "Some."

Delighted with his reaction, Rachel continued, just as casually. "At one of our visits down to see Tash and her family, we caught Mama at the piano. She got all flustered and kept saying how she was too old to learn, and how foolish it was. But then Spence sat down with her to show her a few chords, and you could see, you could just see, how much she wanted to learn. So on Mother's Day, we worked out this big, elaborate plan to get her out of the house for a few hours. Anyway, when she came back, the piano was in the living room. She cried." Rachel blinked the mist out of her own eyes and sighed. "She takes lessons twice a week now, and she's practicing for her first recital."

"That's cool," Nick murmured, obscurely touched.

"Yeah, it's pretty cool." She smiled at him. "I guess it proves it's never too late to try." When she offered a hand, she wanted him to take it as a gesture of friendship and support. "What do you say we walk off some of this pizza?"

"Yeah." His fingers closed around hers, and Nicholas LeBeck was in heaven.

He was content to listen to her talk, to have her laugh shiver over him. Even the shadows of the girls who had weaved in and out of his life faded away. They were nothing compared to the woman who walked beside him, slim and soft and fragrant.

She listened when he talked. And she was interested in what he had to say. When she smiled up at him, those exotic eyes flashing with humor, his stomach tied itself into slippery knots.

He could have walked with her for hours.

"This is it."

Nick pulled up short, standing in almost the exact spot his brother had a few nights before. As his gaze skimmed over the building at her back, he imagined what it would be like if she asked him in. They'd have coffee, and she'd slip off her shoes and curl those long legs up as they talked.

He'd be careful with her, even gentle. Once his nerves settled.

"I'm glad we could do this," she was saying, already taking out her keys. "I hope if you're feeling restless again, or just need to talk to someone, you'll call me. When I file my report with Judge Beckett tomorrow, I think she'll be pleased with the way things are working out."

"Are you?" His eyes locked on hers as he lifted a hand to her hair. "Pleased with the way things are working out?"

"Sure." A little alarm shrilled in Rachel's head, but she dismissed it as absurd. "I think you've taken a step in the right direction."

"Me too."

The alarm continued to beep as she backed up. "We'll have to do this again soon, but I've got to get in now. I have an early meeting."

"Okay. I'll call you."

She blinked as his hand slipped around to cup her neck. "Ah, Nick…"

His mouth closed over hers, very warm, very firm. Her eyes stayed open, registering shock, as her hand flew up to press against his shoulder. His fingers tensed against her neck, and she had the impression of a very lean, very hard body before she managed to pull away.

"Nick," she said again, groping.

"It's okay." He smiled, tucked her hair behind her ear in a gesture that reminded her vividly of his brother. "I'll be in touch."

He strolled away. No…good Lord, he was swaggering, Rachel thought as she stared after him. With her mind whirling, she let herself in. "Oh, boy," she sighed as she paced the elevator.

What now? What now? How could she have been so stupid? Cursing herself, she stomped off the elevator and toward her apartment. This was great, just great. Here she'd been trying to make friends with Nick, and all the while he'd been thinking...

She didn't want to think about what he'd been thinking.

Without taking off her jacket, she paced the apartment. There had to be a reasonable, diplomatic way to handle this, she told herself. He was only nineteen, he just had a crush, she was overreacting.

Then she remembered those limber fingers on the back of her neck, the firm press of those lips, the smooth and practiced way he'd drawn her against him.

Wrong, Rachel thought, and closed her eyes. She wasn't dealing with a child's puppy love, but with a full-grown man's desire.

Dropping down onto the arm of the couch, she dragged her hands through her hair. She should have seen it coming, she told herself. She should have stopped it before it started. She should have done a lot of things.

After twenty minutes of kicking herself, she snatched up the phone. She might be hip-deep in quicksand, but she wasn't going to sink alone.

"Lower the Boom."

"Let me talk to Muldoon," Rachel snapped, scowling at the sound of laughter and bar chatter that hummed through the receiver. "It's Rachel Stanislaski."

"You got it. Hey, Zack, phone for you. It's the babe."

Babe? Rachel thought, narrowing her eyes. "Babe?" she repeated out loud the moment Zack had answered.

"Hey, sugar, I'm not responsible for the opinions of my bartenders." He took a swallow of mineral water. "So you finally realized you couldn't keep away from me."

"Stuff it, Muldoon. We need to talk. Tonight."

He stopped grinning and shifted the phone. "Is there a problem?"

"Damn right."

"Nick breezed through a couple of minutes ago. He seemed fine when he headed upstairs."

"He's upstairs?" she said, calculating. "Just make sure he stays up there. I'm coming right over." She hung up before he could ask any questions.

It wasn't exactly the way he'd planned it, Zack thought as he mixed a couple of stingers. His strategy had been to lie back for a few days, let Rachel simmer. Until she came to a boil—and came looking for him.

She hadn't sounded lonely or aroused or vulnerable over the phone. She'd sounded mad as a hornet.

He cast his eyes up at the ceiling, picturing the apartment overhead, as he automatically added a twist to a glass of club soda. Obviously it had to do with Nick. Where the hell had the boy been all evening? he wondered.

What kind of trouble had he gotten himself into this time? With half an ear, Zack took an order for two drafts, a margarita on the rocks and a coffee, black. Damned if he'd thought the boy was in trouble, Zack reflected. Nick had looked relaxed, calm, even approachable, when he'd checked in. Zack remembered thinking that the date had been a rousing success. And he'd hoped to be able to ease the girl's name out of his brother—along with a bit more salient information.

He didn't figure Nick needed a course in the birds and bees, but he hoped to drop a few hints about responsibility, protection and respect.

A steady girl, a steady job, a stable home. They all seemed to be coming together. So what the hell...

His thoughts broke off as he looked up. Rachel walked in, cheeks flushed from the chilly evening, eyes snapping. As she crossed the room, she peeled off her jacket to reveal one of those soft sweaters she often wore. This one was the color of a good burgundy, with a wide cowl neck that draped softly over the swell of her breasts. It rode her hips, and under it she wore snug black leggings that showed off those first-class legs.

Zack checked to make sure his tongue wasn't hanging out.

She stopped at the bar only long enough to glare at him. "In your office." Without waiting for a response, she strode off.

"Well, well…" Lola watched Rachel swing Zack's office door open, then shut it behind her with a loud click. "Looks like the lady's got something on her mind."

"Yeah." Zack set the last glass on Lola's tray. All he could think was, there was definitely a fire in the hole. "If Nick comes back down, tell him I'm…tied up."

"You're the boss."

"Right." And he intended to remain the boss. He swung through the bar and, taking one bracing breath, marched into his office.

Rachel had tossed her jacket and purse aside, and was pacing. When the door opened, she stopped, swung her hair back and leveled a killing gaze at him.

"Don't you ever talk to him?" she demanded. "Aren't you making any effort to find out what's going on in his head? What kind of a guardian are you, anyway?"

"What the hell is this?" He threw up his hands in disgust. "I don't see or hear from you in days, then you come stalking in here just so you can yell at me. Just simmer down, Counselor, and remember I'm not some felon on the witness stand."

"Don't tell me to simmer down," she tossed back. It felt good, really good, to assuage her guilt and frustration with a pitched battle. "I'm the one who's going to have to deal with him. And if you were any kind of a brother, you would have known. You could have warned me."

Because his confidence as a brother was still at low tide, he hissed out an oath. Rachel echoed it as he shoved her into a chair. "Just sit down and take it from the top. I assume we're talking about Nick."

"Of course we're talking about Nick." She popped up again, and was pushed right back down. "I don't have anything else to discuss with you."

"We'll bypass that for now. Just what is it I should have known and warned you about?"

"That he'd…he'd…" She blew out a breath, struggling for the proper phrase. "That he'd started to think of me as a woman."

"How the hell is he supposed to think of you? As a tuna?"

"I mean as a *woman,*" she said between her teeth. "Do I have to spell it out?"

His brows shot up, then settled again as he reached for a cigarette. "Don't be stupid, Rachel. He's nineteen. I'm not saying he's blind and wouldn't appreciate the way you look. But he's got a girl. He was out with her tonight."

"You idiot." She sprang up again, and this timeshe thumped a fist on his chest. "He was out with *me* tonight."

"Out with you?" With a frown, Zack studied her. "What for?"

"We went to the movies, had a pizza. I wanted to get him to talk a little—informally—so when he called I said sure."

"One step at a time. Nick called you and asked you out on a date."

"It wasn't a date. I didn't think it was a damn date." Since she didn't see anything handy to kick other than Zack's shin, she stalked a circle around his office again. "It seemed to me if we could develop a relationship— A friendship," she corrected hastily. "It would make things easier all around."

Considering, Zack took a drag of his cigarette. "Sounds reasonable. So you took in a flick and had a pizza. What's the problem? Did he get into a fight, give you a hard time?" He stopped, alarmed. "You didn't run into any of the Cobras?"

"No, no, no…" Incensed, she whirled around the room. "Aren't you listening to me? I said he was thinking about me as a woman…as a date. As a… Oh, boy." She let out a long breath. "He kissed me."

Zack's eyes turned into dark, dangerous slits. "Define *kiss*."

"You know damn well what a kiss is. You smack your lips up against somebody's." She spun away, then back. "I should have seen it coming, but I didn't. Then, before I realized what he was thinking, wham!"

"Wham," Zack repeated, trying to stay calm. He took his own turn around the room, bumping his shoulders against hers. "Okay, listen, I think you're making a big deal out of nothing. He kissed you good-night. It's a gesture. He's just a kid."

"No," Rachel said, and her tone had Zack turning back to her. "He's not."

Temper was clawing to gain freedom. As a result, Zack's voice was deadly calm. "Did he try to—"

"No." Recognizing the signs, she cut him off. "Of course he didn't. He just kissed me. But it was the way… Listen, Zack, I know the difference between a casual kiss good-night between friends and—and, well, a move. And I can tell you Nick has a very smooth move."

"Glad to hear it," Zack said between his teeth.

Suddenly drained, she dropped down onto the corner of his desk. "I don't know what to do."

"I'll straighten him out."

"How?"

"I don't know how," he shot back, crushing out his cigarette. "I'll be damned if I'm going to be competing with my kid brother."

The muttered aside had her narrowing her eyes. "I'm not a trophy, Muldoon."

"I didn't mean—" With a shake of his head, he leaned on the desk beside her. "Look, this throws me off course, okay? I figured Nick was out making time with some pretty little teenager whose daddy would want her home by midnight, and now I find out he's coming on to you. If he wasn't my brother, I'd go knock him around a little."

"Typical," she muttered.

He ignored that and tried to think. "It's probably normal for him to develop—or think he's developed—feelings for you. Don't you think?"

"Maybe." She tilted her head to slant Zack a look. "I don't want to hurt him."

"Me either. You could back off, stay unavailable—the way you've tried to be with me."

"I've been busy." All dignity, she lifted her chin. "And we're not talking about you. In any case, I considered that, but I'm supposed to be his co-guardian. I can't do that long-distance. Besides, he talked to me tonight. He really talked, and relaxed, and showed me a little of what's underneath all that defiance. If I cut him off now, just when he's beginning to open up and trust me, I don't know what damage I might do."

"You can't string him along, Rachel."

"I know that." She wanted to lay her head on Zack's shoulder, just for a minute. She looked down at her hands instead. "I need to find a way to let him know I want to be his friend— just his friend—without crushing his ego."

Zack took her hand, and when she didn't pull it away he twined his fingers in hers. "I'll talk to him. Calmly," he added when Rachel frowned at him.

"Actually, I wanted to dump the whole business in your lap, but the more I think about it, the more I'm sure he'd only resent it coming from you. How can you tell him I'm not interested without letting him know we discussed his feelings behind his back?" She shut her eyes. "And I'm not feeling very good about that, either."

"You had to tell me."

"Yeah, I think I did, just like I think I'm going to have to figure out what to do."

He ran his thumb over her knuckles. "We're in this together, remember?"

"How can I forget? But you and Nick are just getting your balance. This is bound to tilt the scales, Zack. I think it's best if I try to handle it." A smile played around the corners of her mouth. "I guess I should apologize for coming here and jumping on you."

"At least it got you here. We'll handle it." He brought her hand to his lips, enjoying the way her eyes darkened and became cautious. "You let him down easy, and I'll let him take it out on me. After all, I can't blame the kid for trying, when I'm doing the same myself."

"One has nothing to do with the other." She pushed away from the desk, but he continued to hold her hand.

"I'm glad to hear it. Feeling better?"

Her lips quirked. "Fighting always makes me feel better."

"Then, sugar, by the time we're through with each other, you should be feeling like a million bucks. I don't suppose you'd like to hang around for a couple of hours until I can close the bar."

"No." Her heart picked up a beat at the thought. A dark, empty bar, blues on the juke, the world locked outside. "No, I have to go."

"I'm shorthanded tonight, or I'd see you home. I'll put you in a cab."

"I can put myself in a cab."

"Okay. In a minute." He caught her by the hips, lifted her, then set her on the desk. "I've missed you," he murmured, nuzzling her neck.

Without thinking—he certainly had a way of making her stop thinking—she tilted her head to give him more access to her skin. "I've been busy."

"I don't doubt you've been busy." He moved up to nip at her earlobe. "But you've been stubborn. I like that about you, Rachel. Right now I can't think of a damn thing I don't like about you."

This was a mistake. Any minute she'd remember why it was a mistake. She was sure of it. "You just want to talk me into bed."

His lips curved before they came down on hers. "Oh, yeah…" He fisted his hands in her hair, and a deep sound of pleasure came from his throat when she arched against him. "How'm I doing?"

"You're making things very difficult for me."

"Good. That's good." He was very close to pressing her back on the desk and doing all the things he'd fantasized about during those long, dark nights he'd lain alone in bed, thinking of her. And she sighed. The soft, broken sound of it seemed to rip something inside his gut. Grinding out an oath, he buried his face in her hair. "I sure pick my spots," he muttered. "On the sidewalk with a mugger, in my office with a barful of customers outside the door. Every time I'm around you I start acting like a kid in the back seat of a parked car."

She had to concentrate just to breathe. As he continued to hold her, just hold her, she found herself stroking his hair, counting his heartbeats, warming toward him in a way that was entirely different from the flash heat of a moment before.

She'd been right about the quicksand, she realized. And she'd been right about not sinking alone. "We're not kids," she murmured.

"No, we're not." Not quite sure he could trust himself, he drew back, taking both her hands in his. "I know it's moving fast, and I know it's complicated, but I want you. There's no getting around it."

"I knew this would happen if I came here tonight. I came anyway." Muddled, she shook her head. "I don't know what that says about me, or about us. I do know it's not smart, and I'm usually smart. The best thing for me to do is walk out the door and go home."

He tugged on her hands, bringing her off the desk and close to him again. "What are you going to do?"

She wavered, caught on the thin edge between temptation and common sense. Images of what could be swam giddily through her head and left her throat dry. Repercussions…she couldn't quite see them clearly, but she knew they existed. And she was afraid they would be severe indeed.

"I'm going to walk out the door and go home." She let out an unsteady breath when he said nothing. "For now."

She grabbed up her jacket, her purse. When she reached the door, his hand closed over hers on the knob. A quick thrill of panicked excitement raced through her at the thought that he would simply turn the lock.

She wouldn't permit it. Of course she wouldn't permit it.

Would she?

"Sunday" was all he said.

Her scattered thoughts scrambled to make sense of the word. "Sunday?"

"I can shift things around and take the day off. Spend it with me."

Relief. Confusion. Pleasure. She had no idea which emotion was uppermost. "You want to spend Sunday with me."

"Yeah. You know, take in a couple of museums, maybe an art gallery, a walk in the park, have a fancy lunch somewhere. I figure most of the time we've spent together so far's been after dark."

Odd…that hadn't occurred to her before. "I guess it has."

"Why don't we try a Sunday afternoon?"

"I…" She couldn't think of a single reason why not. "All right. Why don't you come by around eleven?"

"I'll be there."

She turned the knob, then glanced back at him. "Museums?" she said on a laugh. "Is this on the level, Muldoon?"

"I happen to appreciate art," he told her, leaning forward to touch his lips to hers in a quiet kiss that rocked her back on her heels. "And beauty."

She slipped out quickly. As she walked up to the corner to hail a cab, it occurred to her she hadn't yet decided how best to handle Nick. And she sure as hell hadn't figured out how to handle Nick's big brother.

Chapter 6

Rachel was cursing when her buzzer sounded promptly at eleven o'clock Sunday morning. Securing an earring, she pressed the intercom. "Muldoon?"

"You sound out of breath, sugar. Should I take that as a compliment?"

"Come on up," she said shortly. "And don't call me sugar."

After snapping off the intercom, she flipped off her three security locks, then gave herself one last look in the mirror. She'd forgotten her second earring. Grumbling, she went on a quick search until she found it lying on the kitchen counter beside her empty coffee cup.

It was her day off, damn it. And she resented having it interrupted for work. Not because she'd been looking forward to spending it with Zack. Particularly. It was just that it had been a long time since she'd had a day to wander through museums and galleries, and— She broke off her silent complaining at the knock on the door.

"Come in, it's open."

"Anxious?" Zack commented as he walked in. Then he lifted a brow and took one long look. She was standing in the center of the room, slim and lovely in a bronze-toned suede jacket and short skirt set off by a slightly mannish silk blouse in a flashy blue. She was barefoot, and he found his mouth watering as he watched her perform the feminine and oddly intimate task of securing a shiny gold knot to her ear. "You look nice."

"Thanks. You, too." No, what he looked was sexy, she thought, damn sexy, in snug black jeans, a midnight-blue sweater, and a bomber jacket in soft black leather. But *nice* would have to do. "Listen, Zack, I tried to catch you before you left the bar. I'm sorry I missed you."

"Is there a problem?" He watched as she wiggled one foot into a bronze-colored pump. By the time she'd wiggled into the second, his palms were sweaty and he'd missed what she'd said. "Sorry, what?"

"I said my boss called, about a half hour ago. I've got an attempted murder I have to deal with."

That cut his fantasy off as quickly as a faceful of ice water. "A what?"

"Attempted murder. Alexi's precinct. I can probably plead down to assault with a deadly weapon, but I have to see him today so I can meet with the DA in the morning." She spread her hands. "I'm really sorry I didn't catch you before you came all the way over."

"No problem. I'll go with you."

"With me?" She liked the idea, a little too much. "You don't want to spoil your day off spending it at a police station."

"I'm taking the day off to be with you," he reminded her, and picked up her coat where she'd tossed it over the back of the couch. "Besides, it won't take all day, will it?"

"No, probably no more than an hour, but—"

"So let's get started." He walked to her, then turned her around so that he could slip the coat slowly on one arm, then the other. Lowering his head, he sniffed at her neck. "Did you spray that stuff on for the felon, or for me?"

She shivered once before cautiously stepping away. "For me." Picking up her briefcase, she held it between them like a shield. "I have to go by the office first. We already have a file on the guy. He's been around."

"Okay." He tugged the briefcase away, took her hand. "Let's go, Counselor."

Alex spotted his sister the moment she walked into the station. Since he wasn't any happier than she to be spending his Sunday morning at work, he immediately brightened. Giving Rachel a hard time always lifted his spirits.

Grinning, he strolled over, a greeting on his lips. When he spotted the man hovering around her, the humor in his eyes turned instantly to suspicion. "Rach."

Still clipping her visitor's badge to her lapel, she glanced up. "Alex. They got you, too, huh?"

"Looks like. Muldoon, isn't it?"

"That's right." Zack returned the steady stare and nodded. "Nice to see you again, Officer."

"Detective," Alex corrected. "I didn't hear anything about LeBeck being pulled in."

"I'm not here about Nick." Rachel recognized Alex's unfriendly, aggressive stance. He'd assumed it with every boy and man she'd dated since she'd turned fifteen. "I'm representing Victor Lomez."

"Now that's real slime." But Alex wasn't nearly as concerned about Rachel's client as he was with the reason the big Irishman was carrying her briefcase. "So, did you two run into each other outside?"

"No, Alexi." Rachel commandeered the coffee he was carrying. Though she knew it was worthless, she shot him a warning glance. "Zack and I had plans for the day."

"What kind of plans?"

"The kind that aren't any of your business." She kissed his cheek as an excuse to get close enough to his ear to whisper, "Knock it off." Leaning back, she smiled at Zack. "Grab a seat, Muldoon, and some of this horrible coffee. Like I said, this shouldn't take too long."

"I got all day," he told her as she walked off to a conference room. He turned back to Alex and said blandly, "So, you want to take me down to interrogation?"

Alex told himself he wasn't particularly amused, and gestured with a jerk of his head. "In here'll do." It pleased him to be behind his desk while Zack sat in the chair used to grill witnesses. "What's the story, Muldoon?"

Casually Zack took out a cigarette. He offered one to Alex and lit up when Alex shook his head. "You want to know what I'm doing with your sister." He blew out a stream of smoke, considering. "If you're any kind of detective, you should be able to figure that one out. She's beautiful, she's smart. She's a soft heart in a tough, sexy shell." Taking another drag, he watched Alex's eyes narrow. "Listen, you want it straight, or do you want me to tell you I'm just interested in her legal services?"

"Watch your step."

Because he understood the need to protect what he loved, Zack leaned forward. "Stanislaski, if you know Rachel, you know *she's* been watching my step. Nobody, but nobody, pushes her into something she doesn't want."

"You figure you got her pegged?"

"Are you kidding?" Zack's smile came quickly, and was friendly enough to make Alex's shoulders relax. "There isn't a man alive who really understands a woman. Especially a smart one." When he saw Alex's eyes shift over his shoulder, Zack glanced around. He saw a short, wiry, oily-skinned man being hauled toward the conference room by a uniformed cop. "Is that the one?"

"Yeah, that's Lomez."

Zack hissed smoke through his teeth and swore roundly. Alex could only agree.

At the conference table, Rachel looked up. Though she'd represented Lomez on his last count of assault, she was going over his file. "Well, Lomez, we meet again."

"You took your sweet time getting here." He dropped down in the seat and ignored the hovering cop. But he was sweating. Bungling the mugging meant he'd missed his connection. He hadn't had a fix in fourteen hours. "You bring me a smoke this time?"

"No. Thank you, Officer." Rachel waited until she was alone with her client, then folded her hands over his paperwork. "Well, you really pulled a prize this time out. The woman you attacked was sixty-three. I called the hospital this morning. You should be relieved to know they've bumped her condition up from critical to fair."

Lomez shrugged, his small black eyes gleaming at Rachel. He couldn't keep his hands still. He began to beat a tattoo on the table with his fingertips as he tapped his feet. His system was skidding to a much wilder rhythm. "Hey, if she'd handed over her purse like I told her, I wouldn't have had to get rough, you know?"

God, he sickened her, Rachel thought, fighting to remember she was a public servant. And Lomez, however revolting, was the public. "Knifing a senior citizen isn't going to win you the key to the city. It's sure as hell going to buy you a lock. Damn it, Lomez, she had twelve dollars."

His mouth was dry, and his skin was cold. "Then it wouldn't have cost her a lot to hand it over. You just get me out. That's your job." And the minute he was back on the street, he'd pressure one of the other Hombres to score for him. "I had to sit in that stinking cell all night."

"You're charged with attempted murder," Rachel said flatly.

Lomez tapped his damp hands against his thighs. Even his bones were screaming. "I didn't kill the old bitch."

Rachel wished she hadn't finished the coffee. At least she could have used it to wash some of the disgust out of her mouth. "You stuck a knife in her, three times. The officer responding pursued you as you fled the scene—with the knife and the victim's purse. They've got you cold, Lomez, and your priors aren't going to make the judge think leniency. Your repertoire includes assault, assault and battery, breaking and entering and two counts of possession."

"I don't need a list. I need bail."

"Odds are slim the DA's going to agree to bail, and if he does, it'll be well out of your range. Now I'm going to do what I can to get him to toss the attempted murder. You plead guilty to—"

"Guilty, my butt."

"It's going to be your butt," she said evenly. "You're not going to walk away from this one, Lomez. No matter how many rabbits I pull out of my hat, you're not going to do short time this turn around. Plead guilty to assault with a deadly weapon, it's likely I can swing the judge for seven to ten."

Sweat popped cold on his brow, on his lips. "The hell with that."

Because she was fast running out of patience, she slapped his file closed. "It won't get any sweeter. You cooperate, and I should be able to keep you from spending the next twenty years in a cage."

He screamed at her, then leaped across the table and struck before she had a chance to dodge. The backhanded blow knocked her out of her chair and onto the floor, where he fell on her. "You get me out!" He squeezed his hands on her throat, too wired even to feel her nails rake his wrist. "You bitch, you get me out or I'll kill you!"

At first she could only see his face, the sick rage in it. Then it faded as red dots swam in front of her eyes. Choking, she struck out, smashing the heel of her hand against the bridge of his nose. His blood splattered over her, but his hands tightened.

A roaring filled her ears, buzzing over the wild curses he shouted at her. The red dots faded to gray as she bucked under him.

Then her windpipe was free and she was sucking air down her burning throat. Someone was calling her name, desperately, and she was being lifted, held tight. She thought she smelled the scent of the sea before she fell limply into it.

Cool fingers on her face. Wonderful. Strong hands clasped hard over hers. Comforting. A sigh before waking. Agony.

Rachel blinked her eyes open. Two faces were looming over hers, equally grim, with eyes that held both rage and fear. Woozily she lifted a hand to Zack's cheek, then Alex's. "I'm all right." Her voice was husky, bruises already forming on her throat.

"Just lie still," Alex murmured in Ukrainian, stroking her head with a hand that still throbbed from where it had connected with Lomez's face. "Can you drink some water?"

She nodded. "I want to sit up." As she focused on the room, she realized she was lying on the faded couch in the captain's office. Murmuring her thanks to her brother, she sipped from the paper cup he held to her lips. "Lomez?"

"In a cage, where he belongs." Fighting off the tremors of reaction, Alex lowered his brow to hers. He continued to speak in Ukrainian, kissing her brow, her cheeks, then sitting back on his heels to hold her hand. "You just relax. An ambulance is on the way."

"I don't need an ambulance." Reading the argument in his eyes, she shook her head. "I don't." She glanced down to see that her blouse was gaping open. It was ruined, of course, she thought in disgust. That and her suede skirt were spotted with blood. "His blood, not mine," she pointed out.

"You broke his slimy low-life nose," Alex snapped.

"I'm glad my self-defense class wasn't wasted." When he began to swear, she caught his hand. "Alexi," she began, her voice low, intense. "Do you know what it is for me to accept that you risk your life every day, every night? Do you know I accept only because I love you so much?"

"Don't turn this around on me," he said furiously. "That bastard nearly killed you. He was so far gone it took three of us to drag him off."

She didn't want to think about that just yet. She couldn't. "I played it wrong."

"You—"

"I did," she insisted. "But the point is, we can't change what we are. I won't change, not even for you. Now cancel the ambulance and do something for me."

He called her a name, a rude one, in their native language. It made her smile. "I'm no more of a horse's ass than you. I need to contact my office and explain. I won't be able to represent Lomez under the circumstances."

"Damn right you won't." It was small satisfaction, but he could hope for little more. Gently he touched his fingers to the bruise on her cheekbone. "He's going down, Rachel. I'll make damn sure he goes down for this, if nothing else. There's nothing you or anyone else can do."

"That's for the courts to decide." She got shakily to her feet. "And you will not call Mama and Papa." When he said nothing, she lifted a brow. "If you do, I'll have to tell them about your last undercover assignment. The one where you went through the second-story window."

"Go home," he said, giving up. "Get some rest." He turned away from her to study Zack. His opinion of him had changed a bit, since Zack had been one of the three who'd hauled Lomez off Rachel. Alex had been a cop long enough to recognize murder in a man's eyes, and it had shone darkly in Zack's. He assumed, correctly, that Zack would have dealt with Lomez himself, regardless of cops, if he hadn't been so busy cradling Rachel in his arms. "You'll get her there." It wasn't a question.

"Count on it." He said nothing else as Alex left them.

Unsteady, and far from sure of herself, Rachel tried to smile. "Some date, huh?"

A muscle jumped in his jaw as he studied her spattered blouse. "Can you walk?"

"Of course I can walk." She hoped. The little seed of annoyance his terse question planted helped her get across the room. "Look, I'm sorry things got messed up this way. You don't have to—"

"Do me a favor," he said as he took her arm and led her through the squad room. "Just shut up."

She obliged him, though she was sorely tempted to tell him how foolish it was to indulge in a cab for the few blocks to her building. It was better if she didn't talk, she realized. Not only did it hurt, but she was also afraid her voice would begin to shake as much as her body wanted to.

She'd be alone in a few minutes, she reminded herself. Then she'd be able to indulge in a nice bout of trembling and weeping if she wanted to. But not in front of Zack. Not in front of anybody.

With a drunk's exaggerated care, she stepped out of the cab and onto the sidewalk. Mild shock, she deduced. It would pass. She'd make it pass.

"Thanks," she began. "I'm sorry…"

"I'm taking you up."

"Look, I've already ruined your morning. It isn't necessary to—" But he was already half carrying her to the door.

"Didn't I tell you to shut up?" He pulled open her briefcase to look for her keys himself. White-hot rage had his fingers fumbling. Didn't she know how pale she was? Couldn't she understand what it did to him inside to hear the way her voice rasped?

He pulled her through the door, into the elevator, and jabbed his finger on the button.

"I don't know what you're so mad about," she muttered, wincing a little as she swallowed. "You lost a couple of hours, sure, but do you know what I paid for this suit? And I've only worn it twice." Tears sprang to her eyes, and she blinked them back furiously as he dragged her down the hall to her apartment. "A PD's salary isn't exactly princely." She rubbed ice-cold hands together as he unlocked her door. "I had to eat yogurt for a month to afford it, even on sale. And I don't even like yogurt."

The first tear spilled out. She dashed it away as she walked inside. "Even if I could get it cleaned, I wouldn't be able to wear it after—" She broke off and made an enormous effort to pull herself back. She was babbling about a suit, for God's sake. Maybe she was losing her mind.

"Okay." She let out what she thought was a slow, careful breath. It hitched as it came out. "You got me home. I appreciate it. Now go away."

He merely tossed her briefcase aside, then tugged the coat from her shoulders. "Sit down, Rachel."

"I don't want to sit down." Another tear. It was too late to stop it. "What I want is to be alone." When her voice broke, she pressed her hands to her face. "Oh, God, leave me alone."

He picked her up, moving to the couch to hold her in his lap. Stroking her back through the tremors, feeling her tears hot and damp on his neck. He forced his hands to be gentle, even as the rage and fear worked inside him. As she curled up against him, he closed his eyes and murmured the useless words that always seemed to comfort.

She cried hard, he realized. But she didn't cry long. She trembled violently, but the trembling was soon controlled. She didn't try to push away. If she had, he wouldn't have allowed it. Perhaps he was comforting her. But holding her, knowing she was safe, and with him, brought him tremendous comfort.

"Damn it." When the worst was over, she let her head lie weakly on his shoulder. "I told you to go away."

"We had a deal, remember? You're spending the day with me." His hands tightened once, convulsively, before he managed to gentle them again. "You scared me, big-time."

"Me, too."

"And if I go away, I'm going to have to go back down there, find a way to get to that son of a bitch, and break him in half."

It was odd how a threat delivered so matter-of-factly could seem twice as deadly as a shout. "Then I guess you'd better hang around until the impulse fades. I'm really all right," she told him, but she left her head cuddled against his shoulder. "This was just reaction."

There was still an ice floe of fury in his gut. That was his reaction, and he'd deal with it later. "It may be his blood, Rachel, but they're your bruises."

Frowning, she touched fingers gingerly to her cheek. "How bad does it look?"

Despite himself, he chuckled. "Lord, I didn't know you were that vain."

She bristled, pulling back far enough to scowl at him. "It has nothing to do with vanity. I have a meeting in the morning, and I don't need all the questions."

He cupped her chin, tilted her head to the side. "Take it from someone who's had his share of bruises, sugar. You're going to get the questions. Now forget about tomorrow." He touched his lips, very gently, to the bruise, and made her heart stutter. "Have you got any tea bags? Any honey?"

"Probably. Why?"

"Since you won't go to the hospital, you'll have to put up with Muldoon first aid." He shifted her from his lap and propped her against the pillows. Their vivid colors only made her appear paler. "Stay."

Since the bout of weeping had tired her, she didn't argue.

When Zack came out of the kitchen five minutes later, tea steaming in the cup in his hands, she was out like a light.

She awakened groggy, her throat on fire. The room was dim and utterly quiet, disorienting her. Pushing herself up on her elbows, she saw that the curtains had been drawn. The bright afghan her mother had crocheted years before had been tucked around her.

Groaning only a little, she tossed it aside and stood up. Steady, she thought with some satisfaction. You couldn't keep a Stanislaski down.

But this one needed about a gallon of water to ease the flames in her throat. Rubbing her eyes, she padded into the kitchen, then let out a shriek that seared her abused throat when she spotted Zack bending over the stove.

"What the hell are you doing? I thought you were gone."

"Nope." He stirred the contents of the pot on the stove before turning to study her. Her color was back, and the glazed look had faded from her eyes. It would take a great deal longer for the bruises to disappear. "I had Rio send over some soup. Do you think you can eat now?"

"I guess." She pressed a hand to her stomach. She was starving, but she wasn't sure how she was going to manage getting anything down her throbbing throat. "What time is it?"

"About three."

She'd slept nearly two hours, she realized, and found the idea of her dozing on the couch while Zack puttered in the kitchen both embarrassing and touching. "You didn't have to hang around."

"You know, your throat would feel better sooner if you didn't talk so much. Go in and sit down."

Since the scent of the soup was making her mouth water, she obliged him. After tugging the curtains open, she sat at the little gateleg table by the window. With some disgust, she shrugged out of her stained jacket and tossed it aside. As soon as she'd indulged herself with some of Rio's soup, she would shower and change.

Obviously Zack had found his way around her kitchen, Rachel mused as he came in carrying bowls and mugs on a tray.

"Thanks." She saw his gaze light briefly on the jacket, heat, then flatten.

"I pawed through some of your records while you were out." It pleased him that he could speak casually when he wanted to break something. Someone. "Mind if I put one on?"

"No, go ahead."

Watching the steam, she stirred her soup while he put an old B.B. King album on her stereo. "And they said we had nothing in common."

Relieved that he wasn't going to bring the incident up, she smiled. "I stole it from Mikhail. He has very eclectic taste in music." Once Zack was seated across from her, she spooned up soup and swallowed gingerly. Sighed. It soothed her fevered throat the way a mother soothes a fretful child. "Wonderful. What's in it?"

"I never ask. Rio never tells."

With a murmur of acknowledgment, she continued to eat. "I'll have to figure out how to bribe him. My mother would love the recipe for this." She switched to tea. After the first sip, her eyes opened wide.

"You didn't have honey," Zack said mildly. "But you had brandy."

She took another, more cautious sip. "It ought to dull the nerve endings."

"That's the idea." Reaching across the table, he took her hand. "Feel any better?"

"Lots. I really am sorry you had your Sunday wrecked."

"Don't make me tell you to shut up again."

She only smiled. "I'm starting to think you're not such a bad guy, Muldoon."

"Maybe I should have brought you soup before."

"The soup helped." She spooned up some more. "But not making me feel like an idiot when I was crying all over you did the trick."

"You had pretty good cause. Being tough's not always the answer."

"It usually works." She sipped more of the brandy-laced tea. "I didn't want to let go in front of Alex. He worries enough." Her lips curved. "You know how it is to have a younger sibling who refuses to see things the way you do."

"You mean so you'd like to rap their head against the wall? Yeah, I know."

"Well, whether Alex likes to believe it or not, I can handle my own life. Nick will, too, when the time comes."

"He's not like that creep today," Zack said softly. "He never could be."

"Of course not." Concerned, she pushed her bowl aside. This time she took his hand. "You mustn't even think like that. Listen to me. For two years I've seen them come in and go out. Some are twisted beyond redemption, like Lomez. Others are desperate and confused, either battered by the streets or part of the streets. Working with them, it gets to the point that if you don't burn out or just scab over, you learn to recognize the nuances. Nick's been hurt, and his self-esteem is next to zero. He turned to a gang because he needed to be part of something, anything. Now he has you. No matter how much he might try to shake you loose, he wants you. He needs you."

"Maybe. If he ever starts to trust me, he might be able to turn a corner." He hadn't realized how much it was weighing on him. "He won't talk to me about my father, about what it was like when I was gone."

"He will, when he's ready."

"The old man wasn't so bad, Rachel. He'd never have made father of the year, but—hell." He let out a breath in disgust. "He was a hard-nosed, hard-drinking Irish son of a bitch who should never have given up the sea. He ran our lives like we were green crewmen on a sinking ship. All shouts and bluster and the back of his hand. We never agreed on a damn thing."

"Families often don't."

"He never got over my mother. He was in the South Pacific when she died."

Which meant Zack would have been alone. A child, alone. Her fingers tightened on his.

"He came back, mad as hell. He was going to make a man out of me. Then Nadine and Nick came along, and I was old enough to go my own way. You could say I abandoned ship. So he tried to make a man—his kind of man—out of Nick."

"You're beating yourself up again over something you can't change. And couldn't have changed."

"I guess I keep remembering how it was that first year I came back. The old man was so fragile. He couldn't remember things, kept wandering out and getting lost. Damn it, I knew Nick was running wild, but I didn't have my legs under me. Having to put the old man in a home, watching him die there, trying to keep the bar going. Nick got lost in the shuffle."

"You found him again."

He started to speak again, then sat back with a sigh. "Hell of a time to be dumping this on you."

"It's all right. I want to help."

"You've already helped. Do you want more soup?"

Subject closed, Rachel realized. She could press, or she could give him room. One favor deserved another, she decided, and smiled. "No, thanks. It really did the job."

He wanted to say more, a whole lot more. He wanted to hold her again, and feel her head resting on his shoulder. He wanted to sit and watch her sleep on the couch again. And if he did any one of those things, he wouldn't make it to the door.

"I'll clear it up and get out of your hair. I imagine you'd like some time alone."

She frowned after him as he walked into the kitchen. She had wanted time alone, hadn't she? So why was she trying to think of ways to stall him, keep him from walking out the door.

"Hey, look." She pushed away from the table to wander in after him. He was already pouring the remaining soup in a container. "It's still early. We might be able to salvage some of the day."

"You need rest."

"I had rest." Feeling awkward, she ran water over the bowls he'd stacked in the sink. "We could probably make at least one museum, or catch a matinee. I don't want to think you spent your whole day off mopping up after me."

"Will you quit worrying about my day off?" Zack slapped the container on a shelf in the refrigerator. "I'm the boss, remember? I can take another."

"Fine." She slammed the water off. "See you around."

"Man, you've got a short fuse." Amused, he put his hands on her shoulders and rubbed. "Don't get yourself worked up, sugar. All in all, I had a very eventful day."

She closed her eyes, feeling those rough fingers through the silk of her blouse. "Any time, Muldoon."

He could smell her hair, and he had to fight the urge to bury his face in it. It wouldn't be possible to stop there. "You going to be all right alone? I could call the cop to come stay with you."

"No. I'm fine." Gripping the edge of the counter, she stared hard at the wall. "Thanks for the first aid."

"My pleasure." Damn it, he was stalling when he should be out the door. Away from her. "Maybe we can have an early dinner one night this week."

She pressed her lips together. The way his hands were rubbing up and down her arms made her want to whimper. "Sure. I'll check my schedule."

He turned her around. He couldn't be sure if she moved into his arms or if he'd pulled her there, but he was holding her. Her lips were parting for his. "I'll call you."

"Okay." Her eyes fluttered closed as the kiss deepened.

"Soon." He felt the breath backing up in his lungs as she molded against him.

"Um-hmm…" As his tongue danced over hers, she gave a quick sigh that caught in the middle.

He tore his mouth away to nibble along her jaw. "One more thing."

"Yes?"

"I'm not leaving."

"I know." Her arms curled around his neck as he lifted her. "It's just chemistry."

"Right." Struggling to remember her bruises, he rained soft kisses over her face.

"Nothing serious." She shuddered, nipping at his neck. "I can't afford to get involved. I have plans."

"Nothing serious," he agreed, blood pounding in his head, in his loins. He jerked open a door and found himself facing a closet. "Where's the damn bedroom?"

"What?" She focused, realized he'd carried her out of the kitchen. "This is it. The couch…" She nipped his ear. "It pulls out. I can…"

"Never mind," he managed, and settled for the rug.

Chapter 7

He ripped her blouse. It wasn't only passion that made him grab and tear. He couldn't bear to see her wear it another moment, to see that vivid blue stained with spots of blood.

Yet the sound of it, of the silk rending beneath his fingers, and her gasp of shocked excitement, spread fire through his gut.

"The first time I saw you…" His breath was already short and fast when he tossed the mangled blouse aside. "From the first minute, I wanted this. Wanted you."

"I know." She reached for him, amazed at how deep and ripe a need could be. "Me, too. It's crazy," she said against his mouth. "Insane." Her skin trembled as he tugged the straps of her chemise from her shoulders to replace them with impatient lips. "Incredible."

Glorying in it, she arched against him when he took her breasts in those greedy, rough-palmed hands. Then his mouth— oh, his mouth, hot and seeking—closed over her to tug and suckle. *Hurry,* was all she could think, *hurry, hurry,* and her nails scraped heedlessly up his sides as she dragged his sweater over his head.

Flesh to flesh was what she wanted. Skin already hot, already damp. The feel of his lips against her thundering heart had her locking her fists in his hair, pressing him closer. She fretted for more. Even as the storm built to a crisis point inside her, she met, she ached, and she demanded.

Her fingers dug into his broad shoulders when he slid down, setting off hundreds of tiny eruptions by streaking hungry, openmouthed kisses down her torso. Then back, quickly back, to drown her in desire with his lips on hers.

He couldn't stop himself from taking. No matter that he had once imagined making slow, tortuously slow, love to her on some huge, soft bed. The desperation of what was overpowered any fantasy of what might have been.

She possessed him. Obsessed him. No mystical siren could have stolen his mind and soul more completely.

A button popped from her skirt as he fought to drag it down her hips. He thought he might go mad if he didn't rip aside all obstacles, if he didn't see her. All of her.

Half-crazed, he peeled off her stockings, and the delicate lace that had secured them. Somewhere through the roaring in his brain he heard her throaty cry when his fingers brushed against her thigh. Fighting to hold back, he knelt between her legs, filling himself with the sight of her, slim and golden and naked, her hair tousled around her face, her eyes dark and heavy.

She reared up, too desperate to wait even another moment. Her mouth closed avidly over his, and her fingers tore at the snap of his jeans.

"Let me," she said in a husky whisper.

"No." He slipped a hand behind her back to support her, and brought the other down to cover the source of heat. "Let me."

The volcano he'd imagined erupted at the first touch. Her body shuddered, quaked. And he watched, impossibly aroused, as her head fell back. Not surrender. Even in his own delirium, he understood that she was not surrendering. It was abandonment, the pure, unleashed quest for pleasure. He gave her more, and gave to himself, stroking that velvet fire, letting his tongue slide over hers in a delicious, matching rhythm.

How could she have known that desire could be dark and deadly? Or that she, always so sure, always so cautious, would throw reason to the winds for more of the dangerous delights? No, not just more. All of them, she thought dizzily. All of him. She would have all. Locking her legs around his hips, she took him into her.

She heard his gasp—the first one ended with a groan. She saw his eyes, cobalt now, and fixed on hers as he shifted to fill her. A sword to the hilt. Then he moved, and she with him. Lost in the whirlwind, she heard nothing but the screaming of her own heart.

"The bigger they are," Rachel murmured some time later.

"Hmm?"

Smiling to herself, she lifted one of Zack's hands, let it go and watched it drop limply to the rug. "The harder they fall." She rolled over and propped her elbows on his chest so that she could study him. If she hadn't known better, she would have thought he was sleeping—or unconscious. His breathing had slowed—somewhat—but his eyes were still closed. It had been some time since he'd moved a single muscle.

"You know, Muldoon, you look like you went ten rounds with the champ."

His lips curved. It was about all he had the energy for. "You pack a hell of a punch, sugar."

As a matter of principle, she bit his shoulder. "Don't call me 'sugar.' But, since you mention it, you didn't do too badly yourself."

He opened one eye. "Too badly? I melted you down to a gooey puddle."

True enough, she admitted, but she wouldn't stroke his ego

by agreeing. "I'll say that you have a certain unrefined style that is strangely appealing." She trailed a fingertip down his chest. "But the simple fact is, I had to carry you." That got his other eye open, she thought with satisfaction. "Not that I minded. I didn't have anything else pressing to do this afternoon."

"You carried me?"

"Metaphorically speaking."

His opinion of that was short and rude. "Want to take me on again? Champ?"

She fluttered her lashes. "Any time. Any place."

"Here and now." She was laughing as he rolled her over, but the laughter ended on a hiss of pain when he bumped her bruised cheek. "Klutz," she said as he jerked back and swore.

"I'm sorry."

"Come on, Zack." She smiled, wanting to lighten the concern in his eyes and bring back the laughter. "I was only kidding."

Ignoring that, he turned her head for a closer look at the mark on her cheek. "I should have put ice on that. He didn't break the skin, but it's…"

She could feel the tension hardening his shoulders. Instead of trying to stroke it away, she pinched him. "Listen, Buster, I come from tough stock. I got worse than that wrestling with my brothers."

"If he ever gets out—"

"Stop it." Very firmly she put her hands on either side of his face. "Don't say anything you might regret. Remember, I'm an officer of the court."

"I wouldn't regret it." He tugged her upward until she was sitting beside him. They were circled, he realized, by the tattered remains of her clothes. "And I don't regret this—except for the unrefined style."

She let out an impatient breath. "Look, if you can't take a joke, learn to."

"Wait until I'm finished before you swipe at me, okay? I

swear, you come on faster than a typhoon." He tucked her hair back and kissed her once, hard. "I wasn't going to stay. Not today. I figured a bout of hot sex wasn't the best encore after you'd been strangled."

"I wasn't—"

He interrupted her. "Close enough. You know that I wanted you however I could get you, Rachel. I sure as hell didn't make a secret of it. But it occurs to me that you were upset and vulnerable and I took advantage of that."

She had to wait nearly a full minute before she could speak. "Don't make me mad at you, Muldoon. And don't insult me."

"All I'm trying to say is… I don't know what the hell I'm trying to say," he muttered, and tried again. "Except—well, maybe I could have pulled that stupid couch out instead of using the floor."

Eyes narrowed, she leaned her face close to his. Her eyes were the color of gold doubloons, and just as exotic. "I like the floor. Get it?"

He was starting to feel better. Zack knew that tending to fragility was out of his league. But this tough, hardheaded woman was just his style. Watching her, he picked up her ruined blouse. "I ripped your clothes off."

"Proud of yourself?"

He tossed it aside. "Yeah. I can wait, if you want to put some more on. Then I can rip them off you again."

She bit the inside of her lip, but didn't quite defeat the smile. "Those were ruined anyway. Next time I'll have to bill you for damages. I'm on a budget."

Chuckling, he flicked her earring with his finger. "I'm crazy about you."

Her heart did a fast skip and shudder. The statement was as romantic as a whispered endearment to her. "Hey, don't get sloppy on me."

"Crazy," he said again, amazed and delighted at the faint

blush that stole into her cheeks. "And did I mention that your body makes me wild?"

She was a great deal more comfortable with that. "No." She tilted her head. "Why don't you?"

"From stem to stern," he said, letting his hand speak more eloquently. "Forward and aft. Port and starboard."

"Oh, God." She gave an exaggerated sigh and shiver. "Salty talk. I just love a man out of uniform." More than willing to be aroused, she nuzzled her lips against his. "Tell me something, sailor."

"You bet."

"Which part is the stern?"

"I'll show you." Very gently, he touched his lips to her bruised throat. "Honey, we better pull that couch out before this gets out of hand again."

"Okay." There was something unspeakably erotic about a callused finger stroking the underside of her breast. "If you want."

Though the idea had merit, the couch seemed entirely too far away. "Or we could do it later. Tell you what, if you'd say something in Ukrainian, I'd forget we were on the floor. And I promise to make you forget it, too."

"Why should I say something in Ukrainian?"

"Because it drives me insane."

She tilted her head back. "Are you putting me on?"

"Uh-uh." His tongue traced a slow, teasing circle on her lips. "Go ahead. Say anything."

After a little sigh, she twined her arms around his neck. Against his ear, she murmured the words, then chuckled when he groaned.

"What did it mean?" he demanded, busying himself by nibbling his way along her shoulder.

"Loosely translated? I said you were a big, pigheaded fool."

"Mmm...are you sure you didn't say how much you wanted my body?"

"No. This is how you say that."

She told him, but by the time she was finished, he was already obliging her.

In the dark, he drew her close. They had managed, finally, to pull out the bed. Now they were tangled in her sheets. The afternoon had become evening, and evening night.

"I'd like to stay," he said quietly.

"I know." It was silly, she thought, to be unhappy that he would go. She'd always jealously prized her nights alone. "But you can't. It's too soon to trust Nick overnight."

"If things were different..." Damn, he hadn't expected it to be so frustrating. "I'd like to take you back home with me. I'd like to have you in my bed tonight, wake up with you tomorrow."

"He's not ready for that, either." She wasn't sure she was ready herself. "Until I have a chance to smooth things out with him, and make him understand, it's probably best if he doesn't know we're..."

What were they? The question ran through both their heads. Neither of them voiced it.

"You're right." The mattress creaked as he shifted. "Rachel, I want to be with you again. It doesn't just have to be in bed." He traced the curve of her cheek. "Or on the floor."

"I want to be with you." She touched her fingers to the back of his hand. "It's good. And that's enough."

"Yeah." He was nearly sure it was. "I can take some time Wednesday. How about an early dinner?"

"I'd like that." They fell into silence again, until she sighed. "You'd better go."

"I know."

"Maybe Sunday you and Nick could come to dinner at my parents'. We talked about it before, remember?"

"That would be good." He kissed her again, and the kiss went on and on. "Just once more."

"Yes." She enfolded him. "Just once more."

Rachel shifted the phone to her other ear, scribbled on a legal pad and stared dubiously at the stack of files on her desk.

"Yes, Mrs. Macetti, I understand. What we need are a couple of good character witnesses for your son. Your priest, perhaps, or a teacher." As she listened to the rapid-fire broken English, she wondered if she could catch the attention of any of her harried co-workers and hope that they'd feel sorry enough for her to bring her a cup of coffee. "I can't tell you that, Mrs. Macetti. Our chances are very good for a suspended sentence and probation, since Carlo wasn't driving. But the fact is, he was riding in a stolen car, and…"

She trailed off, carefully folding the page she'd written on. "Uh-huh. Well, as I explained before, it would be rather difficult to convince anyone he didn't know the car was stolen, since the locks had been sprung and the engine hot-wired." Satisfied with the shape of her paper airplane, she shot it out her door. It was as good as a note in a bottle.

"I'm sure he's a good boy, Mrs. Macetti." Rachel rolled her eyes. "Bad companions, yes. Let's hope that this experience will have him keeping his distance from the Hombres. Mrs. Macetti. Mrs. Macetti," Rachel said, trying to be firm, "I'm doing everything I can. Try to be optimistic, and I'll see you in court next week. No—no, really. I'll call you. Yes, I promise. Goodbye. Yes, absolutely. Goodbye."

Rachel hung up the phone, then dropped her head on her desk. Ten minutes of trying to deal with the frantic mother of six was as exhausting as a full day in court.

"Tough day?"

Lifting her head, Rachel spotted Nick in her doorway. He

had her paper airplane in one hand, and a large paper cup in the other.

"Tough month." Her gaze locked on the steaming cup. "Tell me that's coffee."

"Light, no sugar." He stepped in and offered it. "Your note sounded desperate." As she took the first sip, he grinned. "I was coming down the hall, and it hit me in the chest. Nice form."

"I find they make excellent interoffice memos." Another sip and she felt the caffeine begin to pump through her system. "Since you saved my life, what can I do for you?"

"I was just kicking around. Thought maybe we could grab some lunch."

"I'm sorry, Nick." She gestured to the clutter on her desk. "I'm swamped."

"They don't let you eat?" Because he found he enjoyed seeing her here, entrenched in the business of justice, he eased a hip down on the corner of the desk.

"Oh, they throw us some raw meat now and again." Lord, he was flirting with her, she realized. Rachel gauged the files piled in front of her, calculated how much time she had before her meeting with the DA to bargain on a half a dozen cases. It was going to be close. "Actually, I would like to talk to you, if you have a few minutes."

"I'm on six to two tonight, so I've got plenty of minutes."

"Good." She stood, easing by him to close the door. The moment she turned back, she realized he'd taken that gesture the wrong way. His hands went to her waist. She had a moment to think that in a few years that combination of smooth moves and rough manners would devastate hordes of women. Then she managed to slip aside.

"Nick," she began, then hesitated. "Sit down." When he settled in her battered office chair, she sat behind the desk. "We're going on three weeks. I'd like to know how you're feeling."

"I'm cool."

"What I mean is, when we go back in front of Judge Beckett, it's very likely she'll give you probation—unless you make a big mistake in the meantime."

"I don't plan on mistakes." The chair creaked rustily as he leaned back. "Going to jail isn't high on my list these days."

"Glad to hear it. But she may also ask about your plans. This might be the time to start thinking about that, whether you'd like to make the situation with Zack more permanent."

"Permanent?" He gave a quick laugh. "Hey, I don't know about that. I'll probably want my own place, you know. Zack and me...well, maybe we're getting on a little better, but he cramps my style. Kind of hard to have a lady over when big brother can walk in any time." He flicked his green eyes over her face. "Know what I mean?"

An opening, she thought, and dived in. "Do you have a girl?"

His smile was very male and very attractive. "I'm more interested in women. Women with big brown eyes."

"Nick—"

"You know, when I was walking over here, I started to think how getting busted turned out to be a pretty lucky break." He lifted her hand, brushing his thumb over her knuckles before toying with her fingers. His eyes never left hers. "Otherwise, I wouldn't have needed such a great-looking lawyer."

"Nick, I'm twenty-six." It wasn't what she'd meant to say, or how she'd meant to say it, but he only tilted his head.

"Yeah? So?"

"And I'm your court-appointed guardian."

"Kind of an interesting situation." His smile spread. "It'll be over in about five weeks."

"I'll still be seven years older than you."

"More like six," he said easily. "But who's counting?"

"I am." Frustrated, she started to rise, then realized it would be best if she stayed in the position of authority behind the desk.

"Nick, I like you, very much. And I meant what I said when I told you I wanted to be your friend."

"You can't let the age thing bother you, babe." When he rose, she realized she'd miscalculated by staying behind the desk. When he came around to sit on the edge of it, she was trapped between him and the wall.

"Of course I can. I was in college when you were starting puberty."

"Well, I've finished now." He grinned and traced his finger down her cheek. And his eyes narrowed. "Is that a bruise?"

"I ran into something," she said, and tried again. "The bottom line is, I'm too old for you."

He frowned at the bruise another minute, then lifted his eyes to hers. "I don't think so. Let me put it this way. Do you figure a woman shouldn't get tangled up with a guy six years older than she is?"

"That's entirely different."

"Sexist," he said clucking his tongue. "Here I figured you'd be all for equal rights."

"Of course I am, but—" She broke off with a hiss of breath.

"Gotcha."

"Regardless of age—" since that wasn't working, she thought "—I'm your guardian, and it would be wrong, certainly unethical, for me to encourage or agree to anything beyond that. I care about what happens to you, and if I've given you the impression that I'm interested in anything more than friendship, I'm sorry."

He considered. "I guess you take your work pretty seriously."

"Yes, I do."

"I can dig it. No pressure, right?"

Relief made her sigh. "Right." She rose, giving his hand a quick squeeze. "You're all right, Nick."

"You too." They both looked around when her phone began to shrill. "I'll let you get back to serving justice," he told her, then had her mouth dropping open as he brought her hand to his lips. "Five weeks isn't so long to wait."

"But—"

"Catch you later." He strolled out, leaving Rachel wondering if it would help to beat her head against the wall.

Nick was feeling great. He had the whole day ahead of him, money in his pocket, and a gorgeous woman planted in his heart. He had to grin when he thought about the way he'd flustered her. He hadn't realized it could be so satisfying to make a woman nervous.

And imagine a knockout like Rachel worrying about her age. Shaking his head, he jogged down to the subway. Maybe he'd thought she was a couple of years younger, but it didn't matter one way or the other. Everything about her was dead-on perfect.

He wondered how Zack would react when he saw Nick LeBeck strut into the bar one night with Rachel on his arm. He didn't imagine Zack would think of him as a kid when everybody saw he'd bagged a babe like Rachel Stanislaski.

Wrong, he told himself as he hopped on a car that would take him to Times Square. That was no way to talk about a classy lady. What they'd have was a relationship. As the subway car rattled and squeaked, he occupied himself by daydreaming about what they'd do together.

There would be dinners and long walks, quiet talks. They'd go listen to music, and dance. Now and again they'd have a lazy evening snuggled up in front of the television.

Nick considered it a sign of his commitment that he hadn't put sex at the top of the list.

On top of the world, he came out into the bustle and blare of Times Square and decided to use some of his loose change for a little pinball.

The arcade was noisy, and there was a loud rock backbeat

blasting over the metallic sounds of beeps and buzzes. Though he'd missed the freedom of being able to breeze into an arcade any time he chose, he had to admit it felt good to be able to spend money he'd earned.

No sneaking around, no vague sense of guilt. Maybe he didn't have the gang to hang around with, but he didn't feel nearly as lonely as he'd thought he would.

It wasn't something he'd admit out loud, but he was getting a kick out of working in the kitchen with Rio. The big cook had plenty of stories, many of them about Zack. When he listened to them, Nick almost felt as though he'd been part of it.

Of course, he hadn't, Nick reminded himself, using expert body English to play out the ball. There was no possible way he could explain how miserable he'd been when Zack shipped out. Then he'd had no one again. His mother had tried, he supposed, but she'd always been more shadow than substance in his life.

It had taken all her energy to put food on the table and clothes on his back. She'd had little of herself left over once that was done.

Then there had been Zack.

Nick could still remember the first time he'd seen his stepbrother. In the kitchen of the bar. Zack had been sitting at the counter, gobbling potato chips. He'd been tall and dark, with an easy grin and a casually generous manner. Once Nick had gotten up the courage to follow him around, Zack hadn't tried to shake him off.

It was Zack who'd brought him into an arcade the first time, propped him up and shown him how to make the silver balls dance.

It was Zack who'd taken him to the Macy's parade. Zack who had patiently taught him to tie his shoes. Zack who'd clobbered him when he chased a ball into traffic.

And it was Zack who, barely a year later, had left him with

a sick mother and an overbearing stepfather. Postcards and sou-
venirs hadn't filled the hole.

Maybe Zack wanted to make up for it, Nick thought with
a shrug, then swore when the ball slipped by the flipper. And
maybe, deep down, Nick wanted to let him.

"Hey, LeBeck." The slap on his shoulder nearly made Nick
lose the next ball. "Where you been hiding?"

"I've been around." Nick sliced a quick glance at Cash before concentrating on his game. He wondered if Cash would
make any comment about him not wearing his Cobra jacket.

"Yeah? Thought you'd dropped down the sewer." Cash
leaned against the machine, as always, appreciating Nick's skill.
"Haven't lost your touch."

"I've got great hands. Ask the babes."

Cash snorted and lighted a crushed cigarette. His last. Since
Reece had copped less than ten cents on the dollar for the stolen
merchandise, Cash's share was long gone. "Man, the chicks see
that ugly face and you never get a chance to use your hands."

"You've got your butt mixed up with my face." Nick eased
back on his heels, satisfied with his score and the free game
he'd finessed. "Want to take this one?"

"Sure." After stepping behind the machine, Cash began to
bull his way through the game. "You still hanging with your
stepbrother?"

"Yeah, got a few more weeks before we go back to court."

Cash lost the first ball and pumped up another. "You got a
tough break, Nick. I mean that, man. I feel real bad about the
way it went down."

"Right."

"No, man. Really." In his sincerity, Cash lost track of the ball
and let it slip away. "We screwed up, and you took the heat."

Slightly mollified, Nick shrugged. "I can handle it."

"Still sucks. But hey, it can't be so bad working a bar. Plenty
of juice, right?"

Nick smiled. He wasn't about to admit he'd downed no more than two beers in the past three weeks. And if Zack got wind of that much, there'd be hell to pay. "You got it, bro."

"I guess the place does okay, right? I mean, it's popular and all."

"Does okay."

"Must be plenty of sexy ladies dropping in, looking for action."

The neighborhood bar ran more to blue-collar workers and families, but Nick played along. "The place is lousy with them. It's pick and choose."

Cash laughed appreciatively even as he blew his last ball. "Want to go doubles?"

"Why not?" Nick dug in his pocket for more tokens. "So what's going on with the gang?"

"The usual. T.J.'s old man kicked him out, so he's bunking with me. Jerk snores like a jackhammer."

"Man, don't I know it. I put up with him a couple of nights last summer."

"Couple of the Hombres crossed over to our turf. We handled them."

Nick knew that meant fists, maybe chains and bottles. Occasionally blades. It was odd, he thought, but all that seemed so distant to him, distant and useless. "Yeah, well…" was all he could think of to say.

"Some people never learn, you know. Got a cigarette? I'm tapped."

"Yeah, top pocket." Nick racked up another ten thousand points while Cash lit up.

"Hey, I got a connection at this strip joint downtown. Could get you in."

"Yeah?" Nick answered absently as he sent the ball bouncing.

"Sure. I'd like to make that other business up to you. Maybe I'll drop by one night and we'll hang out."

"Forget it."

"No, man, really. I'll spring for the brew, too. Don't tell me slippery LeBeck can't slip out."

"I can get out when I want. Just walk out the kitchen."

"Around the back?"

"Yeah. Zack's usually tied up at the bar until three. Two on Sundays. I can get around Rio when I want to, or take the fire escape."

"You got a place upstairs?"

"Mmm… Your ball."

When they switched positions, Cash continued to question him, making it casual. The cash went in a safe in the office. Business usually peaked by one on Wednesdays. There were three ways in. The front door, the back and through the upstairs apartment.

By the time Nick had trounced him three games in a row, Cash had all he needed. He made his excuses and wandered out to meet with Reece.

He didn't feel good about conning Nick. But he *was* a Cobra.

Chapter 8

Zack stepped out of the shower, grateful the endless afternoon was over. He didn't mind paperwork. Or at least he didn't hate it. Well, the truth was, he hated it, but accepted that it was a necessary evil.

He'd made his orders, paid his invoices and tallied his end-of-the-month figures. Well, maybe he was a week or so behind the end of the month, but still, he figured he was doing pretty well.

And so was the business.

It looked as though he'd finally pulled it out of the hole his father's illness and the resulting expenses had dug. Paying off the loan he'd taken to square things for Nick would pinch a little, but in another year he'd be able to do more than look at boats in catalogs.

He wondered how Rachel would feel about taking a month off and sailing down to the Caribbean. He liked to imagine her lying out on the polished deck, wearing some excuse for a bikini. He liked the idea of watching her hair blow around her face when it caught the wind.

Of course, he'd have to take some time to check the boat out, test the rigging. He thought he'd be able to talk Nick into a day sail, or maybe a weekend. He wanted the two of them to be able to get away—away from the bar, the city, and the memories that tied them to both.

With a towel slung around his hips, he walked to the bedroom to dress. He hoped, sincerely, that the Sunday dinner at the Stanislaskis' would crack the kid's defenses a little more. Whenever Rachel spoke about her family, it made him think of what they—of what Nick—had missed.

All the kid needed was a little time to see how things could be. They were nearly halfway through the trial run, and apart from a few skirmishes, it had gone smoothly enough.

He had Rachel to thank for that, Zack thought as he tugged on a pair of jeans. He had Rachel to thank for a lot of things. Not only had she given him a second chance with Nick, but she'd added something incredible to his life. Something he'd never expected to have. Something he'd—

On a long breath, he stared hard into the mirror. When a man was going down for the third time, he recognized the signs.

Don't be an idiot, Muldoon, he told his reflection. Keep it steady as she goes. The lady wants to keep it simple, and so do you.

It wouldn't do to forget it.

"Hot date?" Feigning disinterest, Nick slouched against the doorjamb. He'd been passing and had caught the way Zack was staring blindly into the mirror.

"Huh? Yeah, I guess you could say that." Zack dragged a hand through his wet hair and scattered drops of water. "I didn't know you were back."

"I'm on at six." For reasons Nick couldn't understand, he was swamped by the memory of the times he'd stood in the bathroom watching Zack shave. How it had made him feel when

Zack slapped shaving cream on his face. "Rio's got beef stew on special tonight. Too bad you'll miss it."

Zack grabbed a shirt. "You take my share or Rio'll make me eat it for breakfast."

Nick grinned, then remembered himself and smirked. "You take a lot of crap from him."

"He's bigger than I am."

"Yeah, right."

Watching Nick in the mirror, Zack buttoned his shirt. "He likes to think he's looking out for me. It doesn't cost me anything to let him. He ever tell you about how he got that scar down the side of his face?"

"He said something about a broken bottle and a drunk marine."

"The drunk marine was going for my throat with that broken bottle. Rio got in his way. The way I see it, I owe Rio a lot more than putting up with his nagging." Tucking in his shirt, Zack turned, grinned. "And you're getting paid to put up with it."

"He's okay." Nick would have liked to ask more, like why a drunk marine had wanted to slice Zack's throat, but he was afraid Zack would just shrug it off. "Listen, if you get lucky tonight, don't worry about coming back."

Zack's fingers paused on the snap of his jeans. Tucking his tongue in his cheek, he wondered how Rachel would take his brother's turn of phrase. "Thanks for the thought, but I'll be home."

"For bed check," Nick muttered.

"Call it what you want," Zack shot back, then bit off an oath. Come hell or high water, they were going to get through one conversation without raised voices. "Listen, I don't figure you're going to climb out the window. Hell, you could do that while I'm here. It could be the lady won't want company overnight."

Mollified, Nick hooked his thumbs in his pockets. "They didn't teach you a hell of a lot in the navy, did they, bro?"

In an old gesture they'd both nearly forgotten, Zack rubbed his knuckles over Nick's head. "Kiss my butt." With his jacket slung over his shoulder, he headed out. "And don't wait up. I'm feeling lucky."

Long after the door shut behind Zack, Nick was still grinning.

Rachel was just unlocking the outside door when Zack strode up behind her. "Good timing," he said, and pressed a kiss to the back of her neck.

"For you, maybe. Everything ran over today. I was hoping to get back and soak in the tub before you got here."

"You want to soak?" The minute they were in the elevator, he had her against the wall. "Go ahead. I'll scrub your back."

"What a guy." When his mouth closed over hers, it hurt, somewhere deep, reminding her just how much she'd wanted to be with him again. "You smell good."

"Must be these." He pulled a paper cone filled with roses from behind his back.

Her heart wanted to sigh, but she resisted. "Another bribe?" She couldn't resist the urge to bury her face in the blooms.

"There was a guy selling them a couple of blocks down. He looked like he could use a couple bucks."

"Softy." She handed him her keys so that he could unlock her door and she could continue to sniff the roses.

"Keep it to yourself."

"It'll cost you." After kicking the door closed with her foot, she dumped her briefcase and laid the spray of roses on a table. "Pay up, Muldoon," she demanded, tossing her arms around him.

There was such joy in it. Heat, yes. And the sweet, sharp ache of need. But the joy was so unexpected, so fast and full, that she laughed against his mouth as he twirled her around.

"I missed you." He continued to hold her, inches off the floor.

"Oh, yeah?" With her hands linked comfortably around his neck, she smiled. "Maybe I missed you, too. Some. How long are you going to hold me up here?"

"This way I can look right at you. You're beautiful, Rachel."

It wasn't the words so much as the way he said them that brought a lump to her throat. "You don't have to soften me up."

"I don't know how to tell you how beautiful—except that sometimes when I look at you, I remember how the sea looks, right at sunrise, when all that color spills out of the sky, kind of seeps over the horizon and falls into the water. Just for a few minutes, everything's so vivid, so… I don't know, special. When I look at you, it's like that."

Her eyes had darkened with an emotion she couldn't begin to analyze. All she could do was rest her cheek against his. "Zack." His name was a sigh, and she knew she would cry any minute if she didn't lighten the mood. "Roses and poetry, all in one day. I don't know what to say to you."

Enchanted, he buried his face in her hair. "That's a first."

"We're not going to get—"

"Sloppy," he finished for her, laughing. "Us? Are you kidding?" But when he sat on the couch, he kept her cuddled in his lap. "Let me see that bruise."

"It's nothing," she said, even as he tilted her head for a closer inspection. "The worst of it was that the word got out and I had to deal with all this sympathy and advice. If those cops had kept their mouths shut, I could have said I'd walked into a door."

"Take off the jacket and sweater."

She arched a brow. "You're such a romantic, Muldoon."

"Can it. I want to see your neck."

"It's fine."

"Which is why you're wearing a sweater that comes up to your chin."

"It's very fashionable."

"Peel it off, babe, or I'll have to do it for you."

Her eyes lit. "Ah, threatening a public official." After kicking off her shoes, she tossed up her chin. "Try it, Buster. Let's see how tough you are."

She didn't put up much of a fight, but the initial wrestling was enough to arouse them both. By the time he had her pinned to the couch, her arms over her head and her wrists cuffed in his hand, they were both breathing hard.

"I took it easy on you," she told him.

"I could see that." Her jacket was crumpled on the floor beside them. Smiling, Zack began to inch her sweater upward, letting his fingers skim over the silky material beneath.

Her breath caught, and released unsteadily. "That's not my neck," she managed as his hand cupped and molded her breast.

"Just checking." Watching her, always watching her, he teased the nipple until it was hot and hard. "You're quick to the touch, Rachel."

His touch, she thought, trembling. Only his.

Slowly, determined to savor every moment, he slipped the sweater up. He released her wrists to tug it off, then clasped them again.

"Zack."

He ignored her flexing hands. "My turn at the helm," he said quietly. "I told you once I wanted to drive you crazy. Do you remember?"

He was. He already was. "I want to touch you."

"You will." He skimmed a fingertip over her neck first, carefully studying the bruises. They were fading to yellow. "I don't want to see you hurt again." Gently he lowered his head to trail a necklace of kisses over the marks. "Not ever again."

"It doesn't hurt." Her pulse jackhammered under his nuzzling lips. "I don't need to be seduced."

"Yes, you do. But you're afraid to be, which makes the whole idea damn near irresistible. You're just going to have to trust me." He shifted so that he could unzip her skirt and slip it off.

"I have places to take you." His mouth lowered to hers, rubbing, then nibbling. "Strange, wonderful places." Then diving deep.

The journey wasn't calm, but she had no choice but to go where he took her. This eagerness for pleasure, this immediacy of need, was still so new that she had no defense against it. His hand slid over her, lingering here, exploiting there, while his mouth devoured hers with a relentless hunger.

No escape, she thought desperately as he brought her close, painfully close, to that first tumultuous release. She was trapped in him, utterly lost in a tangled maze of sensations. She writhed beneath his hand, too steeped in her own needs to know how deliciously wanton her movements were.

"I didn't have time to appreciate these last time." Zack trailed his fingers up the sheer stocking to the pristine white garter. She would think them practical, he knew. He thought them erotic.

With an expert flick of his fingers that had her moaning, he released one stocking, then the other, before tormenting them both by peeling them, inch by lazy inch, down her legs.

He had to kneel on the floor to taste her calves, the backs of her knees, the glorious satin skin of her thighs. She cried out when he slid his tongue beneath her panties to sample the hot, sensitive flesh underneath. Fighting impatience, he tugged them off to give himself the freedom to taste more of her.

As the first wave swamped her, she arched like a bow, leaping into Ukrainian when the aftershocks shuddered through her. Freed, her hands groped for him until they were struggling together to strip off his clothes. Heat to heat, she pressed against him, overbalancing him, until she straddled him and her mouth could merge hotly with his.

"Now" was all he said, all he *could* say, as he gripped her hips.

"I really did mean to take you out," Zack said when they lay on the couch in a tangle of limbs.

"I bet."

He smiled, recognized the sleepy satisfaction in her voice. "Really. We can get dressed and try again."

With a half laugh, she pressed her lips to his chest. His heart was still thundering. "You're not going anywhere, Muldoon. Not till I'm finished with you."

"If you insist."

"That's what free delivery's for. How about Chinese?"

"You're on. Who's going to get up and call?"

She shifted for the pleasure of rubbing her cheek against his skin. "We'll flip for it."

He lost, and Rachel took advantage of the moment to grab a quick, bracing shower. When she came back, her hair damp and curly, a plain white terry-cloth robe skimming her knees, he was pouring them both a glass of wine.

"I think I'm repeating myself," he said, offering her a glass. "But you sure look good wet."

He'd tugged on his jeans, but hadn't bothered with his shirt. Rachel trailed a finger down his chest. "You could have joined me."

"We'd have missed the delivery boy."

"Since he's bringing egg rolls, you have a point." She moved to the kitchen to get some plates, then set them on the table by the window. "And I do have to refuel. I only had time for a candy bar at lunch." Because the mood seemed right, she lit candles. "Nick dropped by the office."

"Oh."

"I wish I had had more time...." She touched match to wick and watched the candle flare. "He caught me between phone calls and before a plea-bargaining meeting."

He watched her move around the room in her practical terry-cloth robe, turning the light into romance with her candles. He wondered if she realized how compelling that contrast was. "You don't have to explain to me, Rachel."

She shook out a match, struck another. It wasn't that she was superstitious, but there was no use taking chances with three on a match. "I have to explain to myself. He wanted to go to lunch, and I just couldn't swing it. I did talk to him about... the situation."

"About the fact that he's fallen in lust with you."

"I wouldn't put it like that." She sighed heavily when the intercom buzzed. After flipping it on, she released the security lock for the delivery boy. "He's simply misinterpreted gratitude and friendship."

Zack took one long look at her in the candleglow. "Whatever you say."

Disgusted, she went back to the table and sat. "You're buying, Muldoon."

He took out his wallet agreeably. He had the tab and the tip ready when the delivery arrived. After carrying three bulging bags to the table, he unpacked the little white cartons. In moments the air was filled with exotic aromas.

"Do you want to tell me the rest?"

"Well..." Rachel wound some noodles around her chopsticks. "I started off explaining the difference in our ages. Umm..." She chewed appreciatively. "He didn't buy it," she said over a mouthful. "He had a very convincing argument, and since I couldn't override it, I changed tactics."

"I've seen you in court," he reminded her.

"I explained the ethics of my being his guardian, and how it wasn't possible for us to go beyond those terms." Thoughtful, she scooped up some sweet and sour pork. "He seemed to understand that."

"Good."

"I thought it was. I mean, he agreed with me. He was very mature about it. Then, when he was leaving, he said how it wasn't so hard to wait five more weeks."

Zack said nothing for a moment. Then, with a half laugh, he picked up his wine. "You've got to give the kid credit."

"Zack, this is serious."

"I know. I know. It's sticky for both of us, but you have to admire the way he turned it around on you."

"I told you he was smooth." After peeking in another carton, she nibbled on some chilled chicken and bean sprouts. "Don't you know any nice teenage girls you could nudge in his direction?"

"Lola's got one," Zack said, considering. "I think she's sixteen."

"Lola has a teenager?"

"Three of them. She likes to say she started young so that she could lose her mind before she turned forty. I can feel her out about it."

"It couldn't hurt. I'm going to try again, though I'm hoping the feeling will pass in another week or two."

"I wouldn't count on it." Reaching across the table, he linked his fingers with hers. "You stick in a man's mind."

"Does that mean you're thinking of me when you're mixing drinks and flirting with the customers?"

"I never flirt with Pete."

She laughed. "I was thinking more of those two 'babes' who drop in. The blonde and the redhead. They always order stingers."

"You are observant, Counselor."

"The redhead's got her big green eyes on you."

"They're blue."

"Aha!"

He shook his head, amazed he'd fallen so snugly into the trap. "It pays to know your regulars. Besides, I like brown eyes—especially when they lean toward gold."

She let his lips brush hers. "Too late." With her head close to his, she laughed again. "It's all right, Muldoon. I can always borrow Rio's meat cleaver if you notice more than her eyes."

"Then I'm safe. I've never paid any attention to those cute little freckles over her nose. Or that sexy dimple in her chin."

Eyes narrowed, Rachel bit his lip. "Get any lower, and you'll be in deep water."

"That's okay. I'm a strong swimmer."

Hours later, when Zack crawled into a cold, empty bed, he warmed himself by thinking of it. It had been nice, just nice, to laugh together over the cardboard boxes and chopsticks. They'd sampled each other's choices, talking while the candles had burned low. Not about Nick, not about work, but about dozens of other things.

Then they'd made love again, slowly, sweetly, while the night grew late around them.

He'd had to leave her. He had responsibilities. But as he settled his body toward sleep, he let his mind wander, imagining what it could be like.

Waking up with her. Feeling her stretch against him as the alarm rang. Watching her. Smiling to himself as she hurried around the apartment, getting dressed for work.

She'd be wearing one of those trim suits while they stood in the kitchen sharing coffee, talking over their plans for the day.

Sometimes they'd steal a quick lunch together, because they both hated to have a whole day pass without touching. When he could, he'd slip away from work so that he could walk home with her in the evening. When he couldn't, he'd look forward to seeing her come through the door, slide onto a stool at the bar, where she'd eat Rio's chili and flirt with him.

Then they would go home together.

One balmy weekend they would set sail together. He'd teach her how to man the tiller. They'd glide out over blue water, with the sails billowing....

The waves were high as mountains, rearing up to slap viciously at the ship. The bellow of the wind was like a thousand women screaming. Burying a fear that he knew could be as destructive as the gale, he scrambled over the pitching deck, clinging to the slippery rail as he shouted orders.

The rain was lashing his face like a whip, blinding him. His red-rimmed eyes stung from the salt water. He knew the boat was out there—radar had it—but all he could see was wall after wall of deadly water.

The next wave swamped the deck, sucking at him. Lightning cracked the sky like a bullet through glass. The ship heeled. He saw the seaman tumble, heard the shout as his hands scrambled on the deck for purchase. Zack leaped, snagging a sleeve, then a wrist.

A line. For God's sake, get me a line.

And he was dragging the dead weight back from the rail.

Wind and water. Wind and water.

There, in a flash of lightning, was the disabled boat. Lower the tow line. Make it fast. As the lightning stuttered against the dark, he could see three figures. They'd lashed themselves on—a man to the wheel, a woman behind him, a young girl to the mast.

They were fighting, valiantly, but a forty-foot boat was no match for the fury of a hurricane at sea. It was impossible to send out a launch. He had to hope one of them could hold the boat steady while another secured the tow.

Signal lights flashed instructions through the storm.

It happened fast. Another spear of lightning, and the mast cracked, falling like a tree under an ax. Horrified, he watched the young girl being dragged with it into the swirling water.

No time to think. Pure instinct had Zack grabbing a flotation device and diving into the face of the storm.

Falling, falling, endlessly, while the gale tumbled his body like dice in a gambler's hand. Black, pitch-black, then the white flare of lightning. Hitting a wall of water that felt like stone. Having it close relentlessly over your head. Like death.

Zack awoke gasping for air and choking against the nightmare water. Sweat had soaked through to the sheets, making him shiver in the chill. With a groan, he let his head fall back and waited for the first grinding ache of nausea to pass.

The room tilted once as he staggered to his feet. From past experience, Zack knew to close his eyes until it righted again. Moving through the dark, he went into the bathroom to splash the cold sweat from his face.

"Hey, you okay?" Nick was hovering in the doorway. "You sick or something?"

"No." Zack cupped a hand near the faucet, catching enough water to ease his dry throat. "Go back to bed."

Nick hesitated, studying Zack's pale face. "You look sick."

"Damn it, I said I'm fine. Beat it."

Nick's eyes darkened with angry hurt before he swung away.

"Hey, wait. Sorry." Zack let out a long breath. "Nightmare. Puts me in a lousy mood."

"You had a nightmare?"

"That's what I said." Embarrassed, Zack snatched up a towel to dry off.

It was hard for Nick to imagine big, bad Zack having a nightmare, or anything else that would make him sweat and go pale. "Uh, you want a drink?"

"Yeah." Steadier now, Zack lowered the towel. "There's some of the old man's whiskey in the kitchen."

After a moment, Zack followed Nick out. He sat on the arm of a chair while Nick splashed three fingers of whiskey into a tumbler. He took it, swallowed, then hissed. "I can't figure out how he had a liver left at the end."

Nick wished he'd pulled pants over his briefs. At least he'd have had pockets to dip his hands into. "I think when he started to forget stuff, it helped him to blame it on the whiskey instead of—you know."

"Alzheimer's. Yeah." Zack took another swallow, let it lie

on his tongue a moment so that his throat could get used to the idea.

"I heard you thrashing around in there. Sounded pretty bad."

"It was pretty bad." Zack tilted the glass, watched the whiskey lap this way and that. "Hurricane. One mean bitch. I never understood why they started naming them after guys, too. Take it from me, a hurricane's all woman." He let his head fall back again, let his eyes close. "It's been nearly three years, and I haven't been able to shake this lady."

"You want to—" Nick cut himself off. "That should help you sleep."

Zack knew what Nick had wanted to ask. And he did want to. It might be best for both of them if they talked it through. "We were off of Bermuda when we got the distress call. We were the closest ship, and the captain had to make a choice. We turned back into the hurricane. Three civilians in a pleasure boat. They'd been thrown off course and hadn't been able to make it to shore before the storm hit."

Saying nothing, Nick sat on the arm of the couch so that he was facing his brother.

"Seventy-five knot winds, and the seas—they must have been forty feet. I've been through a hurricane after it's made landfall. It can be bad, real bad, but it's nothing like it is when it's at sea. You don't know scared until you see something like that. Hear something like that. The lieutenant took a rap on the head, it put him out. We came close to losing some of the crew over the side. Sometimes it was black, so black you couldn't see your own hands—but you could see that water rising up. Then the lightning would hit, and blind you."

"How were you supposed to find them in all that?"

"We had them on radar. The quartermaster could've slipped that ship through the crack of dawn. He was good. We spotted them, thirty degrees off to starboard. They'd tied the kid—little girl—to the main mast. The man and woman were fighting

to keep it afloat, but they were taking on water fast. We had
time. I remember thinking we could pull it off. Then the mast
cracked. I thought I heard the girl scream, but it was probably
the wind, because she went under pretty quick. So I went in."

"You went in?" Nick repeated, wide-eyed. "You jumped
in the water?"

"I was over the side before I thought about it. I wasn't being
a hero, I just didn't think. Believe me, if I had..." He let the
words trail off, then swallowed the rest of the whiskey. "It
was like jumping off a skyscraper. You don't think you're ever
going to stop falling. It was end over end, forever, giving you
plenty of time to realize you've just killed yourself. It was stupid—if the wind had been wrong it would have just smashed
me against the side of the ship. But I was lucky, and it tossed
me toward the boat. Then I hit. God, it was like ramming full-
length into concrete."

He hadn't known until later that he'd snapped his collarbone
and dislocated his left shoulder.

"I couldn't get my bearings. The water kept heaving me
around, sucking me down. It was so black, the searchlight barely
cut through. There I was, drowning, and I couldn't even remember what I was doing. It was blind luck that I found the
mast. She was all tangled up in the line. I don't know how many
times we went under while I was trying to get her loose. My
hands were numb, and I was working blind. Then I had her,
and I managed to get the flotation on her. They said I got the
tow line secured, but I don't remember. I just remember hanging on to her and waiting for the next wave to finish us off.
Next thing, I was waking up in the infirmary. The kid was
sitting there, wrapped in a blanket and holding my hand." He
smiled. It helped to think about that part. Just that part. "She
was one tough little monkey. A damn admiral's granddaughter."

"You saved her life."

"Maybe. For the first couple of months, I jumped off that

deck every time I closed my eyes. Now it's only once or twice a year. It still scares the breath out of me."

"I didn't think you were scared of anything."

"I'm scared of plenty," Zack said quietly as he met his brother's eyes. "For a while I was scared I wouldn't be able to stand on deck and look out at the water again. I was scared to come back here, knowing that once I did, my whole life was going to change. And I'm scared of ending up like the old man, sick and feeble and used up. I guess I'm scared you're going to walk out that door in a few weeks, feeling the same about me you did when you walked in."

Nick broke the gaze first, staring over Zack's shoulder at the shadowy wall. "I don't know how I feel. You came back because you had to. I stayed because there was no place else to go."

There was no arguing with the truth. As far as Zack could see, Nick had summed it up perfectly. "We never had much of a shot before."

"You didn't hang around very long."

"I couldn't get along with the old man—"

"You were the only one he cared about," Nick blurted out. "Every day I'd have to hear about how great you were, how you were making something out of yourself. What a hero you were. And how I was nothing." He caught himself, swallowed the need. "But that's cool. You were his blood, and I was just something that got dumped on him when my mother died."

"He didn't feel that way. He didn't," Zack insisted. "For God's sake, Nick, when I lived with him, he was never satisfied with me, either. I was here, and my mother wasn't. That was enough to make him miserable every time he looked at me. Hell, he didn't mean it." Zack closed his eyes and missed the flicker of surprise that passed over Nick's face. "It was just the way he was. It took me years to realize he was always on my back because it was the only way he knew to be a father. It was the same with you."

"He wasn't my…" But this time Nick trailed off without finishing the sentence, or the thought.

"Toward the end, he asked for you. He really wanted to see you, Nick. Most of the times he came around like that, he thought you were still a little kid. And sometimes—most times, really—he just got the two of us mixed up together. Then he'd yell at me for both of us." He said it with a smile—a smile that Nick didn't return. "I'm not blaming you for staying away, or for holding all those years of criticism and complaints against him. I understand that it was too late for him, Nick. It doesn't have to be too late for you."

"What does it matter to you?"

"You're all the family I've got." He rose and laid a hand on Nick's shoulder, relaxing when it wasn't shoved off. "Maybe, when it comes right down to the bottom line, you're all the family I've ever had. I don't want to lose that."

"I don't know how to be family," Nick murmured.

"Me either. Maybe we can figure it out together."

Nick glanced up, then away. "Maybe. We're stuck with each other a few more weeks, anyway."

It would do, Zack thought as he gave Nick's shoulder a quick squeeze. It would do for now. "Thanks for the drink, kid. Do me a favor and don't mention the nightmare business to anyone."

"I can dig it." Nick watched Zack start back toward the bedroom. "Zack?"

"Yeah."

He didn't know what he wanted to say—just that it felt good, that he felt good. "Nothing. Night."

"Good night." Zack eased back into bed with a sigh, certain he'd sleep like a baby.

Chapter 9

Something had changed. Rachel couldn't put her finger on it, but as she sat between Zack and Nick on the subway to Brooklyn she knew there was something going on between them. Something different.

It made her nerves hum. It made her wonder if she'd made a mistake in bringing the problems of the men who flanked her into her parents' home.

And her problem, as well, she admitted. After all, she wouldn't deny she cared about both of them more than what could be considered professional. She felt a kinship with Nick—the younger-sibling syndrome, she supposed. Added to that, she'd been telling the simple truth when she confessed to Zack that she had a weakness for bad boys.

She wanted to do more for Nick LeBeck than help him stay out of jail.

As for Nick's big brother, she'd long since crossed all professional boundaries with him, into what could only be termed a full-blown affair. Even sitting beside him in the rumbling car, she thought about the last time they'd been together, alone. And it took no effort at all to imagine what it would be like the next time they could steal a few hours.

Her mother was bound to sense it, Rachel mused. Nothing got past Nadia Stanislaski when it came to her children. She wondered what her mother would think of him. What she would think of the fact that her baby girl had taken a lover.

For two people who had vowed not to complicate matters, she and Zack had done a poor job of it, Rachel decided. She'd been so certain she could keep her priorities well in line, accept the physical aspects of a relationship with a man she liked and respected without dwelling on the thorny issue of what-happens-next.

But she was thinking about Zack too much, already slotting herself as part of a couple when she'd always been perfectly content to go along single.

Now, when she imagined moving along without him, the picture turned dull and listless.

Her problem, Rachel reminded herself. After all, they had made a pact, and she never went back on her word. It was something she would have to deal with when the time came. Much more immediate was the nagging sensation that the relationship of the men beside her had taken a fast turn without her being aware of it.

To offset the feeling, she kept up a steady stream of conversation until they reached their stop.

"It's only a few blocks," Rachel said, dragging her hair back as a brisk autumn wind swirled around them. "I hope you don't mind the walk."

Zack lifted a brow. "I think we can handle it. You seem nervous, Rachel. She seem nervous to you, Nick?"

"Pretty jumpy."

"That's ridiculous." She headed into the wind, and the men fell in beside her.

"It's probably the thought of having a criminal type sit down to Sunday dinner," Zack commented. "Now she's going to have to count all the silverware."

Shocked at the statement, Rachel started to respond, but Nick merely snorted and answered for himself. "If you ask me, she's worried about inviting some Irish sailor. She has to worry if he'll drink all the booze and pick a fight."

"I can handle my liquor, pal. And I don't plan on picking a fight. Unless it's with the cop."

Nick crunched a dry leaf as it skittered across the sidewalk. "I'll take the cop."

Why, they're *joking* with each other, Rachel realized. Like brothers. Very much like brothers. Delighted, she linked arms with both of them. "If either of you takes on Alex, you'll be in for a surprise. He's meaner than he looks. And the only thing I'm nervous about is that I won't get my share of dinner. I've seen both of you eat."

"This from a woman who packs it away like a linebacker."

Rachel narrowed her eyes at Zack. "I merely have a healthy appetite."

He grinned down at her. "Me too, sugar."

She was wondering how to control the sudden leap of her heart rate when a car skidded to a halt in the street beside them. "Hey!" the driver called out.

"Hey back." Rachel broke away to walk over to greet her brother and sister-in-law. Bending into the tiny window of the MG, she kissed Mikhail and smiled at his wife. "Still keeping him in line, Sydney?"

Cool and elegant beside her untamed-looking husband, Sydney smiled. "Absolutely. Difficult jobs are my forte."

Mikhail pinched his wife's thigh and nodded toward the sidewalk. "So what's the story there?"

"They're my guests." She gave Mikhail a long, warning look that she knew was wasted on him before calling to Nick and

Zack. "Come meet my brother and his long-suffering wife. Sydney, Mikhail, this is Zackary Muldoon and Nicholas LeBeck."

His eyes shielded by dark glasses, Mikhail took a careful survey. He had a brother's natural lack of faith in his sister's judgment. "Which is the client?"

"Today," Rachel said, "they're both guests."

Sydney leaned over and jammed her elbow sharply in Mikhail's ribs. "It's very nice to meet you, both of you. You're in for quite a treat with Nadia's cooking."

"So I hear." Zack kept his eyes on Mikhail as he answered, and lifted a proprietary hand to Rachel's shoulder.

Mikhail's fingers drummed on the steering wheel. "You own what? A bar?"

"No, actually, I'm into white slavery."

That got a chuckle from Nick before Rachel shook her head. "Go park your car."

As they retreated to the sidewalk, Nick smiled over at Rachel. "I see what you mean now about older brothers. Being a pain must go with the position."

"Responsibility," Zack told him. "We just pass on the benefit of our experience."

"No," Rachel said, "what you are is nosy." Amused, she gestured toward the sound of voices and laughter. Mikhail and Sydney were already at the door of the row house, hugging and being hugged. "This is it." When Rachel spotted Natasha, she gave a cry of pleasure and dashed up the steps.

Hanging back a little, Zack watched Rachel embrace her sister. Natasha was slighter, more delicately built, with rich brown eyes misted with tears, and tumbled raven curls raining down her back. Zack's first thought was that this could not be the mother of three Rachel had described to him. Then a young boy of six or seven squeezed between the women and demanded attention.

"You let in the cold!" This was bellowed from inside the

house in a rumbling male voice that carried to the sidewalk and beyond. "You are not born in barn."

"Yes, Papa." Her voice sounded meek enough, but Rachel winked at her nephew as she lifted him up for a kiss. "My sister, Natasha," she continued, as they stood in the open doorway. "And my boyfriend, Brandon. And," she said when a toddler wandered up to hang on Natasha's legs, "Katie."

"You pick me up," Katie demanded, homing in on Nick. "Okay?" She was already holding up her arms, smiling flirtatiously. Nick cleared his throat and glanced at Rachel for help. When he only got a smile and a shrug, he bent down awkwardly.

"Sure. I guess."

An expert at such matters, Katie settled herself on his hip and wound an arm around his neck.

"She enjoys men," Natasha explained. When her father bellowed again, she rolled her eyes. "Come inside, please."

Zack was struck by the sounds and the scents. Home, he realized. This was a home. And stepping inside made him realize he'd never really had one himself.

The scents of ham and cloves and furniture polish, the clash of mixed voices. The carpet on the stairway leading to the second floor was worn at the edges, testimony to the dozens of feet that had climbed up or down. The furniture in the cramped living room was faded with sun and time, crowded now with people. A gleaming piano stood against one wall. Atop it was a bronze sculpture. He recognized the faces of Rachel's family, melded together, cheek to cheek, flanked by two older, proud faces that could only be her parents'.

He didn't know much about art, but he understood that this represented a unity that could not be broken.

"So you bring your friends, then leave them in the cold." Yuri sat in an armchair, cuddling a sprite of a girl. His big work-

ingman's arms nearly enveloped the pretty child, who had a
fairy's blond hair and curious eyes.

"It's only a little cold." Rachel bent to kiss her father, then
the girl. "Freddie, you get prettier every time I see you."

Freddie smiled and tried to pretend she wasn't staring at the
young blond man who was holding her little sister. But she had
just turned thirteen, and whole worlds were opening up to her.

Rachel went through another round of introductions. Freddie turned the name Nick LeBeck over in her head while Yuri
shouted out orders.

"Alexi, bring hot cider. Rachel, take coats upstairs. Mikhail,
kiss your wife later. Go tell Mama we have company."

Within moments, Zack found himself seated on the couch,
scratching the ears of a big, floppy dog named Ivan and discussing the pros and cons of running a business with Yuri.

Nick felt desperately self-conscious with a baby on his knee.
She didn't seem to be in any hurry to get down. And the little
blond girl named Freddie kept studying him with solemn gray
eyes. He glanced away, wishing their mother would come along
and do something. Anything. Katie snuggled up and began to
toy with his earring.

"Pretty," she said, with a smile so sweet he couldn't help
but respond. "I have earrings, too. See?" To show off her tiny
gold hoops, she turned her head this way and that. "'Cause I'm
Daddy's little gypsy."

"I bet." Unconsciously he lifted a hand to stroke her hair.
"You kind of look like your Aunt Rachel."

"I can take her." Freddie had worked up her courage and
now she stood beside the couch smiling down at Nick. "If she's
bothering you."

Nick merely moved his shoulders. "She's cool." He struggled to find something to say. The girl was china-doll pretty,
he thought, and as foreign to him as Rachel's Ukraine. "Uh...
you don't look a whole lot like sisters."

Freddie's smile bloomed warm and her fledgling woman's heart tapped a little faster. *He'd noticed her.* "Mama's my stepmother, technically. I was about six when she and my father got married."

"Oh." A *step,* he thought. That was something he knew about, and sympathized with. "I guess it was a little rough on you."

Though she was baffled, Freddie continued to smile. After all, he was talking to her, and she thought he looked like a rock star. "Why?"

"Well, you know…" Nick found himself flustered under that steady gray stare. "Having a stepmother—a stepfamily."

"That's just a word." Gathering her nerve, she sat on the arm of the couch beside him. "We have a house in West Virginia— that's where Dad met Mama. He teaches at the university and she owns a toy store. Have you ever been to West Virginia?"

Nick was still stuck on her answer. *It's just a word.* He could hear in the easy tone of her voice that she meant just that. "What? Oh, no, never been there."

Inside the warm, fragrant kitchen, Rachel was laughing with her sister. "Katie certainly knows how to snag her man."

"It was sweet the way he blushed."

"Here." Nadia thrust a bowl into her eldest daughter's hands. "You make biscuits. The boy had good eyes," she said to Rachel. "Why is he in trouble?"

Sniffing a pot of simmering cabbage, Rachel smiled. "Because he didn't have a mama and papa to yell at him."

"And the older one," Nadia continued, opening the oven to check her ham. "He has good eyes, too. And they're on you."

"Maybe."

After smacking her daughter's hand away, Nadia replaced the lid on the pot. "Alex grumbles about them."

"He grumbles about everything."

Natasha cut shortening in the bowl and grinned. "I think

it's more to the point that Rachel has her eye on Zack every bit as much as he has his on her."

"Thanks a lot," Rachel said under her breath.

"A woman who doesn't look at such a man needs glasses," Nadia said, and made her daughters laugh.

When her curiosity got to be too much for her, Rachel opened the swinging door a crack and peeked out. There was Sydney, sitting on the floor and keeping Brandon entertained with a pile of race cars. The men were huddled together, arguing football. Freddie was perched on the arm of the sofa, obviously in the first stages of infatuation with Nick. As for Nick, he seemed to have forgotten his embarrassment and was bouncing Katie on his knee. And Zack, she noted with a smile, was leaning forward, entrenched in the hot debate over the upcoming game.

By the time the table was set and groaning under the weight of platters of food, Zack was thoroughly fascinated with the Stanislaskis. They argued, loudly, but without any of the bitterness he remembered from his own confrontations with his father. He discovered that Mikhail was the artist who had crafted the sculpture on the piano, as well as all the passionate pieces in Rachel's apartment. Yet he talked construction and building codes with his father, not art.

Natasha handled her children with a deft hand. No one seemed to mind if Brandon created a racket imitating race cars or if Katie climbed all over the furniture. But when it was time to stop, they did so at little more than a word from their mother or father.

Alex didn't seem like such a tough cop when he was being barraged by his family's teasing over his latest lady friend—a woman, Mikhail claimed, who had the I.Q. of the cabbage he was heaping on his plate.

"Hey, I don't mind. That way I can do the thinking for her."

That earned an unladylike snort from Rachel. "He wouldn't know how to handle a woman with a brain."

"One day one will find him," Nadia predicted. "Like Sydney found my Mikhail."

"She didn't find me." Mikhail passed a bowl of boiled potatoes to his wife. "I found her. She needed some spice in her life."

"As I recall, you needed someone to knock the chip off your shoulder."

"It was always so," Yuri agreed, shaking his fork. "He was a good boy, but— What is the word?"

"Arrogant?" Sydney suggested.

"Ah." Satisfied, Yuri dived into his meal. "But it's not so bad for a man to be arrogant."

"This is true." Nadia kept an eagle eye on Katie, who was concentrating on cutting her meat. "So long as he has a woman who is smarter. Is not hard to do."

Female laughter and male catcalls had Katie clapping her hands in delight.

"Nicholas," Nadia said, pleased that he was going back for seconds, "you will go to school, yes?"

"Ah…no, ma'am."

She urged the basket of biscuits on him. "So you know what work you want."

"I… Not exactly."

"He is young, Nadia," Yuri said from across the table. "Time to decide. You're skinny." He pursed his lips as he studied Nick. "But have good arms. You need work, I give you job. Teach you to build."

Speechless, Nick stared. No one had ever offered to give him anything so casually. The big, broad-faced man who was plowing through the glazed ham didn't even know him. "Thanks. But I'm sort of working for Zack."

"It must be interesting to work in a bar. Brandon, eat your

vegetables, or no more biscuits. All the people you meet," Natasha continued, saving Katie's glass from tipping on the floor without breaking rhythm.

"You don't meet a whole lot of them in the kitchen," Nick muttered.

"You have to be twenty-one to tend bar or serve drinks," Zack reminded him.

Noting Nick's mutinous expression, Rachel broke in. "Mama, you should see Zack's cook. He's a giant from Jamaica, and he makes the most incredible food. I've been trying to charm some recipes out of him."

"I will give you one to trade."

"Make it the glaze for this ham, and I guarantee he'll give you anything." Zack sampled another bite. "It's great."

"You will take some home," Nadia ordered. "Make sandwiches."

"Yes, ma'am." Nick grinned.

Rachel bided her time, waiting until dinner was over and three of the four apple pies her mother had baked had been devoured. With just a little urging, Nadia was persuaded to play the piano. After a time, she and Spence played a duet, the music flowing out over the sound of clattering dishes and conversation.

She saw the way Nick glanced over, watching, listening. As cleverly as a general aligning his troops, she dropped down on the bench when Spence and Nadia took a break. She held out a hand, inviting Nick to join her.

"I shouldn't have had that second piece of pie," she said with a sigh.

"Me either." It was difficult to decide how to tell her the way the afternoon had made him feel. He wouldn't have believed people lived this way. "Your mom's great."

"Yeah, I think so." Very casually, she turned and began to

noodle with the keys. "She and Papa love these Sundays when we can all get together."

"Your dad, he was saying how the house would get bigger when the kids left home. But now he thinks they'll have to add on a couple of rooms to hold everyone. I guess you get together like this a lot."

"Whenever we can."

"They didn't seem to mind you brought me and Zack along."

"They like company." She tried a chord, wincing at the clash of notes. "This always looks so easy when Spence or Mama does it."

"Try this." He put his hand over hers, guiding her fingers.

"Ah, better. But I don't see how anyone can play different things with each hand. At the same time, you know."

"You don't think about it that way. You just have to let it happen."

"Well…"

She trailed off and, unable to resist, he began to improvise blues. When the music moved through him, he forgot he was in a room crowded with people and let it take over. Even when the room fell silent, he continued, wrapped up in the pleasure of creating sound and feeling from the keys. When he played, he wasn't Nick LeBeck, outcast. He was someone he didn't really understand yet, someone he couldn't quite see and yearned desperately to be always.

He eased into half-remembered tunes, filling them out with his own interpretation, letting the music swing with his mood from blues to boogie-woogie to jazz and back again.

When he paused, grinning to himself from the sheer pleasure it had given him to play, Zack laid a hand on his shoulder and snapped him back to reality.

"Where'd you learn to do that?" The amazement in Zack's voice was reflected in his eyes. "I didn't know you could do that."

With a shrug, Nick wiped his suddenly nervous hands on his thighs. "I was just fooling around."

"That was some fooling around."

Cautious, trying to put a label on the tone of Zack's voice, Nick glanced back. "It's no big deal."

Grinning from ear to ear, Zack shook his head. "Man, to somebody who can't play 'Chopsticks,' that was one whale of a big deal." Pride was bubbling through the amazement. "It was great. Really great."

The pleasure working its way into him made Nick almost as uneasy as the criticism he'd expected. It was then he realized that everyone had stopped talking and was looking at him. Color crept into his cheeks. "Look, I said it was no big deal. I was just banging on the keys."

"That was some very talented banging." With Katie on his hip, Spencer moved to the piano. "Ever think about studying seriously?"

Flabbergasted, Nick stared down at his hands. It had been one thing to sit across the table from Spencer Kimball, and another entirely to have the renowned composer discussing music with him. "No... I mean, not really. I just fool around sometimes, that's all."

"You've got the touch, and the ear." Catching Rachel's eye, he passed her Katie and changed positions with her so that he sat with Nick on the edge of the piano bench. "Know any Muddy Waters?"

"Some. You dig Muddy Waters?"

"Sure." He began to play the bass. "Can you pick it up?"

"Yeah." Nick laid his hands on the keys and grinned. "Yeah."

"Not too shabby," Rachel murmured to Zack.

He was still staring at his brother, dumbfounded. "He never told me. Never a word." When Rachel reached for his hand, he gripped hard. "I guess he did to you."

"A little, enough to make me want to try this. I didn't know he was that good."

"He really is, isn't he?" Overwhelmed, he pressed his lips to Rachel's hair. Nick was too involved to notice, though several pairs of eyes observed the gesture. "Looks like I'm going to have to get my hands on a piano."

Rachel leaned her head against his shoulder. "You're all right, Muldoon."

It took him nearly a week to arrange it, but taking another deep dip into his savings, Zack bought an upright piano. With Rachel's help, he dragged furniture around the apartment to make room for it.

Puffing a bit, her hands on her hips, she surveyed the space they had cleared under the window. "I wonder if it wouldn't be better against that wall there."

"You've already changed your mind three times. This is it." He took a long pull from a cold beer. "For better or worse."

"You're not marrying the stupid piano. You're arranging it. And I really think—"

"Keep thinking, and I'll pour this over your head." He caught her chin to tilt her head up for a kiss. "And it's not a stupid piano. The guy assured me it was the best for the money."

"Don't get started on that again." She eased closer to link her arms around his neck. "Nick doesn't need a baby grand."

"I'd just like to have done a little better for him."

"Muldoon." She pressed her mouth to his. "You did good. When's it supposed to get here?"

"Twenty minutes ago." Wound up, he began to pace. "If they blow this after I went through all that business to get Nick out for a few hours—"

Rachel interrupted him, amused and touched. "It's going to be fine. And I think it was inspired of you to use beer nuts to get him out of the way."

"He was steaming." With a grin, Zack dropped down on the couch. "Argued with me for ten minutes about why the hell he had to go check on a missing delivery of beer nuts when he was getting paid to wash dishes."

"I think he'll forgive you when he gets back."

"Hey up there." Rio's musical voice echoed up the stairway. "We got us one fine piano coming in. Best you come down and take a look."

Rachel tried to stay out of the way—though several times, as they muscled and maneuvered the piano up those steep stairs, she wanted to offer advice. The best part was watching Zack, which she did the entire time the instrument was hauled, set into place and tuned. He worried over the piano like a mother hen, wiping smudges from the surface, opening and closing the lid on the bench.

"That looks real fine." Rio folded his massive arms over his chest. "Be good to have music when I cook. You do right by that boy, Zack. He's going to make himself somebody. You'll see. Now I'm going to fix us something special." He grinned at Rachel. "When you going to bring that mama of yours by here so we can talk food?"

"Soon," Rachel promised. "She's going to bring you an old Ukrainian recipe."

"Good. Then I give her my secret barbecue sauce. I think she must be a fine woman." He started out just as Nick came clattering up the steps. "What's your hurry, boy? Got a fire in your pocket?"

"Damn beer nuts" was all Nick said as he pushed by. He swung into the apartment, ready for a fight. "Listen, bro, the next time you want somebody to—" Everything went out of his mind when he spotted the piano standing new and shiny under the window.

"Sorry about the wild-goose chase." Nervous, Zack jammed his hands in his pockets. "I wanted to get you out so we could get this in." He shifted back on his heels when Nick remained silent. "So, what do you think?"

Nick swallowed hard. "What did you do, rent it or something?"

"I bought it."

Because his fingers itched to feel the keys, he, too, stuck them in his pockets. Rachel nearly sighed. They looked like two stray dogs that didn't know whether to fight or make friends.

"You shouldn't have done that." The strain in Nick's voice made it come out curt and sharp.

"Why the hell not?" Zack shot back. His hands were now balled into fists and straining against denim. "It's my money. I thought it would be nice to have some music around here. So, do you want to try it out or not?"

There was an ache spreading, twisting in his gut and burning the back of his throat. He had to get out. "I forgot something," he muttered, and strode stiffly out the door.

"What the hell was that?" Zack exploded. He snatched up his beer, then set it down again before he gave in to the temptation to hurl the bottle against the wall. "If that little son of a—"

"Hold it." Rachel's order snapped out as she thumped a fist against Zack's chest. "Oh, the pair of you are a real prize. He doesn't know how to say thank you, and you're too stupid to see he was so overwhelmed he was practically on the verge of tears."

"That's bull. He all but tossed it back in my face."

"Idiot. You gave him a dream. It's very possibly the first time anyone ever understood what he wanted, deep down, and gave him a shot at it. He didn't know how to handle it, Zack, any more than you would."

"Listen, I—" He broke off and swore, because it made sense. "What am I supposed to do now?"

"Nothing." Cupping his face in her hands, she pulled it toward hers to kiss him. "Nothing at all. I'm going to go talk to him, okay?" She pulled back and started for the door.

"Rachel." He took a deep breath before crossing to her. "I need you." He watched surprise come into her eyes as he took her hands and brought them to his lips. "Maybe I don't know how to handle that, either."

Something fluttered around her heart. "You're doing all right, Muldoon."

"I don't think you understand." He didn't, either. "I really need you."

"I'm right here."

"But are you going to stay here, once your obligation to Nick is over?"

The fluttering increased. "We've got a couple of weeks before we have to think about that. It's…" Steady, Rachel, she warned herself. Think it through. "It's not just Nick I care about." She tightened her fingers on his briefly before drawing away. "Let me go find him. We'll talk about the rest of this later."

"Okay." He stepped back from her, and from what he was feeling. "But I think we are going to have to talk about it. Soon."

With a quick nod, she hurried down the steps. Rio merely gestured toward the front of the bar, and, grateful she didn't have to talk for a moment, she went out to look.

She found him standing on the sidewalk with his hands balled in his pockets, staring at the late-afternoon traffic. Oh, she knew a portion of what he was feeling. How Zackary Muldoon could get inside you and pull your emotions apart before you had a chance to defend yourself.

Later, she promised herself, she would think about what he'd done to *her* emotions. For now, she would concentrate on Nick.

She stepped up beside him and brushed at the hair on his shoulders. "You doing okay?"

He didn't look at her, just continued to watch the fits and starts of traffic. "Why did he do that?"

"Why do you think?"

"I didn't ask him for anything."

"The best gifts are the ones we don't ask for."

He shifted, meeting her eyes for the barest of moments. "Did you talk him into it?"

"No." Trying to be patient, she took him by the arms so that he had to face her. "Open your eyes, Nick. You saw the way he reacted when he heard you play. He was so proud of you he could barely talk. He wanted to give you something that would matter to you. He didn't do it so you'd be obligated to him, but because he loves you. That's what families do."

"Your family."

She gave him a quick shake. "And yours. Don't try to con me with that bull about not being real brothers. You care just as much about him as he does about you. I know how much it meant to you to walk in there and see that piano. Mama had the same look on her face on Mother's Day, but it was easier for her to show what she was feeling. You just need a little practice."

Closing his eyes, he laid his brow against hers. "I don't know what to say to him. How to act. Nobody's ever... I've never had anybody. When I was a kid, I just wanted to hang around him. Then he took off."

"I know. Try to remember he wasn't much more than a kid himself when he did. He's not going anywhere now." Rachel kissed both his cheeks, as her mother might have done. "Why don't you go back inside, Nick, and do what you do best?"

"What's that?"

She smiled at him. "Play it by ear. Go on. He's dying for you to try it out."

"Yeah. Okay." He took a step back. "You coming?"

"No, I've got some things to do." Some things to think

about, she thought, correcting herself. "Tell Zack I'll see him later."

But she waited after he'd gone in. Standing on the sidewalk, she watched the window. And after a while, very faintly, she heard the sound of music.

Chapter 10

"Yo, Rachel." Pete straightened on his stool and sucked in some of his comfortable stomach when he spotted Rachel swinging through the front door of the bar. "How 'bout I buy you a drink?"

"I might just let you do that." But her smile was for Zack as she hung her coat on one of the hooks by the door. As she crossed the room, she shot a meaningful glance at the blonde who was seductively wrapped around a bar stool, purring an order for another drink while she walked her fingers up Zack's arm. "Busy night?"

Lola juggled a tray as she passed. "That one's on her third stinger," she said to Rachel under her breath. "And those big blue eyes of hers have been crawling all over the boss for two hours."

"That's all she'll do—unless she wants those eyes black-and-blue."

Lola gave a snap of appreciative laughter. "Atta girl. Hey, hold on a minute." With a skill Rachel admired, Lola served a full tray of drinks, emptied ashtrays and replaced an empty basket of chips. "See the brunette by the juke?"

With her lips pursed, Rachel studied the slim jean-clad hips and the waterfall of honey-brown hair. "Don't tell me I have to worry about her, too?"

"No, *I* do. That's my oldest."

"Your daughter? She's gorgeous."

"Yeah. That's why I have to worry. Anyway, Zack's been hinting around about how he'd like Nick to meet some people closer to his own age, so I talked her into coming in, having one of Rio's burgers."

"And?"

"Nick looked. Actually, he was pretty enthusiastic about busing tables tonight. But he didn't make a move in her direction."

"Looking's good," Rachel mused. "It wouldn't bother you if he was interested enough to ask her out?"

"Nick's okay. Besides, my Terri can take care of herself." Lola winked. "Takes after her mom. Keep your pants on," she shouted to the table of four that was signaling to her. "Catch you later."

"Well, now…" Rachel eased onto the stool between Harry and Pete. A glass of white wine was already waiting for her. "What's the latest?"

"Seven-letter word for rapture," Harry told her. "Ending in 'y'."

Rachel smiled into her wine. *"Ecstasy,"* she said, watching Zack.

"Okay!" Pleased with that, he skimmed over the blank spaces in his puzzle. "Here's another seven. Characterized by a lack of substance."

"Perfect," she murmured, shifting her gaze to the blonde, who was leaning her cleavage over the bar. "Try *vacuous*."

"Damn, you're good."

"Harry," she gave him a smile that had him going beet red,

"I'm terrific. Keep an eye on things for me. I want to talk to Nick."

Pete watched her go, sighed. "If I was twenty years younger, thirty pounds lighter, didn't have a wife who'd slit my wrists and still had all my hair…"

"Yeah. Keep dreaming." Harry signaled for another round.

The minute she passed into the kitchen, Rachel took a deep breath. It always smelled like heaven. "Okay, Rio, what's good tonight?"

"Everything's always good." He grinned, wiping his big hands on his apron. "But tonight my fried chicken's number one."

"There must be a drumstick with my name on it. Hey, Nick." Now as at home here as she was in her mama's kitchen, she eased against the counter where he was stacking the dishes. "How's it going?"

"By last count, I've washed six thousand and eighty-two plates." But he smiled when he said it. "Zack mentioned you might be coming by tonight. I've been looking for you."

Rio handed her a plate heaped with fried chicken, creamed potatoes and coleslaw. "If I came by any more often, they'd have to roll me in and out the door."

"You eat." Rio gestured with his spatula before he flipped burgers. "I like to see a woman with hips."

"You're about to." Her willpower was nonexistent when she was faced with Rio's extra-spicy chicken. Rachel began to eat where she stood. "Definitely number one," she said with her mouth full. Rio grinned. "So, did you want to see me about anything in particular?" she asked Nick.

"No." He brushed a hand down her hair. "I just wanted to see you."

Whoops. "Nick, I really think—"

"We've only got a couple of weeks to go."

"I know." She shifted slightly, putting the plate between

them. "In fact, I was able to speak to the DA, tell him about your progress. He doesn't plan on making an objection to the suspended sentence and probation we expect from Judge Beckett."

"I knew I could count on you, but I wasn't just thinking about that."

She knew very well what he was thinking of, and she'd put off dealing with it long enough. "Rio—" she set the plate aside "—I need to talk to Nick for a minute. Can you handle things without him if we go upstairs?"

"No problem. He just wash twice as fast when he come back."

She would be calm, Rachel promised herself as they started upstairs. She would be logical, and she would be in control. "Okay, Nick," she said the minute they stepped into the apartment. And that was all she said, because she found herself being thoroughly kissed. "Stop." Her voice was muffled, but it was firm, and the hands she shoved against his shoulders did the rest.

"I've missed you, that's all." He gentled his grip, then released her completely when she stepped back. "It's been a long time since we had a chance to be alone."

Pressing her hands to her temples, she sighed. "Oh, Nick. I've made a mess of this." The confused churning of emotion was clear in her eyes as she stared at him. "I kept telling myself it would resolve itself, even though I knew it wouldn't." In a gesture that mirrored the helplessness she was feeling, she let her hands drop to her sides. "I don't want to hurt you."

There was a quick warning twist in his gut. People only said that stuff about not hurting you in that particular tone of voice when they were about to. "What are you talking about?"

"About you and me—about you thinking there's a you and me." She turned away, hoping she could find the right words. "I tried to explain it to you before, but I did a poor job of it. You see, initially I was so surprised that you would think of me that way. I didn't—" With a sound of disgust, she turned to face him again. "I'm not handling it any better now."

"Why don't you just say what you mean?"

"I care about you, not only as my client, but as a person."

That all-too-familiar light came into his eyes. "I care about you, too."

When he took a step toward her, she lifted her hands, palms out. "But not that way, Nick. Not…romantically."

His eyes narrowed, and she watched, hurting, as he absorbed the rejection. "You're not interested in me."

"I am interested in you, but not the way you think you'd like me to be."

"I get the picture." Trying to tough it out, he hooked his thumbs in his front pockets. "You think I'm too young."

She thought about the way she'd just been kissed, and let out a long breath. "That argument doesn't seem altogether valid. It should, but you're not a typical teenager."

"So what is it? I'm just not your type?"

When she thought of how much he and Zack had in common, she had to block a quick laugh. "That doesn't work either." Sorry that she was going to hurt him, knowing she had to, Rachel did her best with the truth. "What I feel for you is the same sort of thing I feel for my brothers. I'm sorry it's not what you want, Nick, but it's all I can give." She wanted to reach out, touch his arm, but she was afraid he'd shrug her off. "I'm sorry, too, that I didn't put it just that way weeks ago. I didn't seem to know how."

"I feel like an idiot."

"Don't." She couldn't keep herself from reaching out now, taking his hand in hers. "There's nothing for you to feel like an idiot about. You were attracted, and you were honest about it. And underneath all my confusion and dismay," she added, trying out a smile, "I was very flattered."

"I'd rather you said you were tempted."

"Maybe." Her smile warmed, squeezing his battered heart. "For a moment. I hope it doesn't hurt you to have me say it, but I do want to be your friend."

"Well, you gave it to me straight." And he supposed he would have to accept it. A babe was just a babe, he tried to tell himself. But he knew there was no one else like Rachel. "No hard feelings."

"Good." She wanted to kiss him, but figured it was best not to push her luck. Or his. She did take his other hand. "I always wanted a younger brother."

He wasn't quite ready to take that position. "Why?"

"For the purest of reasons," she told him. "To have somebody I could push around." When he smiled, she felt the first genuine tug of relief. "Come on, get back to work."

She walked down with him, certain they had progressed to the next stage. To reassure herself, she stayed in the kitchen for a few minutes, pleased when she felt no lingering tension from Nick's direction.

When she slipped out, she looked immediately for Zack.

"In the office," Pete told her, grinning. "You should go right on in."

"Thanks." She was puzzled by the chuckles that rumbled around the bar, but when she glanced back, everyone looked busy and innocent. Too innocent, Rachel thought as she pushed open Zack's office door.

He was there all right, big as life, standing in front of his shipshape desk. There was a curvy blonde wrapped around him, clinging like cellophane.

With one brow arched, Rachel took in the scene. The blonde was doing her best to crawl up Zack's body. She nearly had him pinned to the desk, and Zack was tugging at the arms that roped his neck. The expression on his face, Rachel mused—a kind of baffled embarrassment—was worth the price of admission all by itself.

"Listen, honey, I appreciate the offer. Really. But I'm not—" He broke off when he spotted Rachel.

That expression, she decided, was even better. This one had traces of shock, chagrin and apology, all seasoned with a nice dollop of fear.

"Oh, God." He managed to pry one arm from around his neck, and he tried to shake her off, but she transferred her grip to his waist.

"Excuse me," Rachel said, her tongue firmly in her cheek. "I can see you're busy."

"Damn it, don't shut the door." His eyes widened when the blonde shifted to give his bottom a nice, intimate squeeze. "Give me a break, Rachel."

"You want a break?" She glanced back to where the regulars had moved closer, craning their necks to catch the show. "He wants a break," she told them. Very casually, she strolled across the threshold. "Which leg would you like me to break, Muldoon? Or would you prefer an arm? Maybe your neck."

"Have a heart." The blonde was giggling now as she tugged at his sweater. "Help me get her off. She's plowed."

"I'd think a big strong man like you could handle that all by yourself."

"She moves like a damn eel," he muttered. "Come on, Babs, let go. I'll call you a cab."

She was slithering over him, Rachel noted, and with a sigh she took charge. Gripping the blonde's artfully tangled mane in one hand, she tugged. Hard. The quick squeal of pain was very satisfying. Following up on it, Rachel shoved her face close. "You're trespassing, dear."

Babs weaved, gave a glazed-eyed grin. "I didn't see any signs."

"Consider yourself lucky I don't make you see stars." Using the hair as a leash, Rachel pulled the squeaking blonde to the door. "This way out."

"I'll take it from here." Lola slipped an arm around the blonde's waist. "Come on, sweetie, you're looking a little green."

"He's just so damn cute," Babs sighed as she stumbled toward the ladies' room with Lola.

"Call her a cab," Zack shouted. After one heated glare at the grinning faces of his customers, he slammed the door shut. "Listen, Rachel…" Besides being mortified, he was out of breath, and he took a moment to steady himself. "It wasn't the way it looked."

"Oh?" The situation was too entertaining to resist. She sauntered over to his desk, scooted onto the edge and crossed her legs. "How did it look, Muldoon?"

"You know damn well." He blew out a breath, tucked his useless hands in his pockets. "She got herself wasted on a couple of stingers. I came in to call her a cab, and she followed me." His brows drew together when Rachel lifted a hand to examine her nails. "She attacked me."

"Want to press charges?"

"Don't get cute with me." As embarrassing moments went, Zack considered this in the top ten. "I was trying to…defend myself."

"I could see it was a pitched battle. You're lucky you came out of it alive."

"What was I supposed to do, knock her cold?" He paced from one wall to the other. "I told her I wasn't interested, but she wouldn't back off."

"You're just so damn cute," Rachel said, fluttering her lashes.

"Funny," he tossed over his shoulder. "Really funny. You're going to play this one out all the way, aren't you?"

"Bingo." She picked up a letter opener from his desk, tested the point, thoughtfully. "As counsel for the defense, I have to ask if you feel that strutting behind the bar in those snug black jeans—"

"I don't strut."

"I'll rephrase the question." She flicked the tip of the letter opener with her thumb. "Can you say—and I remind you, Mr. Muldoon, you're under oath—can you tell this court you haven't done anything to entice the defendant, to make her believe you were available? Even willing?"

"I never… Well, I might have before you…" As a man of the sea, Zack knew when to cut line. He crossed his arms over his chest. "I take the Fifth."

"Coward."

"You bet." He eyed the letter opener warily. "You don't plan to use that on any particularly sensitive part of my anatomy?"

Letting her gaze skim down, Rachel touched her tongue to her upper lip. "Probably not."

His smile came slowly and was full of relief. "You're really not mad, are you, sugar?"

"That I walked in and found you in a compromising position with a blonde bombshell?" After a quick laugh, she shifted her grip on the letter opener. "Why should I be mad, sugar?"

"You may have saved my life." He thought he'd gauged her mood correctly, but his approach was still cautious. "You don't know what she said she was going to do to me." He gave a mock shudder, and slipped his arms around her, as if for support. "She's a yoga instructor."

"Oh, my." Biting back a grin, Rachel patted his back. "What did she threaten you with?"

"Well, I think it went something like…" He leaned close to her ear, whispering. He heard Rachel's surprised chuckle. "And then…"

"Oh, *my*" was all she could say. She swallowed once. "Do you think that's anatomically possible?"

"I think you'd have to be double-jointed, but we could give it a try."

Wicked laughter gleaming in her eyes, she tilted her head

back. "I don't care what you say, Muldoon. I think you liked being pawed."

"Uh-uh." He nuzzled her neck. "It was degrading. I feel so…cheap."

"There, there. I saved you."

"You were a regular Viking."

"And you know what they say about Vikings…" she murmured as she turned her mouth to his.

"Go ahead," he said invitingly. "Use me."

"Oh, I plan to."

The kiss was long and satisfying, but as it began to heat he tore his mouth from hers to bury his face in her hair.

"Rachel, you don't know how good you feel. How right."

"I know this feels right." Eyes shut tightly, she held him close.

"Do you?"

"Yes. I think…" She let her words trail off into a sigh. She'd been doing a great deal of thinking over the past few days. "I think sometimes people just fit. The way you told me once before."

He drew back, cupping her face in his hands. His eyes were very dark, very intense, on hers. She wasn't entirely sure what she was reading in them, but it made her heart trip-hammer into her throat. "We fit. I know you said you didn't want to get involved. That you have priorities."

She linked her fingers around his wrists. "I said a lot of things."

"Rachel, I want you to move in with me." He saw the surprise in her eyes and hurried on before she could answer. "I know you wanted to keep it simple. So did I. This doesn't have to be a complication. You'd have time to think about it. We have to wait until everything's straightened out with Nick. But I need for you to know how much I want to be with you—not just snatching time."

She let out an unsteady breath. "It's a big step."

"And you don't do things on impulse." He lowered his lips to brush hers. "Think about it. Think about this," he whispered, and took the kiss deep, deep, fathoms deep, until thinking was impossible.

"Zack, I need to—" Nick burst into the office, and froze. He saw Rachel pressed against his brother, her hands fisted in his hair, her eyes soft and clouded.

They cleared quickly enough, and now there was alarm there, and apology. But as Nick stared at them, all he could see was the red mist of betrayal.

She shouted his name as Nick leaped. Zack saw the blow coming, and he let it connect. It rocked him back on his heels. He tasted blood. Instinct had him gripping Nick's wrists to prevent another punch, but Nick twisted away, agile as a snake, and braced for the next round.

"Stop it!" Heedless that the next fist could fly any second, Rachel stepped furiously between them, shoving them apart. "This isn't the way."

Clamping down on his own temper, Zack merely lifted her up and set her aside. "Stay clear. You want to go a round in here?" he said to Nick. "Or take it outside?"

"Of all the—"

"Anywhere you say," Nick snapped, cutting Rachel off. "You son of a bitch. It was always you." He shoved, but the bright hurt in his eyes kept Zack from striking back. "You always had to come out on top, didn't you?" His breathing was labored as he rammed Zack back against the wall. "All this crap about family. Well, you know where you can stick it, *bro*."

"Nick, please." Rachel lifted a hand, but let it drop when he turned those furious eyes on her.

"Just shut up. That whole line of bull you handed me upstairs. You've got real talent, lady, because I was buying it. You knew how I felt, and all the time you're making it with him behind my back."

"Nick, it wasn't like that."

"You lying bitch."

His head snapped back when Zack clipped him with a back-hand. There was blood on both sides now. "You want to take a swing at me, go ahead. But you don't talk to her like that."

Teeth gritted, Nick wiped the blood from his lip. He wanted to hate. Needed to. "The hell with you. The hell with both of you."

He swung on his heel and darted out.

"Oh, God." Rachel covered her face, but it did nothing to erase the image of the hurt she'd seen in Nick's eyes. The dam-age, she thought miserably, that she had done. "What a mess. I'm going after him."

"Leave him alone."

"It's my fault," she said, dropping her arms to her sides. "I have to try."

"I said leave him alone."

"Damn it, Zack—"

"Excuse me." There was a rap on the door, which Nick had left hanging open. Rachel turned and bit back a groan.

"Judge Beckett."

"Good evening, Ms. Stanislaski. Mr. Muldoon, I dropped in for one of your famous manhattans. Perhaps you could mix one for me while I have a conference with your brother's attorney."

"Your Honor," Rachel began, "my client…"

"I saw your client as he roared out of here. Your mouth's bleeding, Mr. Muldoon." She turned and shot a look at Rachel. "Counselor?"

"Perfect timing," Rachel said under her breath. "I'll handle this," she said to Zack. "Don't worry. And once Nick works off a little steam—"

"He'll come back smiling?" Zack finished. His temper was fading, but guilt was moving full steam ahead. "I don't think so. And it's not your fault." He wished he had more than his own empty sense of failure to give her. "He's my brother. I'm responsible." He shook his head before she could speak. "Let me go fix the judge her drink."

He brushed by her. Rachel reached out to stop him, then let her hand fall away. There was nothing she could say to ease the hurt. But she had a chance to minimize the damage with Judge Beckett.

She found the judge looking attractive and relaxed at a table on the far side of the bar. Yet the aura of power the woman had when wearing black robes on the bench wasn't diminished in the least by the trim blue slacks and white sweater she wore tonight.

"Have a seat, Counselor."

"Thank you."

Beckett smiled, tapping rose-tipped nails on the edge of the table. "I can see the wheels turning. How much do I tell her, how much do I evade? I always enjoy having you in my courtroom, Ms. Stanislaski. You have style."

"Thank you," Rachel said again. Their drinks arrived, and she took the time while they were served to gather her thoughts. "I'm afraid you might, understandably, misinterpret what you saw tonight, Your Honor."

"Are you?" With a smile, Beckett sampled her drink. She shifted her gaze to meet Zack's and sent him an approving smile. "And what would you consider my interpretation?"

"Obviously, Nick and his brother were arguing."

"Fighting," Beckett corrected, stirring the cherry around in her drink before biting it from its stem. "Arguing involves words. And, while words may leave scars, they don't draw blood."

"You don't have brothers, do you, Your Honor?"

"No, I don't."

"I do."

With a lift of a brow, Beckett sipped again. "All right, I'll sustain that. What were they arguing about?"

Rachel eased around the boggy ground. "It was just a mis-understanding. I won't deny both of them are hotheaded, and that with their type of temperament a misunderstanding can sometimes evolve into…"

"An argument?" Beckett suggested.

"Yes." Needing to make her point, Rachel leaned forward. "Judge Beckett, Nick has been making such incredible progress. When I was first assigned to his case, I very nearly dismissed him as just another street punk. But there was something that made me reevaluate him."

"Haunted eyes do that to a woman."

Surprised, Rachel blinked. "Yes."

"Go on."

"He was so young, and yet he'd already started to give up on himself, and everyone else. After I met Zack, and found out about Nick's background, it was easy to understand. There's never been anyone permanent in his life, anyone he felt he could count on and trust. But with Zack…he wanted to. No matter how tough and disinterested he tried to act, the longer he was with Zack, the more you could see that they needed each other."

"Just how involved are you with your co-guardian?"

With her face carefully blank, Rachel sat back in her seat. "I believe that's irrelevant."

"Do you? Well." She gestured with her hand. "Continue."

"For nearly two months, Nick has stayed out of trouble. He's been handling the responsibilities Zack has given him. He's de-veloping outside interests. He plays the piano."

"Does he?"

"Zack bought him one when he found out."

"That doesn't seem like something that would make fists fly." A faint smile played around her mouth as she gestured with her manhattan. "You're dodging the point, Counselor."

"I want you to understand that this probationary period has been successful. What happened tonight was simply a product of misunderstandings and hot tempers. It was the exception rather than the rule."

"You're not in court."

"No, Your Honor, but I don't want you to hold this against my client when I am."

"Agreed." Pleased with what she saw in Rachel, what she heard, and what she sensed, Beckett rattled the ice in her glass. "Explain tonight."

"It was my fault," Rachel said, pushing her wine aside. "It was poor judgment on my part that caused Nick to feel, to believe he felt...something."

Beckett pursed her lips. "I begin to see. He's a healthy young man, and you're an attractive woman who's shown an interest in him."

"And I blew it," Rachel said bitterly. "I thought I'd handled it. I was so damn sure I was on top of everything."

"I know the feeling." Beckett sampled a beer nut thoughtfully. "Off the record. Start at the beginning."

Hoping her own culpability would lighten Nick's load, even if it got her thrown off the case, Rachel explained. Beckett said nothing, only nodding or making interested noises now and again. "And when he walked into the office and saw Zack and me together," she concluded, "all he saw was betrayal. I know I had no right to become involved with Zack. Excuses don't cut it."

"Rachel, you're an excellent attorney. That doesn't preclude your having a private life."

"When it endangers my relationship with a client—"

"Don't interrupt. I'll grant that you may have exercised poor judgment in this instance. I'll also grant that one can't always choose the time, place or circumstances for falling in love."

"I didn't say I was in love."

Beckett smiled. "I noticed that. It's easier to beat yourself up about it if you tell yourself love had nothing to do with it." Her smile widened. "No rebuttal, Counselor? Just as well, because I haven't finished. I could tell you you've lost your objectivity, but you already know that. I, for one, am not entirely sure objectivity is always the answer. There are so many shades between right and wrong. Finding the one that fits is something we struggle with every day. Your client is trying to find his. You may not be able to help."

"I don't want to let him down."

"Better you should do what's possible to prevent him from letting himself down. Sometimes it works, sometimes it doesn't. You'll discover how often it doesn't when it's your turn to sit on the bench."

The understanding in Beckett's eyes had Rachel reaching for her wine again. "I didn't know I was that transparent."

"Oh, to one who's been there, certainly." Amused, Beckett tapped her glass against Rachel's. "A few more years of seasoning, Counselor, and you'll make quite a competent judge. That *is* what you want?"

"Yes." She met Beckett's eyes levelly. "That's exactly what I want."

"Good. Now, since I've had a drink and I'm feeling rather mellow, I'll tell you something—off the record. It was almost thirty years ago that I was you. So very close to who and what you are. Things were more difficult for women in our position than they are now. They're far from perfect now," she added, setting her glass aside, "but some of the battles are over. I had to make choices. Those professional-versus-personal choices that men rarely have to make. Do I have a family or do I have a career? I don't regret choosing my career."

She glanced back at the bar, at Zack, and sighed. "Or only rarely. But times change, and even a professionally ambitious woman doesn't have to make an either-or decision. She can have both, if she's clever. You strike me as a clever woman."

"I like to think so," Rachel murmured. "But it doesn't make it any less terrifying."

"That kind of terror makes life worthwhile. I don't think nerves will stop you, Counselor. I don't think anything will. In the meantime, see that you and your client are prepared for the hearing."

When Beckett rose, Rachel was instantly on her feet. "Judge Beckett, about tonight—"

"I came in for a drink. It's a nice bar. Clean, friendly. As for my decision, that will depend on what I see and hear in my courtroom. Understood?"

"Yes. Thank you."

"Tell Mr. Muldoon he makes an excellent manhattan."

With her emotions still in a state of upheaval, Rachel watched Beckett stroll out.

"How bad is it?" Zack asked from behind her.

Rachel merely shook her head, reaching back to take his hand. "She likes the way you mix a drink." Turning to him, she comforted him with a hug. "And I think I've just met another intelligent woman with a weakness for bad boys. It's going to be all right."

"If Nick doesn't come back…"

"He'll be back." She needed to believe it. Needed to make Zack believe it. "He's mad, and he's hurt, but he's not stupid." She gave his hand another quick squeeze and smiled up at him. "He's too much like you."

"I shouldn't have hit him."

"Intellectually, I agree. Emotionally…" Because passion was a part of her life, she shrugged it off. "I've seen my brothers pound on each other too often to believe it's the end of the world. I've got to go." She touched a gentle kiss to his swollen lip. "When he comes back, it's probably best if I'm not here. But I want you to call me when he shows up, no matter what time it is."

"I don't like you going home alone," he said as he walked with her to where her coat was hanging.

"I'll take a cab." The fact that he didn't argue made her realize just how distracted he was. "We're going to work this out, Zack. Trust me."

"Yeah. I'll call you."

She stepped outside and headed down to the corner to hail a cab. Trust me, she'd told him. She could only hope she deserved that trust.

Chapter 11

She nearly called Alex when she got home, but she was afraid that if her brother put out feelers, even unofficially, Nick would only be more furious.

All she could do was wait. And wait alone.

An odd triangle they made, she thought as she wandered restlessly around her apartment with a rapidly cooling cup of tea. Nick, young and defiant, seeing rejection and betrayal everywhere, even as he looked so desperately for his place in the world. And Zack, so innately generous, so fueled by passion and so vulnerable to his brother. And herself, the objective, logical and ambitious attorney who'd fallen in love with them both.

Maybe she should be writing soap operas, she thought as she dropped down on the couch. She curled up her legs, cupping her mug in both hands. If she had the imagination for that, at least she might be able to write herself out of this situation.

Oh, how had it happened? she wondered, and closed her tired eyes. She was the one who had had things aligned so clearly. Hadn't she always known exactly where she was going and how she was going to get there? Every obstacle that could possibly block her path had been considered and weighed. All the options, all the ways of going around or through those obstacles, had been calculated.

All of them.

Except Zackary Muldoon.

By becoming involved with him, by letting her emotions rule her head, she'd made a mess of everything. It was entirely possible that Nick, pumped by hurt and frustration, would race headlong into trouble before the night was over. However understanding and compassionate Judge Beckett was, if Nick broke his probation, she would have no choice but to sentence him.

Even if the sentence was light, how could she forgive herself? How could Zack forgive her for failing? And, worst of all, how could Nick rebound from that final rejection when society put him behind bars?

She wanted to believe he'd go back to Zack. Angry, yes… defiant, certainly…maybe even spoiling for a fight. All those things could be dealt with, if only he went back.

But if he didn't…

The sound of her buzzer had her jolting. Well aware that it was after midnight, she unfolded herself, hoping it was Zack coming by to tell her Nick was safe and sound.

"Yes?"

"I want to come up." It was Nick's voice, edgy and demanding. Rachel had to bite back a cry of relief.

"Sure." She kept her tone light as she released the lock. "Come ahead."

She pressed her fingers against her eyes to push back the tears that filled them. It was stupid to get so emotional. Hadn't logic told her he'd have to come back? Hadn't she said as much to Zack?

But when the knock rapped sharply at her door, she was swinging it open, and the words were tumbling out. "I was so worried. I was going to go after you, but I didn't know where to start to look. Oh, Nick, I'm sorry. I'm so sorry."

"Sorry it blew up in your face?" He shoved the door closed behind him. He hadn't intended to come here, but he'd been walking, walking. Then it had seemed like the only place to go. "Sorry I came in and found you with Zack?"

It was far from over, Rachel realized. What she saw in his eyes was just as dangerous as what had been in them when he'd leaped across the office at Zack. "I'm sorry I hurt you."

"You're sorry I found out what you really are. You're nothing but a liar."

"I never lied to you."

"Every time you opened your mouth." He hadn't moved away from the door, and his hands were balled into fists, white-knuckled, at his side. "You and Zack. The whole time you were pretending to care about me, acting as if you liked being with me, you were making it with him."

"I do care—" she began, but he cut her off.

"I can see what a kick the two of you must've gotten out of it. Poor, pathetic Nick, mooning around, trying to make something of himself because he had a case on the sexy lawyer. I guess the two of you lay in bed and laughed yourself sick."

"No. It was never like that."

"Are you going to tell me you didn't go to bed with him?"

He saw the truth in her eyes before her own temper kicked in. "You're out of line. I'm not going to discuss—"

His hands shot out, snatching the lapels of her robe and swinging her around. Her back rammed hard into the door. The first bubble of fear evaporated in her throat as Nick pushed his face close to hers. All she could see was his eyes, sharp green and glinting with fury.

"Why did you do it? Why did you have to make a fool out of me? Why did it have to be my brother?"

"Nick." She had his wrists now, and she tried to drag them away. But rage had added weight to his sinewy strength.

"Do you know how it makes me feel to know that while I was imagining us you were with him? And he knew. He knew."

Her breath was hitching, but she fought to control it. "You're hurting me."

She thought the statement would come out calm, even authoritative. Instead, it was shaky, and the fear underneath it clear even in his reckless state. His eyes went blank for a moment, then focused on his hands. They were digging into her shoulders. Appalled, he pulled them away and stared at her.

"I'm going."

Sometimes all you had was impulse. Rachel went with it and pressed her back against the door. "Don't. Please. Don't go like this."

There was a churning in his stomach that was pure self-loathing. "I never pushed a woman around before. It's as low as it gets."

"You didn't hurt me. I'm okay."

What she was, he noted, was deathly pale. "You're shaking."

"Okay, I'm shaking. Can we sit down?"

"I shouldn't have come here, Rachel. I shouldn't have jumped on you that way."

"I'm glad you came. Let's leave it at that for a minute. Please, let's sit down."

Because he was afraid she'd stay pressed against the door trembling until he agreed, he nodded. "You've got some things to toss back at me. I figure I owe you that." As he sat, his shoulders slumped. "I guess you'll ask to be taken off the case."

"That has nothing to do with this. But no." She thought about picking up her cold tea, but she was afraid her hands weren't steady enough. "This is personal, Nick. I'm the one who screwed up by blurring the lines. I knew better. There's no excuse." Inhaling deeply, she linked her fingers in her lap.

"What happened between Zack and me wasn't planned, and it certainly wasn't professional."

He gave a quick snort. "Now you're going to tell me you couldn't help yourself."

"No," she said quietly. "I could have. There's always a choice. I didn't want to help myself."

Her answer, and the tone of it, had him frowning. He'd been certain she would try to find an easy way out. "So, you chose him."

"What happened was immediate, and maybe a little over-whelming…" She wasn't certain there were words to describe what had happened between her and Zack. "In any case, I could have stopped it. Or at least postponed it. I didn't, and that fault lies with me. The fact that we were both your guard-ians made it a poor call, but—" She shook her head. "No buts. It was a poor call." Her eyes met his, pleaded for trust. "We never thought of you as poor or pathetic. We never laughed at you. Whatever you think of me, don't let it ruin what you've started to get back with Zack."

"He moved in on me."

"Nick." Her voice held both patience and compassion. "He didn't. You know he didn't."

He did know, wondered if he had always known, that his relationship with Rachel had never been anything more than a fantasy. But knowing it didn't ease the raw wounds of rejection.

"I cared about you."

"I know." Her eyes filled again, and spilled over before she could prevent it. "I'm sorry."

"God, Rachel. Don't." He didn't think he could stand it. First he'd terrified her, and now he was making her cry. "Don't do that."

"I won't." But as quickly as she swiped at the tears, more fell. "I just feel so lousy about it all. When I look back, I can see a dozen ways I should've handled things. I'm usually in control."

Her breath hitched as she fought for composure. "I hate, I really hate, that I've come between the two of you."

"Hey, come on." He was totally at a loss. When he rose to cross to her, he was surprised he didn't leave a trail of slime on her rug. "Listen, take it easy, okay?" He patted her shoulder awkwardly. "I've been dumped before."

All that did was force her to fumble in the pocket of her robe for a tissue. "Don't hate him because of this."

"Don't ask for miracles."

"Oh, Nick, if you could only see through all the mistakes to what you mean to him."

"No lectures." Since her tears seemed to be drying up, he felt he could take a stand on that. "You carry on like you're in love with him." He was stunned when he saw the look in her eyes, the miserable, heartsick look, before they filled again. "Oh, man." While she crumpled into sobs, he readjusted his thinking. "You mean it's not just sex?"

"It was supposed to be." His arm went around her tentatively, and she leaned into it. "Oh, God, how did I get into all this? I don't want to be in love with anybody."

"That's rough." It occurred to Nick that he was holding her close but there weren't any tingles or tugs. The hell of it was, he was feeling almost brotherly. No one had ever cried on his shoulder before, or looked to him for support. "How about him? Is he stuck in the same groove?"

"I don't know." She sniffled, blew her nose. "We haven't talked about it. We aren't going to talk about it. The whole thing's ridiculous. I'm ridiculous." Thoroughly ashamed, she eased back. "Let's just say it's been an emotional night all around. Please, don't say anything to him about this."

"I figure that's up to you."

"Good. I appreciate it." Still shaky, she wiped at a stray tear with the back of her hand. "Don't hate me too much."

"I don't hate you." He leaned back, suddenly exhausted. "I

don't know what I feel. Maybe I thought I could come up here tonight and prove to you I was the better man. Pretty stupid."

"You're both pretty special," she told him. "Why else would a nice, sensible woman like me fall for both of you?"

He turned his head to give her a weak smile. "You sure can pick 'em."

"Yeah." She touched his cheek. "I sure can. Tell me you're going back."

His lips flattened. "Where else would I go?"

That didn't satisfy her. "Tell me you're going back to talk things through with him, to work things out."

"I can't tell you that."

When he started to stand, she took his hand. "Let me go back with you. I want to help. I need to feel as though I've made some of this up to the two of you."

"You didn't do anything but fall for the wrong guy."

She took a great deal of comfort from the familiar smirk. "You may be right. Let me come anyway."

"Suit yourself. You might want to wash your face. Your eyes are red."

"Great. Give me five minutes."

Rachel could feel Nick start to tense up half a block from Lower the Boom. His shoulders were hunched, his brows were lowered, his hands were jammed in his pockets.

Typical, she thought. The male animal ruffles his fur and bares his teeth to show the opposing male how tough he is.

She kept the observation to herself, knowing neither of these males would appreciate it.

"Here's the idea," she said, pausing by the door. "It was a pretty slow night, and it's already after one. We'll wait until the bar closes, and you two can say your piece. I'll be mediator."

Nick wondered if she had any idea how hard it was for him to face what was on the other side of that door. "Whatever."

"And if there are any punches thrown," she added as she pulled the door open, "I'll throw them."

That brought the ghost of a smile to his face. It faded as soon as they stepped in.

Rachel had been right. It was a slow night, as it often was in the middle of the week. Most of the regulars had already headed off to home and hearth. A few diehards lingered at the bar, which Zack was manning alone. Lola was busy wiping down the tables. She glanced up, shot Rachel a satisfied look, then went back to work.

Zack took a pull from a bottle of mineral water. Rachel saw his eyes change, recognized the relief in them before the shutters came down.

"Hey, barkeep—" Rachel slid onto a stool "—got any coffee?"

"Sure."

"Make it two," she said, sending a meaningful glance in Nick's direction.

He said nothing, but he did sit beside her.

"There's an old Ukrainian tradition," she began when Zack set the cups on the bar. "It's called a family meeting. Are you up for it?"

"Yeah." Zack inclined his head toward his brother. "I guess I can handle it. What about you?"

"I'm here," Nick muttered.

"Hey." A man, obviously well on his way to being drunk, leaned heavily on the bar a few stools away. "Am I going to get another bourbon over here?"

"Nope." Carrying the pot, Zack crossed over. "But you can have coffee on the house."

The man scowled through red-rimmed eyes. "What the hell are you, a social worker?"

"That's me."

"I said I want a damn drink."

"You're not going to get another one here."

The drunk reached out and grabbed a handful of Zack's sweater. Considering Zack's size, Rachel took this to be a testament to the bourbon already in his system.

"This a bar or a church?"

Something flickered in Zack's eyes. Rachel recognized it, and was slipping out of her seat when Nick clamped a warning hand on hers.

"He'll handle it," he said simply.

Zack lowered his gaze to the hands on his sweater, then shifted it back to the irate customer's face. When he spoke, his voice was surprisingly mild. "Funny you should ask. I knew this guy once, down in New Orleans. He favored bourbon, too. One night he went from bar to bar, knocking them back, then staggering back out on the street. Story goes that he got so blind drunk he wandered into a church, thinking it was another bar. Weaved his way up to the front—you know, where the altar is? Slammed his fist down and ordered himself a double. Then he dropped dead. Stone dead." Zack pried the fingers from his sweater. "The way I figure it, if you drink enough bourbon so you don't know where you are, you could wake up dead in church."

The man swore and snatched up the coffee. "I know where the hell I am."

"That's good news. We hate hauling out corpses."

Rachel heard Nick's muffled chuckle and grinned. "Truth or lie?" she whispered.

"Probably some of both. He always knows how to handle the drunks."

"He wasn't doing very well with the blonde earlier."

"What blonde?"

"Another story," Rachel said, and smiled into her coffee. "Another time. Listen, would you be more comfortable doing this upstairs, or—" She broke off when she heard a crash from the kitchen. "Lord, it sounds like Rio knocked over the refrigerator." She started to rise and go check. Then froze. The kitchen door swung open. Rio staggered out, blood running down his face from a wound on his forehead. Behind him was a man in a stocking mask. He was holding a very large gun to Rio's throat.

"Party time," he snarled, then shoved the big man forward with the butt of the gun.

"Jumped me," Rio said in disgust as he staggered against the bar. "Come in front upstairs."

There was a quick giggle as two more armed men, their features distorted by their nylon masks, stepped in. "Don't anybody move." One of them accentuated the order by blasting away at the ship's bell over the bar. It clanged wildly.

"Lock the front door, you jerk." The first man gestured furiously. "And no shooting unless I say so. Everybody empty their pockets on the bar. Make it fast." He gestured the third man into position so that the whole bar was covered. "Wallets, jewelry, too. Hey, you." He lifted the barrel of the gun toward Lola. "Dump out those tips, sweetheart. You look like you'd earn plenty."

Nick didn't move. Couldn't. He knew the voice. Despite the distorted features, all three gunmen were easy for him to recognize. T.J.'s giggle and shambling walk. Cash's battered denim jacket. The scar on Reece's wrist where an Hombre blade had caught him.

These were his friends. His family.

"What the hell are you doing?" he demanded as T.J. pranced around the bar, scooping the take into a laundry bag.

"Empty them," Reece demanded.

"You've got to be crazy."

"Do it!" He swung the barrel toward Rachel. "And shut the hell up."

Nick kept his eyes on Reece as he complied. "This is the end, man. You crossed the line."

Behind the mask, Reece only grinned. "On the floor!" he shouted. "Facedown, hands behind your heads. Not you," he said to Zack. "You empty out the cash register. And you—" he grabbed Rachel's arm "—you look like mighty fine insurance. Anybody gets any ideas, I cash her in."

"Leave her the hell—"

"Nick!" Zack's quick and quiet order cut him off. "Back off." As he emptied the till, he watched Reece. "You don't need her."

"But I like her."

Rachel swallowed as the hand tightened on her arm, squeezing experimentally.

"Fresh meat," he called out, smacking his lips. T.J. erupted into giggles. "Maybe we'll take you along with us, sweet thing. Show you a real good time."

The furious retort burned the tip of her tongue. Rachel gritted her teeth against it. The heel of her foot on his instep, she thought. An elbow to his windpipe. She could do it, and the idea of taking him out had her blood pumping fast. But if she did, she knew the other two would open fire.

When Nick strained forward, Reece locked his arm around Rachel's throat. "Try it, dishwasher." His teeth flashed in a brutal challenge. "Do it, man. Take me on."

"Cool it." Reece's attitude toward the woman was making Cash nervous. "Come on, we came for the money. Just the money."

"I take what I want." He watched as T.J. scooped the contents of the till into his sack. "Where's the rest?"

"Slow night," Zack told him.

"Don't push me, man. There's a safe in the office. Open it."

"Fine." Zack moved slowly, passing through the opening of the bar. He had to control the urge to fight, to grab the little sneering-voiced punk and pound his face to pulp. "I'll open it as soon as you let her go."

"I got the gun," Reece reminded him. "I give the orders."

"You've got the gun," Zack agreed. "I've got the combination. You want what's in the safe, you let her go."

"Go on," Cash urged. His hands were sweating on the gun he held. "We don't need the babe. Shake her loose."

Reece felt his power slipping as Zack continued to watch him with cold blue eyes. He wanted to make them tremble. All of them. He wanted them to cry and beg. He was the head of the Cobras. He was in charge. Nobody was going to tell him any different.

"Open it," he said between his teeth. "Or I'll blow a hole in you."

"You won't get what's inside that way." Out of the corner of his eye, Zack saw Rio shift from his prone position. The big man was braced for whatever came. "This is my place," Zack continued. "I don't want anyone hurt in my place. You let the lady go, and you can take what you want."

"Let's trash the dump," T.J. shouted, and swung his gun at the glasses hanging over the bar. Shards went flying, amusing him enough to have him breaking more. "Let's kick butt and trash it." He grabbed up a vodka on the rocks and slurped it down. Then, howling, he hurled the glass to the floor.

The sound of the wreckage, and the muffled cries of the hostages on the floor, pumped Reece full of adrenaline. "Yeah, we'll trash this dump good." Over Cash's halfhearted objections, he fired at the overhead television, blasting out the screen. "That's what I'm going to do to the safe. I don't need a damn woman." He shoved Rachel aside, and she overbalanced, landing on her hands and knees. "And I don't need you."

He swung the gun toward Zack, savoring the moment. He was about to take a life, and that was new. And darkly exciting.

"This is how I give orders."

Even as Zack braced to jump, Nick was springing to his feet. Like a sprinter off the mark, he lunged, hurling full force into Zack as Reece's gun exploded.

There were screams, dozens of them. Rachel swung out with a chair, unaware that one of them was her own. She felt the chair connect, heard a grunt of pain. She caught a glimpse of the mountain that was Rio whiz past. But she was already scrambling over to where Zack and Nick lay limp on the floor.

She saw the blood. Smelled it. Her hands were smeared with it.

The room was like a madhouse around her. Shouts, crashes, running feet. She heard someone weeping. Someone else being sick.

"Oh, God. Oh, please." She was pressing her hands against Nick's chest as Zack sat up, shaking his head clear.

"Rachel. You're—" Then he saw his brother, sprawled on the floor, his face ghostly pale. And the blood seeping rapidly through his shirt. "*No!* Nick, no!" Panicked, Zack grabbed for him, fighting Rachel off as she tried to press her hands to the wound.

"Stop! You have to stop! Listen to me—keep your hands there. Keep the pressure on. I'll get a towel." With prayers whirling in her head, she scrambled up to her feet and dashed behind the bar. "Call an ambulance," she shouted. "Tell them to hurry." Because terror left no room for fumbling, she clamped down on it. Kneeling by Zack, she pushed his hands aside and pressed the folded towel on Nick's wound. "He's young. He's strong." The tears were falling even as she felt frantically for Nick's pulse. "We're not going to let him go."

"Zack." Rio crouched down. "They got away from me. I'm sorry. I'll go after them."

"No." Revenge glittered in his eyes. "I'll go after them. Later. Get me a blanket for him, Rio. And more towels."

"I've got some." Lola passed them to Rachel, then dropped a hand on Zack's head. "He's a hero, Zack. We don't let our heroes die."

"He got in the way," Zack said as grief welled into his throat.

"Damn kid was always getting in the way." He looked at Rachel, then covered her hands with his over his brother's chest. "I can't lose him."

"You won't." She heard the first wail of sirens and shuddered with relief. "We won't."

Endless hours in the waiting room, pacing, smoking, drinking bitter coffee. Zack could still see how pale Nick had been when they rushed him through Emergency and into an elevator that snapped shut in Zack's face.

Helpless. Hospitals always made him feel so helpless. Only a year had passed since he'd watched his father die in one. Slowly, inevitably, pitifully.

But not Nick. He could cling to that. Nick was young, and death wasn't inevitable when you were young.

But the blood. There had been so much blood.

He looked down at the hands that he'd scrubbed clean, and could still see his brother's life splattered across them. In his hands. That was all he could think. Nick's life had been in his hands.

"Zack." He stiffened when Rachel came up behind him and rubbed his shoulders. "How about a walk? Some fresh air?"

He just shook his head. She didn't press. It was useless to suggest he try to rest. She couldn't. Her eyes were burning, but she knew that if she closed them she would see that last horrible instant. The gun swinging toward Zack. Nick leaping. The explosion. The blood.

"I'm going to find food." Rio pushed himself off the sagging sofa. The white bandage gleamed against his dark brow. "And you're going to eat what I bring you. That boy's going to need tending soon. You can't tend when you're sick." With his lips pressed tightly together, he marched out into the hallway.

"He's crazy about Nick," Zack said, half to himself. "It's

eating at him that he didn't round up three armed men all by himself."

"We'll find them, Zack."

"I thought he would hurt you. I saw it in his eyes. That kind of sickness can't be disguised by a mask. He was going to hurt somebody, wanted to hurt somebody, and he had you. I never even thought about Nick."

"It's not your fault. No," she said sharply when he tried to pull away. "I won't let you do that to yourself. There were a lot of people in that bar, and you were doing your best to protect all of them. What happened to Nick happened because he was trying to protect you. You're not going to turn an act of love into blame."

This time, when she put her arms around him, he went into them. "I need to talk to him. I don't think I could handle it if I don't get to talk to him."

"You're going to have plenty of time to talk."

"I'm sorry." Alex hesitated at the doorway. His heart was thumping, as it had been ever since he'd gotten the news. "Rachel, are you all right?"

"I'm fine." She kept one arm firm around Zack's waist as she turned. "It's Nick…"

"I know. When the call came in, I asked to handle it. I thought it would be easier on everybody." His eyes shifted to Zack's, held. "Is that okay with you?"

"Yeah. I appreciate it. I've already talked to a couple of cops."

"Why don't we sit down?" He waited while Zack sat on the edge of a chair and lit another cigarette. "Any news on your brother's condition?"

"They took him into surgery. They haven't told us anything."

"I might be able to find something out. Why don't you tell me about these three creeps?"

"They wore stocking masks," Zack began wearily. "Black clothes. One of them wore a denim jacket."

Rachel reached for Zack's hand. "The one who shot Nick was about five-eight or nine," she added. "Black hair, brown eyes. There was a scar on his left wrist. On the side, about two inches long. He wore engineer's boots, worn down at the heel."

"Good girl." Not for the first time, Alex thought that his sister would have made a damn good cop. "How about the other two?"

"The one who wanted to trash the place had a high-pitched giggle," Zack remembered. "Edgy. Skinny guy."

"About five-ten," Rachel put in. "Maybe a hundred and thirty. I didn't get a good look at him, but he had light hair. Sandy blond, I think. The third one was about the same height, but stockier. At a guess, I'd say the guns made him nervous. He was sweating a lot."

"How about age?"

"Hard to say." She looked at Zack. "Young. Early twenties?"

"About. What are the chances of catching them?"

"Better with this." Alex closed his notebook. "Look, I won't con you. It won't be easy. Now if they left prints, and the prints are on file, that's one thing. But we're going to work on it. *I'm* going to work on it," he added. "You could say I've got a vested interest."

"Yeah." Zack looked at Rachel. "I guess you do."

"Not just for her," Alex said. "I've got a stake in the kid, too. I like to see the system work, Muldoon."

"Mr. Muldoon?" A woman of about fifty dressed in green scrubs came into the room. When Zack started to rise, she gestured to him to stay where he was. "I'm Dr. Markowitz, your brother's surgeon."

"How—" He had to pause and try again. "How is he?"

"Tough." As a concession to aching feet and lower back pain, she sat on the arm of a chair. "You want all the technical jargon so I can show off, or you want the bottom line?"

The next lick of fear had his palms damp. "Bottom line."

"He's critical. And he's damn lucky, not only to have had me, but to have taken a bullet at close range that missed the heart. I put his chances now at about seventy-five percent. With luck, and the constitution of youth, we'll be able to bump that up within twenty-four hours."

The coffee churned violently in his stomach. "Are you telling me he's going to make it?"

"I'm telling you I don't like to work that hard and long on anyone and lose them. We're going to keep him in ICU for now."

"Can I see him?"

"I'll have someone come down and let you know when he's out of Recovery." She stifled a yawn and noted that she'd spent yet another sunrise in an operating room. "You want all the crap about how he'll be out for several more hours, won't know you're there, and how you should go home and get some rest?"

"No thanks."

She rubbed her eyes and smiled. "I didn't think so. He's a good-looking boy, Mr. Muldoon. I'm looking forward to chatting with him."

"Thanks. Thanks a lot."

"I'll be checking in on him." She rose, stretched, and narrowed her eyes at Alex. "Cop."

"Yes, ma'am."

"I can spot them a mile away," she said, and walked out.

Chapter 12

The pain was a thin sheet of agony layered under dizziness. Every time Nick surfaced, he felt it, wondered at it, then slipped away again into a cocoon of comforting unconsciousness. Sometimes he tried to speak, but the words were disjointed and senseless even to him.

He heard a disconcerting beeping, annoying and consistent, that he didn't recognize as his heartbeat on the monitor. The squeak of crepe-soled shoes against tile was muffled by the nice, steady humming in his ears. The occasional prodding and poking as his vital signs were checked and rechecked was only a minor disturbance in the huge, dark lack of awareness that covered him.

Sometimes there was a pressure on his hand, as if someone were holding it. And a murmuring—someone speaking to him. But he couldn't quite drum up the energy to listen.

Once he dreamed of the sea in a hurricane, and watched himself leap off the deck of a pitching ship into blackness. But he never hit bottom. He just floated away.

There were other dreams. Zack standing behind him at a pinball machine, guiding his hands, laughing at the whirl of bells and whistles.

Then Cash was there, leaning on the machine, the smoke from his crooked cigarette curling up in front of his face.

He saw Rachel, smiling at him in a brightly lit room, the smell of pizza and garlic everywhere. And her eyes were bright, interested. Beautiful.

Then they were drenched with tears. Overflowing with apologies.

The old man, shouting at him. He looked so sick as he stumbled to the top of the stairs. *You'll never amount to anything. Knew it the first time I laid eyes on you.* Then that blank, slack look would come over his face, and he could only whine, *Where have you been? Where's Zack? Is he coming back soon?*

But Zack was gone, hundreds of miles away. There was no one to help.

Rio, frying potatoes and cackling over one of his own jokes. And Zack, always back to Zack, coming through the kitchen. *You going to eat all the profits, kid?* An easy grin, a friendly swipe as he went out again.

The gleaming piano—that polished dream—and Zack standing beside it, grinning foolishly. Then the glitter of the overhead light on the barrel of a gun. And Zack—

With a grunt, he threw off sleep, tried to struggle up.

"Hey, hey…take it easy, kid." Zack sprang up from the chair beside the bed to press a gentle hand on Nick's shoulder. "It's okay. You got no place to go."

He tried to focus, but the images around him kept slipping in and out like phantoms in shadows. "What?" His throat was sand-dry and aching. "Am I sick?"

"You've been better." *And so have I,* Zack thought, fighting to keep his hand from shaking as he lifted the plastic drinking cup. "They said you could suck on this if you came around again."

Nick took a pull of water through the straw, then another, but didn't have the energy for a third. At least his vision had cleared. He took a long, hard look at Zack. Dark circles under tired eyes in a pale face prickled by a night's growth of beard.

"You look like hell."

Grinning, Zack rubbed a hand over the stubble. "You don't look so hot yourself. Let me call a nurse."

"Nurse." Nick shook his head, almost imperceptibly, then frowned at the IV. "Is this a hospital?"

"It ain't the Ritz. You hurting?"

Nick thought about it and shook his head. "Can't tell. Feel… dopey."

"Well, you are." Swamped with relief, Zack laid a hand on Nick's cheek, left it there until embarrassment had it dropping away. "You're such a jerk, Nick."

Nick was too bleary to hear the catch in Zack's voice. "Was there an accident? I…" And then it came flooding back, a tidal wave of memory. "At the bar." His hand fisted on the sheets. "Rachel? Is Rachel all right?"

"She's fine. Been in and out of here. I had Rio browbeat her into getting something to eat."

"You." Nick took another long look to reassure himself. "He didn't shoot you."

"No, you idiot." His voice broke, then roughened. "He shot you."

When his legs went watery, Zack sat again, buried his face in his hands. The hands were trembling. Nick stared, utterly amazed, as this man he'd always thought was the next best thing to superhuman struggled for composure.

"I could kill you for scaring me like this. If you weren't flat on your back already, I'd damn well put you there."

But insults and threats delivered in a shaky voice held little power. "Hey." Nick lifted a hand, but wasn't sure what to do with it. "You okay?"

"No, I'm not okay," Zack tossed back, and rose to pace to the window. He stared out, seeing nothing, until he felt some portion of control again. "Yeah, yeah, I'm fine. Looks like you're going to be that way, too. They said they'd move you down to a regular room sometime soon, if you rated it."

"Where am I now?" Curious, Nick turned his head to study the room. Glass walls and blinking, beeping machines. "Wow, high tech. How long have I been out?"

"You came around a couple times before. They said you wouldn't remember. You babbled a lot."

"Oh, yeah. About what?"

"Pinball machines." Steadier now, Zack walked back to the bed. "Some girl named Marcie or Marlie. Remind me to pump you on that little number later." It pleased him to see a faint smile curve Nick's lips. "You asked for french fries."

"What can I say? It's a weakness. Did I get any?"

"No. Maybe we'll sneak some in later. Are you hungry?"

"I don't know. You didn't tell me how long."

Zack reached for a cigarette, remembered, and sighed. "About twelve hours since they finished cutting you up and sewing you back together. I figure if he'd shot you in the head instead of the chest, you'd have walked away whistling." He tapped his knuckles on Nick's temple. "Hard as a rock. I owe you one, a big one."

"No, you don't."

"You saved my life."

Nick let his heavy lids close. "It's kind of like jumping off a ship in a hurricane. You don't think about it. Know what I mean?"

"Yeah."

"Zack?"

"Right here."

"I want to talk to a cop."

"You've got to rest."

"I need to talk to a cop," Nick said again as he drifted off. "I know who they were."

Zack watched him sleep and, since there was no one to see, brushed gently at the hair on his brother's forehead.

"I told you his condition is good," Dr. Markowitz repeated. "Go home, Mr. Muldoon."

"Not a chance." Zack leaned against the wall beside the door to Nick's room. He was feeling a great deal better since they'd brought his brother out of ICU, but he wasn't ready to jump ship.

"God save me from stubborn Irishmen." She aimed a hard look at Rachel. "Mrs. Muldoon, do you have any influence with him?"

"I'm not Mrs. Muldoon, and no. I think we might pry him away once he checks in on Nick. My brother shouldn't be with him much longer."

"Your brother's the cop?" She sighed and shook her head. "All right. I'll give you five minutes with my patient, then you're out of here. Believe me, I'll call Security and have them toss you out if necessary."

"Yes, ma'am."

"That goes for that giant who's been lurking around the corridors, too."

"I'll take them both home," Rachel promised. She looked around quickly as the door opened. "Alexi?"

"We're finished." He couldn't keep the satisfied gleam out of his eyes. "I've got some rounding up to do."

"He identified them?" Zack demanded.

"Cold. And he's raring to testify."

"I want—"

"No chance," Alex said quickly, noting Zack's clenched fists.

"The kid figured out how to do it the right way, Muldoon. Take a lesson. Keep him in line, Rach."

"I'll try," she murmured as her brother hurried off. "Zack, if you're going in there to talk to him, pull it together."

"That son of a bitch shot my brother."

"And he'll pay for it."

With a curt nod, Zack walked by her and into Nick's room. He stood at the foot of the bed, waiting. "How are you feeling?"

"Okay." He was exhausted after his interview with Alex, but he wasn't finished. "I need to talk to you, to tell you. Explain."

"It can wait."

"No. It was my fault. The whole thing. They were Cobras, Zack. They knew when to come in and how, because I told them. I didn't know… I swear to God I didn't know what they were going to do. I don't expect you to believe me."

Zack waited a moment until he got his bearings. "Why shouldn't I believe you?"

Nick squeezed his eyes tight. "I messed up. Like always." He poured out the entire story of how he'd run into Cash at the arcade. "I thought we were just talking. And all the time he was setting me up. Setting you up."

"You trusted him." Zack came around the side of the bed to put a hand on Nick's wrist. "You thought he was your friend. That's not messing up, Nick, it's just trusting people who don't deserve it. You're not like them." When Nick's eyes opened again, Zack took a firm hold of his hand. "If you messed up anything, it was yourself by trying to be like them. And that's done."

"I won't let them get away with it."

"*We* won't," Zack told him. "We're in this together."

"Yeah," Nick said on a long breath. "Okay."

"They're going to kick me out of here so you can get some rest. I'll be back tomorrow."

"Zack," Nick called out as his brother hit the door. "Don't forget the fries."

"You got it."

"Okay?" Rachel asked when Zack came out.

"Okay." Then he gathered her up, held her hard and close. She was slim and small, and as steady as an anchor in a storm-tossed sea. "Come home with me, please," he murmured against her hair. "Stay with me tonight."

"Let's go." She pressed a kiss to his cheek. "I can buy a tooth-brush on the way."

Later, when he fell into an exhausted sleep, she lay beside him and kept watch. She knew it was the first time he'd done more than nod off in a chair in nearly forty-eight hours. Odd, she thought as she watched his face in the faint, shadowy light that sneaked through the windows. She'd never considered herself the nurturing type. But it had been very satisfying to simply lie beside him and hold him until the strain and fatigue of the past few days had toppled him into sleep.

The bigger they are, she thought again, pressing a light kiss to his forehead.

Still, as tired as she was, and as relieved, she couldn't find escape in sleep herself. How daunting it was to realize she'd come to a point in her life where she wasn't sure of her moves.

Love didn't run on logic. It didn't follow neat lines or a list of priorities. Yet, in a matter of days, the bond that had brought them together would be broken. They would go into court, and it would be resolved one way or the other.

Now was the time to face the what-happens-next.

He'd asked her to move in with him. Rachel shifted to watch the pattern of shadows on the ceiling. It could be enough. Or much too much. Her problem now was to decide what she could live with, and what she could live without.

She was very much afraid that the one thing she couldn't live without was sleeping beside her.

He shuddered once, made a strangled sound in his throat before ripping himself awake. Instantly she moved to soothe.

"Shh…" She touched a hand to his cheek, to his shoulder, stroking. "It's all right. Everything's all right."

"Hurricanes," he murmured, groggy. "I'll tell you about it sometime."

"Okay." She rested a hand on his heart, as if to slow its rapid pace. "Go back to sleep, Muldoon. You're worn out."

"It's nice that you're here. Real nice."

"I like it, too." One brow arched as she felt his hand slide up her thigh. "Don't start something you won't be able to finish."

"I just want my T-shirt back." He moved his hand up her makeshift nightie until her warm, soft breast filled his palm. Comfort. Arousal. Perfection. "Just as I thought. This is a completely nonregulation body."

The stirring started low and deep, working its way through her. "You're pushing your luck."

"I was having this dream about the navy." His fatigue had everything moving in slow motion, making it all the more erotic when he slipped the shirt up and off. Her arms seemed to flow over her head and down again like water. "It makes me remember what it was like being at sea for months without seeing a woman." He lowered his mouth to flick his tongue over her. "Or tasting one."

She sighed luxuriously, and even that slight movement heightened his need. "Tell me more." His mouth met hers, so soft, so sweet.

"When I woke up just now, I could smell your hair, your skin. I've been waking up wanting you for weeks. Now I can wake up and have you."

"Just that easy, huh?"

"Yeah." He lifted his head and smiled down at her. "Just that easy."

She trailed a finger down his back as she considered. "I've got only one thing to say to you, Muldoon."

"What?"

"All hands on deck." With a laugh, she rolled on top of him. And it was very, very easy.

"You're not being sensible," she said to Nick as she walked up the courthouse steps beside him, supporting his arm. "It's the simplest thing in the world to get a postponement under the circumstances."

"I want it over," he repeated, and glanced over at Zack.

"I'm with you."

"Far be it from me to fight the pair of you," she said in disgust. "If you keel over—"

"I'm not an invalid."

"You're two days out of the hospital," she pointed out.

"Dr. Markowitz gave him the green light," Zack put in.

"I don't care what Dr. Markowitz gave him."

"Rachel." A little winded from the climb, but still game, Nick shook off her hand. "Stop playing mother."

"Fine." She tossed up her hands, then lowered them again to fuss with Nick's tie, brush the shoulders of his jacket. She caught Zack's grin over Nick's shoulder and scowled. "Shut up, Muldoon."

"Aye, aye, sir."

"He thinks he's so cute with the nautical talk." She stood back to study her client. He was still a little pale, but he would do. "Now, are you sure you remember everything I explained to you?"

"Rachel, you went over the drill a dozen times." Letting out a huff of breath, he turned to his brother. "Can I have a minute with her?"

"Sure." Zack tossed a look over his shoulder. "Hands off."

"Yeah, yeah." The smirk was back, but it was good-natured

rather than nasty. "Listen, Rachel, first I want to tell you how... Well, it was really nice of your family to come by the hospital the way they did. Your mom—" he pushed restless hands in his pockets, then pulled them out again "—bringing me cookies, and all the other stuff. Your father, coming by to hang out and play checkers."

It should have sounded corny, he reflected. But it didn't.

"They came to see you because they wanted to."

"Yeah, but...well, it was nice. I even got a card from Freddie. And the cop—he was okay."

"Alex has his moments."

"What I'm trying to say is, whatever happens today, you've done a lot for me. Maybe I don't know where I'm going, but I know where I'm not. I owe that to you."

"No, you don't." Worried she might cry, she made her tone brisk. "A little, sure, but most of it was right here." She tapped a finger on his heart. "You're okay, LeBeck."

"Thanks. One more thing." He glanced over to be sure Zack was out of earshot. "I know I made things a little sticky before. Zack's been making noises that you might be moving in. I just wanted you to know that I wouldn't be in the way."

"I haven't decided what I'm going to do. Regardless, you wouldn't be in the way. You're family. Got it?"

His lips curved. "I'm getting it. If you decide to throw him over, I'm available."

"I'll keep it in mind." She gave his jacket one last tug. "Let's go."

There was no reason to be nervous, she told herself as she led Nick to the defense table. Her statement was well prepared, and she had a sympathetic judge on the bench.

She was terrified.

She rose with the rest of the court when Judge Beckett came in. Ignoring the twisting in her gut, she gave Nick a quick, confident smile.

"Well, well, Mr. LeBeck," Beckett began, folding her hands. "How time flies. I hear through the grapevine that you ran into a bit of trouble recently. Are you quite recovered?"

"Your Honor…" Puzzled by the break in courtroom routine, Rachel rose.

"Sit, sit, sit." Beckett gestured with the back of her hand. "Mr. LeBeck, I asked how you're feeling."

"I'm okay."

"Good. I'm also informed that you identified the three desperadoes who broke into Mr. Muldoon's bar. Three members of the Cobras—an organization with which you were associated, I believe—who are now in custody awaiting trial."

Rachel tried again. "Your Honor, in my final report—"

"I read it, thank you, Counselor. You did an excellent job. I'd prefer to hear from Mr. LeBeck directly. My question is, why did you identify these men, who a relatively short time ago you chose to protect?"

"Stand up," Rachel hissed under her breath.

Frowning, Nick complied. "Ma'am?"

"Was the question unclear? Shall I repeat it?"

"No, I got it."

"Excellent. And your answer?"

"They messed with my brother."

"Ah." As if she were a teacher congratulating a much-improved student, Beckett smiled. "And that changes the complexion of things."

Forgetting all Rachel's prompting, he took the natural stance. The aggressive one. "Listen, they broke in, busted Rio's head open, shoved Rachel around and waved guns all over the place. It wasn't right. Maybe you think turning them in makes me a creep, but Reece was going to shoot my brother. No way he was going to walk from that."

"What I think it makes you, LeBeck, is a clear-thinking, potentially responsible adult who has grasped not only the basic tenets of right and wrong, but also of loyalty, which is often more valuable. You will likely make more mistakes in your life, but I doubt you will make the kind that will bring you back into my courtroom. Now, I believe the district attorney has something to say."

"Yes, Your Honor. The state drops all charges against Nicholas LeBeck."

"All *right!*" Rachel said, springing to her feet.

"Is that it?" Nick managed.

"Not quite." Beckett pulled the attention back to the bench. "I get to do this." She slapped the gavel down. "Now that's it."

With a laugh, Rachel threw her arms around Nick's neck. "You did it," she murmured to him. "I want you to remember that. You did it."

"I'm not going to jail." He hadn't been able to allow anyone, even himself, to see how much that had terrified him. He gave Rachel one last squeeze before turning to Zack. "I'm going home."

"That's right." Zack held out a hand. Then, with an oath, he dragged Nick into a hug. "Play your cards right, kid, I'll even give you a raise."

"Raise, my butt. I'm working my way up to partner."

"If you gentlemen will excuse me, I have other clients." She gave each of them a highly unprofessional kiss.

"We have to celebrate." Zack caught her hands. There was nothing he could say. Too much that needed to be said. "Seven o'clock, at the bar. Be there."

"I wouldn't miss it."

"Rachel," Nick called out, "you're the best."

"No." She tossed a laugh over her shoulder. "But I will be."

She was a little late. It couldn't be helped. How could she have known she'd get a case of criminal assault tossed at her at six o'clock?

Two years with the PD's office, she reminded herself, grinning a little, as she pushed open the door of the bar.

When the cheer went up, she stopped cold. There were streamers, balloons, and several people in incredibly stupid party hats. A huge banner hung across the back wall.

Next to Rachel, Perry Mason is a Wimp.

It made her laugh, even as Rio hauled her onto his shoulders and carried her to the bar. He set her down, and someone thrust a glass of champagne in her hand.

"Some party."

Zack tugged at her hair until she turned her face for a kiss. "I tried to make them wait for you, but they got caught up."

"*I'll* catch up…" she began. Then her mouth dropped open. "Mama?"

"We're already eating Rio's short ribs," Nadia informed her. "Now your papa is going to dance with me."

"Maybe I dance with you later," Yuri informed his daughter as he swept Nadia off for what was surely to be a polka.

"You invited my parents. And—" She shook her head in wonder. "That's Alex stuffing meatballs in his face."

"It's a private party." Zack clinked his glass against hers. "Nick made up the list. Take a look."

She craned her neck and spotted him at a table. "Isn't that Lola's daughter?"

"She's really impressed that he's been shot."

"It's one of the top ten ways to impress a woman."

"I'll keep it in mind. Want to dance?"

She took another sip of champagne. "I'd bet a week's pay you don't know how to polka."

"You lose," he said, and grabbed her hand.

It went on for hours. Rachel lost track of the time as she sampled the enormous spread Rio had prepared and washed it down with champagne. She danced until her feet went numb and ultimately collapsed to sing Ukrainian folk songs with her slightly snookered father.

"Good party," Yuri said, swaying a bit, while his wife helped him into his coat.

"Yes, Papa."

He grinned as he leaned toward Rachel. "Now I go home and make your mama feel like a girl."

"Big talk. You'll snore in truck on the way home."

He leered at his wife. "Then you wake me up."

"Maybe." She kissed her daughter. "You make me very proud."

"Thank you, Mama."

"You're a smart girl, Rachel. I'll tell you what you should already know. When you find a good man, you lose nothing by taking hold, and everything by letting go. You understand me?"

"Yes, Mama." Rachel looked over at Zack. "I think I do."

"This is good."

Rachel watched them walk out, arm in arm.

"They're pretty great," Nick said from behind her.

"Yes, they are."

"And your brother's not so bad—for a cop."

"I'm pretty fond of him, all in all." With a sigh, she brushed a streamer from her hair. "Looks like the party's over."

"This one is." Smiling to himself, he turned away to help Rio gather up some of the mess. If Nick knew his brother—and he was beginning to believe he did—Rachel was in for another surprise before the evening was over.

Zack tolerated the cleanup crew for nearly twenty minutes before ordering Rio home and Nick to bed. If he didn't get Rachel to himself, he was going to explode. "We'll get the rest tomorrow."

"You're the boss." Rio gave Rachel a wink as he shrugged into his coat. "For the time being."

Zack shook a nearly empty bottle. "There's a little champagne left. How about it?"

"I think I could choke it down." She settled at the bar and, aiming her best provocative look at him, held out her glass. "Buy me a drink, sailor?"

"Be my pleasure." After filling her glass, he slid the bottle aside. "There's nothing I can say or do to repay you."

"Don't start."

"I want you to know how much I appreciate everything. You made all the difference."

"I was doing my job, and following my conscience. No one needs to thank me for that."

"Damn it, Rachel, let me explain how I feel."

Nick swung in from the kitchen. "If that's the best you can do, bro, you need all the help you can get."

The single glance Zack shot in his direction was explosive. "Go to bed."

"On my way." But he walked to the juke and popped in a few quarters. After punching some buttons, he turned back to them. "You two are a real case. Take it from someone who knows you both have weaknesses, and cut to the chase." With a shake of his head, he dimmed the lights and walked out.

"What the hell was that?" Zack demanded.

"Don't ask me. Weaknesses? I don't have any weaknesses."

Zack grinned at her. "Me either." He came around the bar. "But it's nice music."

"Real nice," she agreed, going willingly into his arms to sway there.

"Things have been a little hectic."

"Hmm… Just a little."

"I'd like to talk to you about what I asked you a while back. About moving in."

She shut her eyes. She'd already decided the answer was no. As hard as it was to resist a half a loaf, she would hold out for the whole one. "This may not be the time to go into it."

"I can't think of a better one. The thing is, Rachel, I don't want you to move in."

"You—" She stiffened, then shoved away, nearly toppling him over. "Well, that's just fine."

"What I want—"

"Stuff what you want," she tossed back at him. "Isn't that just typical? After I clean up the mess for you, you brush me off."

"I'm not—"

"Shut up, Muldoon. I'll have my say."

"Who could stop you?" he muttered.

Her heels slapped the floor as she tried to walk off her anger. "You're out of order, Buster. You're the one who kept pushing your way in, pushing your way in." She demonstrated by making shoving motions with her hands. "Just wouldn't take no for an answer."

"You didn't say no," he reminded her.

"That's irrelevant." Facing him, she fisted her hands on her hips. "So, you don't want me to move in. Fine. My answer was an unqualified no anyway."

"Great." He stepped closer so that he had to lean over to shout in her face. "Because I'm not settling for you packing up a few things and coming by to play house. I want you to marry me."

"And if you think— Oh, God." She swayed back, forward, then pressed a hand to his chest for balance. "I have to sit down."

"So sit." He nipped her around the waist and plopped her down on the bar. "And just listen. I know we said no long-term commitments. You didn't want them, and neither did I. But we're turning the page here, Rachel, and there's a whole new set of rules."

"Zack, I—"

"No. You're not going to get me tangled up in an argument." She was too good at winning those, and he'd be damned if he was going to lose this time. "I've thought this through. You've got your priorities, and that's fine." He grabbed her hands, hard. Rachel decided she'd check for broken fingers later. Right now, she couldn't feel anything but amazement. "All you have to do is add one to the list. Me. I didn't plan on falling in love with you, but that's the way it is, so deal with it."

"Me either," she murmured, but he plowed on.

"Maybe you think you don't have room…" His grip tightened, and he ignored her quick yelp. "What did you say?"

"I said, 'Me either.'"

"'Me either' what?"

"You said, 'I didn't plan on falling in love with you,' and I said, 'Me either.'" She let out a long, shaky sigh when his hands slid limply from hers. "But that's the way it is, so deal with it."

"Oh, yeah?"

"Yeah." Perched on the bar, she linked her arms around his neck, lowered her brow to his. Amazing, she thought. He was as scared as she was. "You beat me to it, Muldoon. I was going to turn you down because I love you too much, and I wasn't going to settle for anything less with you than everything. It's had me going in circles for days."

"Weeks." He brought his mouth to hers. "I was going to try to ease you into it, but I couldn't wait. I even talked to your father about my intentions tonight."

Unsure whether to laugh or groan, she drew back. "You did not."

"I plied him with vodka first, just in case. He told me he wanted more grandchildren."

She felt her heart swell. "I'd like to accommodate him."

Something caught in his chest, then broke beautifully free. "No kidding?"

And here it was, she thought, looking down into his eyes. A whole new set of rules. A whole new life for the taking. "No kidding. I want a family with you. I want it all with you. That's my choice."

He cupped her face in his hands. "You're everything I've wanted and never thought I'd have."

"You're everything I wanted," she repeated. "And pretended not to." When she lowered her lips to his, she felt the sting of tears in her throat. "We're not going to get sloppy, are we, Muldoon?"

"Who, us?" He grinned as she slid off the bar and into his arms. "Not a chance."

★ ★ ★ ★ ★